At the billionaire's bidding...
Three billionaires with one thing
on their minds...

Passion

Three powerful, exotic and seductive
novels by bestselling author Lynne
Graham, featuring some of her most
wonderful, ruthless heroes yet.

Lynne Graham
Passion

MILLS & BOON

All the characters in this book have no existence outside the imagination
of the author, and have no relation whatsoever to anyone bearing the
same name or names. They are not even distantly inspired by any
individual known or unknown to the author, and all the incidents are
pure invention.

Mills & Boon, an imprint of Harlequin (UK) Limited, Eton House,
18-24 Paradise Road, Richmond, Surrey TW9 1SR

PASSION © Harlequin Enterprises II B.V./S.`a.r.l. 2011

The Desert Sheikh's Captive Wife © Lynne Graham 2007
The Greek Tycoon's Defiant Bride © Lynne Graham 2007
The Italian Billionaire's Pregnant Bride © Lynne Graham 2008

ISBN: 978 0 263 88759 4

010-0611

Harlequin (UK) policy is to use papers that are
natural, renewable and recyclable products and made from
wood grown in sustainable forests. The logging and
manufacturing processes conform to the legal environmental
regulations of the country of origin.

Printed and bound in Spain
by Blackprint CPI, Barcelona

Lynne Graham was born in Northern Ireland, and has been a keen Mills & Boon® reader since her teens. She is very happily married, with an understanding husband who has learned to cook since she started to write! Her five children keep her on her toes. She has a very large dog, which knocks everything over, a very small terrier, which barks a lot, and two cats. When time allows, Lynne is a keen gardener.

Look out for Lynne Graham's latest exciting novel, *The Marriage Betrayal*, available in July from Mills & Boon® Modern™.

The Desert Sheikh's Captive Wife

LYNNE GRAHAM

CHAPTER ONE

'HAVE I met anyone whom I would like to marry?'
Rashad, Crown Prince of Bakhar almost laughed out
loud as he considered his father's gently voiced question. Engrained good manners, however, restrained such
a blunt response. 'No, I fear not.'

King Hazar surveyed his son and heir with concealed disquiet. His guilty conscience was pricked by
the truth that he had been blessed by Rashad's birth,
for his son was everything a future monarch should
be. His sterling qualities had shone like a beacon during those dark days when Bakhar had suffered under
the despotic rule of Sadiq, Hazar's uncle. In the eyes
of the people, Rashad could do no wrong; he had en-
dured many cruelties, but had still emerged a hero from
the war that had restored the legitimate line to the
throne. Even the rumours that the Crown Prince was
regarded as a notorious womaniser abroad barely raised
a brow, since it was accepted that he had earned the
right to enjoy his liberty.

'There comes a time when a man must settle down,'
King Hazar remarked with all the awkwardness of one

who had never been anything other than settled in his habits. 'And put aside more worldly pursuits.'

His lean and darkly handsome features grim, Rashad stared stonily out at the exquisite gardens that were his father's pride and joy. Maybe when he was older he too would get a thrill out of pruning topiary, he reflected wryly. Although he had a great affection for the older man, father and son were not close. How could they have been? Rashad had been only four years old when he'd been torn from his mother's arms and denied all further contact with his parents. In the following two decades, he had learned to trust nobody and keep his own counsel. By the time he had been reunited with his family, he had been an adult, a survivor and a battle-hardened soldier, trained to put duty and discipline above all other virtues. But on this particular issue he was not prepared to meet his father's expectations.

'I don't want to get married,' Rashad declared levelly.

King Hazar was unprepared for that bold response, which offered neither apology nor the possibility of compromise. Assuming that he had broached the subject clumsily, he said earnestly, 'I believe that marriage will greatly add to your happiness.'

Rashad almost winced at that simplistic assurance. He had no such expectation. Only once had a woman made Rashad happy, but almost as quickly he had discovered that he was living in a fool's paradise. He had never forgotten the lesson. He liked his freedom and he liked sex. In short he enjoyed women, but there was only one space for a woman to fill in his private life and that was in his bed. And just as, when it came to food, he preferred a varied diet, he had no desire to have any woman foisted on him on a permanent basis. 'I'm afraid I cannot agree with you on that issue.'

The older man ignored the decided chill that laced the atmosphere and suppressed a sigh. He wished that he'd had the opportunity to acquire just a smidgeon of his son's superior education and sophistication so that they might talk on more equal terms. Most of all he longed for the ability to deal with the son he loved with a wholly clear conscience, but unhappily that was not possible. 'I have never known us to be at odds. I must have expressed my hopes badly. Or perhaps I took you too much by surprise.'

Rashad folded his wide sensual mouth. 'Nothing you could say will change my mind. I have no desire for a wife.'

'Rashad...' His royal father was aghast at the stubborn inflexibility of that refusal, for his son was not known for his changeability. 'You are so popular with our people that I believe you could marry any woman you chose. Perhaps you are concerned about the type of woman you might be expected to marry. It is my belief that even a foreigner would be acceptable.'

Brilliant dark eyes veiled and grim, Rashad had fallen very still at that reference to the possibility of a foreign bride. He wondered if the older man was recalling his son's disastrous infatuation with an Englishwoman five years ago. The very suspicion of that stung Rashad's ferocious pride. He and his father had buried the ill-fated episode without ever discussing it.

'We live in a modern world. Yet you believe that I must behave exactly as you and my forefathers behaved and marry young to produce a son and heir,' Rashad delivered with cool, crisp diction. 'I do not believe that such sacrifice is necessary. I have three older sisters with a string of healthy sons between them. In the future, one of those boys might stand as my heir.'

'But none of them have a royal father. One day, you will be king. Will you disappoint our people? What have you got against marriage?' the older man demanded in bewilderment. 'You have so much to offer.'

Everything but a heart and faith in womankind, Rashad affixed with inward impatience. 'I have nothing against the institution of marriage. It was right for you but it would not be right for me.'

'At least reflect on what I have said,' King Hazar urged. 'We will talk about this again.'

Having defended his right to freedom as resolutely as he had once fought for the freedom of the Bakhari people from a repressive regime, Rashad strode out through the vast ante-room beyond his father's private quarters. It was thronged with senior ministers and courtiers, who bowed very low as he passed. One after another, guards presented arms and saluted as Rashad progressed through the ancient courtyards and corridors to his suite of offices.

'Oh…I meant to surprise you, Your Royal Highness.' A very attractive brunette with almond-shaped brown eyes and creamy skin, set off by a sleek coil of dark brown hair, straightened from the refreshments she had been setting out in the spacious outer office. In acknowledgement of his arrival, she bent low as did the staff, who had been engaged in answering the phones. 'We all know that you often work so hard that you forget to eat.'

Although Rashad would have preferred privacy at that moment, the courteous formalities expected of a prince were second nature to him. Farah was a distant relation. With modest smiles and light conversation, Rashad was served with mint tea and tiny cakes. Evidently word of his father's hope of marrying him off was out in the élite court circle of Bakhar, so Rashad did not make the mistake of sitting down and prolonging the exchange of pleasantries. He knew that the whole exercise was designed to impress him as to Farah's suitability as a royal bride and hostess.

'I couldn't help noticing your alumni magazine, Your Royal Highness,' Farah remarked. 'You must be proud of having attained a first from Oxford University.'

His level dark deep set eyes shadowed. 'Indeed,' he said flatly, and dismissed her with a polite nod. 'You must excuse me. I have an appointment.'

Having swept up the magazine she had drawn to his attention, Rashad entered his palatial office. He wondered how many previous issues he had ignored and left unread over the years. He had few fond memories of his time as a student in England. In defiance of that thought he leafed through the publication, only to fall still when the fleeting glimpse of a woman's face suddenly focused his attention on one page and a photograph in particular. It was Matilda Crawford arriving at an academic function, her hand resting on the arm of a distinguished older man in a dinner jacket.

Rashad spread the magazine open on his desk with lean brown hands that were not quite steady. It was pure primitive rage, not nerves, that powered him. Matilda's pale blond hair was pulled back from her face, and she was wearing a rather prim high-necked brown dress. But then, her natural beauty required no adornment: she had the fair hair, ivory skin and turquoise-blue eyes of a true English rose. His perfect white teeth gritted as he studied the caption below the photo. She was not named but her partner was: Professor Evan Jerrold, the philanthropist. A rich man—of course a rich man! No doubt another gullible sucker ripe for the plucking, Rashad thought with fierce bitterness and distaste.

He was exasperated that he was still sensitive to the sight of Tilda and the regrettable memories she roused. It had been, however, an unsavoury incident in his life and a reminder that he had human flaws. Five years earlier, Rashad might have been seasoned on the battlefield and idolised by his countrymen as a saviour, but his great-uncle Sadiq had succeeded in keeping him a virtual prisoner in Bakhar. Rashad had lived under constant threat and surveillance. He had been twenty-five years old by the time his father had been restored to the throne and he himself had been eager to take advantage of the freedom that had been denied him.

It had been King Hazar who suggested that Rashad complete his academic studies in England. Rashad might have inherited his mother's intellectual brilliance and his father's shrewdness but, in those days, he had had little experience of the ways of Western females. Within days of his arrival in Oxford, he had become infatuated with an outrageously unsuitable young woman.

Tilda Crawford had been a bar-girl, a one-time exotic dancer and a deceitful gold-digging slut. But she had told Rashad poignant stories about her bullying step-father and her family's sufferings at his hands. She had judged her audience well, Rashad acknowledged with derision. Brought up to believe that it was his duty to help those weaker than himself, he had flipped straight into gallant rescue mode. Duped by her beauty and her lies, he had come dangerously close to asking her to marry him. What a future queen that lowborn Jezebel would have made! The acid bite of the humiliation that had been inflicted on him still had the power to sting Rashad's ego afresh.

He squared his broad shoulders and lifted his proud dark head high. It really was time to draw a line beneath the sleazy episode and consign his regrets to the past. Only now could he see that this feat could scarcely be achieved while the wrongdoers went unpunished. Without a doubt, the requirements of truth and decency had not been served by the dignified silence he had maintained. Indeed, had he not inadvertently made it easier for Tilda Crawford to go on to defraud other wealthy men? He might well save her elderly admirer from a similar trial, he thought with bleak satisfaction. Offenders should be called to account for their sins, not permitted to continue enjoying the fruits of their dishonesty.

Rashad studied the photo of Tilda again and mar-velled at how much better he felt now that he had recog-nised where his ultimate duty lay. Action was required, not strategic withdrawal. He contacted his chief accoun-tant to confirm that not a single payment had yet been received on the interest-free loan he had advanced to the Crawford family. He was not surprised to have his worst expectations fulfilled. He gave the order that the matter should be pursued with diligence. Powered by a strong sense of justice, he tossed the magazine aside.

Pushing the mass of her long blond hair back behind her ear, Tilda studied her mother, Beth, in total consternation and asked for a second time, 'How much do you owe?'

The tear-stained older woman gazed back at her daughter with wretched eyes and repeated the figure shakily. 'I'm sorry; I'm so sorry about this. I should've told you months ago but I couldn't face it. I've been hiding my head in the sand and hoping all the trouble would go away.'

Tilda was in serious shock at the amount of money her mother confessed to owing. It was simply huge. Surely there was some mistake or misunderstanding? She could not imagine how Beth could possibly have got into that much debt. Who would have loaned her perennially cash-strapped parent so much money? How on earth could anyone ever have believed that Beth might repay such a vast sum? She reminded herself that interest charges could be very steep and began to ask more pertinent questions in an effort to establish how and when such a debt had originated.

'When did you take out the loan?'

Beth wiped at her reddened eyes, but did not look directly at her daughter. 'Five years ago…but I'm not sure you could describe it as a loan.'

Tilda was astonished that her mother could have kept it a secret for so long. But she could remember very well how much of a struggle it had been back then just to put food on the table. She was simply bewildered by Beth's uncertainty about whether or not she had taken out a loan. 'Can I see the paperwork?'

The older woman scrambled up and went into the very depths of a cupboard from which she withdrew a plastic container. She shot her daughter a sheepish glance. 'I've had to hide the letters so that you and your brothers and sisters didn't see them and ask me what they were about.'

As a sizeable pile of letters was tipped out onto the table Tilda swallowed back a groan of disbelief. 'How long is it since you were last able to make a payment?'

Pushing her short fair hair off her brow in a nervous gesture, Beth sent Tilda an uneasy look. 'I've never made a payment—'

'Never?' Tilda interrupted in dismay.

'There wasn't the money at first and I thought that I would start making payments when things improved,' the small blonde woman confided, shredding a tissue between her trembling hands. 'But things never did improve enough. There was always a bill or someone needing new shoes or bus fares…or Christmas would come along and I hated disappointing the children. They would go without so much for the rest of the year.'

'I know.' Leafing through the heap of unopened letters, Tilda breathed out and in again very slowly and carefully. She knew she dared not show how appalled she was by what she was finding out. Her mother was a vulnerable woman, prone to panic attacks. She needed her daughter to be calm and supportive. It was, after all, over four years since Beth had last left the house to face an outside world that had become so threatening to her. Agoraphobia, a fear of open spaces, had made Beth's home her prison. But it had not stopped the older woman from working for her living. A whizz with a sewing machine, Beth had a regular clientele for whom she tailored clothes and made soft furnishings. Unfortunately, however, she did not earn very much.

'Exactly how did you get the loan?' Tilda prompted in confusion. 'Surely nobody came to the house to offer you that much money?'

Across the table Beth worried at her lower lip with her teeth and shifted uncomfortably. There was a shame-faced look on her face. 'This is the bit I really didn't want to tell you. In fact, it's why I felt I had to keep it all a secret. It made me feel so guilty and I didn't want to upset you. You see, I asked Rashad for the money and he gave it to me.'

Every scrap of colour ebbed from Tilda's oval face. With her flawless features stretched taut over her delicate bone structure, her turquoise-blue eyes seemed brighter than ever against her pallor. 'Rashad…' she repeated weakly, her heart sinking like a stone and shame grabbing her by the throat. 'You actually asked *him* to help us out?'

'Don't look at me like that!' Beth gasped strickenly, her unhappiness overflowing into tears. 'Rashad once said that we all felt like part of his family, and that that's how families always work in Bakhar—everyone looking out for everybody else. I was convinced he was going to marry you. I thought it was all right to accept his financial help.'

Tilda was aghast at an explanation that rang all too true from a woman as naïve as her mother was. When Rashad had visited her home he had appeared to like her large and boisterous family. In fact, it was only during those occasions that she had ever seen Rashad fully relax his guard. He had played rough-and-tumble games with her brothers, taught one of her sisters mathematical long division and read stories to the youngest. Unsurprisingly, her mother had become a huge admirer of his. Tilda had never had the heart to tell the older woman why and how she and Rashad had broken up. Pushing herself clumsily upright, Tilda walked over to the living-room window. A busy road lay beyond the front garden of the semi-detached house, but Tilda was so lost in a tide of angry, painful thoughts that she was not aware of the traffic.

While she was very loyal to her mother she was cringing at what she had just learned. She was shattered to learn a full five years after the event that her relationship with Rashad had begat a financial angle that she had known nothing about! Surely that must have had a negative effect on Rashad's view of her? She would have died a thousand deaths of shame had she known about that money at the time.

Rashad was fabulously wealthy and very generous. Had he simply taken pity on Beth? Or had he cherished a darker motive? Had he believed that money might make Tilda less nervous of surrendering her body to him? Had he intended it as the purchase price of her virginity? Her pride writhed at that sordid suspicion. Was she being hugely unfair to him? She thought that actions sometimes spoke louder than words. She had not slept with Rashad and he had ditched her without an ounce of compassion or decency.

'I was desperate,' Beth admitted in a stricken undertone. 'I knew it wasn't right but your stepfather had got us into such a mess with the mortgage payments. I was terrified that we were going to end up homeless.'

It took enormous effort but Tilda managed to close a mental door on the potent image of Prince Rashad Hussein Al-Zafar, with whom she'd had the poor taste to fall madly in love at the age of eighteen. That reference to her mother's ghastly second husband helped to distract her. Scott Morrison had married Beth when she was a widow with two young children. On the surface a glib and handsome charmer, he had been a terrible bully, who had systematically robbed his stepfamily of their financial security. The birth of three more children and the stress of dealing with an unfaithful and dishonest husband had led to Beth's panic attacks and her eventual diagnosis of agoraphobia.

'When I asked Rashad for help, he said that he would buy the house and keep it in his name so that Scott couldn't get his hands on it...'

Tilda whirled round, depth-charged by that information out of her recollections and back into the all-too-threatening present. On every front that admission came as a shock to Tilda. 'Are you telling me that Rashad also *owns* this house?' she gasped in horror.

'Yes. At first that made me feel that we were all safe and secure!' the older woman suddenly sobbed.

'Why don't you make a cup of tea while I take a look

at some of these letters?' Tilda suggested, hoping that that routine task would help her mother to calm down. Yet her own self-discipline was being equally challenged by what she had discovered. Although she was determined not to give way to a growing sense of panic, she could not stop Rashad's name from rhyming and purring like a derisive echo at the back of her mind.

Eager to hide the fact that she was frantic with worry, Tilda sorted the mostly unopened letters into rough piles according to date. But flashes of memory kept on attacking her from all sides: Rashad, so breathtakingly handsome she hadn't been able to take her eyes off him the first time she saw him; Rashad, the last time she had seen him, kissing another woman. Having dumped her, he had moved on with breathtaking speed. Her mind was quick to back away from that final recollection and she began reading the letters. Silence fell while she speedily absorbed their contents. Unhappily what she learned from the exercise was not good news.

To begin with, Rashad, or more probably his representatives in the matter, had engaged a London legal firm while ensuring that Beth received advice from another solicitor. The purchase price of the house had been fair. A further substantial amount of money had been advanced to settle several outstanding debts. Wincing as she totted up figures in her head, Tilda became more and more tense. If anything, her mother had underestimated the size of her debt. A contract that allowed for every eventuality had been signed. Her mother had been given a whole year to get her affairs in order before she was asked whether she wished to take out a mortgage to buy the house back or instead opt to pay rent as a tenant. Tilda came on a copy of the tenancy agreement that her mother had signed.

'What made you decide to sign a tenancy agreement?' Tilda queried dry-mouthed.

'The solicitor came to see me here and I had to make a choice about what I was going to do.'

'But you haven't paid any rent, have you?' her daughter prompted, having already seen a worrying missive that referred to rent arrears.

'No. I couldn't afford to.' Beth eyed the younger woman fearfully.

'Not even *one* payment?' Tilda thought that there should have been enough income to at least pay the rent but, as quickly, blamed herself for not having taken more of an interest in the family finances.

'No, not one.' Beth would not meet her daughter's troubled gaze, and Tilda wondered uneasily if there was something that she wasn't being told.

'Mum…are there any other problems?' Tilda pressed.

Beth gave her a frightened look and shook her head. 'Now that you've seen the letters, what do you think?'

Shelving the ESP that was giving her the suspicion there was something else amiss, Tilda knew she could not say what she thought about the letters. Her mother was a loving and caring parent, adored by every one of her five children. She was also extremely kind and hardworking, but when it came to dealing with money or problem husbands Beth was pretty much useless. By ignoring the letters, the older woman had acted as her own worst enemy. More recent missives had taken on the cold, clipped edge of threat. *They were facing eviction from their home.* Tilda felt as if spooky fingers were tightening round her lungs, for the challenge of delivering such terrifying news to her mother was at that moment beyond her. Beth was too frightened even to walk down the drive to the front gate, so how could she possibly cope with the awful upheaval and disgrace of being literally cast out on the street? And if *she* could not cope, how would it affect Tilda's four younger siblings?

'Tilda...' Beth surveyed her daughter with a heavy heart '...I'm really sorry I didn't tell you about this months ago, but I felt so guilty about having married Scott. Everything that's gone wrong for us since then is my fault.'

'You can't blame yourself for marrying him. He didn't show his true colours until after the wedding and now he's out of our lives, so let's not go back there,' Tilda urged in a deliberately upbeat tone. 'Stop worrying about this. I'll look into it and see what I can sort out.'

The buzz of the doorbell sounded extraordinarily loudly in the strained silence.

Dismay tightening her features as she checked her watch, Beth flew upright. 'That'll be a customer. I'd better splash my face with some cold water!'

'Go ahead. I'll answer the door.' Tilda was grateful for that timely interruption, for she did not want to be tempted into soothing her mother by offering empty assurances that everything would come all right. Even in the grip of shock as Tilda still was, she could see little prospect of a happy ending to her family's predicament. After all, only repayment of the debt could settle it and they were all as poor as church mice.

Frustration hurtled through Tilda, who felt as if her brain was suffering from a stress overload. Why, oh, why, had she given up a steady job to pursue an academic qualification for three years? But the decision *had* made sense at the time, offering as it did the prospect of a career with eventual excellent earning potential. Unfortunately it meant that now she had no savings and had a large student loan to pay back. Even though she was currently working full time again in a position with good prospects, she was a junior member of staff and her salary was not generous.

Tilda found her former employer, Evan Jerrold, on the doorstep. Once again Evan had his arms wrapped round a fat roll of curtain fabric. The sight would have provoked a smile from Tilda on a normal day, because in old-fashioned parlance—and he was an old-fashioned man—Evan was sweet on her mother. After a chance meeting with Beth one day when he had given Tilda a lift into work, the older man had gradually become a regular visitor. For months now he had been dreaming up new furnishing projects that gave him ample opportunity to ask Beth to advise him on colour, fabric and style.

Tilda showed Evan through to her mother's workroom at the back of the house. The kindly older man had originally encouraged Tilda to give up her office job and go to university. An academic, who had inherited a thriving family firm, Evan had ensured that Tilda always had a job there during her college vacations. Tilda went into the kitchen to gather up the letters and take them upstairs. She was thinking sadly that Evan, the survivor of a bitter and costly divorce battle, would run a mile once he heard about her mother's financial embarrassments. But, in all probability, nothing more than friendship would have developed between Beth and Evan, anyway, Tilda told herself in exasperation. Since when had she believed in fairy tales?

Her own workaholic father, whom she barely remembered, had been knocked down and killed by a drunk driver when she was five years old. Her mother's subsequent second marriage had been a disaster. Bullied and cowed by Scott, Beth had been in no fit state to protect her children. In Tilda's last year at school, her stepfather had made her work at night in a sleazy club run by one of his cronies.

Tilda forced her straying thoughts back to the present and scolded herself for that momentary slide back into the past. What was needed was action, not time-wasting regret for facts that could not be changed! She reached for the phone and rang the number of the legal firm on the letterhead to ask for an appointment. Humble pleading on the score of extreme urgency won her a late-morning slot the next day. Having arranged several days' leave from her current employment as an accounts assistant, she called her bank and asked how much money she would be allowed to borrow. Her worst fears were fulfilled when the loan officer pointed out that she had no assets and was still on probation in her current job. As she had never been a quitter she contacted three other financial institutions in the hope of receiving a more promising response before she accepted defeat on that issue.

The following day she put on a black trouser suit and caught a train to London. She made a punctual appearance at the imposing legal offices of Ratburn, Ratburn and Mildrop in the City. Ushered into the presence of an urbane, well-turned-out lawyer, she was tense and within minutes it seemed that every word she uttered was worthy only of a stony rebuttal.

'I'm unable to discuss your mother's confidential affairs with you, Miss Crawford.' An explanation of Beth's agoraphobia merely led to a further question. 'Unless, of course, you have acquired power of attorney to speak and act on Mrs Morrison's behalf?'

'No...but I was once quite friendly with Prince Rashad,' Tilda heard herself say, desperate to prove her credentials in some way and win a serious hearing.

The middle-aged lawyer dealt her a cool appraisal. 'I am not aware that His Royal Highness is involved in this matter.'

Tilda became even tenser. 'I appreciate that the loan was ostensibly advanced by a business called Metropolis—'

'I cannot discuss confidential matters with a third party.'

Her full soft mouth compressed. 'Then let me talk it over with Rashad direct. Please tell me how I can get in touch with him quickly.'

'I'm afraid that's not possible.' Before she could pursue the point, the older man stood up to signify that the meeting was at an end.

Less than two minutes later, Tilda was back out on the street again. She was mortified by the reception she had received. She caught the bus to the opulent Embassy of Bakhar, where her request for a phone number or meeting with the Crown Prince was treated with a smiling but dismissive courtesy that gained her not a millimetre of access. The level of security and discretion that appeared to surround Rashad's movements was daunting. Direct contact with him was clearly not to be had for the asking. Her only option was to leave her phone number, which would be passed on to his staff. Throughout her unsatisfactory visit, she was quite unaware of a bearded older man with silvering hair, who had left his office the moment he had seen her name pop up on his computer screen. A troubled frown on his stolid features, he watched her depart from his vantage point on the landing above.

Determined not to be beaten in her quest, Tilda went straight to the nearest library and used the Internet. She was initially infuriated by the discovery that Rashad was currently in London and yet nobody had been prepared to admit that. But when she noticed the date of the charity benefit he was to attend and realised that it was being staged that very day, it lent wings to her thoughts and her feet.

At the reception desk of the exclusive hotel where the benefit was being held, Tilda learned that admission was by invitation only. She paid for an eye-wateringly expensive soft drink so that she could sit in the hotel foyer. Sophisticated women in fashionable cocktail frocks walked in and out of the crowded ballroom. A door was propped wide to facilitate the exit of a man in a wheelchair, and Tilda caught a glimpse of a very tall, powerful male standing about thirty feet inside the room.

Her heart lurched as if she had suddenly been thrown high in the air without warning. It was Rashad, and there was something so achingly familiar in the proud angle of his dark head that she rose to her feet without being aware of it. Her attention roved from the crisp luxuriance of his cropped black hair to the bold lineaments of his strong profile. Below the bright ballroom lights, his skin had the rich sheen of gold, showcasing his well-defined black brows, a thin aristocratic blade of a nose and a fierce sensual mouth set above a hard, masculine jaw line. He was incredibly good-looking in a very exotic, un-English way. Back in the days when she had innocently dreamt of a future as an artist, she had drawn his face over and over again, obsessively attached to every detail of his hawkish features that might have been lifted from an ancient Berber hanging.

He was surrounded by a circle of people. She was willing him to turn his handsome head and notice her at the same moment that she registered that candy-pink female fingernails rested on his arm. For a split second she could not credit that she had not immediately seen the gorgeous brunette in her flimsy short dress flashing an intimate smile up at him. It was as though Tilda's mind had censored that part of her view, only letting her see what she could handle. The last time she had seen Rashad in the flesh five years earlier he had also been with another woman, a sight that had ensured that an extra large dollop of humiliation had been added to her agonised sense of rejection.

Now, as then, pride and anger came to Tilda's rescue. Just as her eyes swerved back onto him, Rashad finally looked in her direction. His keen, dark-as-ebony gaze was trained on her. Not a muscle moved on his lean, strong face. He blanked her as if she didn't exist and her view was cut off as the door swung shut again. In shock at that lack of reaction, Tilda turned pale as death. She went back to Reception and asked to leave a message for Prince Rashad. She hovered while it was being delivered but the minutes ticked slowly past and no answer came back. She sat down again, hollow with physical hunger, for she had not eaten since early morning. But she had no option other than to wait. She dared not leave while there was still an ounce of hope that he might respond to her request for a meeting.

It was almost three hours before Rashad chose to make his departure. Several powerfully built Arab men emerged from the function room and fanned out in an advance guard before Rashad strode into view. He had fantastic carriage, moving with the grace of a prowling panther. His sinuous female companion had to almost run to keep up in her high heels. Tilda could not have broken through the tight cordon of security that kept lesser mortals at bay in the royal presence. She watched as the paparazzi outside flashed cameras and shouted questions. Rashad ignored them and moved down the steps.

'Miss Crawford?'

A dark-skinned older man extended a card to her with a quiet nod and walked on out the door.

Blinking in surprise, Tilda studied the card, which contained an address and a time late the following afternoon. She sucked in a tremulous breath. Rashad was giving her the chance to plead her family's case. But if she had not dutifully waited all those hours like a lowly supplicant for His Royal Highness's attention, she would not have got the concession. Anger stirring afresh, she recognised how Rashad made her suffer: first the whip, then the reward—but only if appropriate humility was displayed.

Reclining back into the comfort of his limousine, Rashad thought about Tilda Crawford, defiantly clad in the sort of masculine clothes he had never liked. Why did she only dress up like that for his benefit? Nothing could detract from such striking natural beauty. Even with her mermaid's mass of curling pale blond hair tied back, her turquoise eyes and the heart-shaped pout of her full pink mouth bare of cosmetic enhancement, she had held every male eye in her vicinity.

Rashad had enjoyed keeping her waiting. He knew what kind of woman she was and he would give no quarter when he dealt with her. In truth, being very tough came naturally to Rashad, who had found restraint and tenderness a much greater challenge. While engaged in picturing Tilda he discovered that a sense of unlimited power could also act as an aphrodisiac. The eager brunette by his side rested a slim, caressing hand on his lean, powerful thigh. With a languid forefinger Rashad depressed the button to screen the windows....

CHAPTER TWO

TILDA sat rigid-backed on the crowded bus that carried her the last mile to her destination. Garbed in what her mother persisted in calling her 'Sunday best'—a long black coat that she wore every winter to go to church—she was striving not to let nerves get the better of her temper.

Unfortunately every time she recalled how Rashad had just *ignored* her at the hotel, a sense of grievance grew inside her. What had she ever done to deserve such discourteous treatment? After all, it was not as though she had even had the slightest suspicion that her mother had asked him for financial help. She pressed cold hands to her hot cheeks as though she could cool the mortified heat that that fact still awakened in her. The whole ghastly business was threatening to tear her apart.

Metropolis Enterprises was housed in a massive contemporary office block. The company comprised a long list of different businesses, which were displayed on the inaugural plaque in the foyer. The building had been officially opened by Prince Rashad Hussein Al-Zafar. She travelled up to the top floor in a glass lift. In the waiting area she sucked in a long desperate breath. For just a moment she thought she couldn't do it, couldn't face asking for time and understanding from a guy who had once torn her heart and her self-esteem to pieces.

'Miss Crawford—come this way.'

Tilda straightened her stiff shoulders and followed the male PA. She was shown into a very large but empty office. Barely had the door closed behind her, however, than another opened across the room and Rashad entered.

His raw physical impact hit her like a tidal wave that swept away rational thought. His fabulously tailored black pinstripe suit oozed designer style, emphasising his wide, powerful shoulders, lean hips and long straight legs. Her heart felt as though it were pounding like mad somewhere in the region of her throat. Meeting eyes as amber gold as a hot sunset, she found it equally hard to catch her breath. For her it was like time rolling back and her response was immediate: her mouth ran dry, her slender length tensing with anticipation. It had been five long years since she had experienced that unsettling little clenching sensation way down low in her tummy and it seriously rattled her.

Surveying her only for the space of a heartbeat, Rashad came to a prowling halt by his desk. His lean strong face hardened on the unwelcome reflection that she bore more than a passing resemblance to some divine snow maiden. The high-necked long black coat provided a dramatic frame for the delicate perfection of her ivory skin and light blond hair. Scarcely divine, he adjusted with inner cynicism, regardless of the purity of her looks. Naturally she knew the effect of her startling beauty. Naturally that aura of artless innocence was a façade designed to ensnare foolish men. He knew that better than anyone.

'Thank you for seeing me.' Tilda shot that at him a little breathlessly, determined to show that she had better manners than he had demonstrated at the hotel.

'Curiosity got to me,' Rashad confided lazily, watching her long honey-brown lashes flutter down over the astonishing turquoise of her eyes, the slight downward pout of her curvaceous pink lower lip. In point of fact, she was still exquisite. A few inches taller and she would have rivalled any supermodel. Five years ago, he had had excellent taste in so far as appearance alone counted. He wondered if she would dare to say no to him now were he to reach for her and, that fast, the stinging heavy heat of arousal engulfed his groin. He gritted his even white teeth at the shock of that instantaneous sexual reaction and killed the frivolous thought that had preceded it. It had not occurred to him that he might still respond to her even when his strong self-discipline and intelligence were in direct opposition to that weakness.

By dint of not quite looking directly at Rashad, Tilda rescued what remained of her concentration and plunged straight to what she saw as the heart of the matter. 'I had no idea that my mother had asked you to loan her money when we were seeing each other. If I had known at the time I would have stopped you getting involved in our family problems.'

Rashad was tempted to laugh out loud at such an implausible claim. *As if!* He strode over to the window, presenting her with his bold chiselled profile. He supposed her ludicrous assertion of ignorance was yet one more example of her old habit of always pleading innocence or having a viable explanation to cover her tracks. The leopard, it seemed, had not changed her spots. Nothing was ever Tilda's fault or her responsibility.

Tilda moved closer in her eagerness to say all that she could in explanation before he could say anything. 'Mum shouldn't have asked you to help, but you shouldn't have given it, either,' she framed in an apologetic tone. 'I mean, how on earth did you ever believe she could pay such a huge amount back? Why didn't you at least tell me what you were thinking of doing before you did it?'

Rashad swung back to face her, for she was stretching credulity too far with that enquiry. A sardonic curve hardened his handsome mouth. 'Surely that wasn't part of your plan?'

Her delicate brows drew together in a slight frown of confusion. 'Plan? What plan? I don't know what you're talking about.'

Rashad surveyed her with derisive cool and he had to admit that she put on a very convincing act. That expression of mystification in her wide turquoise eyes would have persuaded most men that she was speaking the truth. Unhappily for her, past experience had fully armoured Rashad against the lies she might well tell in an effort to awaken his compassion.

The silence felt claustrophobic to Tilda. She did not understand what was wrong or why he had made no response, but she did recognize the scorn gleaming in his narrowed dark gaze. 'Why are you looking at me like that?'

'It astonishes me that you should dare to come into

my presence and criticise my generosity towards your relatives. That might be a wily move with some men, but I find your reproaches offensive.'

Something in that clipped, dark tone chilled her to the marrow and her tension climbed even higher. 'I'm not denying your generosity and I have no wish to be offensive or ungrateful for the spirit that prompted you to give that money. But Mum had no reasonable prospect of ever repaying you and that should have made you think twice about what you were doing.'

His expressive mouth curled. 'Your mother was offered the option of paying rent.'

Tilda recognised that the meeting was already going badly wrong and feared that she was letting her personal pride and animosity get in the way of making a proper clarification of the facts. 'A lot has changed in our lives over the last five years, Rashad. My stepfather has gone. For a while, we lived in chaos. I'm afraid that my mother now suffers from—'

'Stop right there,' Rashad commanded with razor-sharp clarity. 'I have no desire to listen to maudlin sob stories. We are not players in a soap opera, nor do we have a personal relationship. We are dealing with a business matter. Respect those boundaries.'

At that uncompromising rebuke, mortified colour mantled Tilda's cheeks. Sob stories? Was that how her references to her family's plight had struck him five years ago? When she had confided in him, had he viewed her trust in him as an inappropriate and unwelcome demand for sympathy? Yet not once had she told him about the serious shortage of money within her

home! In the same way she had been too ashamed to admit that her stepfather was a good deal worse than just
a work-shy bully and, indeed, had a criminal record.

'Yes, I appreciate that, but—'

'Do not interrupt me when I am speaking. It is very
rude,' Rashad sliced back without hesitation.

'I was only trying to explain my mother's position
and why she has allowed this situation to get out of
hand.' Annoyed by that reprimand, Tilda had to make a
real effort to remain focused and resist the urge to fight
back in self-defence. But keeping her head was very difficult when Rashad was behaving like a stranger. It was
a challenge to believe that he had ever been anything
else. His English had become much more idiomatic and
his manner towards her was brutally cold and distant.
She had never been more conscious of his royal birth
and background. Yet she still found it remarkably hard
not to stare at him for his sheer strength of character had
always drawn her even when she was struggling bone
and sinew to resist him. Her painful awareness of just
how much he had once hurt her was doing nothing to
stabilise her emotions.

'Mrs Morrison's personal circumstances are irrelevant,' Rashad declared. 'Five years have passed. There
has not been a single attempt to service the loan advanced for the settlement of her debts, nor has there
been rent paid according to the tenancy agreement. Such
an abysmal record speaks for itself.'

As Rashad reminded Tilda of those embarrassing realities an uncomfortable flush washed her fair complexion. 'I recognise that Mum has dealt with all this very

badly, but unfortunately I wasn't aware until this week that you owned the house and had also loaned her money.'

At that declaration, his lean bronzed features took on a forbidding aspect. 'Another unlikely excuse? It is hard to credit that you believe the same scam could work twice.'

'*Scam?*' Tilda echoed with an uncertain laugh. 'What scam?'

'Did you think I wouldn't appreciate five years ago that you were doing everything you could to profit from our relationship? It was a scam aimed at milking my interest in you for as much money as you could get. You softened me up with your tear-jerking tales and very prettily you did it. Then your mother begged me to help her to protect you and your siblings from your evil stepfather's spendthrift ways!'

Tilda studied him in horror. 'I just can't believe that you can think that of me or Mum! I only ever told you the truth. I did not try to *milk* your interest in me—what a disgusting term!'

'What else did you do? Nor are your sensibilities as refined as you like to pretend. Why don't we look at the facts? When I first met you, you were working in a bar and dancing in a cage.'

Her turquoise eyes flashed with the blue-gold of a flame in the hottest part of the fire. Temper leapt up so high inside her that she was momentarily left breathless by the impact. Her slim white hands clenched into fists. 'I wondered when you were going to get around to mentioning that again. Since when was bar work on a level with prostitution? I wasn't a lap dancer or a stripper. The one time in my life I danced in a cage for a couple of hours and you never let me live it down!' she launched at him furiously. 'I should never have got involved with you. You were prejudiced against me from the start!'

Brilliant dark eyes gleamed warning gold beneath the lush black fringe of his lashes. 'The past is not up for discussion—'

'Except when it's you making a point?' Tilda was seething at the humiliation of having that ghastly cage episode flung in her teeth five years after the event. So much for Rashad acting like a stranger! Rashad, she thought suddenly, hadn't changed one little bit. He could always be depended on to remind her of the worst possible moments in her life. 'I'm not an immoral or dishonest or greedy person and I never have been!'

Rashad was dimly surprised to register that he was enjoying himself. She was the only woman who had ever dared to raise her voice in his vicinity or tried to argue with him. Once that trait had thoroughly irritated him but now he recognised it for the novelty and the weakness it was. His self-discipline absolute, he elevated a winged ebony brow in mocking encouragement. 'Is that so?'

'Of course it is…' Tilda pushed a trembling hand through the silky stray curls clinging to her warm forehead. 'For some reason you've put together a whole nasty scenario that didn't happen. There was never any plan to get money off you.'

'So…why, in your considered opinion, am I half a million pounds poorer from having known you?'

When Rashad mentioned that particular sum, consternation knocked the breath and the temper out of Tilda. 'Half…a million pounds?' she whispered shakily.

'The sale of the house will recoup some of that loss and the property has at least appreciated as an asset,' Rashad drawled with a complete calm that she found extremely threatening. 'But I assume the rent will never be paid and as for the loan—'

'It can't all come to half a million pounds!' Tilda gasped strickenly.

'Rather more. That is a conservative quote,' Rashad delivered drily. 'I'm surprised that you haven't already worked out the exact amount. I seem to recall that you have a head for figures as good as any calculator.'

Her soft full mouth pursed for she could recognise an insult no matter how well veiled it was. 'But I haven't had access to all the documentation involved.'

'In your role as innocent bystander, naturally not,' Rashad slotted in with an unconcealed derision as frank as a shout of disbelief. 'No matter, I intend to reclaim the debt in full.'

Realising that events were running on without her, Tilda was in a panic. 'You mustn't. If you were willing to give us more time—'

'Until the *next* millennium?'

'Why do you have such a low opinion of me?' Frustration pounded through Tilda, her eyes bright with angry incomprehension again. 'I understand that my family comes out of this looking like freeloaders, but when you won't even let me explain *why*—'

Intent dark golden eyes, heavily enhanced by spiky

black lashes, slammed coolly into hers. 'Let's stick to business.'

'OK. In one more year I hope to be fully qualified as an accountant.'

Rashad raised a brow in surprise. 'How novel…when you were with me, all you could talk about was being an artist.'

It was on the tip of her tongue to point out that the need to earn a living and help her mother raise her siblings had soon put paid to that prospect. She had had to give up her place at art college and find a job instead. But that was not a sacrifice she had ever questioned or regretted.

'I have the ability to earn a decent salary and start paying back what is owed,' Tilda swore with an urgency that betrayed the depth of her concern.

'You have an English saying. A bird in the hand is worth two in the bush. Promises are not of interest to me. If you have nothing more concrete to offer, one might wonder why you went to so much trouble to bring about this meeting,' Rashad drawled, soft and smooth as silk. 'At least, if I didn't know you I might wonder. Knowing you as I do, however, I suspect that you hoped to use your sex appeal as a bargaining chip.'

Tilda was so hugely taken aback by that unjust accusation that her soft mouth opened and shut again. Her coat and her boots covered her head to toe and she wasn't even wearing make-up. There was nothing provocative about her outfit. How did he think she should have presented herself? With a paper bag over her head and her body wrapped in a sack? Pure outrage lit her luminous blue-green gaze. 'How dare you suggest that?'

'But that's what you do. Five years ago you were very careful to withhold your body and play the virgin card to keep me interested.'

Absorbing those words, Tilda breathed in so deep she was vaguely surprised that she didn't spontaneously combust in front of him. 'So this is what you call sticking to business, is it?'

Grim dark golden eyes clashed with hers. 'But I *was* a business proposition as far as you were concerned. You set out to rip me off.'

Tilda snatched in a jerky breath. 'That's outrageous!'

'But true, nonetheless, and if you haven't come here to settle the outstanding debt or at least tender a substantial part of it, why *are* you here?' Rashad enquired very drily.

Her hands clenched into tight fists of restraint for she recognised how he had backed her into a corner and cut off every avenue of escape. If she told the truth and admitted that she had hoped to awaken his compassion by explaining her mother's circumstances, she would vindicate his accusation about her telling sob stories for profit. Her even white teeth set together. 'I hoped that you would give us more time to pay.'

Rashad strolled soundlessly towards her, his pronounced elegance of carriage contriving to hook her attention against her will. But then the very first thing that she had ever noticed about Rashad was the fluid, impossibly sexy grace of his every physical movement. At that memory a tiny betraying little quiver darted through her tummy, tensing her every muscle with defensiveness.

'On what basis would I grant a request for more time?' Rashad drawled lazily. 'I'm a businessman. If you can't raise the money now, there is little chance that you could produce it in the near future.'

'You weren't behaving like a businessman when you commented on the fact that I didn't sleep with you five years ago!' Tilda suddenly shot at him, fed up of playing the game solely by his rules. 'You are totally biased against me!'

Rashad strolled closer. He was so much taller that Tilda felt overshadowed by his proximity. 'Don't waste my time trying to distract me from the issue. I will ask you again—why are you here?'

A faint aromatic hint of sandalwood caught at Tilda's throat and her nostrils and threatened to send her spiralling down into a rich tide of recollection. She was trying to avoid meeting his dark golden gaze, but she could feel his scrutiny and it was as if heat pulsed wherever his brilliant eyes chose to rest. Her mouth tingled, her slender throat tightened. A languorous heaviness was seeping up through her lower limbs, coiling in her belly and sending fingers of awareness darting through her small full breasts.

'For goodness' sake, you know why I'm here,' she argued half under her breath. Being that close to him made her feel dominated and she took a swift step back.

Every imperious line of his lithe hard body taut with command and impatience, Rashad was determined to strip her bare of her manipulative pretences. He closed the distance between them again. 'From my point of view it would appear that you have approached me with nothing to offer but yourself.'

Hot pink flooded her cheeks and she was startled into

a swift upward glance. She was so conscious of his potent authority and strength that she continued to back away from him without even being aware of what she was doing. 'What on earth is that supposed to mean?' she queried half an octave higher.

'I don't think you're that naïve.'

Taut with wrathful incredulity as he confirmed that he meant what she had assumed he could not possibly dare to suggest, Tilda stared up at him, turquoise eyes bright as jewels. 'Are you suggesting that I would try to offer you *sex?*' she gasped.

Cynical amusement filled Rashad, for she acted the affronted virgin with such perfection. 'In the absence of any other option, what else is there?'

At that cruelly mocking confirmation, the anger inside Tilda just cut loose of her restraint and she tried to slap him. But unfortunately her victim had far faster responses and he caught her wrist in midair. 'No... I don't tolerate tantrums!'

'Let go of me!' Tilda gritted in a tempest of fury at having been both insulted and denied any right of reprisal.

'Not until you calm down.' Rashad retained a firm hold on her narrow wrist. He was angry with her but there was a dark, insidious excitement beginning to stir, as well. A desire for what he had once been denied, he told himself harshly. Yet why should he censure himself for what were only natural promptings? He had a powerful libido and she was a very beautiful woman. A mere seventy years earlier, his grandfather had enjoyed a harem of concubines. For a split second, Rashad allowed himself to imagine what it would be like to have

Tilda Crawford entirely at his disposal at any hour of the day. *His alone.* The images that assailed him were so compellingly evocative that they were dispelled only with the greatest difficulty.

'I said—let go!' Tilda was so mad at being held captive like a disobedient child that she attempted to kick him. As he evaded that new potential angle of assault she yanked herself free with a suddenness that sent her careening into the piece of furniture behind her. With a yelp of dismay she fell over the coffee-table and landed on her behind on the other side of it with a loud thump.

'Is it not time that you learned how to control your temper?' With smouldering dark golden eyes, Rashad surveyed her lying in tumbled disarray on his office carpet. He strode forward, reached down and pulled her upright again in one easy motion. 'Are you hurt?'

'No.' Stiff with shame and embarrassment at her loss of control in the presence of the enemy, Tilda shook her head. She tried to make herself apologise and, unfortunately, the words were strangled at the back of her throat. At that moment she hated him with a passion. Yet she had only to connect with his brilliant gaze for a heartbeat to feel the stark rise of yearning that slaughtered her pride.

Rashad studied her lush raspberry-pink mouth and remembered the soft sweet taste of it. He allowed his imagination full sway while he asked himself why he should not turn fantasy into fact. *Tilda at his disposal.* Unleashed from his habitual rigid self-discipline, fierce arousal licked like blazing flames of fire at his lithe, muscular frame. Almost as quickly he reached a decision. He would indulge himself with her. He would indulge his every desire with her until he was sated of that pale blonde perfection.

Why should he not take her? Would it not be the natural justice that he was entitled to claim? Why should he consider the question of honour with a woman of her reputation? He knew what she was. Somewhere he still had the security file that had destroyed his youthful illusions. While he had been with her, she had lied to him, deceived him and slept with other men. Rashad had learnt to his cost that fine principles were a serious weakness and a handicap around Tilda Crawford.

Startlingly aware of the buzz in the tense atmosphere, Tilda was trembling. As she took a step back her hips hit the wall and she braced her slim shoulders against it, gathering up her courage. 'I wasn't offering you sex,' she told him defensively.

Rashad surveyed her with glittering intensity. 'It's the only thing you have to give that I want.'

The silence pulsed and vibrated.

'Are you mad?' Barely able to credit that Rashad could admit that shocking truth to her without betraying even a glimmer of shame, Tilda sucked in a shuddering breath. 'I refuse to believe that you're serious! Sex in return for money? How can you insult me to that extent?'

'Most women consider my attentions an honour. The choice is yours.' His stunning golden gaze narrowed to a smouldering glitter, Rashad let a long brown forefinger push up her chin so that their eyes could meet. 'Make the right choice and you will discover that I can make repayment the sweetest of pleasures.'

Tilda was even more taken aback when that low-pitched forecast made her mouth run dry and butterflies break loose in her tummy. She could not dredge her attention from his lean, strong face or the shimmering gold of his stare. He lowered his arrogant dark head and a pulse beat like a drum pounded through her, leaving every inch of her tense as a drawn bow with anticipation. A little voice told her to move away, raise a hand to keep him away from her, even angle her head back out of reach. She heard the voice but she stayed put, controlled by much more powerful influences. His mouth came down on hers in a slow, languorous tasting that unleashed a host of sensations that she had forced herself to forget. It was a ravishingly potent kiss. Her breasts felt full and constrained by her clothing. A shivery little frisson of wicked delight ran through her slender figure and stirred a deep ache of hunger between her thighs.

Reacting to that shattering response with horror-stricken recoil, Tilda pulled back and spluttered, 'No, thank you very much! Once burnt, twice shy!'

Stunning eyes veiled, Rashad surveyed her with satisfaction.

'So you can still kiss up a storm!' Tilda launched at him furiously. 'But you should be ashamed of yourself for treating me like this!'

Rashad consulted the rapier thin designer watch on his wrist and murmured with smooth regret, 'I have another appointment now. Your time is up.'

'Oh, don't you worry—I'm going all right!' Tilda spun on her heel and hauled open the door with a perspiring palm.

Rashad sent her a sardonic smile. 'You really couldn't expect me to fall for the same fairy stories this time around.'

Her oval face red as fire, Tilda stalked out.

CHAPTER THREE

TILDA got on the train back to Oxford. She was in shock. Everything about her meeting with Rashad had shaken her up. Not least the manner in which she had reacted to that kiss! Her passionate physical response to him had coursed through her like a river in flood and she was furious with herself. Evidently loathing Prince Rashad Hussein Al-Zafar was no defence whatsoever against his persuasive sensuality. What did that say about her intelligence or her self-control?

In that field, Tilda conceded angrily, absolutely nothing had changed in five wretched years. Rashad had still only to touch her to set her on fire with longing. But nobody knew better than Tilda that it was a kind of weakness that could lead to disaster. Her family history bore that out. Her mother, Beth, had only been nineteen when she had fallen pregnant with Tilda and had had to get married in a hurry. Beth's woes had not ended there for her husband had resented his new family obligations. An ambitious young lawyer, he had been a neglectful husband and an uninterested parent. Five years later, Beth had become a widow and an easy mark for Scott

Morrison's promises of undying devotion. Madly in love, Beth had conceived her third child just a few months into the relationship and had rushed back into marriage with seriously unhappy results.

Tilda suppressed a sigh. Although she felt guilty acknowledging it, she had tried to learn by her mother's mistakes and had resolved that no man would ever be allowed to come between her and her wits, or her education, for that matter. In the early teenage years she had had little interest in boys. Scott's bullying, drinking and womanising had put her off the entire male sex, while she had done what she could to support her mother and help out with the younger children.

At eighteen years old, she had been in her last year of school. When Scott had told her that he had fixed her up with part-time work as a waitress in a nightclub managed by one of his seedy friends she had been incensed, for she had already had a weekend job in a supermarket. Unfortunately whenever Tilda had dared to defy Scott, he had taken his temper out on the rest of her family, who had been much less able to stand up to him. Within a week the continual arguments and her mother's distress had vanquished Tilda's resistance. While dutifully agreeing with Beth that, yes, she would earn more money, she had known that the extra hours and late nights would scarcely be conducive to the intensive studying she had been doing for her final exams.

From the outset Tilda had hated the attention that her looks had drawn from the customers. The club had attracted slick, high-earning professionals and wealthy students and spoilt young men who had drunk too much and thought the female staff were fair game. Tilda had soon realised why the manager only seemed to hire waitresses who were more than ordinarily attractive. Some of them had regularly slept with the clientele in return for gifts or cash and their liberal ways had encouraged custom.

Tilda had worked there only a fortnight before she had first seen Rashad. His supple, sexy aura as he had descended the stairs had caught her eye first. When he had turned his head and locked dark golden eyes with hers, she had literally stopped breathing. Mentally it had been like running into a solid brick wall and seeing stars. She had found it impossible not to keep gazing around to see where he was, or to steal another transfixed glance at him. Every time she had looked, she had found that he was looking, too, and, even though that had embarrassed her, she had been helpless to resist temptation.

A big dark-haired guy had approached her towards the end of that evening. 'Fancy coming to a party tonight?' he asked, his foreign accent roughening his pronunciation.

'No, thanks,' she said flatly, turning away.

'I'm Leonidas Pallis and I have a friend who wants to meet you.' He dropped a card and a hundred pound note down on the tray she was holding. 'Party kicks off around midnight. That should cover your cab fare.'

'I said, no, thanks.' Her cheeks scarlet, Tilda thrust the banknote back at him and walked away.

Soon afterwards, a waitress called Chantal came over to speak to her. 'You really riled Leonidas. Don't you know who he is? He's the grandson of a Greek tycoon and he's absolutely loaded. He gives incredible tips and throws amazing parties. What's your problem?'

'I'm just not interested in mixing with the customers outside working hours.' Tilda could also have mentioned that she had school the next day, but the manager had banned her from admitting that she was still a schoolgirl as he had said it might give the club a bad name.

When she emerged into the car park at closing time, a surprising number of vehicles were still there. She heard a vigorous burst of male laughter. Her heart sank when she spotted the Greek guy drinking from a bottle and leaning up against the bonnet of a Ferrari with his mates. Then she saw Rashad straightening up and moving towards her. Something very like panic gripped her but her feet were frozen to the spot. He was so stunningly handsome she was mesmerised by the clean, hard-boned lines of lean dark features.

'I'm Rashad,' he murmured softly, and he extended his hand with a formality that took her entirely by surprise.

'Tilda,' she breathed, just touching his lean brown fingers.

'May I drive you home?'

'I get a lift with one of the other girls.'

Unexpectedly, Rashad smiled as if such an explanation was perfectly acceptable to him. 'Of course. It is very late. Will you give me your phone number?'

That charismatic smile threatened her defences and she battened down the hatches, terrified of what he was making her feel. 'No, sorry. I don't date club members.'

The following evening the club manager, Pete, cornered her. 'I hear you blew away our new royal VIP last night,' he accused.

'Royal?' Tilda parroted, wide-eyed.

'Prince Rashad, the heir to the throne of Bakhar and a string of oil wells.' Pete dealt her an angry look. 'Our two best customers—Leonidas Pallis and Sergio Torrente—brought him in. Those guys are minted, too. They spend thousands here and I don't want any stupid little girl offending them. Is that clear?'

'But I haven't done anything.'

'Do yourself a favour. Smile sweetly and give the prince your phone number.'

Pete changed the table rota so that, on her next shift, Tilda was serving the VIP table. Now that she knew who Rashad was, she noticed his thickset bodyguards trying unsuccessfully to stay in the background. Uneasily aware of his royal status, she tried very hard to put him out of her mind. But he dominated her every thought and response. It was as if an invisible wire attached her to him, so that she noticed his every tiny move. In comparison with him, his companions were immature. He seemed to be the only one of the group graced with morals or manners. He didn't drink to excess, he didn't fool around, he was always courteous. He was also absolutely, totally gorgeous and it did not escape her attention that every girl in the place had her eye on him.

The night she tripped and dropped a tray of drinks, everything changed. While his rowdy mates laughed at the spectacle she made, Rashad sprang to his feet and immediately helped her up from the floor.

'You are unhurt?'

Her hand trembled in his and she connected with brilliant dark eyes enhanced by luxuriant ebony lashes.

'When you fell my heart stopped beating,' he breathed in a raw undertone.

That was the moment she went from being infatuated with his vibrant dark good looks to falling head over heels in love with him, but she still pulled her hand free with muffled thanks and hurriedly walked away. She saw it as being sensible and protecting herself from a broken heart. What future was there in loving a guy who was only a temporary visitor to her country and, even worse, destined to be a king? His two friends approached her later that evening. Making it clear that the shy stolen glances that betrayed her attraction to Rashad had not passed unnoticed, Leonidas and Sergio virtually accused her of being a tease.

'How much do you want to go out with him?' Leonidas demanded contemptuously, peeling off notes from the thick wad in his wallet.

'You're not rich enough!' Tilda snapped in disgust.

She went home in tears that night only to find her stepfather, Scott, drunkenly upbraiding her mother with the club manager, Pete's, complaint that Tilda had an unfriendly attitude towards the customers. The next weekend Pete told her that she had to stand in for one of the cage dancers who had called in sick. She refused. Threatened with the sack and worn down by what felt like everybody's criticisms, she gave way, reasoning that the bikini-style outfit exposed no more than she would have revealed at the swimming pool. She persuaded herself that nobody really looked at the dancers except as gyrating bodies that added to the club atmosphere.

When Rashad arrived, a birthday cake was brought

in for his benefit. Tilda still recalled the instant when he had registered who was dancing in the cage: the shock and consternation, the distaste he had been unable to hide. In the same moment cage dancing had gone from being what Tilda had told herself was essentially harmless to the equivalent of dancing naked and shameless in the street. When Rashad studiously averted his attention from her as though she were putting on an indecent display, she fled from the cage and refused to get back into it again. Chantal later revealed that Tilda had been set up.

'It's the prince's twenty-fifth birthday. Sergio and Leonidas thought it would be a laugh to get you into the cage. They paid Pete to fix it for them.'

Tilda never did tell Rashad that truth. Telling tales about his best friends wouldn't have got her very far. Instead, she blamed herself for not having had the guts to tell Pete where to get off. Eyes red from tears, she put on her uniform and got on with her usual waitressing. Already promised a full-time summer job at the firm owned by Evan Jerrold, she consoled herself with the prayerful hope that she would not be serving drinks for much longer. Unhappily, however, new employment would mean that she was unlikely to ever see Rashad again.

When she finished her shift, she emerged from the club to find the weather was wet and unseasonably cold, and that the girl who usually gave her a lift had gone off to a party without telling her. Shivering while she was trying to call a cab on her mobile, she tensed when a silver Aston Martin Vanquish pulled up in front of her with a throaty growl. Rashad sprang out and studied her in silence across the bonnet and she knew he wouldn't ask anything of her because he had asked before and she had said no. He was too proud to ask again. Tears made her eyes smart; she still felt so utterly humiliated that she had let herself be pressed into dancing in the cage.

As Rashad walked round the bonnet and reached out to open the passenger door one of his bodyguards skidded up at speed to do it for him and prevent him from lowering himself to such a mundane task.

'Thanks,' she said gruffly and got in. At that moment she was not aware of having made a decision. She just couldn't muster the mental resistance to walk away from him again. She told herself that if she kept things as light as though it were a holiday romance she wouldn't get hurt.

'You'll have to tell me where you live,' Rashad murmured as calmly as if she had been getting into his car every night for months.

'Happy birthday,' she said in a wobbly voice, as the excessively emotional surge of tears was still threatening her composure.

At the traffic lights he reached for her hand and almost crushed it within the fierce hold of his. 'In my country we stopped putting people in cages when slavery was outlawed a hundred years ago.'

'I shouldn't have agreed to do it.'

'You did not wish to?'

'Of course not—apart from anything else, I'm not a dancer.'

'Don't do it again,' Rashad told her with innate authority and instantly she wanted to do it again just to demonstrate her independence. She had to bite her lip not to respond with the defiance that she had acquired to hold her own with her stepfather.

And so it began: a relationship that attracted a great deal of unwelcome comment from others. Leonidas Pallis made it clear that he regarded her in much the same light as a call-girl. Sergio Torrente, the sleek, sophisticated Italian who completed the trio of friends, seemed equally disdainful of Tilda's right to be treated with respect, but was not quite so obvious about revealing the fact. Had she been less green about the strength of male bonding, she might have realised then that with such powerful enemies her relationship with Rashad was utterly doomed to end in tears.

As the hateful Leonidas Pallis put it, 'Why can't you keep it simple?' Tilda heard him ask Rashad this during a night out. 'Boy meets girl, boy shags girl, boy dumps girl. You don't romance waitresses!'

As her revolting stepfather put it: 'Well, you can thank me for getting you the job that's about to make your fortune. Tell him you like cash better than diamonds.'

Offered the chance to rent a room in a student house for the summer, she grabbed it to escape Scott and quit working at the club. At the same time she started her temporary job in the accounts department at Jerrold Plastics. The weeks that followed were the happiest but also the stormiest of her life, because Rashad laid down the law as if he were her commanding officer and did not adapt well to disagreement. She was challenged to keep his hands off her, but whenever passion threatened to overcome prudence she backed off fast. She was a virgin, well aware that she came from a very fertile line of women, and she was totally terrified of getting pregnant. She honestly believed, too, that keeping serious sex out of the equation would lessen the pain when Rashad returned to Bakhar.

Tilda was yanked out of those unsettling recollections only when the train pulled into the station. While she queued for the bus, she began putting the recent knowledge she had gained into those memories and she winced at the picture that began to emerge. Although she had had no idea of it, there had been a whole hidden dimension to her relationship with Rashad. That financial aspect encompassed, not only the embarrassing level of her family's indebtedness, but also a seemingly brazen reluctance on her family's part to pay rent or pay off the loan. Was it any wonder that over time Rashad had become suspicious of her motives and decided that all along she must have been a gold-digger out for all she could get?

Sex… *It's the only thing you have to give that I want.* Still outraged by that declaration, Tilda could find no excuse for him on that score. Obviously that was all he had ever wanted from her and the brutal way he had ditched her had spelt out the same message. She was proud of the fact that she had not slept with Rashad five years earlier. But just as swiftly the false courage of offended pride and anger started to wane in the face of reality. When she began walking down the road where she lived her steps got slower and slower as she neared her home. After all, what had she achieved? She had got nowhere with Rashad. He was tough, resolute and ruthless. Emotion never got in the way of his self-discipline. Sadly, the strength, intellect and tenacity that she had once admired also made Rashad a lethally effective opponent.

Tilda was wrenched from her reflections by the startling sight of her former stepfather climbing into his beat-up car outside her home. As the older man had never demonstrated the smallest interest in maintaining contact with Katie, James and Megan, his three children by her mother, Tilda was taken aback. 'What are you doing here?' she asked in dismay.

'Mind your own bloody business!' Scott Morrison told her, his heavy face flushed with aggression below his thinning blond hair.

Seriously concerned, Tilda watched him shoot his vehicle back out onto the road. Why had he been visiting the house? He had come at a time when her mother would be alone. She went straight into Beth's workroom. Her mother was sobbing and the room was in turmoil. Curtains were heaped on the floor in a tangle and a chair had been turned over. Perhaps most telling of all, the older woman's purse lay open on the ironing board with only a few coins spilling out of it.

'I bumped into Scott outside. Has he been taking money off you again?' Tilda asked baldly.

Beth broke down and, piece by horrible piece, the whole story came tumbling out. When Scott had found out several years earlier that Rashad was the current owner of the house, he had accused Beth of defrauding him of his share of the property. Ever since then Beth had been living in fear of Scott's visits and giving way to his threats and demands for money. While she soothed the distraught older woman, Tilda's anger grew for she finally understood why Beth had found it impossible even to pay rent. From behind the scenes, Scott Morrison had still been bleeding Tilda's family dry.

'Scott got what he was entitled to when the divorce settlement went through the court. He has no right to anything more. He's been telling you lies. I'm going to get the police, Mum—'

'No, you can't do that.' Beth gave her a look of horror. 'Katie and James would die of shame if their father was arrested—'

'No, they'd die of shame at what's been going on here, what you've been putting up with on their behalf! Silence protects bullies like Scott. Don't you worry…I'll sort him out,' Tilda swore, furious with herself for not even suspecting what had been going on behind all their backs. The divorce had not gotten rid of Scott after all and working for a living had never been his way.

She was hanging her coat below the stairs when she noticed that the post had arrived. She tensed at the sight of the familiar brown envelope and scooped it up. Yes, just as she had feared it *was* yet another missive from Rashad's solicitors. Taking a deep breath, she tore it open. Nervous perspiration broke out on her brow as she realised what the letter was. It was a written notice asking her mother to leave the house within fourteen days. As the rent was in arrears the landlord, it stated, would go to court seeking possession at the end of the month.

Tilda took the letter upstairs. She just could not face giving it to her mother at that moment. From the window she watched her sisters, seventeen-year-old Katie and nine-year-old Megan, walking up the drive in their school uniforms. James was shambling along in their wake, a tall gangling boy of fourteen, who had still to grow into his very large feet and deep bass voice. Her brother, Aubrey, currently in his fourth year of studying medicine, would be home later. Tilda was deeply attached to all of her siblings. They had gone through so much unhappiness when Scott had been making their lives hell but they had stayed close. They were good kids, hard-working and sensible. What would losing their home mean to them? *Everything.* It would shatter her family, because Beth's agoraphobia would ensure that the older woman could not cope. When Beth fell apart at the seams, what then? Aubrey would probably drop out of med school and Katie would find it impossible to study for her A-levels.

There was only one way out, only one way of protecting her family from the horror of being put out on the street: Rashad.

Rashad…and sex. It would most probably be a major disappointment to Rashad, whose womanising exploits filled endless pages in the tabloid newspapers, to discover that Tilda did not possess a single special sexy talent to offer in the bedroom. Nothing but ignorance. It would serve him right, Tilda reflected, tight-mouthed. Even so, common sense urged that she would have to ensure that he wrote off all the debts and the house as well before it dawned on him that she really wasn't worth the sacrifice of that much money. She shuddered, shame enveloping her from head to toe. She would be selling herself like a product in return for cash.

She reminded herself that if she hadn't been so fearful of heartache and pregnancy, she would have ended up in bed with Rashad while she had been dating him. But it would have been different back then, because she had truly loved him and had certainly believed that he had more feelings for her than he had finally demonstrated. Would she be able to have sex just for the sake of it? Presumably other women did. There was no point being over-sensitive to the reality that she really had no choice if she wanted to protect the people she loved from having their lives devastated.

Standing by the window, she called Metropolis Enterprises on her mobile and asked to speak to Rashad. Various very well-trained personnel tried to head her off and make her settle for much smaller fry. She persisted with the reminder that she'd had an appointment with the prince earlier that day and added that he would be very annoyed if he did not receive her personal call.

Rashad was in a meeting when the message flashed up on his BlackBerry. *Tilda.* A slow, chilling smile curved his wide, handsome mouth as he took the call in his office. So, the fish was biting. He felt like a shark about to attend a banquet. She was his. Finally his to enjoy. At his leisure in a place of his choosing and for as long as he wanted her. He would make all the rules and she would really, really hate that. His brilliant dark golden eyes gleamed with anticipation. He pictured her greeting him when he returned from a long trip abroad and knew instantly where he would accommodate her. Somewhere where her talent for infidelity could not possibly be exercised. A discreet location where she had nothing to do but devote herself to being his sexual entertainment. He could think of no place more suitable than his late grandfather's desert palace.

'How may I be of assistance?' Rashad drawled smoother than the most expensive silk in tone.

Instantly Tilda wanted to reach down the phone and slap him, for she knew that he knew exactly why she was ringing. She swallowed her pride with difficulty. 'I'm willing to accept your offer.'

'What offer?'

Her short upper lip dampened with perspiration. 'You said it was the only thing I had to offer that you wanted.'

'Your body,' Rashad filled in gently, savouring every syllable. 'You. We'll have to meet to discuss the rules.'

'What rules?' she protested. 'I just want to know that that eviction order won't proceed.'

'Meet me tomorrow afternoon at my town house.' He quoted the address and a time. 'We'll sort out the details of our future association. You'll be living abroad. I can tell you that now.'

As Tilda parted her lips to argue with that alarmingly unexpected assurance, Rashad concluded drily, 'It will be as I say.'

At that juncture he terminated the call. He would not compromise on any point. The rules would not be negotiable. Everything would be as he wanted it to be. The sooner she learned that and accepted it, the better.

CHAPTER FOUR

EVAN JERROLD brought his elegant Jaguar car to a halt in the exclusive London residential square. 'Good luck,' he said cheerfully.

'Thank you.' Tilda opened the passenger door of the luxury vehicle with a sense of relief, since telling lies made her uncomfortable. Evan had offered her a lift when her mother had mentioned that Tilda was heading to London that afternoon. Asked why she was taking time out of work, Tilda had told the first fib that had occurred to her—that she was attending a job interview. It had then occurred to her that the excuse of a new job could well be the perfect cover, if Rashad stuck to his insistence that she travel abroad.

'Now remember I'll give you an excellent reference. I'll call back in an hour because you may be finished by then,' Evan told her.

Tilda was embarrassed. 'There's no need.'

The older man gave her a wry smile. 'If I have to drop you home again, it'll give me another excuse to see your mother. Don't think I haven't noticed that her spirits are very low just now.'

Clambering out of the car, Tilda almost winced at his insight, grateful that her siblings were less perceptive. She mounted the steps to the imposing front door, nerves leaping through her like jumping beans that couldn't settle.

'Tilda!' Evan called after her. 'You forgot your bag.'

Tilda hurried back down the steps to take it from him, apologising and thanking him in one urgent breath. Admitted to the town house by a manservant, she was shown to a seat in the large stylish hall. She wondered if Rashad's household staff still routinely greeted his every appearance on bended knee, touching their very brows to the floor in the need to demonstrate respect to the heir to the throne. A couple of minutes later, a bearded older man with greying hair appeared and came to a sudden halt at the sight of her, an expression of surprise skimming his thin intelligent face. With a scrupulously polite dipping of his head in acknowledgement of her presence, he walked past her and went out.

Tilda was ushered upstairs into a very grand drawing room. She was pleased to note that the manservant bowed rather than knelt. 'Miss Crawford, Your Royal Highness.'

Rashad surveyed her with dark eyes as cold as Arctic ice. Clad in a casual grey hooded jacket and black trousers, she should have looked ordinary. But the unassuming clothes simply accentuated her beauty and the slender grace of her figure. Several irrepressible curls were already springing loose above her brow with a silvery fair abundance that hinted at the full glory of her hair when it was worn loose. Memories stirred and, with the image, a surge of arousal, which he rigorously sought to control.

'Take a seat,' Rashad told her huskily.

Eyes bright as slivers of pure turquoise above cheekbones stung pink by the spring breeze, Tilda shot him an edgy glance. Once again he was formally dressed in a superb charcoal-grey business suit teamed with a white shirt and a cobalt-blue silk tie. He looked amazingly handsome. And grim. Well, that was at least familiar, she told herself in an effort to gain control of herself. Rashad in censorious mode was nothing new to Tilda. When she had been dating him, she had sometimes felt as if he was putting her through a meticulous self-improvement programme. Feeling uncomfortably warm, she unbuttoned her jacket, removed it and sat down stiffly in an armchair.

'It was tasteless to allow your current lover to bring you here,' Rashad said with derision, 'but very much in line with the kind of childish defiance I expect from you.'

Tilda drew in some oxygen to steady herself and focused on his hand-stitched shoes. *Childish?* She reminded herself of the eviction order and of the vast amount of money outstanding and told herself that a few insults wouldn't hurt her. On the other hand, wrong assumptions had to be righted. 'Evan is old enough to be my father. I once worked for him. That's all.'

Rashad dealt her an unimpressed appraisal. 'You attended an academic dinner with him and he's a wealthy man.'

'How did you know about that dinner? He's a family friend and he needed a partner for the event. His bank balance doesn't come into it.' Her eyes were bright with the anger and resentment firing through her tense body.

'I appreciate that you really don't like me and have a very low opinion of me. So please explain—what am I doing here?'

'Look in the mirror,' Rashad advised without hesitation.

Tilda had somehow expected him to contradict her when she had accused him of not liking her. His failure to do so shook her and she could not silence the words that sprang to her lips. 'What sort of a guy wants to have a relationship with a woman he dislikes?'

'Define relationship.'

Discovering that she was suddenly super-sensitive to his every word and potential putdown, Tilda coloured to the roots of her pale hair. She got the message: his sole interest in her was physical. 'You mentioned rules,' she framed curtly, studying her tightly linked hands, telling herself that she needed to grow a thicker skin.

'No other men. I expect total fidelity.'

Tilda was so outraged by his self-assurance as it came at her like a bolt from the blue that she leapt to her feet. 'What the heck do you think I am? I've never been unfaithful to anybody!'

Rashad vented a harsh laugh of disagreement. 'I know you slept with other men while you were with me five years ago!'

Tilda blinked and then focused unbelieving turquoise eyes on his lean, vibrant face. Hauteur and fierce reserve were etched in every angular line of his startlingly handsome features. She registered in dismay that there could be no doubt that he actually believed what he was saying. 'I can hardly credit that you're accusing me of something so despicable! Why would you choose to believe something like that about me? I mean, for goodness' sake, why would I be seeing you and carrying on with other guys at the same time?'

'I was purely a business proposition.'

Her hands knotted into fists of frustration. 'So why didn't I grab you the first chance I got?'

'Playing hard to get made me keener.'

Tilda appreciated that he had long since explained any inconsistencies in her behaviour to his own satisfaction. He had made the cap fit even if it didn't belong to her. 'I did not sleep with anyone else while I was with you...what is your problem, Rashad? I was in love with you!' she launched back at him, angry with him and angry with herself for feeling cut to the bone by his demeaning misconceptions. She had found it hard enough to deal with the idea that he thought her avaricious, but to learn that he also thought she was a slut had to be the ultimate slap in the face.

'So you wanted me to believe.'

'Who are these men I'm supposed to have slept with?' she demanded furiously.

'I see no point in rehashing your past misdemeanours.' The twist of his wide, sensual mouth had more than a hint of disdain.

Undaunted, Tilda lifted her chin to a pugnacious angle. 'Whereas I'm happy to rehash them, because the allegations you have made are completely untrue!'

'I'm bored with this discussion. It's ancient history.' Rashad rested forbidding dark eyes on the animated oval of her face, wondering what she hoped to achieve with her futile protestations of innocence. 'Naturally I have seen the proof of those allegations.'

'Well, I want to see that proof!'

'That is not possible. Nor am I prepared to argue with you on this issue.'

Tilda was trembling with vexation. 'You can't confront me with accusations of that nature and then deny me the right to respond.'

His dark gaze narrowed and flashed a hard golden challenge. 'It is my belief that I can do whatever I want. If you don't like it that way, you are of course free to leave.'

Tilda was so wound up that she was on the brink of tears of fury. The dark, intimidating power of him faced her like a solid stone wall as implacable as his expression. He would not back down or compromise. His potent strength had been honed by experiences that were tougher than any she would ever know. Pinning her taut lips together, Tilda made her stiff knees bend and she lowered herself slowly back into the armchair. It was an acknowledgement of defeat that savaged her pride, but she knew that if she staged a pitched battle with him she would lose. And so, unhappily, would her family. Rashad was convinced she was a gold-digging trollop and he had evidently thought that way about her for a long time. No longer did she need to marvel at the brutality with which she had been dumped, she reflected bitterly. Whether she liked it or not, she would have to save her defence for a more promising moment. Pale as milk, and with the effort that self-discipline demanded, she folded her hands together.

'Rules,' she prompted woodenly.

'You make an effort to please me.'

Tilda dared to lift her head. 'Would you care to elaborate on that?' she pressed shakily.

'No half measures. I tell you what I want and you strive to deliver,' Rashad specified silkily. 'In where you live, in what you wear, in how you behave, in everything that you do.'

A Stepford wife without the wedding ring, Tilda thought in horror. A living, breathing puppet with a puppeteer pulling her strings at every turn. She was aghast at the prospect of Rashad taking control of her life to that extent, but not at all surprised by his expectations, for telling people what to do and how to do it came very naturally to the future King of Bakhar. Unfortunately doing as she was told when it was Rashad doing the telling did not come naturally to Tilda. While she had no problem accepting authority in other areas of her life, a rebellious demon of resentment had ignited inside her five years ago whenever Rashad had laid down the law.

'I…I thought you just wanted to sleep with me,' Tilda muttered in a small tight voice. 'Why do you have to make such a production out of it?'

'Pleasure deferred has a keener edge.' Rashad noted the fact that her thin fingers were digging convulsively into the fabric of the garment folded across her lap. She was all worked up and could not hide the fact. It did not fit his image of her and it troubled him.

Why do you have to make such a production out of it? He marvelled at that gauche comment and the implication that sex on her terms was nothing worth getting excited about. But how likely was it that so experienced a woman could also be that naïve? Most probably she was trying to manipulate him again and win his sympathy. Was anything about her real? Was her every expression and word part of an act designed to deceive? Once, she had played the innocent so well, pulling back from his passion to ensure that he lived in a torment of unslaked desire for her. That recollection roused the blazing anger and bitterness that he had kept taped down for five long years. He had wanted her as he had never wanted any woman—before or since.

'Whatever,' Tilda mumbled, loathing the level coolness of Rashad's intonation, wondering what had happened to the markedly conservative streak that had once set him apart from his much more liberal companions. No doubt, such sensitive and civilised niceties had long since bitten the dust beneath the tidal wave of uninhibited sexual licence he had been enjoying ever since he had left her. How dared he accuse her of infidelity when he had betrayed *her?* She hated him for dragging her pride in the dust. She hated him for judging her unfairly, for his determination to have the last word. She really, *really* hated him.

'On the other hand, there's no reason why you shouldn't give me a preview of what I can expect from you,' Rashad declared, the rich, dark timbre of his accented drawl smoother and softer than the most exclusive silk.

Her silvery fair head raised, jewelled eyes locking to his with instant consternation. 'A…a preview?' she parroted unevenly.

'I think you understand perfectly.'

And Tilda froze. It was a test, she was sure of it! She could not credit that he could expect her to go to bed with him there and then. Suddenly she was all for him making as much of a production of that event as he pleased. Indeed, anything that might keep that act of intimacy in the future rather than the present got her vote. Her shaken blue-green eyes tangled reluctantly with his.

His smouldering dark golden gaze was hot as a flame on her oval face. Her heart started a slow, thudding pound behind her breastbone. She was in a state of alert that left her too tense to breathe and with her tongue glued to the roof of her dry mouth. She was maddeningly aware of the heaviness of her breasts and the tingling tenderness of her nipples. Liquid heat was pooling like a rich swirl of honey in her pelvis. She shifted in her seat, suddenly unable to sit still, feeling the familiar hunger build like a dam about to break its banks and wash away her barriers.

'Come here...' Rashad urged thickly, swooping down to grasp her hand and tug her upright, impelling her straight into the proximity she would have done almost anything to avoid.

Before Tilda could even attempt to suppress her response to him, he claimed her soft, full lips with a hungry growl of resolve. The hot, hard insistence of his mouth on hers was shockingly demanding. He gave her no opportunity to deny him and the erotic plunge of his tongue into the tender interior of her mouth made her shiver violently in reaction against his big, powerful frame. Her heartbeat was racing.

Every sense she possessed was reeling from the impact. The taste of him was addictive. Her hands rose to his broad shoulders initially to steady herself and then to feverishly close there. Her fingers dug into the expensive cloth of his jacket as though she needed that support to stay upright in the dizzy world of seductive sensation that enthralled her. Every kiss made her long with frantic impatience for the next. He pushed up her sweater and closed a hand on one lush full breast in a bold caress. He thrust her light cotton bra from his path and chafed a straining pink nipple. She whimpered in shock and excitement. Her knees threatened to fold under her. There was a tight band of tension across her belly, a tormenting feeling of need that made her push against him in blind demand for assuagement.

Rashad clamped his hands to her hips to urge her closer to the raging heat of his desire. He was as hard as iron. She wasn't resisting a single move he made. Raw triumph flooded him with all-male energy. Too well did he recall how she had once become as unresponsive as a marble statue in his arms. He bent down and scooped her off her feet at decisive speed. The sooner he satisfied his desire for that slim, perfect body of hers, the better. She had the morals of an alley cat. As she had said herself, making a production out of the event was most inappropriate. For what reason would he wait?

Tilda gasped for air to ease her oxygen-starved lungs. Trembling like a leaf in a high wind, she opened anxious eyes to focus on Rashad's lean darkly handsome face above hers. He had snatched her up into his powerful arms as though she weighed no more than a doll. 'Where are we g-going?' she stammered.

Rashad kicked open a door with controlled force. He had appointments to keep, not to mention a flight to New York scheduled. He didn't care. Just for once in his life he was going to do what he wanted to do, not what he *should* do! He wanted her now; he did not want to wait one hour longer. Had he not waited five years already? He settled her down on his bed and immediately undid the clip that confined her hair. He sank caressing hands into the tumbling mass and drew it across her slight shoulders so that it fell almost to her waist in a glorious snaking tangle of platinum-blond ringlets.

Aghast to find herself on a bed when mere minutes earlier she had been safe in a drawing room, Tilda stared up at him wide-eyed. The Rashad she remembered would never have kissed her like that and swept her off into a bedroom without hesitation. He had treated her with respect and restraint. She was stunned by the change in him. Even briefly deprived of his caresses her body leapt and tingled with a sensual aftershock so powerful that it almost hurt not to drag him down to her again. 'Rashad...'

Rashad unbuttoned his jacket with a masculine air of purpose. Scorching golden eyes assailed hers with fierce intensity. 'Here in my bed we will seal our new understanding.'

'Now?' Tilda was appalled by that declaration of intent. She would not let herself think about how her enthusiastic response to his passion could only have encouraged him to believe that it was fine to regard her as a midmorning sexual snack. 'I mean, right here and now?'

Rashad surveyed her with compelling force. 'It is my wish.'

He was dangerously accustomed to instant acquiescence with his expressed wishes and immediate gratification, Tilda acknowledged in a daze. She was already battling to come to terms with the idea of willingly becoming Rashad's plaything, his possession, his little toy. Suddenly the sheer weight of such expectations was too much for her to handle at that moment.

'I can't!' she gasped. 'Not right now anyhow.'

Rashad had not considered that possibility. A lean brown hand clenched in frustration and then loosened again for the depth of his reserve had made the concealment of his every private reaction instinctive. The ache of sexual arousal was so sharp and frustrating that it felt like a physical pain. 'Then we must wait until you reach Bakhar.'

Tilda flushed to her hairline when she realised the meaning he had mistakenly taken from her outburst. She lowered her head, knowing she was not about to correct him and wondering if that made her a terrible cheat. Like one of those women who famously feigned continual headaches? But before she could let her thoughts stray in that direction, all of what he had just said finally sank in and she raised shaken turquoise eyes. 'You're planning to take me back to Bakhar with you?'

'I have a palace in the desert. The harem is tailor-made for a woman like you.' Rashad was thinking with savage satisfaction of Tilda in the Palace of the Lions, isolated by the remote location from the temptations of the rest of the world and forced to depend only on him for company and amusement. That would soon sort her out. She would be his very personal project. There would be no more lies, no more deceits and no more pretence.

Outraged and convinced he was joking in a very unfunny way, Tilda slid off the bed and hurriedly sidestepped him while trying not to look as if she was running away. She paused by the door. 'I know you've got to be teasing me. You once told me that there was no such thing as a harem anywhere in Bakhar.'

Rashad gave her a sardonic appraisal, enjoying her disbelief and the hint of panic she couldn't hide. It was but a small repayment for the sexual disappointment she had just dealt him. *Again.* She had had no business giving him such encouragement when she could not offer him release. But hadn't that been typical of her? To yield just a provocative taste of her exquisite body to tantalise and tease him?

'I mean, I know you're too civilised to try and treat me like a concubine…or something,' Tilda proffered in a small, tight voice of deep audible suspicion.

'My grandfather had hundreds of concubines. We don't talk about it. It's not politically correct these days. But the royal household always had concubines. Most of them were gifts from their families. It was considered an honour to enter the royal harem and a good way of gaining the favour of the ruling family,' Rashad confided lazily, watching her gorgeous eyes widen and her ripe lower lip part from the upper in disquiet. 'Alas, I will have to satisfy myself with only you, but think of all the attention you'll get. At least you won't have to compete with other women or share me.'

'I'm not going to be anybody's concubine, especially not yours!' Tilda shot at him vehemently, yanking open the door and hastening out into the corridor.

Rashad, who had never thought of himself as an imaginative man, pictured Tilda reclining in something very flimsy on a bed in the Palace of the Lions, counting the days and the hours until he would visit her there. He found that vivid mental image so deeply attractive that it was an effort to move on from it to consider more practical aspects. When had anyone last lived at the old palace? He would have to throw an army of servants into the ancient building and refurbish it from roof to basement for occupation. It would be a huge task. His staff would be kept extremely busy.

'How long are you expecting me to stay in Bakhar for?'

'For as long as I want you in my bed.' Rashad thrust open the drawing-room door.

Tilda swallowed painfully. 'If I agree—'

'You've already agreed.'

'You have to write off the loan and sign the house back to Mum.'

His colourful reverie most effectively dispersed by that evidence of her financial acuteness, Rashad surveyed her with hard dark eyes. 'You think you'll be worth that much money?'

Tilda promised herself that somehow, some day, some way, she would get revenge for what he was doing to her. Pale as death, she knotted her restive hands together and veiled her angry, mortified gaze. 'It's what you think that matters,' she pointed out flatly. 'But if you want me to hand myself over body and soul and put my whole life on hold for goodness knows how long, I need to know that my family's going to be all right while I'm away.'

'There speaks the martyr,' Rashad murmured with scorn.

Tilda would not allow herself to react to that inflammatory comment. 'When will you stop the eviction proceedings?'

'The day you fly into Bakhar. That will give you ten days at most to get organised.'

Tilda dealt him a stricken look of condemnation. 'You can't do it that way!'

'I don't trust you, so the pressure stays on. There will be no room for renegotiating in the hope of more favourable and lucrative terms and no opportunity for you to renege on the deal.' Having glanced out the window and noted the expensive Jaguar awaiting her return, Rashad turned his arrogant dark head to study her with chilling intensity. 'In the meantime, you should be careful to be on your very best behaviour.'

'Best behaviour?' Her brow furrowed. 'What are you talking about?'

'Your lover has come back to pick you up. But you can't get into his car again, or be alone with him or any other man now. I'm a very suspicious guy and I will have you watched from the moment you leave this house until you reach Bakhar. If there is so much as a hint of flirtation or questionable behaviour, the deal is off and the eviction proceedings will go ahead.'

Tilda stared back at him in mute incredulity and horror. 'You're threatening me.'

'I am warning you that if you disappoint me you will

suffer punitive consequences. Get rid of your elderly chauffeur now. The clock is already ticking,' Rashad murmured with lethal cool.

Tilda dug into her bag for her mobile phone and rang Evan in haste. She told him that it would be quite some time until she was free to leave and that there was absolutely no point in him waiting for her.

'Excellent. I was always convinced that with the correct approach you would find it very easy to follow instructions,' Rashad drawled lazily.

Tilda quivered with rage and frustration. She felt as if a tornado were locked inside her and fighting for exit. But she dared not explode; she dared not offend or antagonise him because he had the power to rip her family apart. She wanted to tell him how much she hated him. Instead, loathing seethed inside her and she had to hold it in.

Someone knocked on the door and entered to address Rashad in his own language.

'I have to leave for the airport,' Rashad imparted. 'I will have you conveyed home. I'll be in touch with further directions.'

Her silvery fair head lifted, turquoise eyes burning brilliant blue. 'Yes, Your Royal Highness. Anything else?'

'I'll be sure to let you know.' Emanating a positive force field of masculine power and authority and untouched by her silent hostility, Rashad sent her a shuttered glance of cool, calm satisfaction.

From the drawing-room window above, Tilda watched him climb into his big black limo. Ten minutes later she got into the Mercedes that had been ordered to take her home. All she would let herself think about was the story she would tell her family. She practised a breezy smile and a cheerful voice. Her surrender on Rashad's terms would be totally wasted if her mother suspected even a hint of the unlovely truth.

'I've got fantastic news. Rashad has just offered me a terrific job,' she told Beth Morrison when she got home again. 'It will pay well enough to eventually clear all the money that we owe.'

The older woman was initially astonished, but her palpable relief soon silenced her surprised questions. 'Of course! You came first on your accountancy course, so Rashad will be getting a top-notch employee. I'm so glad I wasn't wrong about him. I always thought Rashad was a decent and trustworthy young man,' Beth contended happily. 'Where will you be working?'

'Bakhar.'

'Oh, my goodness, this new job will be abroad! I should've thought of that possibility,' her mother exclaimed. 'We'll all miss you so much. Are you sure this is the right thing for you?'

'Oh, totally.' Tilda kept right on smiling although her jaw was beginning to ache.

Her supposed new career move was the sole topic of discussion amongst her siblings that evening. As none of them was aware of the severity of the family financial problems, the assumption was that Tilda had won her dream job. 'I suppose working abroad will be a nice change for you,' Aubrey, her brother, commented vaguely before he went back upstairs to swot. A year her junior, he was exceptionally clever and, like many intellectual people, quite removed from the practicalities of life.

Her teenaged brother, James, gave her an impressed look. 'You can earn a fortune tax-free in the Middle East!'

'Will you go to work on a camel every morning?' her little sister, Megan, asked hopefully.

Her other sister, Katie, was more thoughtful and less easily convinced by the surface show of normality. As the sisters got ready for bed in the room they shared, the teenager's blue eyes were troubled. 'What was it like for you seeing Rashad again? Didn't you just hate him?'

'No, I got over all that a long time ago,' Tilda whispered, not wanting to waken Megan.

'But you've never really gone out with anyone since him.'

Turning her head to the wall, Tilda shut her eyes tight. 'That's nothing to do with Rashad. I mean, relationships aren't for everyone,' she muttered. 'I've had a few dates—they just haven't led anywhere.'

'Because you're not interested...the guys always are—'

'I haven't got time for a man.'

'You had time for Rashad when he was around.'

Stinging tears foamed up behind Tilda's lowered lids. She swallowed back the ache in her throat and told herself not to be so foolish. She then lay awake for half of the night fretting about how her family would manage a hundred and one different tasks without her help. She was also aware that she had to sort out Scott. Those twin concerns screened out the even bigger worry about how she would handle Rashad. The next morning she handed in her notice at work and when she had finished for the day she caught the bus to her stepfather's house.

'What do you want?' Scott demanded menacingly on the doorstep.

'If you ever try to take money from my mother again, I'll report you to the police,' Tilda told him. 'If you threaten or hurt any member of my family, I'll also go straight to the police, so leave us alone!'

The furious resentment with which the older man hurled a tide of abuse at her convinced her that her warning would scare him off. Like most bullies, Scott usually avoided people who fought back and concentrated his aggression on milder personalities.

She was waiting for another bus when her mobile phone went off.

'I thought your stepfather was history,' Rashad's voice remarked with crystal clarity in her ear.

Surprise almost made Tilda jump a foot in the air. 'I thought you were in New York!'

'I am.'

'So how do you know I'd been at my stepfather's house?'

'My security staff are superb at surveillance. I told you I would watch over you,' Rashad drawled lazily. 'Why were you visiting Morrison?'

Tilda cast a harried and cross glance up and down the street, which was as busy as most residential areas were at that time of the evening. But there was no sign of anyone paying her particular attention; if there had been she was in the right mood to give them a piece of her mind. 'None of your business. I can't imagine why you're taking the trouble to put Nosy Parkers on my trail!'

'Nothing is too much trouble when it comes to my

favourite concubine.' An unholy grin of amusement slowly curving his handsome mouth and putting his formidable cool reserve to flight, Rashad relaxed his lean, powerful body back into his office chair and listened to the line being cut with a furious click. There was a powerful buzz to his every exchange or encounter with Tilda. That truth disturbed him…

CHAPTER FIVE

THE car door of the Mercedes opened. The chauffeur bowed low and the bodyguards fanned out. Her heart beating very fast, Tilda climbed out and walked into the hotel, striving to appear indifferent to all the heads turning to look in her direction. The lift was held for her benefit. Moments later, she was ushered into an opulent suite and shown straight into a bedroom where a complete change of clothes awaited her.

Her palms were damp as she unbuttoned the jacket of the ordinary navy trouser suit she had worn. She undressed with great care. Leaving home had upset her and keeping up the cheerful front had been a challenge. It was her second visit to this London hotel. Her first had taken place over a week earlier, when a couple of hours had passed while she had been comprehensively measured for a new wardrobe. Both trips had been organised by an anonymous voice over the phone. She'd had to put on pressure to find out exactly when she would be flying out to Bakhar. From Rashad himself, she had heard not a word. While she was by no means keen for any unnecessary contact with him, that silence had done nothing to lessen her apprehensions about her future.

Tilda donned the cobweb-fine silk and lace lingerie. Each item was a perfect fit. She had never known anyone who wore stockings. She liked her underwear plain and comfortable, not designed to present the female body in a provocative way. The gossamer-thin bra and briefs offered nothing in the way of concealment. In spite of the warmth of the room she shivered. She slid into the beautifully made blue dress and eased her feet into the delicate high-heeled shoes. She was reaching for the matching light coat when the very expensive mobile phone lying on the bed rang.

After a moment of hesitation, she answered it. 'Hello?'

'Leave your hair loose,' Rashad murmured huskily.

It was an effort to find her voice. 'Right.'

'The phone is yours. It enjoys enhanced security. Wear the jewellery. I'm looking forward to seeing you at the airport.' Rashad rang off.

Moving with as much enthusiasm as an automaton, Tilda tucked the fancy phone into the designer handbag on the bed. A jewel box reposed on the dressing table. She flipped it open, anxious eyes widening at the sight of the dazzling platinum and diamond set pendant and drop earrings. Her hands all thumbs, she put the jewellery on. She unclasped her hair and reached for a comb. He had always loved her hair. A tremor ran through her slender length. At that instant she was tempted to hack her hair off to within a few inches of her scalp.

But how would her desert prince react? Suppose that hair was her main attraction in his eyes? Suppose he took one look at her shorn of her crowning glory and rejected her at the airport? It was not a risk she could afford to take. Her lovely face tightening, she tidied her hair and slid into the light coat. Her reflection in the mirror mocked her, for the conservative outfit adorned with the eye-catching jewellery was very stylish. On the surface she looked like a lady, she conceded bitterly, but both she and, more importantly, *he* knew that beneath the elegant restraint of her outer garments she was dressed like his favourite concubine.

She travelled to Heathrow in an enormous limousine embellished with tinted windows. She was walking through the airport terminal when someone called her name. She came to a surprised halt and turned her head and was instantly targeted by a blinding onslaught of flashing cameras borne by running people. In the commotion questions were shouted at her while the security team accompanying her banded round her in a protective huddle and urged her on.

'How does it feel to be the Crown Prince's latest lady?'

'Turn this way, luv…let us get a shot of the sparklers round your neck!'

'Are you flying out to meet the Bakhari royal family?' A woman yelled, trotting alongside her and extending a microphone. 'Is it true you first met when Prince Rashad was up at Oxford?'

Aghast at the attention and the intrusive interrogation, Tilda sped on almost at a run and kept her head bent down to discourage further photos being taken. Another couple of bodyguards came rushing up in support of their beleaguered colleagues and hastily ushered her out of the main concourse, down a corridor and into a private room.

Her dismayed eyes collided without warning with Rashad's searing golden scrutiny. Although the austere classic lines of his lean, strong face bore his customary air of detachment, Tilda felt as jolted as if she had stuck her finger into a live electric socket: wrath emanated from him in a force field. He inclined his arrogant dark head in a clear signal for her to approach him. She would have preferred to stay where she was. On the other hand she did not want to run the risk of being ordered around in front of his staff, all of whom were clumped in a corner being careful to neither speak nor look in their direction.

'I will deal with this matter after we board.' Rashad's low-pitched intonation somehow achieved the same stinging effect as the flick of a whip.

Tilda's sense of intimidation was put to flight by a surge of annoyance. Here she was packaged and presented from head to toe and from the skin out as His Royal Highness had commanded. She had done exactly as she had been told. She had not put a foot wrong. What was the matter with him? Was he never satisfied? Her life promised to be hell for the duration of their relationship, she thought angrily. But she was quick to remind herself that the reward was that, within twenty-four hours, all immediate threat to the stability of her family would be eradicated.

She stole a grudging glance at Rashad from below her honey-brown lashes and her tummy flipped with an immediacy that infuriated her. He was breathtakingly handsome. Yet there was something more compelling than mere good looks in his lean, sculpted features, something that ensnared her and made her want to look again and again. Five years earlier, she had been hopelessly addicted to him and wildly in love. A deep pang of pain assailed her at that recollection and chilled her to the marrow. No, she promised herself staunchly, never again would she allow her more tender emotions to overwhelm her in Rashad's radius. She could not afford to make herself that vulnerable again.

His private jet was large and the interior so sumptuous it took Tilda's breath away. She sank into an extremely comfortable seat and braced herself for take-off while ruminating over what might have annoyed him. Was it the startling interest that the press had demonstrated in her at the airport? Well, that was scarcely her fault. He was a fabulously wealthy womaniser and royal into the bargain. The paparazzi adored him and tracked his movements round the globe. His social life filled gossip-page columns every month and occasionally even attracted headlines.

Soon after the plane had left the runway, Rashad undid his seat belt and rose from his seat with swift movements. 'You may now answer my questions.'

Tilda, who had only flown a couple of times in her entire life, relaxed her white-knuckled grip on the arms of her seat and opened her eyes. 'What is wrong?' she asked, shaking her pale blond head in bewilderment. 'I've done nothing and I already feel like I'm on trial.'

Rashad surveyed her with lustrous dark eyes of suspicion. He could not recall when he had last come so close to losing his temper. Her luminous turquoise eyes rested on him in seemingly innocent enquiry. But the very fact that she had contrived to home in on his one oversight and take advantage of it convinced him that once again she was acting.

'Why did you tip off the press about our travel plans?'

Tilda blinked, letting the ramifications of that far-reaching question sink in. Outrage flashed through her. 'Now just you listen here,' she gasped, struggling to undo her seat belt with furious hands.

Rashad crouched down on a level with her. 'No, you listen,' he urged soft and low and deadly in warning. 'If you shout, you will be overheard and you will embarrass my staff. Impertinence and discourtesy are much disliked in Bakhar.'

Fit to be tied, Tilda trembled with rage and chagrin. 'You're the only person who makes me feel like this—'

Rashad undid the seat belt that had defeated her with a deft flick of one hand and subjected her to the full assault of his stunning dark golden eyes. 'You are strong-willed. I'm the only person who stands up to you.'

Tilda scrambled up and took herself over to the other side of the cabin. Her oval face flushed, she spun round again before he could remind her that it was rude to turn her back on him. 'You're also the only person who continually makes me the target of unjust accusations. Surely that is some excuse for a loss of temper?' she whispered back at him vehemently, her hands balled into fists of restraint by her side. 'I've never had any contact with the press. I haven't a clue about how to go about tipping them off, either.'

Rashad dealt her a sizzling appraisal. 'I cannot accept that. Five years ago the paparazzi barely knew of my existence and my association with you was never revealed in print. But today, even though I have never yet appeared in public with you, the paparazzi were waiting for your arrival. They have already identified you and made reference to our past acquaintance. Who else could have whetted their appetite with such details?'

'How would I know? It wasn't me!' Tilda protested.

'Sooner or later, you will have to tell me the truth,' Rashad delivered with hard resolve. 'Lies are at all times unacceptable to me.'

Tilda ground her teeth together. 'I'm not lying to you. Why would I tip off the press? Do you think I'm proud of the reason why I'm allowing myself to be flown out to your country?'

'Enough,' Rashad shot at her in a warning growl, marvelling at her ability to stand there looking so exquisitely beautiful while she went for him like a spitting, clawing tigress. But he meant every word that he had spoken. He would not settle for lies. She had strength and intelligence. He was convinced that if he was tough enough with her, those virtues would rise nearer the surface.

Tilda picked a seat as far away from him as she could. Silence fell, and it was a silence laden with angry tension. A sun of impotent rage was rising inside her. According to *him*, everything that went wrong was her fault and now she couldn't even shout at him. Where was the justice in that? How dared he blame her for the level of press interest in his fast-lane life with models and actresses? From where did he get the brass neck to continually take the moral high ground? In comparison she lived a life of unblemished virtue. So, she wasn't perfect? So what! Was he?

Temper still simmering, Tilda shot him a furious glance. 'Do you really think that I have any wish to be publicly known as your trollop?'

Rashad had to dig deep into his reserves to maintain silence in the face of such unbridled provocation. His *trollop*? He set his perfect white teeth together and flexed long, shapely brown fingers. Once the jet landed, his staff reappeared to disembark and Rashad was approached by his current senior aide, Butrus. A professor of law and an excellent administrator, the older man made a rather strained enquiry as to what designation he should place on Tilda's visa to enter Bakhar.

Rashad's anger, all the more powerful for being denied utterance, was still intense. Wrathfully impatient of the bureaucracy of petty detail that the royal family had always been exempt from, Rashad responded in his own language and with an unashamed resolution that none would dare to question. 'She is my woman. She does not require a visa.'

Butrus froze, then went straight into retreat and bowed very low. An electric silence enveloped them all, his entire staff falling still. An almost imperceptible hint of colour demarcating his high cheekbones, Rashad realised that for the first time in his life he had shown his stormy emotions in public. As quickly, he decided that his candour might have shocked but it had not been a mistake. He closed a fierce hand over Tilda's pale, delicate fingers. He could not possibly keep her a secret from those closest to him and, although he had not planned to make such a dramatic announcement, at least, he reasoned, nobody was now in any doubt about her non-negotiable status in his life.

'You're hurting my hand,' Tilda stretched up on tiptoe to snap.

Rashad immediately loosened his possessive hold, but he did not let her go. She was his now, he thought with satisfaction. She was in Bakhar with him. He smoothed her crushed digits between a caressing forefinger and thumb and retained her hand in his. Taken aback by that response to her waspish complaint, Tilda looked up at him. A slow-burning smile slashed his beautiful mouth. Engulfed in that unexpected warmth, she felt dizzy and breathless.

Across the cabin, Butrus watched that visual exchange of smiles in sincere wonderment before hastily averting his attention from the display. All of a sudden he finally understood why the Palace of the Lions was being prepared for occupation and he was appalled by his misinterpretation of his royal employer's meaning. How could he have been so foolish as to credit that the Crown Prince might defy the conventions to the extent of importing a foreign mistress? Instead, Prince Rashad had taken a refreshingly traditional path to matrimony, which would bring great joy to his family and the entire country of Bakhar. A marriage by declaration. Was it not truly typical of their heroic and fiercely independent prince that he should choose a bride and bring her home without any of the usual fuss? As soon as his employer had left the plane, Butrus got on the phone to break the happy tidings to King Hazar's closest advisor, Jasim, and ensure that scandalous rumours could gain no ground whatsoever in the royal household. He was little disappointed by the discovery that the happy tidings were not quite the surprise he had envisaged.

Tilda was quite unprepared for the roasting heat of Bakhar midafternoon and briefly forgot that she was demonstrating her supreme disdain for Rashad by not speaking to him. 'Is it always this hot?'

Even this faintest hint of criticism of the Bakhari climate made Rashad square his broad shoulders. 'It is a beautiful day. There are no gloomy grey skies here in early summer.'

An air-conditioned limo pulled up and whisked them past a very large new airport terminal. The vehicle carried them only a couple of hundred yards before setting them down again beside a large white-and-gold helicopter. Boarding, she sat down on a fitted cream sofa and tried not to gape at the space and comfort surrounding her.

The panoramic view soon stole her attention. The helicopter followed a craggy line of mountains and flew over green fertile valleys before reaching the desert interior. Her first glimpse of the great ochre-coloured sand dunes rolling towards the horizon enthralled her. Far below she saw a camel train trekking out into the great emptiness and, once or twice, encampments of black tents. Children chased the shadow of the helicopter and waved frantically, and still the desert stretched like a vast, endless golden ocean ahead of them.

'How much farther?' she was finally moved to ask.

'Another ten minutes or so.' Rashad had instructed the pilot to give them a scenic grand tour and the flight had been much longer than necessary. Although he usually found a fresh sight of the country he loved an energising experience, he had barely removed his keen dark gaze from Tilda's delicate, feminine profile. His hunger to possess her was stabbing at him like a knife.

He had watched while she knelt laughing on the seat and waved back at the Bedouin children with youthful enthusiasm. *Joie de vivre,* the French called it, and that sparkling quality of joy had once had enormous appeal for a male who had grown from a solemn little boy into a very serious young man. The emotion Tilda showed so freely had been a powerful source of attraction. Exasperation made him suppress those memories. The present, he told himself bleakly, was more relevant. Yes, she was very desirable. But had he not bought her into his bed? Where was the appeal in that? Or in her lies?

Picking up on the dry note in his rich dark drawl, Tilda went pink. She smoothed down her dress and sat down in a more circumspect fashion. 'Will I be able to shout at you when we arrive wherever we're going?'

'No. I tell you what I want and you strive to deliver,' Rashad reminded her with immense cool.

A little quiver of nervous tension rippled through Tilda for there was a shimmering golden light in his gaze. 'What if I disappoint you?'

'You won't.'

Tilda sucked in a stark breath.

'I think you'll learn fast,' Rashad murmured lazily.

Her face burning, Tilda turned her head away and

saw an immense building perched on the rocky hillside directly ahead. The helicopter swooped in over the outer walls and landed. She stepped out into the fresh air, her fascinated eyes climbing the weathered battlements of the ancient gate tower ahead.

'Welcome to the Palace of the Lions,' Rashad intoned, feeling the pulse of his mobile phone as it sought his attention. He tensed and then reached into his pocket to switch it off. He had always taken his duties very seriously, and it was an act that cost him a tussle with his conscience, but he was determined not to be distracted from Tilda. For just a few precious hours he would forget his royal responsibilities.

Beyond the tower lay a yet more imposing entrance dominated by very tall carved doors. 'It's an incredibly old building,' Tilda remarked, struggling not to be intimidated. 'Is this where you live?'

'It belongs to me but I have only stayed here occasionally. One of my ancestors built the palace. When our people were nomads this was the seat of power in Bakhar. My grandfather died, our main city grew in size and this building gradually fell into disuse.'

They passed into a vast echoing entrance hall. Light flickered and danced over the glinting reflective surfaces of the tiny coloured mirror tiles set into the intricately patterned ceiling. Tilda glanced through doorways and saw tantalising glimpses of rooms furnished in a highly exotic mix of Victorian and middle-eastern décor that dated back at least a century in style. The palace appeared to be well and truly stuck in a time warp.

'My goodness,' Tilda remarked helplessly. 'It's like walking into a time capsule.'

Rashad tensed. Presented with an enormous challenge and a tiny timeframe his staff had done their best, but had felt forced to concentrate on matters such as the plumbing, the electrical fixtures and the lack of air-conditioning.

'Totally fascinating,' she confided, craning her neck to admire an ancient hanging on the wall depicting a robed horseman waving a sword in the bloodthirsty heat of battle.

A servant appeared and fell to his knees in front of Rashad. He broke into a flood of apology, for Rashad had given a command that under no circumstances was he to be disturbed. The man laid a phone at his royal employer's feet with an air of entreaty.

Rashad compressed his handsome mouth and repeated his instruction. A hundred and one matters, and a hundred and one people at court, in government and from abroad, demanded his attention every day—and he never, ever took a day off. But this particular day was different: he was with Tilda. Obviously he had not been firm enough in his command. He stepped over the phone.

'Is there a problem?' Tilda enquired, peering back at the hapless older man literally wringing his hands and muttering laments. 'He seems a bit upset.'

'Drama is the spice of life to my people.'

Angling her bright gaze back to Rashad, Tilda lifted her chin and finally said what had been simmering at the back of her mind for hours. 'I didn't tip off the press and I can't imagine why you think I would've done.'

'Many women revel in that sort of public attention.

There are also those who choose to make money by sell-ing personal information to the paparazzi.'

That inflammatory comeback tensed her narrow spine into rigidity and she decided to give him the re-sponse he deserved. She spun round, platinum-fair curls falling in silvery streamers round her exquisite face, her jewelled eyes hurling a challenge. 'Actually I don't plan to sell my story of what it's like to be a prince's concubine until I go home again.'

The atmosphere sizzled like oil heated to boiling point.

Dense black lashes sweeping low on his scorching golden gaze, Rashad strolled silently back to her, in-trigued by her continuing defiance. 'Perhaps,' he mur-mured very softly, 'you won't want to go home again. I can be very persuasive.'

Tilda had wanted to annoy him and the tenor of his reply took her by surprise. 'Of course I'll want to go home again...I'll be counting the days!'

'Or you'll be doing whatever it takes to hold my in-terest so that you can stay. Today you stop running away and start learning.' A lean brown hand lifted to brush a straying strand of pale hair back from her cheekbone in a confident gesture of intimacy. She backed up against the cold solid wall, her breath catching in her throat. He traced the pouting cupid's bow of her upper lip with his thumb and gently opened her mouth to graze the soft moist underside. Her legs went limp and stinging aware-ness made her nipples pinch into painfully tight buds. It was a fight to contain the wanton shock of fascina-tion travelling through her.

'I don't run away,' she told him frantically. *'Ever!'*

'Once, you ran faster than a gazelle every time I got too close. I'm a hunter. I enjoyed the chase.' Rashad let his forefinger dip sexily between her peach-soft lips and retreat again. He watched her pupils dilate and the slender white expanse of her throat extend as she tipped her head back in instinctive female invitation. 'But you always wanted me. You may fight with me, but you are begging for my mouth right now.'

Her long brown lashes fluttered. It took enormous effort to concentrate again. Angry pain slashed through that mental fog because for a long, timeless moment she had craved the heat of his mouth on hers as badly as a life-giving drug. 'I'm not begging,' she muttered, forcing a laugh that sounded horribly strangled.

Rashad gazed down at her with a languorous heat that made her tremble. 'Don't worry—you will.'

Tilda braced a hand on the wall and pushed herself away from him with a lack of coordination that infuriated her. She was trembling, maddeningly aware of every fluid shift of his lithe, powerful body so close to hers. Her mind threw up a dangerous image of Rashad pushing her back against the wall with the passion that was so much a part of him, the passion he so rarely freed from restraint. The knot of tension in her pelvis tightened and she recognised it for the hunger it was. The fact that her hostility didn't stop her responding to him shook her up badly.

Rashad shot her pale, taut profile a glittering appraisal and closed a shapely brown hand over hers. 'Let me show you the harem.'

'I can hardly wait.' Although colour now mantled her

cheeks, Tilda lifted her head high. She remembered his dark sense of humour so well. She remembered how he had once teased the life out of her. A sharp pang of regret gripped her for that lost time and had the effect of simply hardening her resolve.

'I didn't tip off the press,' she told him afresh.

'So you say.' His audible indifference to such a plea incensed her.

'And five years ago, I didn't sleep with anyone else.'

Rashad expelled his breath in a long-suffering hiss. Why did she keep on reminding him of her infidelity? He did not want to be reminded. Why did she not appreciate that every denial merely acted as a prompt to unsavoury memories?

Mounting a vast stone staircase by his side and determined to ignore the discouraging silence that had met her valiant claim, Tilda swallowed hard. 'I'd like to see the proof you said you had of my so-called misdemeanours.'

'Some day I will let you see it.' Rashad flashed her an impatient look. As she could have no idea how conclusive his proof was she was probably hoping to argue her way out of the evidence of her deceit. Unhappily for her, he had complete faith in the source of the information he had received.

'Why not now?'

'I have heard enough of your lies. Silence is preferable.' His lean, darkly handsome face was resolute. 'In time, I expect you to accept the futility of lying to me.'

Tilda yanked her hand forcibly free of his. 'So you intend to make it impossible for me to defend myself. I'm damned if I do speak up and damned if I don't. But why would any man want a lying, cheating gold-digger?'

Rashad made no answer. He refused to rise to the bait. He was beginning to appreciate that whenever she was most desperate to keep him at a distance she started fighting with him.

Aggrieved by his lack of response, Tilda murmured dulcetly, 'Maybe you only like bad girls.'

At that crack, Rashad surveyed her with pure predatory appreciation. Where she was concerned that was true. When he looked at her, when he thought about her, her sins were never at the forefront of his mind. His desire ran too hot and strong to be denied. With her turquoise eyes as vivid as polar stars, she glowed with beauty and quicksilver energy. The ache at his groin came close to pain. Never had he felt such powerful need to possess a woman. Suddenly all his patience just vanished. He strode forward and swept her up off her feet and headed for his bedroom.

'What the heck are you doing?' Tilda launched at him in astonishment.

'We've waited long enough to be together.' Rashad thrust at a door with a broad shoulder to force it wider and kicked it shut in his wake.

Tilda spread a decidedly panicky glance round the echoing bedroom, which seemed to her to have very little else in it beyond the highly ornate four-poster bed that sat on a dais. 'I thought I was going to get a tour of the harem!'

'Some other day, when I have the strength to resist you.' Rashad lowered her to the floor and stripped off her coat, an imprisoning hand splaying across the soft swell of her hips in case she dared to stray anywhere out of his reach. He bent his arrogant dark head, golden eyes smouldering over her like tiny flames, and tasted her soft full mouth.

It was as though every time he touched her he sent another brick flying out of her wall of defence, leaving her more at risk and less able to hold out against him the next time. His insistent kiss jolted her like a bolt of lightning shooting down her spine and made her go back for more. Her heart raced and her body quivered against the hard, masculine promise of his. He pried her lips apart for the erotic plunge of his tongue. Her tummy flipped with sheer excitement. She could not withstand her need to touch him. Her hands slid beneath his jacket to trace the warm, hard contours of his powerful chest beneath the fine shirt.

Rashad raised his head, luxuriant ebony lashes lifting to frame golden eyes alight with hunger. He eased her dress off her narrow shoulders and let it slide down to her feet in a heap. She was startled, for she had not realised that he had already unzipped the garment. Suddenly feeling very exposed in her flimsy bra and briefs, she wrapped her arms round herself.

'Don't embarrass me by acting as though you are shy,' Rashad derided, long brown fingers enclosing her wrists to uncross her arms again. Such pretence from her hit the rawest of nerves and his annoyance with her was intense. 'I hate anything false. Fake modesty leaves me cold. Why would I even want you to be a virgin?'

Tilda jerked back from him in a defensive movement.

Why would I even want you to be a virgin? That scornful demand faded the pink from her cheeks. He recognised the hollow light in her clear eyes and, disturbed by that awareness, he reached for her again, determined to break through her resistance.

'Did you think that pretence is what I want from you?' Rashad demanded in a roughened undertone. 'It was not my intention to cause you pain. But this time I want only what is real from you.'

Tilda was shaken that he had noticed that he had hurt her feelings, because she had believed she was better at hiding her feelings. He framed her face with his lean hands and took her mouth with ravishing sweetness and spellbinding sensuality. She stopped thinking and let her response take over. He curved her slender, unresisting body to his, drinking in the scent of her creamy white skin and the telling unsteadiness of her breathing. Lifting her onto the bed, he stood back to discard his tie and unbutton his shirt.

Her limbs felt heavy where they lay on the crimson silk spread and there was a liquid heat burning low in her belly. She could not take her eyes off the light golden slice of male torso he had revealed: muscle rippled across the solid wall of his chest as he took off the shirt, and black whorls of hair dusted his pectorals and arrowed down in a silken furrow across the flat slab of his stomach. Her mouth ran dry.

Rashad surveyed her with smouldering appreciation and the mattress gave under his weight. Tilda rolled away. Rashad laughed and hauled her back to him with easy strength. 'You are so beautiful,' he told her thickly, tasting her luscious mouth again, dipping his tongue between her parted lips with a dark sensuality that left her trembling. 'You want me, too.'

She shut her eyes for fear that he could read that truth there. The tiny moments when he wasn't touching her were already a torment. Like a doll, she was incapable of independent action and it was the very strength of her desire for him that kept her trapped. He pressed his hard, sensual mouth against the tiny pulse going crazy below her collar-bone and she gasped and arched her narrow spine. He pulled her back against him to unclasp her bra. A groan of male satisfaction sounded in his throat when her small, high breasts tumbled free. He teased the swollen pink peaks with skilful fingers, before he bent over her and used his mouth to toy with the straining buds. Every bitter-sweet sensation darted straight as an arrow to the hot damp pulse between her thighs and increased the ache there.

'Rashad…oh, please…'

Rashad looked down at her with heavily lidded eyes, lashes so long they almost hit his superb cheekbones. Somewhere outside he heard the sharp crack of rifles releasing a hail of bullets and he frowned.

'What's that?' she mumbled breathlessly, her fingers delving into the luxuriant depths of his black hair.

'Someone has probably got married and the guards are showing their appreciation.' Although that was the most likely explanation, Rashad was tense as only a former soldier could be in such circumstances. Then he heard the drone of aircraft. As he leapt off the bed and snatched up his shirt a jet flew overhead. Barely twenty seconds later, he heard the heavy whop-whop of more than one helicopter approaching.

'Rashad? What's happening?' Tilda prompted apprehensively.

'Get dressed.' An urgent knocking sounded on the door. The noise was almost drowned out by the ear-splitting whine of another jet flashing over the palace.

Rashad answered the door.

'Please forgive the intrusion, Your Royal Highness,' a senior manservant delivered anxiously, 'but I have been asked to inform you that the Prime Minister is about to arrive. He most humbly requests an audience with you.'

Every scrap of colour in Rashad's lean, strong face ebbed. He turned the colour of burnt ashes, because he could only think that something had happened to his father. For what other reason would the Prime Minister come to see him without having organised the visit in advance?

'Rashad?' Tilda pressed worriedly.

Rashad looked through her as if she had suddenly become invisible. At speed he donned his tie and jacket. 'Do not on any account leave this room, or speak to anyone, until I return.'

CHAPTER SIX

RASHAD had only got as far as the landing when he recalled his mobile phone, which he had switched off, and he immediately put it on again. He cursed the selfish streak of recklessness that had caused him to ignore the phone's demands barely thirty minutes earlier. Almost immediately, the ringtone sounded again and he answered it. Informed that his royal parent was waiting to speak to him, he was bewildered.

'My son,' King Hazar boomed on the line as if he were addressing a packed audience chamber, 'I am overjoyed!'

'You are in good health, my father?' Rashad breathed in astonishment.

'Of course.'

Rashad was still shaken by the fear that had seized him. 'Then, why has the Prime Minister flown out to the desert to speak to me?'

'The occasion of your marriage is of very great importance to us all.'

Rashad came to an abrupt halt at the head of the stone staircase. 'My...*marriage?*'

'Our people do not wish to be deprived of a state wedding.'

'Who said that I was married, or even getting married?' Rashad managed to ask in as level a voice as he could muster.

'A journalist contacted your sister, Kalila, in London and showed her a photo taken at the airport. Kalila contacted me and e-mailed that picture of Tilda for us all to see. She is very beautiful and a magnificent surprise. I should have sat up and taken more notice the day I heard you were having the old palace refurbished!'

Rashad was thinking fast and realising that so many facts were already out in the family and public arena that he could not simply dismiss the story out of hand. He had been frankly appalled by the presence of the paparazzi at Heathrow—the rumours must have been flying around about his relationship with Tilda before he'd even got his jet off the ground in London! So much for discretion and privacy! He was even more taken aback by his father's hearty enthusiasm at the news that his son had married a woman he had never met.

'When you proclaimed that Tilda was your woman and required no visa, old Butrus almost had a heart attack until it dawned on him that you must already be married to her to make such an announcement. And, even had you not been—' the king chuckled in the best of good humour '—according to the laws of our royal house once you declared Tilda yours before witnesses, it was a marriage by declaration. The statute that saved your grandfather's skin was never repealed.'

Rashad found it necessary to lean back against the

wall for support. A marriage by declaration—a law
hastily trotted out to clean up the scandal after his licen-
tious grandfather had run off with his grandmother with
not the slightest intention of doing anything other than
bedding her. It was still legal? He felt as if the bars of a
cage were closing round him.

'My father…' Rashad breathed in deep.

'As if you would bring any woman other than your
intended bride into Bakhar!' the older man quipped.
'No man of honour would sully a woman's reputation.
I had only to hear Tilda's name spoken and at once I
knew she was your bride and that we had a wonderful
celebration to arrange. Was she not the woman who
gained your heart five years ago?'

As the king waxed lyrical on the subjects of true love
and lifelong matrimonial happiness Rashad grew a great
deal grimmer at his end of the phone. There might be
sunlight beyond the window, but a giant dark cloud was
now obscuring his appreciation of it. He had broken the
rules only once and now he was to pay the price with
his freedom. What insanity had seized him when he
had taken the risk of bringing Tilda into Bakhar? It had
been an act of utter recklessness and, in retrospect, he
could not fathom what had driven him to the point of
such incredible folly.

Rashad went downstairs to greet the Prime Minister
and his entourage. He accepted hearty congratulations,
elaborate greetings and compliments for his bride and the
news that a two-day public holiday had already been declared at the end of the month to mark the occasion of his
state wedding. He did not even pale when he was in-

formed that formal announcements had been made on the state television and radio services and that bridal good wishes were pouring in from every corner of Bakhar.

It was a full hour before he was in a position to return to Tilda. He was still suffering all the outrage and disbelief of a male who had never put a foot wrong in his life, but now had made one fatal error. He had no doubt whatsoever that Tilda would be ecstatic at the news that she was not a concubine but a wife, and that at the very least they would have to stay married for a year.

Fully dressed, Tilda was pacing the floor. Sporadic outbreaks of gunfire and the extraordinary amount of air traffic had frightened her into wondering if the palace was under attack. When silence had fallen, she had finally succumbed to the most sickening fear that Rashad had not reappeared because he had been taken prisoner, wounded or killed. Her response to that suspicion was much more emotional than she would have liked to admit and had informed her that her hatred ran only skin deep. While it was perfectly all right to loathe Rashad when he was in front of her and enjoying full health, when she was assailed by a vision of him lying somewhere hurt and unattended she felt sick and wanted to rush to his aid. For that reason, she was on the very brink of disobeying orders and leaving the room when the door opened.

'Where on earth have you been all this time?' she shot at Rashad in instant fury at his reappearance, when it became immediately obvious that her fears had been nonsensical: not a strand of his luxuriant black hair was out of place and his superb tailored suit was immaculate. 'I've been frantic with worry!'

'Why?' Rashad asked, ebony brows pleating.

'The gunfire…your instructions…all those jets and helicopters flying in and round about!' Tilda slung at him shakily.

'There is no cause for alarm. Natural caution urged me to ask you to stay here. But the outbreak of excitement was a celebration and the result of a misapprehension.' Rashad shrugged a broad shoulder with something less than his usual cool. 'The misunderstanding is entirely my fault. The whole country thinks that I have brought you back to Bakhar as my wife.'

Tilda was so taken aback by that information that she simply stared at him, noting that his lean, strong face was unusually pale and taut. 'For goodness sake, why would anyone think something like that?'

'Circumstances have conspired to make it the only acceptable interpretation of events,' Rashad pronounced with great care. 'I acknowledge that I did wrong in bringing you here. No woman has ever travelled home to Bakhar with me before. The intervention of the press in London and their awareness of our previous relationship only added strength to the rumour that you are, at the very least, my intended bride.'

Tilda blinked. 'So what now?'

Rashad frowned. 'According to my father we are already married in the eyes of the law, because I referred to you as my woman in front of witnesses.'

Puzzled by the first part of that explanation, Tilda easily picked up on the second part and slung him an angry look of disdain. 'You called me *that*? When?'

'Before we alighted from the jet. But I can put my

hand on my heart and swear on my honour that I intended no insult to you.'

'Of course you did—you described me as your woman as though I was a possession! It's medieval!'

'You feel as though you belong with me. I meant that you were part of my life,' Rashad growled. 'Now you are in truth a part.'

'In the eyes of the law…we're *already married?*' Tilda parroted in sudden shock as his original meaning finally sank in on her. 'How can that be?'

'Many years ago, my grandfather abducted my grandmother and created a huge scandal. He always acted first and thought afterwards. To smooth matters over it was considered necessary to pass a law that allowed him to claim that she was his wife from the moment he said she was in the presence of witnesses. That law relates only to the royal family and it has not been repealed.'

'But such behaviour and laws of that sort are still downright medieval! With relations like that, I'm amazed that you had the nerve to criticise *my* family.' Tilda shook her head in a daze, her thoughts tumbling about in turmoil while she attempted to reason with clarity. 'Well, the obvious solution to all this ridiculous confusion is that you just tell the truth. You are, after all, *very* fond of telling me that lies are always unacceptable to you.'

As that proposal was made, a tiny muscle pulled taut at the corner of Rashad's unsmiling mouth. 'The truth would now appear to be that, according to Bakhari law, we are legally married.'

'If that is so, I really do think that it would serve you right,' Tilda admitted helplessly. 'But, as I wouldn't stay married to you even if you had a gun to my head, the divorce can't come quick enough!'

'This is a serious matter.'

A bitter edge had already entered Tilda's thoughts and coloured them. She was remembering how madly in love she had been five years earlier. In those days she would've made any sacrifice to marry her desert prince. Were they really and truly married? No doubt that fact explained why he was as grave as though he were attending a funeral. She was obviously the very last woman alive that he would have willingly chosen to be his wife.

'I expect it is serious. But if I'm married to you, then I must have some rights.' Her beautiful eyes concealed by her lashes, she turned her head away from him, determined not to reveal that she was upset. 'Or have you got another list of threats to hold over me to ensure that I do exactly as you want me to do?'

That candid question hit Rashad like a bucket of icy water on hot skin. Until she had come back into his life, he had never threatened a woman, nor ever dreamt that he might do so. Now he was confronted head-on with his harsh treatment of Tilda. Once, she had betrayed his trust and inflicted a wound for which he had never forgiven her. But that, Rashad acknowledged heavily, was no defence for a misuse of power to mete out punishment. His father's talk of marriage and the photo of Tilda with Jerrold had reawakened Rashad's bitter anger and encouraged him to pursue what he believed to be justice. But from the instant he had seen Tilda again, far less acceptable motives and desires had powered him. No longer could he marvel at the disastrous consequences that he had unleashed on both of them.

'No. There will be no more threats.' His lean and darkly handsome face sober, Rashad surveyed her with dark, unreadable eyes. 'I should never have used coercive tactics.'

Surprised by that total turnaround, Tilda lifted her pale blond head. 'You're admitting that?'

'I can do nothing less when I look at the situation I have created. I was in the wrong and for that I apologise.' Voicing those words of sincere regret cost Rashad a great deal of pride for he had never had to apologise before. 'I harboured anger from the past and it blinded me to what was right.'

Tilda could only think of her own anger, nourished and kept alive by hurt. She thought of the fact that she had never let any man so close to her again. She thought of how she had felt just minutes earlier when she had been afraid that he might have been injured. A giant tide of fear engulfed her at that point as she appreciated that her feelings for Rashad ran much deeper than was safe or sensible.

'I will never threaten you again,' Rashad promised her levelly. 'Instead, I am asking you for your co-operation.'

'Are we really and truly married?' Tilda prompted uncertainly.

'Yes,' Rashad confirmed.

'But I expect you'll do whatever it takes to get us out of the marriage as fast as you possibly can,' Tilda remarked in a tone that was a tad brittle.

Rashad studied the wall to one side of her with frowning attention. Divorce would entail her departure from Bakhar. He discovered that that prospect had no appeal for him whatsoever. Surely, he reasoned, a hasty marriage and an even hastier divorce would only compound the errors he had made? A marriage was a marriage, no matter how it had been entered into. In the same way a wife was a wife, deserving of his support and respect. He should at least try to make a success of their alliance, he decided with sudden purpose. He would have to learn to put all memory of her past behind him.

'A quick divorce is not an option I would wish to choose.' Rashad rested dark golden eyes, gleaming with renewed energy, back on her. 'There is no reason why we should not attempt to make the best of our predicament.'

'Meaning?' Suddenly maddeningly aware of the smouldering appraisal resting on the swollen contours of her pink mouth, Tilda tensed. Without warning she found that she was reliving the melting pleasure of his hungry mouth roaming over her breasts and the pulsing ache at the secret heart of her body. She sucked in a fractured breath, embarrassed by her susceptibility.

Taut with arousal, Rashad made a valiant attempt to overcome the barrier of his fierce pride and build a bridge that might take him from coercion to acceptance. He moved closer. 'Waking or sleeping, you are in my every thought. My hunger for you is no greater than yours for me. I want to be with you.'

Tilda swallowed the lump in her throat and hated herself for being tempted. But he was only interested in getting her into bed. That was all he had ever been interested in, she told herself wretchedly. Yet her body still tingled with the sexual responsiveness that only he could awaken. It incensed her that she knew exactly what he was talking about. Every day, every hour, her every thought was centred on him, to the point of obsession. But that was a truth she despised and would never admit to him.

In any case, she had much more important things to worry about. Within the space of an hour every seeming certainty had vanished. It seemed shameful to her that she should long to walk into his arms and forget everything both past and present because of passion. What would sharing a bed with Rashad fix or clarify? Where were her pride and her common sense? First and foremost, she was in Bakhar for the sake of her family. She reminded herself that she had yet to see evidence that the threat against their security had been lifted.

'What I need right now is the assurance that that eviction order has been cancelled,' she murmured tautly.

A faint rise of dark blood marking the angular line of his classic cheekbones, Rashad fell still. 'It has been.'

As the tense pool of silence gathered Tilda worried uncomfortably at her full lower lip. 'And the house—has it been signed back to my mother?'

'Of course.'

'The outstanding loan has been settled?'

Rashad inclined his proud dark head in immediate acknowledgement.

'I would like to see all that in writing.' Tilda closed her restive hands together in front of her. In an effort to conceal her discomfiture, she was struggling to be as businesslike as he had once urged her to be.

'If that is your wish. I will ensure that you see the documentation.' Affronted though he was by that lack of trust in his word, Rashad made no further comment. He told himself that he should not be surprised that financial matters were her first consideration. Had he not always known that money meant more to her than anything else? He could not quell the rise of his distaste.

Tilda's fingers curled in on themselves too tightly for comfort. 'And I would also like to see the proof you said you had of my affairs with other men.'

Rashad veiled his icy gaze, determined not to surrender to that particular demand. Confronting her with unassailable evidence of her youthful promiscuity would only antagonise her at a time when he needed her co-operation. If she refused to conduct herself as his wife, his father and the rest of his family would be, at the very least, severely embarrassed. Indeed, all too many innocent people were at risk of suffering the consequences of his bad judgement and lack of foresight.

'I'm afraid that's not possible.'

He looked apologetic and he sounded apologetic, but Tilda was not convinced. She was parting her lips to tell him so when he voiced an apology at the interruption and answered his mobile phone.

His lean bronzed profile taut, he compressed his wide, sensual mouth. 'My sisters, Durra and Tibah, have arrived.'

In a large reception room downstairs she was immediately approached by two fashionably dressed women, who looked to be in their forties and, as such, a good deal older than Tilda had expected. Both spoke excellent English and greeted their brother with an affection laced with deferential restraint.

'The king has asked that you bring Tilda to him today so that he can meet her.' A small plump brunette with a bustling air, Durra greeted Tilda with warm words of welcome.

'There are a great many preparations to be made,' Tibah added with enthusiasm. 'The next few weeks will be very exciting! I do hope you can come now. We try not to keep our father waiting.'

Tilda noticed that Rashad looked very much as though he had been carved out of solid granite. Her heart and self-image slowly sank to her toes while she kept a resolute smile pinned to her taut mouth. She was painfully aware of Rashad's low opinion of her and felt that he could only loathe the prospect of introducing her as his bride to the father he esteemed. His siblings regarded him with barely concealed tension until he inclined his sleek dark head in agreement. He clapped his hands and a servant appeared from beyond the door. He issued instructions.

'We will leave immediately,' he murmured without expression.

His sisters flew back to Jumiah with them. The Great Palace where the royal family lived was situated several miles outside the flourishing capital city. As soon as the helicopter landed, Durra and Tibah parted from Rashad and Tilda to return to their apartments within the palace complex. A vast carved stone building enhanced by formal gardens and fountains, it was a much newer property than Tilda had expected to see and she made a surprised comment.

'The old palace was badly damaged during the war. It had also taken on unfortunate associations after two decades of my great-uncle's misrule,' Rashad explained. 'This new palace was built as a symbol of hope for the future.'

'It's colossal but very impressive.' Tilda shot him a strained glance and suddenly abandoned the stilted conversation in favour of honesty. 'Is there no way I can avoid having to meet your father?'

His stubborn jaw line clenched hard. 'In wishing to admit you so immediately to his presence, the king seeks to honour you.'

Tilda went pink with discomfiture. 'You misunderstood my meaning. Oh, never mind.'

'My father is a kind man. Not unreasonably, he has assumed that there is honest affection between us.'

The backs of Tilda's eyes stung in receipt of that sardonic reminder but she lifted her chin. To add insult to injury, Rashad proceeded to give her several tips on how to be polite and respectful in the presence of Bakhari royalty. 'There's nothing wrong with my manners,' she told him tightly. 'I'm not going to be rude.'

'I did not intend to cause offence.' Rashad was merely annoyed that she should have to enter such a crucial meeting without any preparation whatsoever.

Feeling wretchedly unsuitable for the honour being extended to her, Tilda was ushered into the audience room. King Hazar was a tall, spare man in his sixties, garbed in traditional robes that added to his quiet aura of dignity.

The kindliness of his unexpectedly friendly smile took her aback and instantly released the worst of her tension. He welcomed her to Bakhar in slow, careful English, embraced his son with enthusiasm and informed Tilda that he would be happy to regard her as another daughter. Very polite conversation ensued about the sights of Oxford, as well as the vagaries of the English climate. It dawned on Tilda that, far from being aghast at or even worried by his son's sudden marriage to an Englishwoman, the older man seemed genuinely delighted.

Under cover of this gentle dialogue, she studied Rashad from below her lashes. His lean bronzed profile was lit by the sunshine piercing the window behind him. As if aware of her attention, he turned his arrogant dark head. His tawny gaze met hers and her tummy performed an instant somersault of response. Colouring, she dragged her attention from him again. Goodness, he was gorgeous, she thought helplessly, and she was married to him. Really and truly married. The shock of that was still sinking in. With difficulty she returned her concentration to the conversation.

Rashad was wondering to himself exactly why his royal parent was so overjoyed by his supposed marriage. Had the older man feared that his son would remain single for the rest of his days? Was almost any wife better than no wife on his father's terms? Was that why not a single awkward question had yet been asked of either of them?

The king said that it was of great importance that Tilda receive support and guidance to enable her to feel at home within the royal household and in the country beyond the palace walls. 'Unlike your late mother, your wife will lead a life in the public eye,' his father remarked gravely. 'It is only sensible that Tilda should be helped to prepare for that role in advance of your wedding.'

What wedding? Tilda almost asked, just managing to bite back the startled query, for she was very much afraid of saying the wrong thing. She stole another covert glance at Rashad and noted that he seemed quite unfazed by that same reference. She suspected that he might be rationing information on a strict need-to-know basis and resentment stirred in her.

'I'm not convinced that Tilda should take on a public role,' Rashad countered.

Tilda tried to ignore Rashad's lack of enthusiasm for her taking on the responsibilities that went with being his wife. Naturally he felt like that, she told herself impatiently. There was no need whatsoever for her to take that personally. Unhappily this common-sense conviction did not prevent her from feeling cut to the bone and deemed a loser before she even got to run the race.

His father looked amused. 'My son, you cannot marry an educated and accomplished young lady and hope to keep her all to yourself. Why, the crown office has already had a request for your wife to open the new surgical wing of the hospital next month! All such matters will be more easily dealt with if Tilda has had the opportunity to study our history, etiquette and language, so that she may be comfortable wherever she travels within our borders.'

In the aftermath of the revealing meeting, Tilda was in a tense and unhappy daze. It appeared that some big fancy wedding was in the offing to satisfy convention. The very idea of that made her feel uncomfortable, because she was no actress. What was more, pretending to be Rashad's wife promised to be a serious challenge. Evidently it was regarded as something of a full-time occupation if she was to be put in training for the role. But, worst of all, Rashad was expecting her to take part in a massive pretence and enact a cruelly deceptive masquerade to fool people who were trustingly offering her sincere affection and acceptance. His family all seemed so *nice!* In her opinion only a truly horrid and insensitive person could feel anything other than guilt-stricken.

CHAPTER SEVEN

'You did very well with my father. He was most impressed,' Rashad commented, resting a lean hand at the base of Tilda's spine to guide her in the direction of his wing of the palace.

'I was so nervous I hardly said a word,' Tilda confided anxiously. 'I know next to nothing about you and your family and I was terrified of saying something that would reveal that. Your sisters are older than I expected. Why did you never talk about your family when you were a student?'

'Five years ago, my father and my sisters still felt like strangers to me.'

'But why?' Tilda questioned in bewilderment.

'My three sisters are the children of my father's first wife, who died of a fever after Kalila's birth. I am the son of his second marriage. When I was four years old my father was badly hurt in a riding accident,' Rashad explained. 'His uncle Sadiq stepped in as Regent and then used the opportunity to take the throne by force. My father was still bedridden when Sadiq took me from my family and held me as a hostage.'

'For how long?'

'Until I was an adult. Sadiq had no son of his own and he named me as his heir to keep certain factions happy. I was sent to a military academy and then I went into the army. My family's safety was dependent on Sadiq's goodwill.'

Tilda was appalled. 'My goodness, why did you never tell me any of this before? I mean, I knew about Sadiq and the war, but I didn't realise you'd been separated from your family when you were only a little boy.'

'I have never seen the wisdom of dwelling on misfortunes.'

'Your mother must have been devastated.'

'I believe so. I never saw her again. She fell ill when I was a teenager but I was not allowed to visit her.'

For perhaps the first time, Tilda understood the source of the unrelenting strength and self-discipline that lay at the heart of Rashad's character. As a child he must have suffered great loneliness and grief at being denied his family and it had hardened him. He had learnt to hide his emotions and make an idol of self-sufficiency. It was little wonder that he did not give his trust easily.

They crossed a marble forecourt screened by trees and lush vegetation. Daylight was fading as the sun slowly sank in a spectacularly beautiful sky shot with shades of peach, tangerine and ochre. Beyond the extensive greenery sat a substantial building. 'My home here at the palace is extremely private,' Rashad remarked.

In a magnificent circular entrance hall large enough

to stage a concert, Tilda came to a halt. 'The king mentioned something about a wedding.'

Rashad waved away the eager and curious servants who had all clustered below the stairs, and whom Tilda did not notice. He pushed open a door and stepped back. Tilda preceded him into a very large reception room decorated very much in the Eastern style with sumptuous sofas and a carpet so exquisite that it seemed a sin to actually walk on it.

'There will be a state wedding held for us at the end of the month. It cannot be avoided,' Rashad murmured. 'My people expect such a show and to do otherwise would be to create a great deal of comment.'

Tilda was rigid with disbelief, but she made no immediate response. She felt as though she were sinking into quicksand and only she was aware of the emergency. She could not credit that he simply expected her to go along with all such arrangements as though they were a genuine couple!

Rashad continued to pursue his deliberate policy of politely ignoring the tense signals Tilda was emanating. If he set an example, it was possible that in time she would learn to mirror his behaviour. 'May I call for dinner to be served?' he asked. 'I don't know about you, but it seems like a very long time since we last ate a proper meal and I confess that I am hungry.'

That reference to food was the proverbial last straw for Tilda. Her tension gave suddenly as she spread her hands wide in a helpless gesture of frustration. 'I can't do this, Rashad…I really can't! How do you manage to act as though everything's normal?'

'Discipline,' he told her quietly.

'Well, it's freaky and unnatural,' Tilda told him feelingly. 'We have to talk about this—'

'Why? Nothing can be changed. We're married. I am your husband. You are my wife. We must do what is expected of us.'

'Sacrifice doesn't come naturally to those of us who were not raised to be royal and perfect!' Tilda declared.

His strong jaw line set. 'I am not trying to be perfect.'

'Your father and your sisters are lovely. What a welcome they've given me!' Tilda shook her silvery fair head, struggling to find the right words with which to voice her deep unease at the role that had been forced on her. 'Doesn't deceiving them into believing that we're a real couple bother you?'

'Of course it does, but it is the lesser of two evils. I can only regret the actions that brought us to this point. But I also accept that the truth would shame and distress, not only my family, but also our people. A respectful pretence is the best option on offer to us.'

Tilda was very tempted to look for something large and heavy and throw it at him in the hope of extracting a less logical and dispassionate response. 'But this is a total nightmare.'

Accustomed to her love of exaggeration, Rashad surveyed her with glinting golden eyes of appreciation. Even after a day that would have taxed most women to the edge of hysteria she still looked absolutely amazing: glorious hair, glorious skin, glorious eyes, glowing and full of life. Out of politeness, courtiers, government officials and staff had tried not to stare at her, but the pure impact of her beauty had proved too much for many. That she had not betrayed the smallest awareness of that attention had impressed him. He had felt proud of her.

'Not a nightmare,' Rashad chided gently.

'Well, it is a nightmare for me!' Tilda condemned, her temper finally letting rip in the face of such indifference to her feelings. 'I don't routinely lie to people. I can't feel comfortable faking stuff. I don't have the first idea about how to act like your wife—'

'I can help you. You should have entered our apartments, met the servants and accepted their flowers and congratulations. You would then have ordered dinner.'

Her generous pink mouth fell wide. What servants? She had not seen any servants! And why was he talking about food again? After a day when she had reeled dizzily from one shock into the next, was that truly all he could think about?

'Or, you could have gone straight upstairs with me to bed,' Rashad framed, willing to exchange one hunger for another that became more pressing every time he looked at her. His intent gaze acquired a smouldering light as it roamed over her lovely face and slim, shapely figure. 'I can tell you now that sex is a high priority on my list. Meet my expectations there and I will regard you as the perfect wife.'

Tilda was almost dumbfounded with rage. For once, she could see that he had had no thought of being facetious. He was set on being candid and helpful when he informed her that his priorities were as basic as Neanderthal man's had no doubt been. Sex and food.

'I do not aspire to be the perfect wife, and if that was

the pep talk that was supposed to act as inspiration it was a killer!' Tilda launched at him. 'You asked for my co-operation. As I seemed to have very little choice, I went along with that, but I had no idea how big a charade you were expecting me to dish up!'

Lean, darkly handsome face taut, Rashad breathed, 'Our marriage does not have to be a charade.'

'And I don't have to be a concubine within this stupid fake marriage if I don't want to be!' Tilda flung that declaration and folded her arms, pride and fortitude prompting her to take a stand. She was willing to co-operate when it came to the marriage ceremony, but that was enough. Anything more than co-operation would have to be earned. Rashad was at the very foot of that particular learning curve…and his hints about sex and food were unlikely to increase his chances of achievement.

'Tilda…'

'Just you dare say one more word about how best to meet your expectations and, I swear, I'll scream until you gag me!' Tilda threatened, her voice half an octave higher in tone. 'You're not persuading me. You are so spoilt, so used to women who fall over themselves to do whatever you want—'

'Where am I going wrong with you? Perhaps I'm talking too much when action would be preferable.' Strolling forward, Rashad treated her to a fierce look of masculine challenge and, without hesitation, he pulled her into his arms.

Tilda was so disconcerted by that move in the middle of their argument that she lost valuable seconds when she might have gone into retreat. In the interim, Rashad ravished her mouth with his and set off a shattering sexual chain reaction throughout her slender body. Even though she knew she should not, she kissed him back, bruising her lips with the wild hot urgency that had risen like a crazy fever inside her, her hands delving into his black hair like possessive claws. She wanted him, wanted him, *wanted* him…just like a concubine? A favourite concubine? Those mocking words and the memory of how he had threatened to teach her to beg for his sexual attention, returned to haunt her. In an abrupt movement she tore herself free of his lithe hard body and literally tottered away a few steps on legs that didn't feel strong enough to keep her upright.

Rashad was trembling, his body screaming for release. *You're not persuading me,* she had said. Outrage roared through him when he grasped the significance of those words. What was it that Tilda found persuasive? What did it take to make Tilda surrender? As the answer came his fists clenched and he hated her as much as he wanted her and the force of that internal turmoil threatened to rip him apart.

'How much?' he intoned in a wrathful undertone. 'How much of a financial inducement do you want to share my bed?'

Shock at that question turned Tilda's flushed face white. Did he still think so little of her? Of course he did. Had she not agreed to sleep with him in return for having a very large debt written off? Her fire of anger was doused, but she was appalled at being directly confronted with his belief that she would do anything for cash.

'I don't want your money,' she whispered tightly,

forcing out the denial between tremulous lips. 'Please don't make me an offer like that ever again.'

Rashad was eager to believe that he had misinterpreted her behaviour. 'Then why do you deny us what we both desire?'

Sucking in a steadying breath, Tilda spun back to him, her bright eyes veiled to a wary glimmer. 'Sex isn't so simple for me as it is for you. I may have been willing to protect my family at the cost of my pride, but I'm not for sale any more. I'm sorry if you think that's dishonest,' she muttered defensively, 'but I think that it's a fair enough exchange if I agree to act like your wife and jump through all the right hoops to please everyone. I'll keep up the performance for as long as you ask, as well. That will be enough of a challenge when I can't possibly think of myself as your wife in any real way.'

Striving to control his hunger for her, Rashad regarded her with passionate force. 'Did I misunderstand what you meant by persuasion?'

A strangulated laugh was wrenched from Tilda. 'Oh, yes. But don't worry about it. All I'm asking for is a separate bedroom.'

'And that is what you want?' Rashad was frowning. He could barely credit what she was saying. She was his wife. She already *felt* like his wife. Was that really how she felt?

'*All* that I want from you, believe me.' Tilda would not look at him again for she had little faith in what she was saying even though pride had demanded that she say it. She wanted him with every fibre of her being but she would not let herself sink to the level of sleeping with a man who assumed he might have to pay her for his pleasure. He was his own worst enemy, she thought painfully. A few pleasing words, even a fleeting reference to the beauty of the desert sunset, and he could have had her for nothing. But flattery and romantic allusions to sunsets had never been Rashad's style.

'It will be as you wish. I have work to do. Excuse me,' Rashad responded with scrupulous politeness.

The door closed and the silence folded in. She expelled her breath in a long jagged surge. Her fingers lifted to the reddened and tingling contours of her lips and something like a sob tugged at her vocal cords, forcing her to grit her teeth and fight for self-control.

She dined solitarily later that evening in a state dining room with superb marble walls and floor. She ate everything that was put in front of her and tasted nothing. What had gone so badly wrong between herself and Rashad that he could think she was so cheap? Why was he so convinced that she had gone with other men behind his back? He was logical, intelligent. What was the proof of her infidelity that he evidently considered irrefutable? She knew that for the sake of her self-esteem she had to find out.

Sitting there alone, she remembered how madly in love with Rashad she had once been. She recalled cherished memories of fun, sweetness and passion. Once, a car had backfired in the street. Assuming that it was gunfire, Rashad had thrown her to the ground and protected her with his body. The sheepish expression on his face in the aftermath had been comic, but she had been touched to the heart to realise that, at a moment when he had honestly believed that he was in danger, he had instinctively put her safety before his own.

Nobody had ever really tried to look after Tilda before and, although she had scoffed at the idea, she had liked it because, for too long, she'd had to be the strong one in her family and look out for everyone else's interests. She had leant on Rashad and found him wonderfully supportive, even while the power of her passion for him had terrified her as much as it excited her. Determined not to be hurt, she had believed that she was in full control of her emotions. Then, out of the blue, he had dumped her and all her proud illusions had crumbled faster than the speed of light.

One day everything had seemed fine, the next it had been over. Rashad had arranged to take out her for a meal. She had sat waiting for him to pick her up. Time had crept on and he hadn't arrived, hadn't phoned, either. She had tried to call him on his mobile and there had been no answer. The next day, frantic with worry that something had happened to him, she had called round at the house he had rented and his staff had refused her entry. No explanation, no apology, nothing. Believing that in some way she must have offended him, she had gotten angry then and had decided to sit him out. For several days she had lived in denial of her growing misery until, one evening, when she just hadn't been able to bear being without him any longer, she had found out from a friend where he was and had gone in search of him.

The party had been at Leonidas Pallis's apartment. Through the crush, she had seen Rashad on a sofa with a sinuous redhead wrapped round him. Rashad, who supposedly didn't like such public displays of intimacy, had been kissing the girl. Something had died inside Tilda and all her proud pretences had fallen apart as she had fought her passage back to the exit. She had been convinced that he had ditched her and replaced her with a more sexually available girlfriend. There had been a desperate irony to the fact that it had been only then that she had fully appreciated how much she loved him.

As Tilda let herself recall the terrible hurt of Rashad's betrayal five years earlier, her chin came up. No way was she going to give Rashad the chance to put her through those agonies again! She might still be drawn to him like a stupid moth to a candle flame, but that didn't mean she had to surrender to her weakness or let him suspect that it existed. Events had made them more equal, she told herself bracingly. She was trading co-operation rather than sex in return for the debts he had written off. At least being partners in a pretend marriage left her with some dignity and he was already discovering that he could not treat a wife like a concubine.

Tilda straightened her slight shoulders, turquoise eyes luminous with purpose. She might not feel as though they were married but, goodness, she intended to be the *perfect* wife in public. By the time she left Bakhar, Prince Rashad Hussein Al-Zafar and his family would feel that he was losing a woman who had been an absolute solid gold asset to him. And not if he offered her a million pounds, not even if he begged on his knees, would she stay with him!

CHAPTER EIGHT

In the privacy of his office, Rashad watched the film footage for the third time. The camera, obviously wielded by a man hopelessly enthralled with Tilda's exquisite face, followed her every move at a children's concert. In front of a camera she was a natural and highly photogenic, and the Bakhari media industry had succumbed to their first bout of celebrity fever. When his sisters had taken Tilda shopping in Jumiah, the traffic had been brought to a standstill because interest in Tilda had been so great that drivers had abandoned their cars to try and catch a glimpse of her in the flesh.

Alarmed by the size of the crowds that had swiftly formed that morning, Rashad had wasted no time in tripling the size of Tilda's protection team. He had also put a more experienced man in charge of her security. She was incredibly popular. He ran the footage of the concert again and absorbed the lingering shots of his wife's radiant smile, her relaxed warmth with the children and the interest she showed in everyone she spoke to. Her intelligence and charisma attracted much admiring comment. Tilda might now look like a beautiful fashion queen, but when a toddler left a sandy handprint on her dress she just laughed and brushed herself down. In less than a month she had become the best-known face in Bakhar, next to his father's and his own.

So, who was it who had said that the camera never lied? Was this the same woman who had once deceived him, extracted money from him and slept with other men? Was the fact that she *still* hadn't slept with him ongoing evidence of the existence of that other unscrupulous persona? Was she simply a fantastic actress? Was she giving the people what they wanted, just as she had once played the innocent for his benefit? After all, he was willing to concede her innocence was what he had wanted most when he'd first met her. Then, he had been too idealistic to desire a succession of different women in his bed. What he had wanted most was a wife. Tilda had struck him as a pearl beyond price and he had put her on a pedestal.

Lean, powerful face grim, Rashad froze Tilda's image on screen. The woman in the film was a more adult version of the girl he remembered and he was deeply disturbed by the fact. Second time round, armed with the knowledge of her greed and promiscuity, he had expected to easily detect her insincerity and her other flaws. But Tilda was contriving to keep her dark side remarkably well hidden from him and from the whole of Bakhar. Few people were all bad or all good, he reminded himself impatiently. Wasn't it possible that she had seen the error of her ways and changed them? How could he doubt her guilt even for a moment? For wasn't that what was really bothering him? He had so far failed to match the woman enchanting everyone with her charm with the greedy, scheming wanton she was supposed to be at heart.

In a sudden movement Rashad straightened to his full height and unlocked the safe. He had to go right to the back of it to find the slim security file he sought. Put together by a British private detective, it was written in English. Rashad remembered what a battle he had had to understand that language on the day he'd read it and shock had made his brain freeze. He still felt queasy just looking at the cover of the file with her name on it. He reminded himself that it had come to him direct from an impeccable source. He felt that he needed to read it again, but he believed it would be unduly disrespectful to Tilda to even open that unsavoury file now, two days before their wedding.

His tension eased, his brilliant gaze simmered gold. The day after tomorrow, Tilda would be one hundred per cent his. She would have no grounds to complain of medieval laws and customs. There could be no suggestion that their union was anything other than legal and above-board. A wolfish smile of satisfaction slashed his wide, sensual mouth. Aware that he needed her co-operation before their state wedding made them the most married couple in Bakhar, he had played a waiting game of restraint. But restraint had its limits: his bride would lie in his bed on their wedding night.

The phone rang to inform him that Tilda's family were about to arrive. Rashad glanced at the file still in his hand and thrust it into his briefcase. Determined to award her mother and siblings every courtesy and frankly curious to meet them all again, Rashad left his office to be at Tilda's side. He had not actually been invited to be so, but he was prepared to rise above that small slight.

Tilda wrapped her arms exuberantly round Katie and Megan and had she had a third arm she would have hugged her brother James, as well, who gave her hair an affectionate tug and stepped back out of reach with a laughing complaint when she tried to hug him. Aubrey was shaking his head over the astonishing splendour and size of the palace.

'So much for the accounting job you mentioned!' Katie teased. 'Here you are decked out in designer gear, living in the lap of luxury and about to marry the love of your life. Obviously you took one look at each other and went overboard again. The only thing that stops it all being perfect is Mum not being here with us.'

Tilda sighed in agreement. 'I know. She's ecstatic that I'm getting married to Rashad but really sad she can't be here with us.'

'Mum is a lot happier and less nervy,' the youthful blonde confided. 'Aubrey thinks that having to miss your wedding might be just what it takes to push her into getting the professional help she needs.'

Having chatted to her parent regularly on the phone since leaving home, Tilda was well aware that Beth was in a much healthier and stronger frame of mind since she had been able to stop worrying about her debts. Stress, Tilda thought ruefully, might well have made her mother's condition worse. An end to Scott's threatening visits would also have helped.

'Rashad!' Megan suddenly yelled and tore across the room, only to fall still in sudden uncertainty several feet from the male she had once idolised.

Laughing at that noisy and enthusiastic welcome, Rashad strode straight up to the girl and bent down to speak to her.

'He's, like, totally the fairy-tale prince.' Katie rolled admiring eyes and groaned. 'So handsome, likes kids, always polite and charming. I mean, why the heck did you two ever break up? A silly row?'

'Something like that.'

'There's something that you should know. Remember the reporters cornering you at the airport?' Katie murmured uneasily. 'That was James's fault and he feels awful about it.'

'How on earth could it have been James's fault?' Tilda questioned.

'Dad—Scott.' Katie grimaced. 'James phones Scott sometimes, and James let drop about you and Rashad. It's a fair bet that Scott passed on the news to someone, maybe made a bit of money out of it.'

Tilda was relieved to find out who had been responsible, but disturbed by the fact that her younger brother had been in contact with his father. She took a deep breath and told her sister that Scott had been taking money from their mother. Katie scolded Tilda for not telling her sooner and promised to warn James.

Tilda found her attention roaming back continually to Rashad. His arrival had bowled her over. It was a challenge to take her eyes off his lean, darkly beautiful features. But then, she had seen precious little of him over the past month. Her days had been filled with history, language and etiquette lessons, not to mention dress fittings, shopping trips, innumerable social meetings with Rashad's extended family and several informal public appearances.

Every night she had fallen into bed exhausted and lain awake listening in vain for Rashad coming home, because his bedroom was so far from hers that she had no hope of hearing his return. Slowly but surely, his cool detachment had begun to infuriate her. A member of his staff had brought her a sealed envelope containing all the documents pertaining to the transfer of the family home back into her mother's name and the writing off of the loan. She had sent him a very polite note of thanks.

But it had not achieved the desired response, for he had not come looking for her. She had more or less told him to leave her alone and Rashad, who had never, ever done what she told him to do before, *was* leaving her alone. Initially she had told herself that this proved that there had been no real substance to his assurance that their marriage did not have to be a charade. But it had soon dawned on her that demanding a separate bedroom had been a sure-fire way of ensuring that their relationship remained a sham. Though it galled her to admit it, she wanted much more from him.

Rashad's working day began very early. A lie-in had become an unknown treat for Tilda because the minute Rashad left the building she raced down the corridor and across a courtyard to his room to check that his bed had actually been occupied the night before. Well aware that he had a very racy reputation as a womaniser, Tilda had developed a need to continually check that he wasn't doing anything suspicious. She was now as well acquainted with Rashad's daily schedule as any seasoned member of his staff.

He rose at five in the morning to go riding across the desert sands. He showered at six. He often breakfasted and dined with his father, or had a working meal with staff. He rarely ate lunch. He worked extremely hard. He had gone abroad on business twice and she hadn't slept a wink while he was away for worrying that he might be making up for those weeks of celibacy. Every day he sent her flowers or, if he had seen little of her, he phoned her. If she was silent or sulky, he did the talking. His manners were outrageously good, his reserve impenetrable. She was convinced that he could hold a pleasant conversation with a brick wall. He remained breathtakingly impervious to her most tart remarks. At times, she had wanted to screech down the phone like a shrew to get a reaction from him but if that had happened she'd have felt horribly childish.

Now she watched him speaking to each of her siblings and receiving an overwhelmingly positive response from each of them. He was good with people, quick to set them at their ease, she acknowledged grudgingly. Even Aubrey was smiling and James, often silenced by teenaged awkwardness, was talking away happily.

'Where is your mother?' Rashad asked Tilda in a quiet aside a few minutes later. 'Did the journey overtire her? Has she gone upstairs to lie down?'

Tilda went instantly into defensive mode. 'She's not here. She couldn't come.'

Rashad shot her a perturbed glance. 'Why not?'

Her turquoise eyes sparked. 'I'm not going to tell you and risk being accused of telling sob stories.'

'Tilda,' Rashad chided, gleaming dark as midnight eyes resting on her in level enquiry.

Her face went pink, her mouth running dry. When he looked directly at her a thousand butterflies were set loose in her tummy and it seriously embarrassed her. 'OK. Mum suffers from agoraphobia. It's more than four years since she even went out of the front door of her home. She never goes out. She *can't.*'

His ebony brows pleated in consternation. 'Agoraphobia? You should have told me about this.'

'Why? You were in the process of having my mother evicted. You didn't want the human-interest tales then. It's too late to talk like Mr Compassionate now,' Tilda told him accusingly.

'I was hard on you, but I would never be unjust,' Rashad countered evenly. 'Someone should have given me the true facts of the matter.'

Tilda was determined not to let him off the hook. 'You wouldn't have been interested.'

'I had good reason for mistrust. Five years of inaction followed by a last-minute plea from you? But you must draw a line under that period because your family is now my family. I will do whatever is within my power to ensure that your mother receives the very best treatment available.' Rashad gazed down at Tilda's mutinous oval face. 'The day after tomorrow is our wedding day.'

Tilda released a theatrical long-suffering sigh. 'Like I could forget that!'

Rashad flung back his imperious dark head and laughed with genuine appreciation. The day could not come soon enough for him.

'All I can say is…you look amazing,' Katie said dreamily.

Tilda did a little twirl in front of the cheval-mirror. Her wedding gown was glorious: pristine white and cut to enhance her graceful figure, it had the deceptively simple designer elegance that came from style and sumptuous fabric. Her two sisters looked delightful in matching dresses the colour of burnished copper, which had been fitted in London. Rashad's eldest sister, Durra, was acting as a matron of honour for the first ceremony which would be followed by the Bakhari ceremony, a few hours later.

The phone was brought to Tilda. It was her mother, Beth. The older woman's happiness was patent in spite of the thousands of miles that separated mother and daughter. Beth explained that Rashad had arranged for a video link to be set up in her home so that Beth could watch the ceremonies. A lump formed in Tilda's throat. His consideration where her family was concerned was surprising her yet again. Once he had realised that her siblings would be leaving directly after the wedding ceremony because both Aubrey and Katie had exams coming up, he had organised a fun sightseeing tour for them to enjoy the day before.

She rang Rashad to thank him for the video link.

'It was nothing,' he protested.

'It means everything to Mum.' Tilda went into the *en suite* bathroom for privacy and added, 'She thinks this wedding is real, so it's a really big deal for her.'

'For me, as well, and for Bakhar,' Rashad murmured coolly.

'I didn't mean it that way…oh, for goodness' sake, just because you never say *anything* without thinking!' Tilda groaned.

'Tilda?' Katie knocked on the door. 'What are you doing?'

Tilda emerged with sparkling eyes, still talking on the phone. 'Oh, I'm just arguing with Rashad, Katie. Nothing new there—'

'Tilda,' Rashad drawled huskily. 'Make no mistake. This is a real wedding…'

Rashad, devastatingly handsome in a superb grey morning suit, worn with a silk waistcoat and striped trousers, awaited her in a beautifully decorated room filled with all his closest relatives. The Christian marriage service, conducted by a chaplain attached to the British embassy, was short and sweet, but the simple words of the ceremony had a familiarity that had a lingering resonance for Tilda. Rashad slid a platinum ring on her finger and she returned the favour with a matching band on his. For the first time she felt married, for the first time he felt like her husband and she felt like a wife.

'You look fantastic in white,' Rashad confided huskily.

Meeting his appreciative gaze, Tilda tingled. After the bride and groom had posed for formal photographs with

King Hazar, Tilda was whisked off at speed to be prepared and presented afresh as a traditional Bakhari bride.

Assisted from her gown by half a dozen pairs of helpful hands, lost in a crowd of chattering women, Tilda was ushered into a palatial bathroom. A scented bath liberally sprinkled with rose petals awaited her. While she bathed, she heard music striking up in the room next door and smiled. There was a marvellous atmosphere of fun in the air. She emerged wrapped in a towel and learnt that she had only completed the first step of the all-important bridal preparations. She submitted to having her hair rinsed with what one of her sisters-in-law explained was an extract of amber and jasmine. It left her tresses silky smooth and deliciously perfumed.

After being placed on a couch, Tilda was gently massaged with aromatic oil and she relaxed for the first time that day. Durra asked her if she would mind having her hands and feet ornamented with henna. Acquiescing, Tilda looked on in fascination while, for the sake of speed, two women embarked on painting delicate lacelike ochre patterns on her slender hands and feet. Refreshing mint tea was served.

'Men are not usually very good at waiting for what they want,' Durra contended cheerfully, 'but Rashad is an exceptional man. It is years since my brother first mentioned your name to us and here you are, his bride at last.'

Surprise made Tilda tense. 'You knew about me then…I mean, Rashad told you about me?'

Durra gave her an anxious apologetic look. 'Perhaps I shouldn't have mentioned it.'

'No, not at all,' Tilda soothed, because she was pleased to learn that Rashad had considered her of sufficient importance in his life to have told his family about her. At the same time, though, it made her even more determined to find out what had so totally destroyed his faith in her. Had he seen her with a work colleague or another student that summer? Misinterpreted what he had seen? Did he have a problem with jealousy? Had someone lied about her?

A diversion was created by the arrival of a brass-bound wooden box inlaid with mother-of-pearl. Tilda eased up the lid and displayed, to a chorus of 'oohs' and 'aahs,' an intricate headdress of beaten golden coins and an incredible quantity of ornate turquoise jewellery. Evidently last worn by Rashad's mother on the occasion of her marriage, the antique necklaces, earrings and bracelets had been passed down through many generations of brides.

Tilda sat while her hair was styled and her make-up done. Her sisters' steadily widening eyes warned her that the end result was likely to be very different from what she was accustomed to. A wonderfully colourful hand-embroidered and beaded kaftan was extended for her admiration. Only when she was finally dressed was she allowed to see herself in the mirror.

'Welcome to the sixteenth century!' Katie whispered cheekily in Tilda's ear.

From her kohl-lined, glittering turquoise-shadowed eyes to the silvery fairness of her hair, which fell like a gleaming sheet of silk below the bridal headdress, there was a dazzling barbaric splendour to her appearance.

Tilda wondered if Rashad would go for the traditional Bakhari bride look and she rather thought he would.

She was led into a huge richly decorated room filled with people, but the only person she was truly aware of was Rashad. He wore an army dress uniform in royal-blue and gold, a sword hanging by his side. Her heart skipped a beat as soon as she saw him. She let the inner wall of her pride soften for an instant and admitted to herself that she didn't just find Rashad madly, insanely sexy and attractive. That was only a part of what drew her to him. The truth was that she had never got over the secret conviction that he was the love of her life. Although he had hurt and disappointed her, he had still awakened feelings stronger than any other man could hope to match. She still loved him. Perhaps, she reasoned ruefully, now that they were husband and wife, it really was time that she stopped fighting with him and gave him a second chance.

On cue, Rashad gripped her hand and murmured with flatteringly impressed conviction. 'You look so beautiful—it is wrong of me to think it, but every man here must envy me.'

Delighted that she had been correct in assuming that the medieval theme would be a winning success, Tilda drifted dreamily through the ceremony that followed. Her heart open to her emotions and her love acknowledged, she felt curiously at peace with herself. The reception started with a lavish feast. She sat by Rashad's side in their carved thronelike chairs and, with a calm smile on her lips, watched a ceremonial display of dancing with swords, whips and bloodthirsty shouts. After the folk dances came poetry readings and songs and the presentation of magnificent gifts. They went out onto a balcony to watch a camel race taking place beyond the walls.

In the noisy debate that took place at the end of the race, Rashad closed a hand over hers and tugged her back indoors and down a quiet staircase. 'Now at last we can be alone.'

'We can just vanish in the middle of it all?'

Rashad surveyed her with scorching golden eyes and brought his hungry mouth down on hers with passionate force. As an answer it was very effective. Her consciousness of the world around her went into a crazy tail-spin until he lifted his imperious dark head again.

'You've spent virtually the whole of the last month ignoring me!' Tilda recovered enough to splutter.

'But you made it plain that you wanted to be left alone,' Rashad reminded her darkly, walking her down the stairs at a pace she could manage in her long dress and high heels. 'You said you wanted to sleep apart from me.'

As Tilda paused to look up at him a sensual frisson of awareness slivered through her body. 'Not tonight, *but*—'

'No conditions,' Rashad slotted in.

'Just one tiny one,' Tilda told him winsomely, noting the way his devouring gaze was glued to her and feeling an intoxicating sense of her feminine power. 'You have to tell me what really happened five years ago. I want to know what made you turn against me.'

Seriously disconcerted by that demand, Rashad

breathed, 'You want to rake up the past on our wedding night? Are you crazy?'

'Don't I have a right to know?'

'Yes,' he conceded, but with a reluctance she could feel, 'but not tonight.'

Tilda supposed he had a point and his admission that she had a right to know mollified her a little. Even so, she did not want to drop the subject until she had received an answer that she could depend on. 'What sort of evidence do you have?'

'A security file,' Rashad divulged, in the hope that revealing the source of his knowledge would persuade her into a diplomatic retreat. He could see no point in putting either of them through the discomfort of examining evidence that she would only find degrading.

Tilda was taken aback by that admission. 'And how the heck did you get hold of a security file?'

'It's been in my possession for a while. No one else has seen it,' he grated tightly. 'Right now it's in my briefcase.'

Satisfied by that admission, if a little spooked by the strength of his reaction, Tilda said nothing more; he'd listened to her request and acted on it. Tomorrow or the next day would be soon enough to resurrect the past. For the present, Tilda realised that she was more interested in making the most of her wedding day.

CHAPTER NINE

THE magnificent main bedroom suite, which neither Rashad nor Tilda had occupied before, was bedecked with flowers and bore more than a passing resemblance to a fairy-tale bower. Tilda was enchanted.

Rashad watched her reverently touch a snowy-white lily blossom. He moved forward to grasp her hand gently in his. 'This is my wedding gift to you.' He threaded a stunning oval diamond ring onto her finger. 'A betrothal ring. We were never engaged but I would like this ring to signify a new beginning for us.'

Her eyes prickled. The diamonds glittered with breathtaking brilliance. She was very touched by what he had just said, because he was offering her heart's desire. More than anything else she wanted to believe that she had a proper future with him. His choice of gift told her so much more than he would have managed to say. 'It's absolutely gorgeous.'

Rashad detached the coin headdress from her hair with great care and set it aside. Beautiful dark eyes serious below his luxuriant black lashes, he removed the turquoise jewellery piece by piece. 'It meant much to me to see you wear these gems.'

'Did anyone ever tell you how amazing you look in army uniform?' Tilda muttered helplessly.

'No,' Rashad said truthfully, and an amused smile lightened his solemn expression.

'Well, you do,' she told him gruffly.

'I want you so much I hurt,' Rashad breathed not quite steadily, letting the tip of his tongue delve between her readily parted lips.

As he leant closer she felt the hard evidence of his arousal through his clothing and a combination of nerves and excitement gripped her. He detached his sword belt and undid his jacket. She tugged it off him with hands that were clumsy with impatience. She had waited too long for him. She wondered if he would realise that he was her first lover. She hoped so. Then he would have to accept how wrong he had been about her and she supposed she would graciously accept his heartfelt apologies.

He undid the tight sash at her waist and unzipped the ornate and heavy kaftan, easing the rich fabric down slowly over her hips. Desire sparked low in her pelvis and she pressed her slim thighs together in embarrassment. Tiny little tremors were running through her slender figure. She stretched up and found his wide, sexy mouth again for herself. He held her there entrapped, one lean hand braced to her spine, the ripe swell of her breasts crushed by the powerful wall of his chest. As he captured her lips with shattering urgency her heart thumped an upbeat tempo inside her ribcage and a delicious surge of heat warmed her belly. His tongue plundered the soft recesses of her mouth, teaching her a wickedly erotic rhythm that made her whimper low in her throat with surprise and pleasure.

Golden eyes smouldering like the heart of a fire, Rashad set her back from him and removed the gossamer fine silk slip she wore. 'So many unnecessary layers,' he complained thickly.

Still clad in bra and briefs, Tilda reddened, wildly conscious of his appraisal as he shed his uniform. Watching in guilty fascination, she thought how beautiful he was from the smooth golden skin of his wide, sculpted shoulders to the hard, muscular breadth of his chest and his long, lean, hair-roughened thighs. Her admiring scrutiny jolted to a sudden halt just below the low-slung waistband of his boxers, where the explicit outline of his bold maleness was all too obvious to her disconcerted eyes. Hastily she glanced away, a tiny frisson of mingled response and alarm gripping her.

'Come here,' he urged.

'Can we do this really slowly?' Tilda asked abruptly.

Surprise and amusement made Rashad smile. With quiet confidence he let his long brown fingers feather through her pale silky ringlets in a soothing motion. 'What are you scared of? Surely not of me?'

Tilda went pink, mortified that she had let herself down with that nervous and all-too-revealing question. 'Don't be daft.'

Unhooking her bra with deft assurance, Rashad vented a husky sound of satisfaction and lifted his hands to cup the full, firm mounds of creamy flesh that tumbled free. 'I promise that you will know only pleasure in this bed tonight.'

Tilda remained tense. 'I'm not as experienced as you seem to think.'

His stubborn jaw line tautened, for he did not want to think of anything that might awaken thoughts of the men with whom she had betrayed his trust. He shut out that statement and wiped the very memory of it from his mind. If he let anger touch him again he feared that his promise of a new beginning would become empty, meaningless words and so he made no answer. Instead, he bent his head to kiss her into silence again and he stroked the delicate coral pink buds that crowned her breasts with skilful fingers.

The liquid sensation at the juncture of Tilda's thighs became a knot of almost painful anticipation. She sucked in an audible breath, but a gasp of disconcertion was wrenched from her when he pulled her down across his thighs, though she had no thought of protest. He used his tongue to lash a lush, pouting nipple with wicked expertise. He followed that bold caress with the gliding graze of his teeth, tormenting the tender peaks into rigid, straining points.

'Rashad…' she gasped, her hips squirming in a forlorn attempt to assuage the throb of need he had awakened.

'You like that?' Venting a soft laugh of satisfaction, Rashad framed her face with lean brown fingers to hold her still. 'I think you will like everything I do.'

He tasted her swollen mouth with erotic urgency and eased a hand beneath her hips to remove her last garment. Suddenly aware that she was totally naked, Tilda tensed and there was a hint of insecurity in the way her tongue twinned with his. Rising with her in his strong arms, he tumbled her gently down amongst the pillows. Removing his boxer shorts, he joined her on the bed. His rawly appreciative gaze feasted on the pale rounded contours of her shapely body. She lay there, her entire skin surface buzzing with a wanton response that not even an attack of almost paralysing shyness could kill.

'I want to please you,' Rashad muttered huskily. 'Just as you will wish to please me.'

'Please you?' she whispered uncertainly.

He took her hand and closed her fingers round that part of him that she had rigorously avoided looking at. The size of him dismayed her, even while the offer of such blatant intimacy fascinated her. Her face flamed at the iron-hard heat and satin smoothness of his rigid shaft. Uncertain though she was, curiosity took over. When he rested back against the pillows and groaned with uninhibited pleasure, answering heat slivered through her and centred on the damp, tender heart of her.

'How am I doing?' Tilda whispered shakily

'Too well for my control.' Rashad laced possessive fingers in her hair and devoured her luscious mouth in an almost punitive kiss while he spread her back against the pillows. He skimmed teasing fingers through the pale blond curls below her belly and she shivered, madly, wantonly aware of the hot, moist heat of that hidden place. He found the tenderest spot of all and she moaned and pushed her flushed face into his shoulder, alternately taut and melting with delight in response. She was wildly sensitive to his erotic skill. Her head moved restively back and forth, her spine incurving in a helpless attempt to release the unbearable tension rising inside her. He tested the slick, wet heat of her with a single finger. Consumed by the sheer force of her own response, she cried out, her senses scattered with need.

She had never dreamt that she could want and crave as she did at that moment. 'Rashad...please!'

But only when the ache for fulfilment had become a torment did he angle her back, sliding lithely and surely between her thighs. She was frantic by that stage, urging him on with eager, clutching fingers. With an earthy sound of male pleasure he eased a path into her delicate passage, restraining himself with difficulty as she was very tight.

'You feel marvellous,' he breathed raggedly.

Tilda was past speech, all her needs pent up in the violence of the hunger he had aroused and the astonishing newness of what he was making her feel. Only when he deepened his penetration did she feel discomfort. It took her entirely by surprise and was swiftly followed by a sharp stab of pain as he completed his possession. That final pang wrung an involuntary cry from her lips.

'Tilda...' In bewilderment, Rashad angled back from her and stared down at her. For a split second he had thought he felt a barrier, but he could not bring himself to voice what he believed would be a foolish question. Of course she could not have been a virgin. Of course it must have been his imagination. 'Have I hurt you?'

'No...no,' she mumbled, scarcely knowing what she was saying for she was not in the mood for a post-mortem. All momentary discomfort now forgotten, her body was tingling and aching with desire. She was on the thrilling edge of a sensual precipice, her excitement eager and ready to fly high again. That quickening sensation of overwhelming need made her feverishly impatient and she arched up to him in a wholly instinctive movement of encouragement.

With a roughened groan, Rashad succumbed to her provocative invitation and embedded himself again in the sweet oblivion of her body. The hot, virile glide of his flesh within hers submerged her in a sensual world of the purest pleasure. Enthralled by the discovery, she rose up to him and he thrust again. The potent masculine rhythm that he set increased her hunger for him, banishing all awareness of everything but the excitement he had unleashed. At a delirious peak of ravenous need, she reached a glorious climax and abandoned herself to the sweet convulsions of writhing pleasure that engulfed her.

Afterwards, enveloped in a heavy languor, she wondered abstractedly if she would ever move again. Inside she felt like warm, melting honey and buoyantly happy. She was amazed by how close she now felt to Rashad. He kissed her slow and deep and then rolled over, carrying her with him. Content to be held, she snuggled into him, revelling in the achingly familiar scent of his skin. Beneath her cheek, his heart had a steady, reassuring beat.

With a rueful sigh, Rashad eased her up level with him and subjected her to the onslaught of frowning dark golden eyes. 'I hurt you…I'm sorry.'

'You noticed, didn't you? But you are so stubborn,'

Tilda murmured rather tenderly, running a slim forefinger along the taut line of his passionate mouth. 'So stubborn that you won't put two and two together and come up with the right answer. Well, it seems that I'll have to do it for you. I was a virgin.'

Rashad frowned down at her in disbelief. 'That's not possible,' he muttered half under his breath.

Tilda pulled herself up against the pillows and winced at the unexpected pang of tenderness that reminded her of how intimately entwined they had been just minutes earlier.

In an equally sudden movement, Rashad sat up, dislodging the bedding. He went very still when he saw the evidence of her lost innocence on the white sheet. He was so stunned to appreciate that he had not been mistaken in his suspicions that he was silenced. There could have been no other men in her life, not even *one* other man, or even a single serious affair. It should have been impossible but he looked down into her clear, expectant eyes and knew it was not, for there was fearlessness in that look that challenged him to disbelieve her again.

'So now you have to explain yourself...and a little humility would go a long way,' Tilda told him gently, positively basking in a sense of power and willing to offer helpful hints. 'Are you just a paranoiacally jealous guy? Because I really do need to know, if that's the problem.'

'That's not the problem,' Rashad breathed stiltedly.

'I want to see that file—'

'That is impossible.' Rashad could now imagine nothing more disastrous than to show her the sleazy file that had destroyed his faith in her. What an insult that would be to add to the original injury!

'You don't have a choice.'

'I have wronged you. I have misjudged you.' His head was pounding, he could barely think straight. He was fighting to absorb and contain the shock of what he had just found out. But he could not yet move beyond it because the fallout from that misjudgement five years back had been too great. 'I can only ask for your forgiveness.'

Tilda was seriously dissatisfied with that wooden response. She did not know exactly what she had expected from him but an ongoing refusal to do as she asked was not acceptable. 'The file?'

'No. I'm sorry.' In one strong movement, Rashad sprang out of bed, determined to get his head straight before he risked saying one more word to her. But, really, all he was conscious of was an enormous surge of bitterness and shame. 'I need a shower.'

In angry stupefaction, Tilda watched as his long, powerful golden back view vanished into the *en suite* bathroom. It didn't really matter to him, she thought painfully. She felt so horribly rejected. It didn't really matter that he had been her first lover, after all. Had she honestly believed that he would think that she was somehow more special? Wasn't that pathetic of her? All her hurt and anger turning destructively inward, she slid off the bed. What a fool she had made of herself! Why was she always doing that with him? She loved him, he lusted after her. Nothing had changed in five years. She was still looking for what she couldn't have, still hoping to somehow win what he didn't have to give her!

Despising her nakedness, she snatched up the wedding kaftan and wriggled her way into it, twisting round to do up the zip with frantic hands. She angled a shamed glance back at the tumbled bed, seeing it as the scene of her humiliation. Why had she thought a wedding ring would change anything? But why, most of all, had she allowed herself to believe that sexual intimacy would somehow make everything all right between them? She was on the way back to her own room when she recalled his grudging admission that the file he had mentioned was in his briefcase. Her eyes flashed. Without hesitation, she changed direction and headed for his office suite.

In the tiled wet room, Rashad stood with clenched fists under the powerful flow of the water. What did he say to her? Where were the words that could express his regret for his lack of trust? He was convinced that there were no words adequate to such a massive challenge. Especially after what he had gone on to do to Tilda and her family. He could blame only himself for the fact that he had added the pursuit of revenge to his tally of sins. Shame cut through him as keenly as the slash of a knife. He forced his taut shoulders back against the cold tiles. A boiling knot of rage was forming in place of his usual reasoned restraint. He shuddered at the memory of that file and what it had cost her…and him.

Such slander could only have been authorised at the very highest level. Sweat broke on Rashad's brow. He looked back five years. He remembered his father's lukewarm attitude to the prospect of his son taking an English wife. The king had urged his son to wait and consider before embarking on such an important commitment. Accustomed to independent, decisive action, Rashad had resented the suggestion that he could not be trusted to choose his own wife. No comment had been made when Rashad had let it be known that the relationship was at an end. Now Rashad was suspicious of what he had regarded at the time as his father's tactful silence. All his life he had awarded absolute loyalty to his parent. But he also knew that if the older man had sanctioned the sordid destruction of Tilda's reputation, he would never be able to forgive him for it. It was an issue, he recognised bleakly, that had to be dealt with immediately.

Rifling through Rashad's briefcase, Tilda finally came on what she sought. Swallowing hard, she withdrew the slim folder. She pushed the case back under the desk and returned to her bedroom, wondering if Rashad had noticed yet that she was missing and, if he had, what he would do about it. In the distance she could hear the sound of lively music and revelry: the royal wedding guests were still celebrating.

She sat down on the bed and opened the file. Her heart was in her mouth and she scolded herself, for all she was expecting to see was the source of the misunderstanding that she believed must have taken place—possibly, the name of a male friend had been erroneously linked with hers. Her address was given as the student house in which she had rented a room that summer. What she was not prepared to see was a fabrication of lies that listed a string of men, whom she had never heard of, and declared that they had all stayed overnight in her room. It was very precise as regards dates and times. Evidently she had been the victim of a sordid character assassination. She was devastated by the realisation that Rashad could have believed her capable of such rampant promiscuity.

Just as suddenly she was flooded with an explosive mix of rage and pain. When was enough enough? What did it say about her that she was willing to take whatever Rashad threw at her? Five years ago his rejection had destroyed her pride, her peace of mind and her happiness. Having encouraged her to care about him, he had broken her heart in the cruellest way available to him. When she had approached him recently in search of some compassion, he hadn't had a scrap of pity to spare. He had treated her like the dirt beneath his royal feet! He had offered her the chance to pay off the debts with her body. Only her concern for her family's future had persuaded her to agree to those degrading terms.

Yet when Rashad's ruthless plans had run aground and blown up in his face and he had needed *her* support, had she refused? Oh, no, she hadn't refused him anything but immediate sexual gratification! How could she have been so understanding? So ready to make allowances and forgive? In a passion of denial and self-loathing, she peeled off the kaftan and stalked through to the bathroom to wash her face clean of make-up. In the dressing room she dragged out fresh underwear, a shirt and cotton trousers, choosing from her own clothes, not from the designer wardrobe he had bought her. She was leaving him, she was going home to her mum. He could get stuffed! He could keep the fancy togs and all the ancestral jewellery, as well. She set the diamond engagement ring on the chest by the bed. She wasn't hanging on to that as though it were a sentimental keepsake! Her throat was thick with tears. It was better to travel light.

Tying her hair back, she put on a jacket and checked her passport. She ripped a sheet of paper out of a notebook and put it on top of the file, which she left lying on the bed. She wrote: 'You don't deserve me. I'm never coming back. I want a divorce.'

Only when she reached a side entrance of the palace did she appreciate that her bodyguards had seemingly come out of nowhere to follow her every step of the way. Consternation assailed her, because, not only had she hoped to make a sneaky exit, but she had also thought that she was barely recognisable in her plain and ordinary outfit.

'You would like a car, Your Royal Highness?' Musraf, the only English speaker in her protection team, asked with a low bow.

'Yes, thank you. I'm going to the airport.' Tilda endeavoured to behave as though a late run to the airport on her wedding night was perfectly normal. But the *Royal Highness* appellation almost totally unnerved her, because she had not known she was entitled to that label and it made anonymity seem even more of a forlorn hope.

Within minutes a limousine pulled up. Ushering her into it, Musraf enquired about the time of her flight.

'I want to go to London—but I haven't organised it yet,' Tilda informed him loftily.

She was assured that all such arrangements would be made for her. A private room was made available to her the instant she arrived at the airport. There she sat for two hours before being taken out to a private jet with the colours of the royal household painted on the tail fin. She crept aboard, feeling it was rather cheeky to leave Rashad by fleeing the country in one of his own aircraft. As it occurred to her that a wife who vanished within hours of a state wedding would cause him rather more serious embarrassment than that, she came up with an invented cover story for Musraf to relay to Rashad.

'Say my mother's not well and that's why I left in a hurry,' she instructed him helpfully before take-off.

Dawn was breaking when the jet landed in the U.K. Tilda had slept several hours and felt physically refreshed, but her spirits were at rock-bottom. Her protection team stayed close and while she was struggling to work out how to dismiss them politely her mobile phone rang.

'It's Rashad,' her husband murmured, making her stiffen in dismay. 'I'll see you at the town house in an hour.'

'Are you saying that you're in London, too?' Tilda vented in a hastily lowered voice that was the discreet version of a shriek. 'That's impossible!'

'One hour—'

'I'm going to see Mum—'

'*One hour*,' Rashad decreed.

'I won't be—'

'If you're not there I will come to Oxford for you,' Rashad informed her with ruthless clarity. 'You are my wife.'

Her face burning, Tilda thrust the phone back in her

bag. He must have flown out of Bakhar very shortly after she had. His wife? His accidental wife would have been a more accurate description. How many women got married without even getting a proposal? Her teeth gritted. Well, if Rashad was that determined to stage a confrontation, he could have one with bells on! She had done nothing to be ashamed of. Although dating him in the first place struck her as being a hanging offence; he'd looked like trouble with a capital *T*. From start to finish, that was what he'd proved to be.

But even as she fought in self-defence to keep her furious defiance at a high, she remained miserably conscious of how devastating she had found the contents of that file. Actually seeing in print the kind of stuff that Rashad had believed her capable of had ripped any sentimental scales from her eyes. Love was a total waste of time with a guy who could happily make love to a woman he believed to be a total slut. That file had also resurrected the terrible pain that he had inflicted on her five years earlier. Well, there would be no more of it. He had done enough damage.

It was closer to two hours before Rashad strode into the drawing room of the town house where, just six weeks earlier, he had enforced his terms for their relationship. From the window, Tilda had watched him arrive and her chest had tightened and her breathing had shortened as though she was on the brink of a panic attack. She didn't want to notice that he looked drop-dead gorgeous in a very snazzy black designer suit. She didn't want to feel a hot, quivery sensation of near dizziness when she inadvertently collided with his smouldering tawny gaze.

Dark vibrations of anger were rippling through Rashad. 'You went into my briefcase to see that file.'

Her chin came up. 'I'd have blown up a safe to get a look at that file and I'm really glad I did.'

'That's not and will never be an excuse to walk out on our marriage.'

'I didn't walk, Rashad. I ran! And where were you? What was your reaction to the discovery that everything you accused me of, everything you dared to think about me, was hopelessly wrong?' Tilda demanded grittily, her wide eyes burning with tears. 'You went for a shower.'

Rashad vented a phrase in Arabic that sounded like a curse. 'I was in shock—I was upset—'

'Since when did you do "upset"?' Tilda threw at him bitterly. 'I've seen you cold, angry, scornful, silent. I've never seen you shocked or upset. Heaven forbid that anyone might suspect you have any real emotions!'

Rising to that challenge, Rashad settled blazing golden eyes on her. 'I was schooled from an early age not to reveal what I thought or I felt. Initially, that training was aimed at ensuring I had good manners, but before I was much older my safety and that of others often depended on my ability to stay in control. I have never had the freedom to parade my emotions as you do.'

Reminded of his background, Tilda squirmed and felt guilty, but she could not help feeling that her hurt was increased by the extent of his rigid self-discipline.

'Of course I was upset,' Rashad added in fierce continuance. 'How could you doubt it? The filthy lies in that file destroyed what we had found together five years ago.'

Her lashes lifted on mutinous turquoise eyes. 'No,

you did that. You believed those filthy lies. You didn't give me a chance, not one single chance to speak up in my own defence.'

Rashad spread lean golden hands in a sudden driven movement that betrayed the level of his stress. 'I believed the source of that file to be above reproach. When I realised last night that the contents were an unforgivable tissue of lies designed to destroy our relationship, I had to know *who* was responsible. For that reason I approached my father first to find out if he had ordered the fabrication of that file.'

'Your *father?*' she echoed in surprise.

His lean, strong face was set in grim, angular lines. 'He was most distressed when I showed it to him. He had never seen it before.'

Fabrication or not, Tilda was aghast at him having showed that file to King Hazar. 'You actually showed the file to him?'

Rashad expelled his breath in a taut hiss. 'I wanted him to see for himself how you were maligned. He was appalled because he believes that he was indirectly responsible. He was concerned when I told him five years ago that I wanted to marry you.'

'You wanted to marry me way back then?' Tilda whispered in utter astonishment at that declaration.

'Let me explain this without interruptions,' Rashad urged, strain marking the set of his stubborn jaw line. 'My father is a man who did not become a ruler until he was past middle age. When I met you, he was still new to the throne and nervous of many things. A son and heir proposing to marry a foreigner was a source of worry to him.'

'Yes,' Tilda conceded rather numbly.

'He shared his anxiety with his closest adviser, who was at the time in charge of Bakhar's secret service. No course of action was discussed. My father did not feel he could interfere. But when I later told him that my relationship with you was over, he did wonder if the adviser had taken independent action. But he chose not to question him or mention the suspicion to me and both those omissions have been on his conscience ever since. He called in Jasim, who is now his closest aide. Jasim worked for my father's advisor five years ago. He was aware of the file and very troubled by what was done,' Rashad related heavily.

'At least someone knows right from wrong,' Tilda muttered.

'Jasim was silent for fear of losing his position. His former employer is now dead. Jasim saw you when you visited the embassy in London last month and when you came to my house. He believed that I had discovered the truth about the file and he informed my father that you and I appeared to be seeing each other again.'

'But nobody came clean and owned up about the file until it was too late to matter.' Tilda had gone from shock that Rashad had been hoping to marry her five years earlier to overwhelming bitterness that the happiness that they had had then had been cruelly stolen from them. 'And nobody's going to pay for what was done to me or my reputation, either.'

Rashad was watching her every move. 'Haven't we all paid many times over?'

A sharp little laugh was dragged from Tilda. She

turned from him to stare sightlessly out of the window overlooking the handsome early Victorian city square. 'I don't think five years of consorting with gorgeous supermodels and actresses and socialites was that much of a penance for you, Rashad.'

Rashad turned an ashen shade below his bronzed skin. He was willing her to look at him and she would not. There was a distance in her that he had never seen before. He did not know what to say to her. He could not deny the supermodels, or the actresses or the socialites, but not one of them had been blonde because it would have reminded him too much of her. Not one of them had brought him happiness. Not one of them had been her.

'I did not forget you. I was never able to forget,' he breathed flatly.

Tilda was unimpressed. 'Only because of the insult to your pride. That rankled with you. You wanted revenge.'

'I wanted you back—'

'You wanted revenge. As if it wasn't enough that you just dumped me without a word. As if it wasn't enough that I had to see you kissing another woman. As if it wasn't enough that you left my mother loaded with debt!' Tilda flung at him chokily, striving not to parade her emotions in the manner he had described.

In response to that hail of accusations, his tawny gaze remained bleak. 'What you say is true. I have no defence to offer.'

'But do you know what your biggest sin is? That you didn't care enough about me or what we had to confront me or even doubt that file!' Tilda condemned fiercely, raging resentment finally breaking through her hollow sense of bitterness. 'You put your pride first.'

'I wouldn't now,' Rashad murmured in a roughened undertone.

'Oh, yes, you would. Last night, instead of concentrating on me, you went for a blasted shower and then you went off to see your father! You wanted someone to blame. You couldn't put me or my feelings first even then,' she accused shakily.

'That is not how it was.' Rashad drew in a deep shuddering breath. 'I was so angry at what we had lost—'

'You didn't lose me; you dumped me!'

Lean, vibrantly handsome features taut over his superb bone structure, Rashad dealt her a resolute dark golden appraisal. 'I know how many mistakes I have made with you, but I won't give up trying. I refuse to accept that the past should be allowed to wreck our marriage.'

'But that marriage is less than I deserve and I'm not settling for it,' Tilda protested vehemently. 'Your father is also obviously dead set against even having me in the family, although he was too well mannered to reveal those reservations to me.'

'My father is not against you,' Rashad asserted with assurance. 'Did I not tell you how much he regretted his doubts when I first knew you? It seems that ever since he has been haunted by the fear that he was responsible for the end of our relationship. He is very pleased that we are married and most impressed by the way you have taken on a public role.'

Tilda shook her silvery fair head. 'But I'm only your wife now because your revenge rebounded on you. When I saw that file, I just felt sick with anger that you had believed that rubbish... I couldn't ever forgive you for that.'

'But you are still my wife and it would go against my very nature to let you leave me,' Rashad responded quietly. 'I will do everything within my power to keep you. My bad judgement caused this. I believe that I can make our marriage what you deserve.'

The tears that she refused to shed were strangling her. Her throat ached and she could barely swallow. He was blaming himself for everything and, contrary as she was, she didn't like that. She was conscious of how hard he worked in every corner of his life. He carried a huge load of responsibility. It seemed wrong that he should feel forced to work at his marriage, as well. It had been his father's weakness and reluctance to be honest with his son that had created the situation. Rashad had been set up for a fall just like her and he was a warrior, born and bred, and he had responded with natural aggression.

She hated the fact that she was already making excuses for him. She felt like someone hovering indecisively while the last lifeboat was lowered from a sinking ship. That sinking ship was her image of what it would be like for her to live in a loveless marriage. In such a union, she would never feel truly necessary or special to him and she would always be forced to keep the emotional stuff low-key for fear of making him feel uncomfortable. The very knowledge that she wasn't loved would only make her continually try harder to be the best possible wife, and the most she could ever hope for in return would be appreciation and acceptance.

Involuntarily, driven by forces stronger than her will-power, Tilda stole a glance at Rashad and it was as if her very body was screaming at the threat of having to survive without him. For once, that response had nothing to do with his dazzling sexual magnetism. He might as well have chained her to him, she acknowledged bitterly, for there was a deep abiding need within her to be with him and to grasp at whatever closeness he could offer. Even though deep down inside she was still seething with indignant pain and anger over that hateful file, she knew that she still loved him enough for both of them. Walking off into the sunset with her pride intact was only going to make her wretchedly unhappy.

In an effort to bolster her mood, Tilda reminded herself that she had seriously undervalued her importance to Rashad when he was a student. She had assumed that all he had ever been after was a good time—primarily a good time in bed—while instead he had been making plans to marry her. Energised by that tantalising information, she fixed glimmering turquoise eyes on him. 'Were you in love with me five years ago?'

Rashad froze. He looked like a guy confronted by a firing squad without warning. 'I…' A tiny muscle pulled taut at the edge of his wide, sensual, unsmiling mouth. 'I liked you very much.'

It was a response that would have delighted her had they both been aged around ten years old.

Recognising that he had said the wrong thing, Rashad said abruptly, 'If I say I loved you, will you stay with me?'

And that telling response from Rashad, who barely uttered a word without triple-checking it in moments of stress, shed blinding light on his motives for Tilda. Never had she felt more ashamed of herself. She had him over a barrel. Within twenty-four hours of the televised state wedding she had scarpered. Angry, hurt and humiliated and needing to hit back the only way she knew how, she had run away. Doubtless Rashad thought her behaviour had been very immature. He had had to follow her and try to persuade her to return to Bakhar with him. What choice did he have? If his wife abandoned him he, along with every Bakhari, would feel they had lost face because he had picked the wrong wife. It wasn't fair to ask him if he had loved her.

'I think we should have some breakfast. Have you eaten?' Tilda enquired woodenly in a change of subject aimed at politely and quickly burying her stupid question and his revealing response.

His winged ebony brows drew together. She could see him struggling to master his bewilderment. 'No. I could not eat.'

Tilda drew in an irregular breath. She trod over to the bell in the wall and pressed it. The silence swirled like a stormy sea full of dangerous depths. A manservant appeared and she ordered breakfast in slow, careful Arabic.

Shaken up by the question she had asked, Rashad had felt able to tell her anything she wanted to hear, even if it meant lying for the first time in his life. But he had only felt that way for about ten seconds, for free speech or lies struck him as extremely dangerous in the current climate. He knew exactly how he felt about her. She was his wife with all that encompassed and he wanted, quite naturally, to take her home again.

'You are learning quickly,' Rashad murmured a shade unevenly, stunning golden eyes screened by the thick black wedge of his lashes to a bright glimmer.

Tilda wondered whether he meant the language or how to kill stone-dead the sort of emotional scene that she knew he found excruciating. 'I think I'd like to take the opportunity to see my mother while we're here,' she informed him prosaically.

'An excellent idea.'

'Both of us should visit,' she added, in case he had not yet got the message she was trying to give.

'Of course.'

The silence rushed back round them again.

'So, are we having a honeymoon?' Tilda heard herself ask rather loudly in the hope that he would comprehend the meaning of that less-than-subtle query.

Rashad stayed very still and then a charismatic smile flashed across his beautiful mouth, all the strain there put to flight by that query. 'It was already planned. Why do you think I've been working so hard in recent weeks? I needed to free up some time.'

That smile made Tilda's heart flip and the inside of her mouth run dry. That smile had sufficient pulling power to make her run up a mountain. She wanted to race across the room and fling herself at him like an eager puppy. She thought it fortunate that just at that moment the announcement that breakfast awaited them prevented her from embarrassing him to that extent.

When Tilda and Rashad visited her mother's home later that day in what Tilda felt was a welcome distraction after all the drama, they found Evan Jerrold cosily enjoying afternoon tea and home-made scones. Beth was overjoyed by the arrival of her daughter and son-in-law and Evan quickly excused himself. But Rashad spoke to the older man at some length, while Tilda talked to her mother. She was very pleased when the older woman confided that Evan had persuaded her to walk out of the front door and sit in his car just a few feet away for a few minutes the previous day.

'And you managed to do that without having a panic attack?' Tilda was amazed, because all Beth's children had made repeated efforts to coax their mother into trying to fight her phobia rather than totally surrendering to it.

'Evan's so confident. It did take me nearly two weeks to work myself up to walking out the front door. But I have to learn how to manage now that you're married to Rashad. Aubrey will be leaving home soon, as well,' Beth pointed out. 'I need to be more independent.'

The older woman passed her daughter several letters that had come for her. While Beth made fresh tea, Tilda went through her post. The final envelope was addressed in unfamiliar handwriting. She tore it open and withdrew a sheet of paper. It bore a poor quality photocopied image of a blonde woman dancing in a cage. A pulse started beating very fast at the foot of Tilda's throat. She peered at it in horror. It could have been her, or just as easily it could've been someone else. It was impossible to tell. Below the image, a mobile phone number was printed.

'I've made more tea!' Beth called as Tilda ducked into the dining room to make a call in private.

'I'll only be a couple of minutes.' Tilda closed the door and rang the number.

She recognised Scott's voice the moment he answered. Her tummy gave a sick lurch and she snatched in a steadying breath. 'It's Tilda. Why did you send me that picture?'

'I've got some actual photos of you doing your little dance.'

Her fingers tightened round her mobile phone. 'I don't remember anyone taking photos that night. I don't believe you.'

'It's up to you what you want to believe. But now you're royalty, those photos must be worth a packet. I reckon Rashad would pay a tidy sum to keep them all to himself.' Her former stepfather loosed a seedy chuckle. 'Of course, if you're not interested, just say. A half-naked blond princess in a cage would go down a treat with the gutter press.'

Tilda felt sick. Scott Morrison was blackmailing her. Had someone taken photos of her? His creepy mate, Pete, perhaps? She had no idea. A half-naked blond princess in a cage would be a much bigger source of humiliation to Rashad and his family than a runaway wife. She cringed at the prospect of such pictures appearing in print. 'How much do you want for the photos?'

'I thought you'd see it my way and keep it in the family. I want fifty grand.'

Although she was as white as a sheet, Tilda decided to call his bluff. 'Then I'll have to go to Rashad for the money because I don't have access to that kind of cash.'

'Leave him out of it,' Scott hastened to tell her, his agitation at the suggestion that she involve Rashad audible. 'Keeping you on a shoestring, is he? How much cash can you raise in a hurry?'

'Maybe five thousand,' she mumbled shamefacedly for she knew she was doing the wrong thing. Everyone knew it was stupid to give way to blackmail. She knew it, too, but just the idea of Rashad seeing a photo of her in that cage again made her feel physically ill. She was convinced it would mean the end of her marriage. She had not spent any of the allowance that Rashad had put in a bank account for her. She told herself that using Rashad's money to get the photos back was a lesser evil than embarrassing him with the pictorial proof of her teenaged mistake.

Scott argued volubly, and then finally said he'd accept the payment if that was the best she could offer.

The door opened and Tilda gave a nervous start. Rashad was framed in the doorway. He quirked a sleek dark brow that questioned her obvious tension.

'I'll send you a cheque,' Tilda told Scott gruffly and hurriedly finished the call.

'Is there something wrong?' Rashad enquired, beautiful dark golden eyes welded to her pale, anxious face.

'No, nothing…just a stupid bill I forgot about. Embarrassing,' she mumbled, her teeth near to chattering at the very thought of him finding out what she was planning to do.

'My staff will take care of it. Let me have the details,' Rashad instructed.

'No, I'll see to it myself. When are we flying back to Bakhar?'

'Only when you wish.'

Tilda studied his gold silk tie with fixed attention. She did not dare meet his gaze, for he was far too keen and clever an observer. After that nasty little chat with Scott, Bakhar somehow seemed to shine like a safe haven on a wonderfully distant horizon. 'Could we leave tonight?'

When Rashad spoke, his surprise at that request was patent in his dark deep drawl. 'I thought you might prefer somewhere more cosmopolitan for our honeymoon…Paris, Rio—'

'The Palace of the Lions. You never did get around to showing me the harem,' Tilda reminded him, feeling that that remote desert location would be comfortingly out of reach of Scott and his machinations.

CHAPTER TEN

'GOOD heavens...you and your grandfather might have been identical twins!' Tilda studied the photo of the long-departed Sharaf in his ceremonial robes with fascination, because she could see from where Rashad had inherited his classic bone structure.

Rashad splayed a possessive hand to her stomach to angle her back into connection with his lithe, powerful body. 'My father says his father's genes skipped a generation and turned up in me. Although I would like to believe that the likeness is only skin-deep, I definitely didn't inherit my father's mild temperament.'

'Have you abducted any women?' Tilda teased a little unevenly, physical contact with his lean, masculine frame stirring her into immediate awareness. Her nipples were pinching into tingling tension beneath the light cotton dress she wore.

'No. But if you hadn't agreed to give our marriage another chance I would have abducted you.'

Her eyes rounded in disbelief. 'Are you serious?'

Above her head, Rashad was trying not to smile. Nothing would have persuaded him to let her go. He bent his handsome dark head and his even white teeth gently grazed the tiny pulse point just below one soft feminine ear lobe. She shivered helplessly, warmth pooling in the pit of her tummy.

'Are you?' she repeated less evenly.

'I told you I wouldn't let you go in London.'

Cooler air brushed her breasts as he undid her wrap and stripped it gently down over her arms. She stood naked and captivated in the circle of his arms. He explored the sensitive peaks of her pouting breasts with a carnal skill that left her vibrating with quivering response against him. 'We only got up an hour ago,' she whispered.

'It's hard work being my favourite concubine,' Rashad intoned thickly.

'Is it?' she contrived to ask jerkily as long fingers smoothed down over her stomach to flirt with the silvery fair curls at the apex of her thighs.

'And when you signed up for the long haul of being a wife, the working conditions got much tougher. I hope you know how to stand up for your rights because I intend to take full advantage of having you within reach twenty-four hours a day.'

A breathless giggle was her sole response to that assurance. The unpleasantness of that episode with Scott had shaken her up, but she had sent the cheque. Surely, since he'd got what he wanted, any photos he had would be returned to her at her mother's address? Anyway, she might only have spent a week at the Palace of the Lions with Rashad, but she was happy. They'd never had the luxury of so much time together, and the more they were with each other, the less they wanted to be apart. She could see their reflections twinned in the mirror on the antique wardrobe. Her pale blond hair was bright as a banner against the darkness of his, her breasts wantonly bare beneath his bronzed hands. She thought she looked shameless. Shameless and fulfilled. With a certain indolent look in his gorgeous dark eyes, a particular note in his deep drawl, he could make her literally weak with longing. Her heart was pounding and her legs were trembling. She was leaning back against him to stay upright, wildly, dizzily conscious of his every caress.

With an earthy groan of satisfaction, Rashad explored the lush damp heat at the heart of her body. Spinning her round, he curved his hands to the soft swell of her hips and hoisted her up onto the table behind her. Her lashes lifted, passion-glazed eyes flying wide with disconcertion on his lean, dark, intent face.

'You'll like it,' Rashad growled in persuasion.

Before she could react, he parted her soft mouth and probed its moist interior with an erotic thrust of his tongue in a move that was as provocative as it was effective. He opened her thighs and touched her in ways that left her alternately whimpering and breathless, barely able to contain the throbbing ache of hunger that possessed her. Only when he had pitched her to a tormented edge of need did he tilt her back and plunge into her. Raw excitement sent a wave of blinding pleasure splintering through Tilda, and then another and another, until she was sobbing with mindless delight.

It was quite some time afterwards before she found voice and reason again. She was lying in bed where Rashad had carried her. At the high point of ecstasy she thought she might have screamed. Her face burned and she kept her eyes closed because she wasn't quite ready to look him in the eye yet. Five years earlier it had been the very intensity of what he could make her feel that had put her so much on her guard with him. Letting go of those defences gave her a wonderful sense of freedom.

A long taunting forefinger skimmed lazily down her spine. 'You liked it a lot,' Rashad husked, flipping her over and kissing her until she finally opened her eyes. 'I liked it even more. You are as passionate as I, and I don't have to restrain myself with you.'

Tilda focused on his lean, strong face and brushed weak fingers along the sensual line of his beautiful masculine mouth. He was wild in bed and she was discovering that she really loved that lack of inhibition.

His winged dark brows pleated in dismay and he drew back from her in a sudden movement. 'I forgot to use a condom.'

'Oh…well.' Tilda gave a vague accepting twitch of a slim shoulder and immediately began picturing a miniature Rashad with serious dark eyes, or a tiny bustling version of Durra chattering at every step. Although conceiving so early in their marriage was not what she would have planned, she was conscious of a warm feeling of anticipation.

Rashad studied her tautly. 'I might have gotten you pregnant,' he extended as though she might not have worked out that risk for herself.

'Well, it wouldn't be the end of the world, would it?'

'You wouldn't mind?'

'No, if it's meant to be, it's meant to be. I like children.'

His lean, darkly handsome face relaxed. He pulled her into his arms. 'You're amazing, but I shouldn't think we have anything to worry about,' he told her. 'We've been here for a week. Would you like to go to Cannes for a while? I own a house there.'

With a drowsy smile, Tilda rested her head on his shoulder. 'If you like.'

'Do you like?'

'Hmm…' she whispered, her eyes drifting shut, because she had decided that she would like anywhere as long as he was there with her.

Four weeks later, their honeymoon, which had been extended twice, was almost over. They had enjoyed a lengthy sun-soaked stay at Rashad's gloriously secluded estate in the South of France. He'd had been called away on business the day before. He was due back today, and Tilda was packing her jewellery in preparation for their departure later on. She was mentally taking note of the fact that once again her breasts felt a little tender. Her period was also ten days late. She had no intention of saying anything to Rashad until she had seen a doctor, but she suspected that she might have fallen pregnant. In fact, she was quite excited at the idea that she might already be carrying their first child and just a little worried that Rashad would be rather less enthusiastic.

As Rashad was expected to father the next generation of royals, having a family would naturally have featured on their future agenda. But it was very early in their marriage for her to have conceived. Although she knew that Rashad would act as if it were the best news he had ever heard, even if he didn't really feel that way, she was afraid that he would secretly regard a pregnant wife as a much less attractive option.

Heaving a sigh, she studied herself in the mirror, striving to imagine how she would look with a bigger bosom, no waist and a large tummy. Being of a practical disposition, Tilda scolded herself for agonising over what could not be changed. He wasn't in love with her and she knew it would be silly to try and pretend that that didn't make a difference. Her looks and how active she could be in and out of bed had to be crucial factors in the continuing success of their relationship. There would be no more flying here, there and everywhere, whenever the fancy took them, and water-skiing or horse riding might be too taxing, as well. They both enjoyed such activities, but now she would have to take her exercise in moderation. Would he get bored with her then?

In an abstracted mood she studied the glittering brilliance of a diamond bracelet. Rashad's most recent gift, it was as stylish as her engagement ring. She had also acquired a necklace and earrings. He had given her some gorgeous pieces. He was wonderfully generous. It was as though nothing pleased him more than pleasing her. Reminding herself of that truth, she walked out to the shaded terrace and sat down on a comfortable seat.

Beautiful mature gardens ran down to the beach. The estate also had an extensive stable. Tilda had never learned to ride, but Rashad and his family were horse-mad. He had coaxed Tilda out of her nerves and up onto the back of a doe-eyed mare. Able to relax on a horse that had only one speed—plodding—she had gone riding on the beach with him every morning. Well, she had plodded and watched him galloping very glamorously through the surf. He was a keen amateur polo player and he looked amazingly sexy on a horse.

Most evenings they had eaten out, dining everywhere from the grand restaurants in Cannes to the terraces below the palm trees. His reserve was fading fast. He was talking to her a lot more, teasing her more easily, as well. Their relationship had changed since that ghastly business over the file had come out into the open. More and more she was seeing the guy who had stolen her heart five years earlier.

Occasional arguments disturbed the peace and were usually settled in bed. Rashad was very energetic, very passionate and very stubborn. He had a will of iron and a naturally forceful personality. He was always going to be bossy. He was always going to think he knew best about most things. What was infuriating was how often he was right. She was totally, absolutely in love with him, she acknowledged dizzily.

'Tilda?' Rashad strode out onto the terrace, looking spectacularly handsome in a lightweight beige suit. 'I've been looking everywhere for you.'

'I didn't know you were back. I was enjoying the view.' Tilda registered that his lean bronzed features were unusually grave.

'Would you come inside? We have to talk,' Rashad told her.

Tilda got up slowly and smoothed down her skirt with uncertain hands. She had a tight, nervous feeling in her tummy. ESP was telling her that something was wrong, seriously wrong. She entered the room that

Rashad used as an office. He lounged back against the edge of the desk, brilliant dark eyes resting reflectively on her.

'You know, for some reason, I feel like a misbehaving kid called into the headmaster's office,' Tilda confided tightly.

'Take a seat,' Rashad murmured gently.

Tilda sat down, but her back stayed poker-straight, because she knew she was not imagining the tense atmosphere.

'I'm going to ask you something and I would like you to be honest. What is your opinion of me as a husband?'

Tilda blinked and then opened her eyes very wide. 'S-seriously?' she stammered.

'Seriously.'

'Why are you asking me?'

'Indulge me just this once.'

'Well…you're marvellous company, even tempered…and patient. Great in bed.' Her face burned as Rashad elevated a questioning aristocratic brow that suggested she was barking up the wrong tree with her comments. 'Generous, thoughtful, fair.'

'I sound like a saint and I am not. You must be more candid and mention my faults.'

'I didn't say you had any faults,' Tilda disclaimed instantly, feeling that she was being steadily backed into a corner for some reason that she had not yet contrived to comprehend. 'Apart from being too clever for your own good sometimes.'

Rashad lifted a sheet of paper from the desktop and held it up for her to see. Tilda blenched, for it was the same photocopied picture of a woman dancing in a cage that Scott had sent her before. 'Where did you get that from?'

'Your mother forwarded it with your post. There was nothing on the envelope that indicated that it might be confidential, and it was opened by one of my staff, who thought it was a party invitation.'

Tilda extended her hand for the page and read the words below. 'Next instalment due,' it said, alongside Scott's phone number and address.

'It's been dealt with,' Rashad informed her quietly.

But shock and apprehension had made Tilda feel light-headed and sick, and she startled him as much as she startled herself at that moment by bursting into floods of tears.

Astonished and dismayed, Rashad lifted her out of the seat with a groaned apology. He smoothed her hair back from her damp brow. 'I think this may qualify as a too-clever-for-my-own-good moment,' he breathed rawly. 'I didn't intend to upset you. That was the very last result I wanted.'

'What did you expect when you showed me that horrible picture?' Tilda gasped chokily as he passed her a tissue and she mopped up. 'I was hoping I'd never have to see it again!'

Rashad banded his arms round her. 'You wouldn't have had to see it, if you had come to me with the first demand.'

Tilda stiffened and finally dared to look up at him. 'How do you know about that?'

'I saw Scott last night. That's where I was yesterday. Naturally, the instant I saw that picture, I knew that it could only have been sent to you as a form of threat. I confronted Morrison. There *are* no photos in existence of you dancing that night at the club.'

'Are you certain of that?'

'Yes,' Rashad confirmed. 'If he had had a genuine photo of you, he would have copied that, instead of using a stranger's on a photocopy.'

Tilda flushed. 'I suppose I should have thought of that.'

'It was an amateur effort to extort money. He wasn't clever enough to use a computer to fake a photo of you. It has been a very distasteful experience for you nonetheless. What was the first letter like?'

'The same picture was used,' she admitted tautly.

'You received it when we visited your mother. That was Morrison you spoke to on the phone regarding the bill that required payment, wasn't it?'

She nodded uncomfortably.

Dark deep-set eyes very direct in gaze, Rashad spread lean, shapely hands in a very expressive movement. 'It shames me that you would not come to me for help and support with this matter.'

'And rake up that cage business again? I'd sooner have died!' Tilda told him with a feeling shudder. 'I suppose that you already know that I paid Scott five thousand pounds?'

'Yes, and there's no hope of retrieving it, either. He's spent it.' Rashad grimaced with distaste. 'He's a nasty specimen, but he would never have dared to trouble you, had you come to me with his attempt to blackmail you. He's scared of me.'

'There's no real photos of me dancing in that cage… you're *sure?*' Tilda prompted, because she was still concerned and could not quite accept as yet that the threat had been removed.

'Certain.'

'I feel such an idiot now for having paid up.' She sighed. 'But I was just so horrified at the idea of some horrible sleazy-looking photo appearing in the newspapers and embarrassing you.'

'Even if there had been a photo we would have lived it down. I am more wise and tolerant than I was when you first knew me,' Rashad said wryly. 'I'm not that easily embarrassed.'

Tilda was amazed at his attitude. 'Do you mean that?'

'Of course I do.'

'Good. Then it's about time that I told you that it was your friends who put me in that cage to dance. They paid the manager to get me into it because it was your birthday!'

Rashad was very much disconcerted by this revelation. Tilda quite enjoyed that turning of the tables. She told him that she had found out that Scott had been taking money from her mother for several years, and that Morrison had most likely been behind the appearance of the paparazzi at the airport that day. He looked grim but was convinced that her former stepfather would cause no further annoyance.

'In my eyes, a husband's most basic role is to protect his wife from harm,' Rashad shared tautly. 'Yet you could not trust me enough to tell me that Morrison was blackmailing you.'

'It wasn't that I didn't trust you. I felt so guilty about the cage episode.'

'You have no need to feel guilty. But perhaps you did

not have enough faith in me because I have been too slow to tell you what you mean to me.' His lean strong face was taut. 'Five years ago, you were everything I had ever wanted in a woman. In an instant I fell deeply in love with you. That's all it took.'

Tilda stared up at him in unconcealed surprise.

'You were my dream, my prize after many disappointments. I had been alone a long time. But I knew you did not feel the same way as I did—'

'Rashad,' she broke in emotively.

'I believed that if you had felt as much for me as I did for you, that you would have slept with me.'

Tilda was shaken by that candid admission. 'That's just not true. I really loved you, but I thought there was no future in it. I mean, you were going to be a king some day and I didn't want to be hurt. I thought if I kept our relationship light that it wouldn't hurt so much when you went back to Bakhar.'

'I had no idea. Wasn't it obvious that I was serious about you?'

'No. I was also terrified you would get me pregnant,' she admitted in a rush. 'I had a thing about that then— Mum always seemed to fall pregnant so easily.'

Rashad cupped her face with unsteady hands. 'If only we had talked about the things that really matter, but I didn't know how to. I just expected you to *know* what was in my heart.'

'But I did really love you an awful lot,' Tilda told him unsteadily. 'When you dumped me, it felt like my world had ended.'

His lustrous dark eyes were suspiciously bright and

he bowed his handsome head over hers with a husky groan. 'I adored you. I would have given up everything for you, even the throne, and I think my father knew it, which gave him more reason to fear your power over me.'

Tilda was so close to him she could barely breathe and it still wasn't close enough. He had adored her, too? He crushed her to him and she rejoiced in his emotion.

'In five years without you, I was never once happy again. I am ashamed to admit it, but even if you had been a gold-digger I think you would still be my wife because I love you so much.'

'How long have you been in love with me?'

'For five years I called it hatred. I never got over you,' Rashad confessed in a driven undertone.

'Don't you realise how much I still love you?'

Rashad studied her with doubt in his candid gaze.

'But how could you?'

'You say sorry very nicely. You're great with black-mailers, too. You're very handsome. You make me happy. I suppose that's the most important thing of all. When I'm with you, I'm just so happy!'

'You love me?' His spellbinding smile was beginning to curve his lips.

Tilda stretched up and kissed him, and that was all the encouragement he needed to kiss her back—breathless.

'Oh, and I think I might be pregnant,' she shared in an afterthought, deciding that she would never keep anything from him again. 'And I'm pleased.'

Rashad laughed out loud and surveyed her with near reverence. 'I must be the luckiest man alive.'

Feeling very much like the luckiest woman, Tilda let

her eyes drift dreamily shut as he carried her off to bed. She suspected that the end of their honeymoon would be postponed for yet another few days....

Almost three years later, Tilda watched Rashad hunker down to open welcoming arms to his son and daughter.

Sharaf was almost two, a solid little boy who was tall for his age with black hair and blue eyes. Pyjama-clad, the child hurled himself at his father with a shout of delight and immediately started chattering. Rashad tucked his son under one arm and murmured gentle encouragement to the baby crawling laboriously towards him. Bethany was nine months old. Blond and brown-eyed, she had her father's charismatic smile and her mother's temper. As the Persian rug beneath her rumpled and impeded her progress she burst into tears and threw herself flat to sob. Rashad scooped her up and soothed her with an ease that revealed how comfortable he was handling his children. The little girl clung like a limpet and patted his face, beaming at him with love and approval.

It was the weekend and Tilda and Rashad often spent weekends at the Palace of the Lions, where privacy was usually assured. Sharaf had proved such a delight to his parents that they had decided to have another baby as soon as possible after his birth. He was a delightful child, forward for his age and very active. Tilda had had two straightforward pregnancies and was planning on waiting awhile before contemplating a third.

Her mother had recently married Evan Jerrold and was living in much more comfortable circumstances. It had taken a year and professional help for Beth to overcome her agoraphobia. It had been a tough challenge for her, but she was now a regular visitor to Bakhar. Tilda had been delighted by Beth's remarriage, for she had always liked Evan and she no longer worried about her parent in the same way that she once had. Her brother, Aubrey, had qualified as a doctor and Katie was at university. Her younger siblings, Megan and James, were doing well at school. It was a source of great satisfaction to Tilda that she was still able to see a lot of her family. She often visited London with Rashad.

The king was a regular visitor to their home in the Great Palace for he was very fond of children. Tilda had become very relaxed around the unassuming older man. She led a very busy but fulfilling life. She had supervised the renovation of the Palace of the Lions. She also realised how lucky she was to always have ready assistance with the children and she made the most of it. She had taken up painting again, although she had privately reached the conclusion that, although she enjoyed the pursuit she was possibly a more talented accountant than she would ever be an artist. Even so, Rashad, who could hardly draw a recognisable stick figure, was hugely impressed by her every artistic endeavour and embarrassingly quick to show her work off to visitors.

Tilda lifted Bethany from her husband's arms. Their baby daughter was yawning. 'She's sleepy.'

Rashad leant down and claimed his wife's luscious mouth with a brief but hungry insistence that made her dizzily aware of his potent masculinity. She went pink and thought about how much she had missed, for he had been in New York for a week. Sometimes Tilda and the children travelled with him, but it wasn't always practical. Together they put Sharaf and Bethany to bed. They enjoyed such quiet family moments. Rashad told his son a bedtime story while Tilda gave their daughter a drink and tucked her into her cot.

'At last,' Rashad groaned, tugging her into his arms in the privacy of their bedroom. 'I couldn't wait to get back to you tonight.'

'Hmm…' A blissful smile on her lips, Tilda leant into the heat of his big, powerful body. 'Did I ever tell you how happy you make me?'

'I can live with being told again.' Stroking her hair back from a delicate cheekbone with tender fingers, Rashad studied her with possessive intensity. 'But I couldn't live without you… I love you more every day….'

The Greek Tycoon's Defiant Bride

LYNNE GRAHAM

CHAPTER ONE

WHEN the limousine appeared, a perceptible wave of anticipation rippled through the well-dressed cliques of people gathered on the church steps. Two cars had already drawn up in an advance guard, from which muscular men wearing dark glasses and talking into walkie-talkies had emerged to fan out in a protective cordon. At a signal from the security team the chauffeur finally approached the passenger door of the limo. The buzz in the air intensified, heads craning for a better view, eyes avid with curiosity.

Leonidas Pallis stepped out onto the pavement and immediately commanded universal attention. A Greek tycoon to his polished fingertips, he stood six feet three inches tall. A staggeringly handsome man, he wore a black cashmere overcoat and a designer suit with an elegance that was lethally sexy. That cutting-edge sophistication, however, was matched by a cold-blooded reserve and ruthlessness that made people very nervous. Born into one of the richest families in the world and to parents whose decadence was legendary, Leonidas had established a wild reputation at an early age. But no Pallis in living memory had displayed his extraordinary brilliance in business. A billionaire many times over, he was the golden idol of the Pallis clan and as much feared as he was fêted.

Everyone had wondered if he would bother to attend the memorial service. After all, just over two years had passed since Imogen Stratton had died in a drug-fuelled car crash. Although she had not been involved with Leonidas at the time, she had enjoyed an on-off association with him since he'd been at university. Imogen's mother, Hermione, swam forward to greet her most important guest with gushing satisfaction, for the presence of Leonidas Pallis turned the event into a social occasion worthy of comment. But the Greek billionaire cut the social pleasantries to a minimum— the Strattons were virtual strangers. While Imogen was alive he had neither met them nor wished to meet them and he did not have an appetite for fawning flattery.

Ironically the one person he had expected to greet him at the church, his only surviving acquaintance in the Stratton family circle, had yet to show her face: Imogen's cousin, Maribel Greenaway. Refusing an invitation to join the front pew line-up, Leonidas chose a much less prominent seat and sank down into it with the fluid grace of a panther. As quickly, he wondered why he had come when Imogen had despised such conventions. She had revelled in her fame as a fashion model and party girl. Living to be noticed and admired, Imogen had loved to shock even more. Yet she had worked hard at pleasing him until her absorption in drugs had concluded his interest in her. His hard-sculpted mouth flattened. Ultimately, he had cut her out of his life. Attending her funeral had presented a challenge and the fallout from that rare inner conflict had been explosive. The past was past, however, and like regret, not a place Leonidas had ever been known to visit.

* * *

Maribel nosed her elderly car into the parking space. She was horribly late and in a fierce hurry. At speed she re-angled the driving mirror and, with a brush in one hand and a clip gripped between her teeth, attempted to put her hair up. Newly washed and still damp, the shoulder-length fall of chestnut was rebellious. When the clip broke between her impatient fingers she could've wept with frustration. Throwing the brush aside, she smoothed her hair down with frantic fingers while simultaneously attempting to get out of the car. From the minute she'd got up that morning everything had gone wrong. Or perhaps the endless line of mini-disasters had begun the night before, when her aunt Hermione had phoned to say dulcetly that she would quite understand if Maribel found it too difficult to attend the memorial service.

Maribel had winced, gritted her teeth at that news and said nothing. Over the past eighteen months her relatives had made it clear that she was now *persona non grata* as far as they were concerned. That had hurt, since Maribel cherished what family connections she had left. Even so, she fully understood their reservations. Not only had she never fitted the Stratton family mould, but she had also broken the rules of acceptance.

Her aunt and uncle set great store on looks, money and social status. Appearances were hugely important to them. Nevertheless, when Maribel had been orphaned, her mother's brother had immediately offered his eleven-year-old niece a home with his own three children. In the image-conscious Stratton household Maribel had had to learn how to melt into the background, where her failings in the beauty, size and grace stakes would awaken less censure and irritation. Those years would have been bleak, had they not been enlivened by Imogen's effervescent sense of fun. Although Imogen and Maribel had had not the slightest thing in common, Maribel had become deeply attached to the cousin who was three years her senior.

That was the main reason why Maribel was determined that nothing should be allowed to interfere with her sincere need to attend the service and pay her last respects. *Nothing,* she reminded herself doggedly, not even a powerful level of personal discomfiture. That sense of unease exasperated her. Over two years had gone by. She had no business still being so sensitive—*he* didn't have a sensitive bone in his body.

Her violet-blue eyes took on a militant sparkle and her chin came up. She was twenty-seven years old. She had a doctorate and she was a university tutor in the ancient history department of the university. She was intelligent, level-headed and practical. She liked men as friends or colleagues, but had reached the conclusion that they were far too much hassle in any closer capacity. After the appalling upheaval and the grieving process that she had had to work through in the wake of Imogen's sudden death, Maribel had finally found contentment. She liked her life. She liked her life very much. Why should she even care about what *he* might think? He had probably never thought about her again.

In that mood, she mounted the church steps and took the first available seat near the back of the nave. She focused on the service, looking neither right nor left while her sixth sense fingered down her taut spine and her skin prickled. Self-conscious pink began to blossom in her cheeks. *He* was present. She knew he was present and didn't know how. When she couldn't withstand temptation any longer, she glanced up and saw him several rows ahead on the other side of the aisle. The Pallis height and build were unmistakable, as was the angle of his arrogant dark head and the fact that at least three extremely attractive females had contrived to seat themselves within easy reach of him. Involuntarily she was amused. Had Leonidas been a rare animal, he would long ago have been hunted to extinction. As it was, he was dazzlingly handsome, totally untamed and a notorious womaniser. He mesmerised her sex into bad behaviour. No doubt the women hovering near him now would attempt to chat him up before the end of the service.

Without warning, Leonidas turned his head and surveyed her, the onslaught of his brilliant dark deep-set eyes striking her much like a bullet suddenly slamming into tender flesh. Her fight-or-flight response went into overdrive. Caught unawares and looking when she would have given almost anything to appear totally impervious to his existence, Maribel froze. Like a fish snared by a hook and left dangling, she felt horribly trapped. Mustering her self-discipline and her manners, she managed to give him a slight wooden nod of polite acknowledgement and returned her attention to the order of service in her hands. The booklet trembled in her grasp. She breathed in slow and deep and steadied her hold, fighting the riptide of memory threatening to blow a dangerous hole in her defences.

The glamorous blonde who slid into the pew beside her provided a welcome diversion. Hanna had belonged to the same modelling agency as Imogen. Indifferent to the fact that the vicar was speaking, Hanna lamented at length about the traffic that had led to her late arrival and then took out a mirror to twitch her hair into place.

'Will you introduce me to Leonidas Pallis?' Hanna stage-whispered as she renewed her lip gloss. 'I mean, you've known him for ever.'

Maribel continued to focus her attention on the service. She could not credit that once again a woman was trying to use her to get to Leonidas and she was quick to dismiss the idea that she could ever have been deemed an acquaintance of his. 'But not in the way you mean.'

'Yeah, you were like living as Imogen's housekeeper or whatever in those days, but he must still remember you. Have you any idea how rare that is? Very few people can claim *any* sort of a connection with Leonidas Pallis!'

Maribel said nothing. Her throat felt as if a lump of hysteria were wedged at the foot of it and she was not the sort of woman who threw hysterical fits. It was ironic that she could only think about Imogen, who had set her heart on a man she could not have, a man who would never care enough to give her the stability she had so desperately needed. Sometimes it had been very hard for Maribel to mind her own business while she had lived on the sidelines of her cousin's life, forced to witness her every mistake. The discovery that she herself was equally capable of blind stupidity had been hugely humiliating and not a lesson she was likely to forget in a hurry.

Hanna was impervious to the hint that silence might be welcome, adding, 'I just thought that if you introduced me, it would look more casual and less staged.'

Casual? Hanna was wearing a candy-pink suit so tight and so short she could barely sit in it. The feathery hat-confection in her long, streaming blonde hair was overkill and would have been more appropriate at a wedding.

'Please…please…please. He is so absolutely delicious in the flesh,' the other woman crooned pleadingly in Maribel's ear.

And a total, absolute bastard, Maribel reflected helplessly, only to be very much shocked by such a thought occurring to her in church and on such a serious occasion. Face colouring with shame, she cleansed her mind of that angry, bitter thought.

Leonidas had decided to be amused by that stony little nod from Maribel. The only woman he had ever met who refused to be impressed by him. A challenge he had been unable to resist, he acknowledged. His heavily lidded dark gaze roamed at an indolent pace over her, noting the changes with earthy masculine appreciation. Maribel had slimmed down, the better to show off the abundant swell of her full breasts and the voluptuous curve of her hips. The spring sunlight arrowing though a stained glass window far above glinted over hair the colour of maple syrup, skin like clotted cream and a generous mouth. Not beautiful, not even pretty, yet for some reason she had always contrived to grab his attention. Only this time he believed that he could finally understand why he was looking: she had the vibrant, sensual glow of a sun-ripened peach. He wondered if he was responsible for awakening that feminine awareness. Just as quickly, he wondered if he could seduce her into a repeat performance. And, on that one lingering look and that one manipulative thought, his slumbering libido roused to volcanic strength and sharpened his interest.

* * *

As the service drew to a close Maribel was keen to melt back out of the church in a departure as quiet as her arrival. That urge intensified when she noted the immediate surge up the aisle by her aunt and cousins, who were clearly determined to intercept Leonidas before he could leave. Unfortunately, Maribel's passage was blocked by Hanna.

'Why are you in such a hurry?' Hanna hissed, when Maribel attempted to ease past her stationary figure. 'Leonidas was looking in this direction. He's already noticed me. I asked you for such a tiny favour.'

'Someone as beautiful as you doesn't need an introduction,' Maribel whispered in sheer desperation.

Hanna laughed and preened. With a toss of her rippling golden tresses, she sashayed out into the aisle like a guided missile ready to lock onto a target. Several inches shorter, Maribel used the blonde as cover and ducked out in her wake to speed for the exit like a lemming rushing at a cliff. It wasn't cool to be so keen to avoid Leonidas, but so what? Mindful of the reality that her aunt no longer wished to acknowledge her as a member of the family, Maribel knew that it was her duty to embrace a low profile. In her haste, however, she cannoned into the photographer lying in wait beyond the doors. Wondering why she was spluttering an apology when the man was assailing her with furious abuse, Maribel rubbed the shoulder that had been bruised by the collision and hurried on out and back to the car park.

Unreceptive to the many opposing attempts to gain his attention, Leonidas strode out to the church porch. He was thoroughly intrigued by the mode and speed of his quarry's flight, because Maribel was, as a rule, wonderfully well mannered and conservative. He had expected her to hover unwillingly out of politeness and speak to him. But she had not even paused to converse with the Strattons. While his protection team prevented the lurking paparazzo from snatching a photo of him, he watched Maribel approaching a little red car. For a small woman, she moved fast. Lazily, he wondered if she was the only female who had ever run away from him. Exasperated, he inclined his handsome dark head to summon Vasos, his head of security, to his side and gave him a concise command.

As Hermione Stratton, closely followed by her two daughters, surged to a breathless halt by his side, Leonidas spoke conventional words of regret before murmuring in his dark, deep voice, 'Why did Maribel rush off?'

'Maribel?' The older woman opened her eyes very wide and repeated the name as if she had never heard of her niece.

'Probably racing home to that baby of hers,' the tallest, blondest daughter opined with more than a touch of derision.

Although not an ounce of his surprise showed on his lean bronzed features, Leonidas was stunned by that careless statement. Maribel had a baby? *A baby?* Since when? And by whom?

Hermione Stratton pursed her mouth into a little *moue* of well-bred distaste. 'I'm afraid that she's a single parent.'

'And not in the fashionable category. She was left in the lurch,' her daughter chipped in, smiling brightly at Leonidas.

'Typical,' her sister giggled, rolling inviting big blue eyes up at him. 'Even with all those brains, Maribel still made the biggest mistake in the book!'

* * *

Five minutes after leaving the church, Maribel pulled off the road again to shed her black knitted jacket because she was overheating like mad. An attack of nerves always made her hot. Inside her head was an uninvited image of how Leonidas had looked in church. Breathtakingly beautiful. What else had she expected? He was still only thirty-one years old. Her hands clenched round the steering wheel. For a tiny moment, while she allowed her emotions to gain the upper hand, her knuckles showed white. Then slowly, deliberately, she relaxed her grip. She refused to concede that she had experienced any kind of emotional reaction and concentrated instead on being thoroughly irritated by her foolish and trite reflection regarding Leonidas' good looks. After all, shouldn't she have moved far beyond such juvenile ruminations by now?

Her rebellious mind served up painful memories and she gritted her teeth and literally kicked those thoughts back out of her head again. She slammed shut the equivalent of a mental steel door on recollections that would only stir up the feelings she was determined to keep buried. Clasping her seat belt again, she drove off to pick up her son.

Ginny Bell, her friend and childminder, lived in a cottage only a field away from Maribel's home. The older woman was a widow and a former teacher currently studying part-time for a master's degree. Slim and in her forties, with her black hair in a bob, she glanced up in surprise when Maribel appeared at her back door. 'My goodness, I wasn't expecting you back so soon!'

Elias abandoned his puzzle and hurtled across the kitchen to greet his mother. He was sixteen months old, an enchanting toddler with curly black hair and tobacco brown eyes. All the natural warmth and energy of his temperament shone in his smile and the exuberance with which he returned his mother's hug. Maribel drank in the familiar baby scent of his skin and was engulfed by a giant wave of love. Only after Elias's birth had she truly understood the intensity of a mother's attachment to her child. She had revelled in the year of maternity leave she'd taken to be with her baby. Returning to work even on a part-time basis had been a real challenge for her, and now she was never away from Elias for longer than a couple of hours without eagerly looking forward to the moment when she would get back to him again. Without even trying, Elias had become the very centre of her world.

Still puzzled by Maribel's swift return, Ginny was frowning. 'I thought your aunt and uncle were hosting a fancy buffet lunch after the service.'

Maribel briefly shared the content of her aunt's phone call the night before.

'My goodness, how can Hermione Stratton exclude you like that?' Ginny exclaimed, angrily defensive on the younger woman's behalf because, as a long-standing friend, she knew how much the Strattons owed to Maribel, who had loyally watched over Imogen while the model's family had given their daughter and her increasingly erratic and embarrassing behaviour a wide berth.

'Well, I blotted my copybook by having Elias and I can't say that I wasn't warned about how it would be,' Maribel countered with wry acceptance.

'When your aunt urged you to have a termination because she saw your pregnancy as a social embarrassment, she was going way beyond her remit. You had already told her that you wanted your baby and you're scarcely a feckless teenager,' Ginny reminded the younger woman with feeling. 'As for her suggestion that you wouldn't be able to cope, you're one of the most capable mothers I know!'

Maribel gave her a rueful look. 'I expect my aunt gave her advice in good faith. And to be fair—when Hermione was a girl it *was* a disgrace for a child to be born out of wedlock.'

'Why are you so magnanimous? That woman has always treated you like a Victorian poor relation!'

'It wasn't as bad as that. My aunt and uncle found it hard to understand my academic aspirations.' Maribel moved her hands in a dismissive gesture. 'I was the oddball of the family and just too different from my cousins.'

'They put a lot of pressure on you to conform.'

'But even more on Imogen,' Maribel declared, thinking of her fragile cousin, who had craved approval and admiration to such a degree that she had been able to handle neither rejection nor failure.

Elias squirmed to get down from his mother's lap so that he could investigate the arrival of the postman's van. He was a lively child with a mind that teemed with curiosity about the world that surrounded him. While Ginny went to the door to collect a parcel, Maribel gathered up all the paraphernalia that went with transporting a toddler between different houses.

'Can't you stay for coffee?' Ginny asked on her return.

'I'm sorry. I'd love to, but I've got loads of work to do.' But Maribel turned a slight guilty pink for she could have spared a half-hour. Unfortunately seeing Leonidas again had shaken her up and she craved the security of her own home. She scooped up Elias to take him out to her car, which was parked at the back door.

Her son was big for his age and lifting him was becoming more of an effort. She hefted him into his car seat. He put his own arms into the straps, displaying the marked streak of independence that sometimes put him at odds with his mother. 'Elias do,' he stated with purpose.

His bottom lip came out and he protested when she insisted on doing up the clasp on the safety belt. He wanted to do it himself, but she was determined not to give him the opportunity to master the technique of locking and releasing it. Having learnt to walk at an early age, Elias was already a skilled escape artist from chairs, buggies and play-pens.

Maribel drove back out onto the road and slowed down to overtake a silver car parked by the side of it. It was a bad place to stop and she was surprised to see a vehicle there. A hundred yards further on, she turned into the sun-dappled rambling lane overhung by trees that led to what had once been her home with her parents. She had inherited the picturesque old farmhouse after her father died and it had been rented out for many years. When the property had finally fallen vacant, everybody had expected her to sell up and plunge the proceeds into a trendy urban apartment. The discovery around the same time that she was pregnant, however, had turned Maribel's life upside down. After she had revisited the house where she had all too briefly enjoyed a wealth of parental love and attention, she had begun to appreciate that bringing up a child alone was going to demand a major change of focus and pace from her. She would have to give up her workaholic ways and make space in her busy schedule for a baby's needs.

Ignoring the comments about how old-fashioned and

isolated the property was, she had quietly got on with organising the refurbishment of the interior. Situated in a secluded valley and convenient to both London and Oxford, the farmhouse, she felt, offered her the best of both worlds. The convenience of having a good friend like Ginny living nearby had been the icing on the cake, even before Ginny had suggested that she take care of Elias while Maribel was at work.

'Mouse…Mouse…Mouse!' Elias chanted, wriggling like an eel and pushing at the door as Maribel unlocked it.

An extremely timid Irish wolfhound, Mouse was hiding under the table as usual. He would not emerge until he was reassured that it was only Maribel and Elias coming home. Struggling out from below the table because he was a very large dog, Mouse then welcomed his family with boisterous enthusiasm. Boy and dog rolled on the floor in a tumbling heap. Elias scrambled up. 'Mouse…up!' he instructed, to the manner born.

For a split-second, a flash of memory froze Maribel to the spot: Leonidas seven years earlier, asking when she planned on picking up the shirts lying on the floor. There had been that same note of imperious command and expectation, but not the same successful result because, intimidating though Leonidas was, Maribel had never been as eager to please as Mouse. Another image swiftly followed: Leonidas so domestically challenged and so outraged by the suggestion that he was helpless without servants that he had put an electric kettle on the hob.

Her son's yelp of pain jerked Maribel out of her abstraction. Elias had stumbled and bumped his head on the fridge. Tiredness made him clumsy. Maribel lifted him and rubbed his head in sympathy. Tear-drenched, furious brown eyes met hers, for the reverse side of his warmth and energy was a strong will and a temper of volcanic strength and durability. 'I know, I know,' she whispered gently, rocking him until his annoyance ebbed and his impossibly long black lashes began to droop.

She took him upstairs to the bright and cheerful nursery she had decorated with painstaking care and enjoyment. Removing his shoes and jacket, she settled him down in his cot with soothing murmurs. He went out like a light, yet she knew he wouldn't stay horizontal for very long. In sleep, he looked angelic and peaceful, but awake he could lay claim to neither trait. She watched him for a couple of minutes, involuntarily drawn into tracing the physical likeness that could only strike her with powerful effect on the same day that she had seen his father again. She wondered if her son was the only decent thing that Leonidas Pallis had ever created. It was a fight to get a grip on her thoughts again.

Accompanied by Mouse, Maribel went into the small sunlit room she used as a study and got straight down to marking the pile of essays awaiting her attention. Some time later, Mouse barked and nudged at her arm with an anxious whine. Ten seconds after that warning, she heard the approach of a car and she pushed back her chair. She was walking into the hall when she registered that other vehicles appeared to be arriving at the same time. Her brow furrowed in bewilderment, for she received few visitors and never in car loads.

Glancing out of the window, she stilled in consternation, for a long gleaming limousine now obscured her view of the garden and the field beyond it. Who else could it be but Leonidas Pallis? Her paralysis lasted for only a moment before she raced into the lounge, gathered up the toys lying on the rug and threw them into the toy box, which she thrust at frantic speed behind the sofa. The bell went even before she straightened from that task. She caught a glimpse of herself in the mirror: her blue eyes were wide with fear, and her face was pale as death. She rubbed her cheeks to restore some natural colour while apprehension made her mind race. What the heck was Leonidas doing here? How could he possibly have found out where she lived? And why should he have even wanted to know? The bell rang again in a shrill, menacing burst. She recalled the Pallis impatience all too well.

A dark sense of foreboding nudging at her, Maribel opened the door.

'Surprise…surprise,' Leonidas drawled softly.

Unnerved by the sheer smoothness of that greeting, Maribel froze and Leonidas took immediate advantage by stepping over the threshold. Her hand fell from the door as she turned to face him. After what had been a mere stolen glimpse in church, she got her first good look at him. His suit and coat were exquisitely tailored, designer-cut and worn with supreme *élan*. His height and breadth alone were intimidating, but for a woman his lean sculpted bone structure and utterly gorgeous dark, deep-set eyes had the biggest impact. Nor was that effect the least diminished by the fact that those ebony eyes were as dangerously direct and cutting as a laser beam. A tiny pulse began beating horribly fast at the foot of her throat, interfering with her ability to breathe.

'So what ever did happen to breakfast?' Leonidas murmured with honeyed derision.

A crimson tide of colour washed away Maribel's pallor

in a contrast as strong as blood on snow. Shock reverberated through her as he punched an unapologetic hole through the mind-block she had imposed on her memories of that night after Imogen's funeral, just over two years earlier. Flinching, she tore her gaze from his, hot with shame and taut with disbelief that he should have dared to throw that crack at her in virtually the first sentence he spoke. But then what did Leonidas not dare? The last time she had met his gaze, they had been a good deal closer and he had shaken her awake to murmur with quite shattering cool and command, 'Make me breakfast while I'm in the shower.'

In remembrance, a wave of dizziness washed over her and her tummy flipped as though she had gone down too fast in a lift. She would have done just about anything to avoid the recollection of his cruel amusement that morning. She had been gone by the time he'd emerged from that shower. She had buried her mistake as deep as she could, confiding in nobody, indeed resolving to take that particular secret to the grave with her. She was ashamed of the events of that night and all too well aware that Leonidas had not even a passing acquaintance with sensations like shame or discomfiture. She was dismayed by the discovery that, even after two years, her defences were still laughably thin. So thin that he could still hurt her, she registered in dismay.

'I would sooner not discuss that,' Maribel enunciated with a wooden lack of expression.

Exasperated by that prissy response, Leonidas snapped the front door shut with an authoritative hand and strolled into the front room. Her taste had not changed, he noted. Had he been presented with pictures of house interiors he could easily have picked out hers. The room was full of plants, towering piles of books and faded floral fabrics. Nothing seemed to match and yet there was a surprising stylishness and comfort to the effect she had achieved.

'Or why you bolted from the church today?' Leonidas queried, his rich, dark, accented drawl smooth as silk, but infinitely more disturbing.

Feeling trapped but determined not to overreact, Maribel studied his elegant grey silk tie. 'I wasn't bolting—I was simply in a hurry.'

'But how unlike you to disregard the social rituals of the occasion,' Leonidas censured softly. 'Yet another unusual experience for me. You are the only woman who runs away from me.'

'Maybe I know you better than the others do.' Maribel could have clapped her hand to her mouth in horror after that verbal reprisal simply tripped off her tongue without her even being aware that it was there. She was furious with herself, for in one foolish little sentence she had betrayed the fear, the anger, the bitterness and the loathing that she would have very much preferred to keep hidden from him.

CHAPTER TWO

LEONIDAS was not amused by that retaliation. The devil that lurked never far below his polished granite surface leapt out. While women of all ages fawned on him and hung on his every word, Maribel, it seemed, still favoured the acerbic response. He had never forgotten the one surprisingly sweet night when Maribel had used honey rather than vinegar in her approach. He had liked that; he had hugely preferred that different attitude, since he had neither taste nor tolerance for censure.

His brilliant eyes gleamed in liquid-gold warning below his luxuriant black lashes. 'Maybe you do,' Leonidas acknowledged without any inflection at all.

For a long, wordless moment, Leonidas took his fill while he looked at her, his gaze roaming over her with a boldness that came as naturally to him as aggression. His attention lingered on her strained violet-blue eyes, dropped to the luscious fullness of her mouth as it pouted against her peach-soft skin, and finally wandered lower to scan the full glory of her hourglass curves. It was a novelty to know that, this time around, she would most probably slap him if he touched her. After all, it wouldn't be the first time.

He almost smiled at the memory: his very first and still quite unique experience of female rejection.

Madly aware of that unashamedly sexual appraisal and unable to bear it any longer, Maribel flushed to her hairline and breathed curtly, 'Stop it!'

'Stop what? 'Leonidas growled, strong arousal now tugging at him, in spite of the powerful sense of intuition that warned him that there was something wrong. Even as he glanced back at her face, he picked up on her fear and wondered why she was scared. She had never been scared around him before, or so reluctant to meet his gaze. A faint sense of disappointment touched him, even while he wondered what was wrong with her.

'Looking at me like that!' For the first time in two long years, Maribel was hugely conscious of her body and she was furious that she could still be so easily affected by him.

Leonidas loosed an earthy masculine laugh. 'It's natural for me to look.'

Her slim hands coiled into fists of restraint. 'I don't like it.'

'Tough. Aren't you going to offer me coffee? Ask me to take off my coat and sit down?' Leonidas chided.

Maribel felt like a bird being played with by a cat and she snatched in a fractured breath. 'No.'

'What *has* happened to your manners?' Unasked, Leonidas peeled off his coat in a slow graceful movement that was curiously sexy and attracted her unwilling attention.

Maribel dragged her guilty eyes off him again, gritting her teeth, literally praying for self-discipline. He came between her and her wits. He brought sex into everything. He made her think and feel things that were not her choice. No matter how hard she fought it, there was a shameful hum of physical awareness travelling through her resisting body. He had always had that effect on her, *always*. Leonidas had provoked a sense of guilt in Maribel almost from the first moment of their meeting.

In a fluid stride, Leonidas closed the distance between them and lifted a hand to push up her chin and enforce the eye contact she was so keen to avoid. 'Was it the service? Did it upset you?'

He was now so close that Maribel trembled. She was taken aback by the ease with which he had touched her. She did not want to recall the fleeting intimacy that had broken down all normal barriers. She did not want to be reminded of the taste of his mouth or the evocative scent of his skin. 'No...it was good to remember her,' she said gruffly.

'Then what's the problem?' Mesmeric dark golden eyes assailed hers, powered by a larger-than-life personality that few could have withstood.

Her throat ached with her tension. 'There isn't one,' she told him unevenly. 'I just wasn't expecting you to call.'

'I'm usually a welcome visitor,' Leonidas murmured lazily, his relaxed rejoinder quite out of step with the keen penetration of his gaze.

As Maribel strove to keep a calm expression on her oval face her teeth chattered together behind her sealed lips for a split-second before she overcame that urge. 'Naturally I'm surprised to see you here. It's been a long time and I've moved house,' she pointed out, struggling to behave normally and say normal things. 'Did my aunt give you my address?'

'No. I had you followed.'

Maribel turned pale at that unnervingly casual admission. 'My goodness, why did you do that?'

'Curiosity? A dislike of relying on strangers for information?' Leonidas shrugged with languid cool. An infinitesimal movement out of the corner of his eye turned his attention below the table where a shaggy grey dog was endeavouring to curl its enormous body into the smallest possible space in the farthest corner. 'Theos...I did not even realise there was an animal here. What is the matter with it?'

Maribel seized on the distraction of Mouse's odd behaviour with enthusiasm. 'He's terrified of strangers and when he hides his head like that he seems to think he's invisible, so don't let on otherwise. Friendly overtures frighten him.'

'Still collecting lame ducks?' Leonidas quipped and, as he turned his head away, he caught a glimpse through the window of a hen pecking in the flower bed at the front of the house. 'You keep poultry here?'

His intonation was that of a jet-setter aghast at her deeply rural lifestyle. Maribel was willing to bet that Leonidas had never before been so close to domestic fowl, and in another mood she would have laughed at his expression and rattled on the window to chase the hen away from her plants. Unable to relax, she resolved to treat him as she would have treated any other unexpected visitor. 'Look, I'll make some coffee,' she proffered, thrusting open the kitchen door.

'I'm not thirsty. Tell me what you've been doing over the past couple of years,' he invited softly.

A chill ran down her taut spinal cord before she turned back to him. He couldn't know about Elias, she reasoned inwardly. Why should he even suspect? Unless someone had said something at the service? But why the heck should anyone have mentioned her or her child? As far as her relatives were concerned she was a geek who led a deeply boring life. Scolding herself for the unfamiliar paranoia that was ready to pounce and take hold of her, Maribel tilted her chin. 'I've been turning this place into a habitable home. It needed a lot of work. That kept me busy.'

Leonidas watched her hands lace together in a restive motion and untangle again. She folded her arms and shifted position in a revealing display of anxiety that any skilled observer would have recognised. 'I believe you have a child now,' he delivered smooth as glass, and all the time as his own tension rose he was telling himself that he had to be wrong, his suspicions ridiculously fanciful.

'Yes—yes, I have. I didn't think you'd be too interested in that piece of news,' Maribel countered in a determined recovery, forcing a wry smile onto her taut lips, while wondering how on earth he had found out that she had become a mother. 'As I recall it, you used to give friends with kids the go-by.'

Leonidas would have been the first to admit that that was true: he had never had any interest in children and found the doting fondness of parents for their offspring a bore and an irritation. Nobody acquainted with him would have dreamt of wheeling out their progeny for him to admire.

'Who told you I'd had a child?' Maribel enquired a shade tightly.

'The Strattons.'

'I'm surprised it was mentioned.' While fighting to keep her voice light, Maribel was wondering frantically what she would say if he asked her what age her child was.

Would she lie? *Could* she lie on such a subject? She was in a situation that she would have done almost anything to avoid. She did not believe that she could lie about such a serious matter and still live with her conscience. 'Was it the "left-in-the-lurch" version?' she asked.

A rare smile of amusement slashed the Greek tycoon's beautifully shaped mouth. 'Yes.'

'That's not how it was,' Maribel declared, attempting not to stare, because when he smiled the chill factor vanished from his lean, hard-boned features and banished the forbidding dark reserve that put people so much on their guard.

Without warning, distaste that she had slept with another man assailed Leonidas and killed his momentary amusement on the subject. He marvelled at that stab of possessiveness that ran contrary to his nature. His affairs were always casual, hampered by neither emotion nor sentimentality. But then, he had known Maribel for a long time and he had become her first lover. Perhaps that had been inevitable, he reasoned, still in search of the precise trigger that had fired him into making that discovery, more than two years earlier. Once he had discovered how she felt about him, the awareness had lent a strangely enjoyable intimacy to their encounters.

'How was it?' he heard himself ask, and it was the sort of question he never asked, but he was determined to satisfy his curiosity.

Maribel was disconcerted by that enquiry and she spread her hands in a jerky motion. Her tension was climbing steadily. 'It wasn't complex. I found myself pregnant and I wanted the baby.'

Leonidas wondered at her wording. Why no reference

to the father? Another one-night stand? Had he given her a taste for them? Had he ever really known her? He would have sworn that Maribel Greenaway was one of the last women alive likely to embrace either promiscuity or unmarried motherhood. Her outlook on life was conservative. She went to church; she volunteered for charity work. She wore unrevealing clothes. A frown line dividing his sleek ebony brows, his gaze skimmed over the view through the kitchen doorway. There, however, his attention screeched to an abrupt halt and doubled back to re-examine the brightly coloured, magnetised alphabet letters adorning the refrigerator door. Those letters spelled out a familiar name. A powerful sense of disbelief gripped him.

'What do you call your child?' Leonidas murmured thickly.

Maribel went rigid. 'Why are you asking me that?'

'And why are you avoiding answering me?' Leonidas shot back at her.

A horrible cold knot twisted tight inside her stomach. It was not something she could hide, not something she could lie about, for her child's name was a matter of public record. 'Elias,' she almost whispered, her voice dying on her at the worst possible moment.

It was the name of his grandfather and also one of his, and she pronounced it correctly in the Greek fashion, El-lee-us, not as someone English might have said it. Leonidas was so much shocked by that awareness that he was struck dumb, as he could not initially accept that what had only been the mildest of craziest suspicions might actually turn out to be true.

'I always liked the name,' Maribel told him in a last-ditch attempt at a cover-up.

'Elias is a Pallis name. My grandfather had it and so also do I.' Hard dark eyes rested on her with cold intensity. 'Why did you choose to use it?'

Maribel felt as though an icy hand were closing round her vocal cords and chest and making it impossible for her to breathe properly. 'Because I liked it,' she said again, because she could think of nothing else to say.

Leonidas swung away from her, lean brown hands clenching into fists of frustration. He had no time for mysteries or games that were not of his own making. His chequered life had taught him many things, but patience was not one of them. He refused to believe what his brain was striving to tell him. He did not do unprotected sex. A risk-taker in business and sport and equally fearless in many other fields, he was cautious when it came to contraception, always choosing the safe approach. He did not want children. He had never wanted children. Even less had he ever wished to run the risk of giving some woman a literal gun to hold to his head and his wallet. For what else could an unplanned child be to a man of his extreme wealth? A serious liability and a complication he could do without. It was a mistake he had always thought he was too smart to make. But he was well aware that the night after Imogen's funeral he had been in a very bizarre mood and he had abandoned his usual caution. More than once.

Maribel surveyed Leonidas with a surge of reluctant perception. Severe tension held his lean, powerful body taut. He was staggered and he was appalled, and she quite understood that. She did not blame him for his carelessness in getting her pregnant. It was true that she had felt rather differently when she had first discovered her condition, but the passage of time had altered her perspective.

After all, Elias had enriched her life to an almost inde-scribable degree and she could hardly regret his concep-tion.

'Let's not discuss this,' she murmured gently.

That suggestion outraged Leonidas. How could a woman with her extraordinary intellect say something so foolish? But was it possible that she could have given birth to his child without even letting him know that she was pregnant? Surely it had to be impossible? His logic refused to accept her in such a role—she was a very conventional woman. Yet why else had she named her child Elias? Why was she so nervous? Why was she irrationally trying to evade even discussing the matter?

'Is the child mine?' Leonidas demanded harshly.

Her natural colour had ebbed and with it the strength of her voice. 'He's mine. I see no reason to add anything else to that statement.'

'Don't be stupid. I asked a straight question and I will have a straight answer. What age is he?'

'I'm not prepared to discuss Elias with you.' Dry-mouthed, her heart beating so fast she felt nauseous, Maribel straightened her spine. 'We have nothing to talk about. I'm sorry, but I would like you to leave.'

Leonidas could not give credence to what he was hearing. In all his life he had never been addressed in such a fashion. 'Are you out of your mind?' he breathed in a raw undertone. 'You think you can throw this bombshell at me and then tell me to go away?'

'I didn't throw anything at you. You reached your own conclusions without any assistance from me. I don't want to argue with you.' Her blue eyes were violet with a curious mix of defiance and entreaty.

'But if I hadn't reached the correct conclusion, you would surely have contradicted me,' Leonidas reasoned with harsh bite. 'As you did not, I can only assume that you believe Elias to be my child.'

'He is mine.' Maribel linked her hands tightly together to prevent them from trembling. 'I'm quite sure you don't want my advice, but I'll give it all the same. Please consider this issue in a calm and logical way first.'

'Calm? Logical?' Leonidas growled, affronted by that particular choice of words.

'Elias is healthy, happy and secure. He lacks nothing. There is no reason for you to be concerned or involved in any way in our lives,' Maribel told him tautly, willing him to listen, understand and accept those facts.

Rage was rising in Leonidas with a ferocity he had not experienced since his sister had died when he was sixteen. How dared she seek to exclude him from his child's life? Elias had to be *his* child, *his* son. Had it been otherwise, Maribel would have said so. But bewilderment held him back from the much more aggressive response ready to blast from him. Why was she trying to get rid of him if Elias was his child? What kind of sense did that make?

'Did you assume I wouldn't want to know? Is that what lies at the foot of this nonsense?' Dark eyes shimmering gold, Leonidas studied her in wrathful challenge. 'Are you presuming to believe that you know how I would feel if I had a child? You do not know. Even I do not know when such news comes at me out of nowhere!'

The atmosphere was so hot and tense Maribel would not have been surprised to hear it sizzle and see it smoke.

'When was he born?' Leonidas demanded.

Her neck and her shoulders ached with the tension of her

rigid stance. All the legendary force of the Pallis will was trained on her in the onslaught of his fierce dark gaze. Never had she been more conscious of his strength of character and it occurred to her that parting with a few harmless facts might actually dampen down his animosity. She gave the date.

The silence seemed to last for ever. In the circumstances and with such a date, Leonidas knew immediately that there was virtually no chance that anyone else could have fathered her child. 'I want to see him.'

Maribel went white and shook her head in urgent negative, chestnut brown hair flying round her cheeks in a glossy fall. 'No. I won't allow that.'

'You won't...*allow*...that?' Leonidas breathed in rampant disbelief.

Maribel wished that there had been a more diplomatic way of telling him that. Unhappily, she had no precedent to follow because people didn't say no to Leonidas Pallis. 'No' was not a word he was accustomed to hearing. 'No' was not a word he knew how to accept. From birth he had had every material thing he had ever wanted or asked for, while being starved of the much more important child-hood needs. But he had survived by tuning out the emotional stuff, getting by without it. Now when he desired something, he simply went all out to take it and sensible people didn't get in his way. He was as ruthless as only a very powerful personality could be when he was crossed. She knew very well that her refusal struck him as a deeply offensive challenge and just how unfortunate that reality was.

'I won't allow it,' she whispered apologetically while she stood as straight and stiff as a statue, struggling not to feel intimidated.

But Leonidas was already striding past her to snatch up the photo frame on a corner table. 'Is this him?' he breathed in a thickened undertone, staring down with a strong air of bemusement at the snap of the smiling toddler clutching a toy lorry.

It was natural human curiosity, she told herself, fighting to control the sense of panic clawing at her. 'Yes,' she conceded in reluctant confirmation.

Leonidas scanned the photo with an intensity that would have stripped paint. He studied the little boy's olive skin and black curly hair and his dark-as-jet eyes. Although he could never recall looking at any other child with the slightest interest and had absolutely no basis for comparison, he thought that Elias was, without a shade of doubt, the most handsome baby he had ever seen. From his level eyebrows to his determined little chin, he just oozed strong Pallis genes.

'Please go, Leonidas,' Maribel urged tautly. 'Don't make this a battle between us. Elias is a happy child.'

'He is also self-evidently a Pallis,' Leonidas pronounced in a bemused tone, his Greek accent more marked than usual.

'No, he's a Greenaway.'

Lush black lashes swept up on sizzling dark golden eyes. 'Maribel…he is a Pallis. You cannot call a dog a cat just because you want to, and why should you want to?'

'I can think of many reasons. Now that you've forced me to satisfy your curiosity, will you leave?' Maribel was trembling. She was tempted to snatch that precious picture of her son from his lean brown hand. All her protective antenna were operating on high alert.

'Acquit me of a motive as superficial as that of mere

curiosity,' Leonidas censured. 'You owe me an explanation—'

'I owe you nothing and I want you to go.' Swallowing back the thick taste of panic in her throat, Maribel moved forward and snatched up the phone. 'If you don't leave right now, I'll call the police.'

Leonidas gave her a disconcerted glance and then threw back his handsome dark head and laughed out loud. 'Why would you do something so mad?'

'This is my home. I want you to leave.'

'In the same hour that I find out that you may be the mother of my only child?' Innate caution and shrewdness were already exercising restraint on Leonidas. He knew it would be most unwise to acknowledge Elias as his before stringent DNA testing had been carried out and the blood bond fully proven by scientific means. Yet he knew in his bones that Elias was his child. He did not know how he knew but he did, and he was already reaching the conclusion that the situation could have been a great deal worse. At least he had Maribel to deal with, and not some mercenary, calculating harpy without morals.

'I *will* call the police,' Maribel threatened unsteadily, terrified that Elias would waken and make some sound upstairs, and that Leonidas would immediately insist on going up to see him.

Leonidas slung her a confounded look and flung his arms wide in a gesture that was expansively Greek and impressive. 'What is the matter with you? Is this hysteria? Are you at risk of robbery or assault? Is that why you need to talk garbage about calling the police?'

Her eyes were as bright a purple-blue as wild violets, an impression heightened by her pallor and tension. 'I want you to forget you came here and forget what you think you may have found out. For all our sakes.'

'Is there some other guy hanging around who thinks that Elias is his child?' Leonidas enquired grimly, seizing on the only motive he could think of that might explain why she was so eager for him to stage a vanishing act.

A band of tension was starting to pound behind Maribel's smooth brow and tighten there like a painful vice. Standing up to Leonidas Pallis in such a mood was like being battered by a fierce storm. 'Of course not.' Distaste showed openly in her oval face. 'That's a really sleazy suggestion.'

'Women do stuff like that all the time,' Leonidas told her cynically, and he was not wholly convinced by her denial. Having watched Imogen manipulate Maribel, he had soon appreciated that, while Maribel might be exceptionally brainy, she could also be very gullible when her emotions were engaged. 'If that isn't the problem, spare me the theatrical speeches about forgetting I came here. How likely is that?'

'Just this once I'm asking you to think about someone other than yourself. If that's theatrical, I'm sorry, but that's how it is.' With an unsteady hand, Maribel pushed the hair back from her cheekbone.

Leonidas gave her a quelling look of granite hardness. 'I'm not listening to this claptrap. Where is Elias?'

Maribel stepped into the hall and yanked open the front door with a perspiring hand. 'I'll get the police, Leonidas. I mean it. I've got nothing to lose.'

'My business card. Call me when you come to your senses.' Leonidas settled a card down on the table.

'I won't be changing my mind any time soon,' Maribel declared defiantly.

Leonidas came to a halt in front of her. Dangerous dark golden eyes slammed down into hers. 'You want to start a war? You think you can handle that? You think you can handle me?' he growled. 'You could never handle me.'

'But I have to, because I will not accept you in any part of my son's life. I'll do whatever it takes to protect him from you!' Maribel swore in a feverish rush, determination etched into every rigid line of her small, shapely figure.

'Protect him from me? What are you trying to say? You become offensive and without reason.' Lean. dark features set with chilling intent, Leonidas shot her a forbidding appraisal. 'Why? I expected better from you. Is this some sort of payback, Maribel? Are you angry that it took me two years to look you up?'

Maribel wanted to kill him and it was not the first time he had filled her with so much rage and pain that she barely knew what she was thinking any more. Nobody could be more provocative than Leonidas Pallis. Nobody knew better how to put the metaphorical boot in and hurt. Sensible people did not make an enemy of him. But then a sensible woman, she thought in an agony of bitter self-loathing, would never have gone to bed with him in the first place.

'Why would I be?' Maribel murmured helplessly. 'I don't even like you.'

Virtually nothing shocked Leonidas as, while he'd been growing up, he had seen all the worst facets of human nature as paraded by his dysfunctional mother, but that declaration from Maribel shocked him. He had always viewed her no-nonsense front as a defensive shell. He regarded her as a caring, sympathetic woman with a genuine soft centre, sadly condemned to have her good nature taken advantage of by the users and abusers of the world. But in the space of half an hour, Maribel had turned everything he believed he knew about her upside down and gone out of her way to attack and insult him.

Yet, from what he could work out, she appeared to be the mother of his child. He wondered if stress was making her hysterical, if she just couldn't cope with the situation. He did not accept that she didn't like him. He knew she loved him and he had known that almost as long as he had known her. She was not a changeable woman. That she had given birth to his child, rather than choose to have a termination, struck him as perfectly understandable.

Lean, darkly handsome face bleak, Leonidas climbed into his limousine. A Pallis and an alpha male personality to the core of his aggressive being, he wasted no time in making his next move. Lifting the phone, he called the executive head of his international legal team and asked for a copy of Elias Greenaway's birth certificate to be obtained. He gave the details and ignored the staggered silence that fell at the other end of the line, because Leonidas Pallis never explained his actions to anyone, or laid out the full details of a situation unless he chose to do so.

'In the morning, I also want a full briefing with regard to my rights as a father in this country.'

Furiously angry and in fighting mode, Leonidas marvelled afresh at Maribel's offensive behaviour and unreasonable attitude. As he recalled her words his hostility grew ever stronger. To refuse him his natural desire to see the child! To suggest that the child should be protected from him and would be better off without him! His sense of honour was outraged by the shameful accusations she had dared to make.

And, all the while, he kept on seeing images of Maribel flashing him that defiant look, her luscious pink mouth taut with censure. His shimmering dark eyes scorched and hardened. How could she have had his baby without telling him? When the photo of the little boy came to mind, however, he tensed, for he preferred being angry with Maribel to thinking about the matter that lay at the heart of it all.

CHAPTER THREE

ELIAS was grizzling noisily for attention by the time that Maribel finally emerged from her overwrought stance behind the front door. The limousine, with its accompanying cavalcade, was long gone.

Recovering her wits, Maribel hastened upstairs and swept her son from his cot with an enthusiasm that made him laugh and shout with pleasure; there was nothing Elias loved more than good old-fashioned horseplay. Trembling, Maribel lifted him high and then hugged him tight, knowing that she would want to die if anything happened to him. She had done the right thing in sending Leonidas away; she *knew* she had done the right thing.

But what were the chances that Leonidas would stay away? Maribel looped her damp hair off her anxious brow. Leonidas, who was mentally primed only to do what he wanted to do, and likely to want to do what he was told he could not or should not do? Elias had the same bloody-minded competitive trait. Maybe it was a male thing. She took Elias out into the garden with Mouse. While her son and the wolfhound ran about doing nothing much that she could see but hugely enjoying themselves, Maribel sat on the swing and let her memory take her back seven years…

* * *

Imogen had bought a house in Oxford and had persuaded Maribel, who had then been a student, to move in and take care of the property for her. Maribel had been happy to reduce her expenses and take care of the domestic trivia that Imogen, who had often been away from home, couldn't be bothered with. Imogen had been twenty-three, and her career as a fashion model had failed to reach the dazzling heights she'd craved. An indomitable party girl, Imogen had wasted no time in introducing herself to Leonidas Pallis when she'd run into him at a nightclub. At the time Leonidas had been a student at Oxford University.

'He is so rich money means nothing to him. His party was *amazing*!' Imogen, a tall, strikingly lovely blonde in a trendy short dress, was so excited that her words were tripping over each other. 'He's an A-list celebrity and so cool, he just freaks me out. Oh, and did I mention what a total babe he is?'

Listening to that artless flood of confidence, Maribel was more worried than impressed, because Imogen was all too easily influenced by the wrong people. The advent of an infamous Greek playboy, who crashed cars and abseiled down skyscrapers for thrills, struck Maribel as very bad news. Dating the heir to the Pallis billions, however, very much enhanced Imogen's earning power as a model. Suddenly she was in great demand, rubbing shoulders with the rich and famous and flying round the world to shoots, weekend parties and endless vacations.

'He's the one…he's the *one*. I want to marry him and become a Greek tycoon's fabulously wealthy wife. I'll die if he dumps me!' Imogen gasped at the end of the first fortnight, and that same night she dragged Leonidas in to meet Maribel without the slightest warning.

Clad in tartan pyjamas, and curled up with a research

paper on carbon dating and a mug of hot cocoa clutched in her hand, Maribel was appalled when Imogen simply walked into her bedroom with Leonidas in tow.

'This is my cousin, Maribel, my best friend in the whole world,' Imogen declared. 'She's a student like you.'

Lounging in the doorway, Leonidas gave Maribel a lazy smile of amusement and the shock of his intense attraction hit Maribel like an electric charge. She didn't know where to look or how to handle it, since the even bigger shock was that she had the capacity to feel that way! Up until that point, Maribel's dating forays had been unenthusiastic and always disappointing. One guy had got friendly with her only to steal her work, and another had tried to get her to do his assignments for him. Then there were the many who expected sex on the first date and the others who drank themselves into a stupor. None of them had given her goose-bumps or, indeed, an instant of excitement—until Leonidas appeared on the horizon.

And Maribel being Maribel, she was sick with guilt at being attracted to her cousin's man. That very first night, she shut out that awareness and refused to allow herself to take it out again. In the month that followed, she barely saw Imogen, who stayed in Leonidas' properties in Oxford, London and abroad. And then, just as suddenly, the brief affair was over, just one more fling in Pallis terms, but it had meant a great deal more to Imogen, who had adored the high life.

'Of course, if you want the right to live in the Pallis world, you've got to share Leonidas and not be possessive.' Imogen tried to act as if she didn't mind watching Leonidas with her replacement, a young film starlet. 'With the choice he's got, you can't expect him to be satisfied with one woman.'

'Just walk away,' Maribel urged ruefully. 'He's a cold, arrogant bastard. Don't do this to yourself.'

'Are you crazy?' Imogen demanded in shrill disbelief. 'I'll settle for whatever I can get from him. Maybe in a few weeks, when he's fed up with the movie star, he'll turn back to me again. I'm somebody when I'm with him and I'm not giving that up!'

And true to her resolve, Imogen's ability to make Leonidas laugh when he was bored ensured that she retained him as a friend. Perhaps only Maribel cringed when she appreciated that Imogen was quite willing to ridicule herself if it amused Leonidas. Then there was a fire at Leonidas' Oxford apartment and Imogen invited him to use her house while she was working abroad.

Maribel's animosity went into override because Leonidas proved to be the house guest from hell. Without a word of apology or prior warning, he took over and moved in his personal staff, including a cook and a valet, not to mention his bodyguards. His security requirements squeezed her out of her comfortable bedroom into an attic room on the second floor. Visitors came and went day and night, while phones rang constantly and scantily clad and often drunken and squabbling women lounged about every room.

After ten days of absolute misery, Maribel lost her temper. Up until that point, she wasn't even sure Leonidas had realised that she was still residing in the house. On the morning of the eleventh day, she confronted him on the landing with a giggling brunette still tucked under one arm.

'May I have a word with you in private?'

A sleek ebony brow elevated, because even at the age of twenty-four Leonidas was a master of the art of pure insolence. 'Why?'

'This is my home as well as Imogen's, and, while I appreciate that in her eyes you can do no wrong, I find you and your lifestyle utterly obnoxious.'

'Get lost,' Leonidas told the brunette with brutal cool.

Studying him in disgust, Maribel shook her head. 'Possibly you are accustomed to living in the equivalent of a brothel where anything goes, but I am not. Tell your women to keep their clothes on. Send them home when they become drunk and offensive. Try to stop them screaming and playing loud music in the middle of the night.'

'You know what you need?' Dark golden eyes hot with a volatile mix of anger and amusement, Leonidas anchored his hands to her hips and hauled her to him, as if she were no more than a doll. 'A proper man in your bed.'

Maribel slapped him so hard her hand went numb, and he reeled back from her in total shock. 'Don't you ever speak to me like that again and don't touch me either!'

'Are you always like this?' Leonidas demanded in raw incredulity.

'No, Leonidas. I'm only like this with you. You bring out the very best in me,' Maribel told him furiously. 'I'm trying to study for my exams…okay? Under this roof, you are not allowed to act like an arrogant, selfish, ill-mannered yob!'

'You really don't like me,' Leonidas breathed in wonderment.

'What's to like?'

'I'll make it up to you—'

'No!' Her interruption was immediate and pungent,

because she was well aware of how he got around the rules with other people. 'You can't buy yourself out of this one. I don't want your money. I just want you to sort this out. I want my bedroom back. I want a peaceful household. There isn't room here for you to have a bunch of live-in staff.'

That evening, she came home to find all her possessions back in her old room and that there was blissful silence. She baked him some Baklava as a thank-you and left it with a note on the table. Two days later, he asked when she was going to pick up his unwashed shirts from the floor. When she explained that her agreement with Imogen did not include such menial duties for guests and that hell would freeze over before she touched his shirts, Leonidas asked how he was supposed to manage without household support.

'Are you really that helpless?' Maribel queried in astonishment.

'I have never been helpless in my life!' Leonidas roared at her.

Of course he *was*—totally helpless in a domestic capacity. But a Pallis male took every challenge to heart and Leonidas felt that he had to prove himself. So he burned out the electric kettle on the hob, ate out for every meal and tried to wash his shirts in the tumble drier. Pity finally stirring, she suggested his staff came back but lived out. An uneasy peace was achieved, for Leonidas could, when he made the effort, charm the birds from the trees. She was surprised to discover that he was actually very clever.

Two days before he moved into his new apartment, he staggered in at dawn hopelessly drunk. Awakened by the noise he made, Maribel got out of bed to lecture him about the evils of alcohol, but was silenced when he told her that it was the anniversary of his sister's death. Shaken, she listened but learned little, as he continually lapsed into Greek before finally commenting that he didn't know why he was confiding in her.

'Because I'm nice and I'm discreet.' Maribel had no illusions that he was confiding in her for any other reason. She knew herself to be plump and plain. But that was still the night when Maribel fell head over heels in love with Leonidas Pallis: when she registered the human being who dwelt beneath the high-gloss sophistication, who could not cope with the emotional turmoil of his bad memories.

The day he moved out, and without any warning of his intention, he kissed her. In the midst of a perfectly harmless dialogue, he brought his mouth down on hers with a hot and hungry demand that shook her rigid. She jerked back from him in amazement and discomfiture. 'No!' she told him with vehemence.

'Seriously?' Leonidas prompted, his disbelief patent.

'Seriously, no.' Her lips still tingling from the forbidden onslaught of his, she backed away from him and laughed to cover her embarrassment. It was her belief that he had kissed her because he had very little idea of how to have a platonic friendship with a woman.

Knowing how Imogen still felt about him, she felt so guilty about that kiss that she confessed to her cousin. Imogen giggled like a drain. 'Someone must've dared Leonidas to do it! I mean, it's not like you've got the looks or the sex appeal to pull him on your own, is it?'

Her earliest memories of Leonidas were bitter-sweet, Maribel acknowledged as her thoughts drifted back to the present. Leonidas had cast a long dark shadow that had somehow always been present during the years that followed. When Maribel had occasionally met him again through Imogen, she had utilised a tart sense of humour as a defence mechanism. While putting together billion-pound business deals, Leonidas had continued to run through an unending succession of gorgeous women and make headlines wherever he went. Imogen, however, had worked less and had become more and more immersed in her destructive party lifestyle. Over a year before her death, Leonidas had stopped taking Imogen's phone calls.

Maribel caught Elias as he ran past her and pulled him onto her lap where he lay, totally convulsed by giggles. Her eyes overbright, she resisted the urge to hug him again and let him wriggle free to return to his play. He was so happy. She did not believe that Leonidas had ever known that kind of happiness or security. Elias depended on her to do what was best for him. She did not believe that any father was better than no father at all; she *refused* to believe that.

Leonidas was conscious of annoyance when he saw Elias Greenaway's birth certificate: he had not been named as the father. 'I want DNA-testing organised immediately.'

The three lawyers seated on the other side of the table tensed in concert. 'Where a couple are unmarried, DNA tests can only be carried out with the mother's consent,' the most senior of the trio imparted. 'As your name isn't on the birth certificate, you don't have parental responsibility either. May I ask if you have a cordial relationship with Miss Greenaway?'

The Greek tycoon's gaze flared gold and veiled. 'It's Dr

Greenaway, and our relationship is not up for discussion. Concentrate on my rights as a parent.'

'Where there is no marriage, the UK legal system favours the mother. If you have the lady's agreement to DNA-testing, to sharing parental responsibility and to granting reasonable access to the child, there won't be a problem,' the lawyer enumerated with quiet clarity. 'Without that agreement, however, there would considerable difficulty. Applying to a court would be your only remedy and, in general, the judge will regard the mother and custodial parent as the best arbiter of the child's interests.'

Always cool under pressure, Leonidas pondered those disconcerting facts, his lean, dark face aloof. Although nobody would have guessed it, he was very surprised by what he was finding out. 'So I need her consent.'

'It would be the most straightforward approach.'

Leonidas recognised what went unsaid but invited no further comment. He knew that there were wheels within wheels. For a man of his wealth, there was always a way of circumventing the rules. When winning was the goal, and it was usually the *only* goal for Leonidas, the concept of fair play had no weight and the innocent often got hurt. That was not, however, the route he wished to follow with Maribel, who had once been sincerely appalled to catch Imogen cheating at a board game. For the moment he was prepared to utilise more conventional means of persuasion…

Maribel lifted her office phone and jerked out of her seat the instant she heard Leonidas' rich, dark-chocolate drawl in her ears. 'What do you want?' she demanded, too rattled to even attempt the polite small talk usually employed at the outset of a conversation.

'I want to talk to you.'

'But we spoke yesterday and I'm at work,' Maribel protested in a near whisper, panic squeezing the life from her vocal cords.

'You're free for an hour before your next tutorial,' Leonidas informed her. 'I'll see you in five minutes.'

Suddenly Maribel wished she were the sort of woman who put on make-up every day, instead of just on high days and holidays. She dug frantically into her bag to find a mirror and brushed her hair, while striving not to notice that her sleepless night was etched on her face and in the heaviness of her eyes. A split-second after that exercise, she was outraged by her instinctive reaction to his phone call. Instead of mustering her wits and concentrating on what was important, she had spent those precious moments fussing over her appearance. A waste of time, she told herself in exasperation, glancing down at her ruffled green shirt, trousers and sensible pumps. Only Cinderella's fairy godmother could have worked a miracle with such unpromisingly practical material.

Leonidas strolled in with the unhurried grace that was so much a part of him. Deceptively indolent dark golden eyes skimmed over her taut expression and he sighed. 'I'm not the enemy, Maribel.'

Maribel lifted her chin, but evaded too close a meeting with his incisive gaze. But that single harried glimpse of his lean strong features still lingered in the back of her mind. The bold, sculpted cheekbones, the imperious blade of a nose and the tough jawline were impressive even before the rest of him was taken into account. She had always got a kick out of looking at Leonidas. Denying that urge to look and enjoy hurt to an almost physical degree.

Desperate to relocate her composure, she sucked in a steadying breath. 'Coming here to see me is indiscreet,' she told him stiffly. 'This is a public building and my place of work. A lot of people would recognise you. You attract too much notice.'

'I cannot help the name I was born with.' His fluid shrug somehow contrived to imply that she was being wildly irrational. 'You must've known that we would have to talk again. Possibly I felt that you would be less likely to threaten me with the police here.'

'Oh, for goodness' sake, you knew I wasn't really going to call the police to get rid of you!' Maribel's patience just snapped at that crack. 'And since when were you afraid of anything? I can see the headlines even as we speak. ATTEMPTED ARREST OF GREEK TYCOON, because you know perfectly well that your bodyguards wouldn't give you up to anybody! Do you really think I would risk inviting that kind of attention?'

'No?' Leonidas filed away the obvious fact that she had a healthy fear of media exposure. Considering the many women who had boasted in print of an intimate association with him, he wondered if he should be offended by her attitude. She had always been so different from the women he was accustomed to that he was never quite sure what she might say or how she might react.

'Of course I wouldn't. I can't believe that you would want that either. In fact I'm sure you've thought seriously about things since yesterday.'

'Obviously.' Leonidas leant back against the edge of her desk and stretched out his long powerful legs, a manoeuvre that had the effect of virtually trapping her by the corner next to the window. The office was no bigger than a large broom cupboard and it contained a second desk because it was a shared facility. He surveyed her with assessing cool. Even tiredness could not dim the crystal clarity of those violet eyes. As for the outfit, it looked drab at first glance, but the snug fit of the shirt and the trousers at breast and hip enhanced the proud curves and intriguing valleys of her fabulously abundant figure. She was woman enough to make many of her sex seem as flat and one-dimensional as cardboard, he conceded, assailed by a highly erotic recollection of Maribel all rosy, warm and luscious at dawn. The instant tightening at his groin almost made him smile, for it was some time since he had reacted to a woman with that much enthusiasm.

Subjected to one sensual flash of his bold, dark golden gaze, Maribel went rigid. She was aghast at the languorous warmth spreading through her and at the swollen feel of her breasts within the confinement of her bra. As her tender nipples tightened she folded her arms in a jerky movement. 'So, if you've thought seriously…'

'I still want answers. At least, be realistic.' His brilliant eyes now screened to a discreet glimmer below lush black lashes, his drawl was as smooth as silk. 'What man would not, in this situation?'

Maribel didn't want to be realistic. She just wanted him to go away again and stop threatening the peace of mind that she had worked so hard to achieve. 'What do I have to do to make you understand?'

'See both sides of the equation. Be the logical woman I know you to be. To ask me to walk away without even knowing whether or not the child is mine is absurd.' The complete calm and quiet of his voice had an almost hypnotic effect on her.

'Yes, but…' Maribel pinned her lips closed on the temptation to speak hasty words '…it's not that simple.'

'Isn't it?' Leonidas countered. 'Clearly *you* believe that Elias is my son. If you didn't believe that, you would have swiftly disabused me of the idea.'

Maribel stiffened, her eyes reflecting her indecision. 'Leonidas…'

'Every child has the right to know who his father is. Until I was seven years old, I believed my father was my mother's first husband. But, after the divorce, it emerged that someone else was the culprit. I know what I'm talking about. Are you planning to lie to Elias?'

'Yes…*no*! Oh, for goodness' sake!' Maribel gasped, raking her chestnut hair off her troubled brow with an anxious hand, as his candour had disarmed her. 'I will do whatever is best for Elias.'

'One day Elias will be an adult, and you will lose him if you lie to him about his parentage.' Leonidas dealt her a cool dark appraisal. 'You hadn't thought of that aspect, had you? Or about the fact that Elias has rights, too.'

Maribel blenched at that unwelcome reminder.

'And what if something happens to you while he is still a child? Who will take care of him then?'

'That's dealt with in my will.'

Any pretence of relaxation abandoned at that admission, Leonidas was as still as a panther about to spring. 'Do I figure in it?'

Tense as a bow string, Maribel slowly shook her head.

The silence folded in as thick and heavy as a fog.

With reluctance, Maribel looked back at him. Leonidas was studying her with a chilling condemnation that cut her to the bone. It was obvious that he had already reached his own conclusions as to her son's parentage. Her heart sank, since she had no way of convincing him otherwise, no magical method of turning back time and ensuring that he did not find out what she had believed he would have been perfectly happy not to know. 'All right,' she said gruffly, her slim shoulders slumping, for she felt as battered as if she had gone ten rounds with a heavyweight boxer. 'You got me pregnant.'

Leonidas was startled by the strong sense of satisfaction that gripped him and relieved that he had not had to exert pressure. As he had anticipated, Maribel had listened to her conscience. So, the boy was his. The boy was a Pallis: the next generation of the family. His ancient trio of great-aunts would be overjoyed at the continuation of the Pallis bloodline, while his more avaricious relatives would be heartbroken at being cut out in the inheritance stakes. Although Leonidas had long since decided that he would neither marry nor reproduce, it had not until that moment occurred to him that he might father a son and heir with so little personal inconvenience.

'I knew that you wouldn't lie to me,' he intoned with approval.

But Maribel felt very much as though she had failed. She knew that decent standards were a weakness in his vicinity. She knew his flaws. Yet she was still ensnared by the stunning gold of his eyes glinting below the dense black fringe of his lashes. He could still take her breath away with one scorching glance.

In a lithe movement Leonidas abandoned his misleadingly casual stance against the desk and straightened his lean, powerful body to his full imposing height. He reached for her taut, clenched fingers, straightening them out with confidence to draw her closer. 'You've done the right thing,' he murmured lazily. 'I respect you for telling me the truth.'

'That's good, because I think that telling you the truth was one of the most pointless things I've ever done.' Her slender fingers trembled in the hold of his as she fought the insidious force of his sensual charisma. Once bitten, for ever shy, she reminded herself frantically. He had almost destroyed her self-esteem more than two years earlier. Imogen and a whole host of other women had somehow managed to do casual with Leonidas, but Maribel had felt as though her heart were being ripped out slowly while she was still alive. And the horror of it had lasted for weeks, months, afterwards.

'How so?' Leonidas could feel the trepidation she was struggling to hide and marvelled at it, for he could think of no reason for her continuing apprehension. His thumb massaging her narrow wrist in a soothing motion, he gazed down at her, his attention lingering on the ripe pink fullness of her mouth. As the rich tide of sexual arousal grasped him he made no attempt to quell it. In fact he was enjoying the astonishing strength of his reaction to her. Seducing Maribel, he was recalling, had been unexpectedly sweet, and it would certainly take care of all the arguments now. 'I'm not angry with you.'

'Not at the moment…no,' Maribel agreed, dry-mouthed, in response to the perceptible change in the atmosphere. Her heart was thumping as fast as a car being revved up on a race track. It was as if time had slowed down, while her every physical sense went on hyper-alert. Her breath catching in her throat, she fought to stay in control.

'We were careless,' Leonidas commented in a husky undertone, wondering if he should lock the door and take full advantage of the moment.

'I wasn't…you were,' Maribel muttered, unable even with her brain in a state of sensual freefall to let him get away with making such an unfair claim.

'I left my wallet in the limo and you wouldn't let me phone for it to be brought in, so I had no contraception—'

'I didn't want your chauffeur and your wretched security team to know what you were doing!' Maribel protested, her cheeks burning at the memory of her embarrassment.

Leonidas gave her a smile of unholy amusement. 'I stayed the night with you. So what?'

'I don't want to talk about it.' Maribel recognised the treacherous intimacy of the discussion. Fighting the wicked draw of his dark animal magnetism, she turned her head away.

He lifted a lean brown hand up to flick a straying strand of amber-coloured hair back from her pale brow. Incredibly aware of his proximity, Maribel quivered. She could feel her whole body leaning towards him. It was as if he had pressed a button and her spine had crumbled. There was a craving in her that overpowered common sense. There was a wild longing for the forbidden and, try as she might, she could not stamp it out.

'You make *this* complicated,' Leonidas muttered thickly, a big hand splaying to the feminine curve of her hip to ease her up against him before she could step out of reach. 'But for me it's simple.'

She knew it was not simple, she knew it was complicated. She even knew that it was a hideous mistake and that she was going to hate herself later. But when he bent his handsome dark head, she still found herself stretching up on tiptoe so that she wouldn't have to wait a split-second longer than necessary to make physical contact. And whatever else Leonidas was, he was an overpoweringly physical male. His lips claimed hers with a red-hot hunger and demand that she felt right down to her toes. His tongue tasted her and she shivered. He pushed against her, banding her closer with strong hands, unashamedly letting her feel the hard thrust of his erection. Answering heat flared low in her belly and she gasped beneath his marauding mouth. Her fingers dug into his broad shoulders. With no recollection of how they had got there, she yanked her hands guiltily off him again. Forcing herself to break free of his arms hurt as much as losing a layer of skin.

Violet-blue eyes blazing with resentment at his nerve, Maribel launched herself clumsily back out of reach. Her shoulders and hips met the filing cabinet behind her and provided merciful support, because her legs felt as sturdy as quaking jelly. 'What the hell are you playing at?' she snapped at him in furious condemnation, angry over her weakness and the hateful inevitability of his having taken advantage of it. 'Is this because I showed you the door at my home yesterday? Did I insult your ego? You have just found out that you're the father of my son! And what do you do? You make a pass at me!'

'Why not?' Having followed his natural inclinations and met with a very encouraging response, Leonidas was in no mood to apologise, particularly not when he was stifling a staggeringly powerful desire to simply haul her back into his arms. 'I think I'm behaving very well. I'm willing to accept responsibility—'

'You've never accepted responsibility for a woman in

your life!' Maribel launched at him with a bitterness she could not conceal.

'I'm willing to accept responsibility for Elias.'

'But you're so busy being a player that you've just shown me all over again why I can't stand the thought of you in my son's life!' Maribel slung at him, the raw force of her emotions ringing from her voice. Her entire body was tingling with almost painful sensitivity and a stark sense of what could only be described as deprivation. Shame over her loss of control threatened to choke her.

'You'll have to learn to stand it and me, because I have no intention of staying out of my child's life.' Hard dark-as-midnight eyes sliced back at her like gleaming rapier blades of warning challenge. 'Elias is a Pallis.'

'No matter what it takes, I swear that I will prevent you from gaining access to him,' Maribel threw back at him with clenched fists.

Leonidas released his breath in a slow, derisive hiss. 'Give me one good reason why you should behave that way.'

'Just look at what being born a Pallis did to you!' Maribel sent him a furious appraisal, because the brazen self-assurance he exuded only reminded her of the dignity she had surrendered in his arms. 'You're irre-sponsible. You have no respect for women. You're a commitment-phobe—'

Derision engulfed by incredulous indignation, Leonidas growled. 'That is outrageous.'

'It's the truth. Right now, Elias would be a novelty to you like a new toy. You only take business seriously. You have no concept of family life or of a child's need for sta-bility. How could you after the way you were raised? I'm not blaming you for your deficiencies,' Maribel told him in a driven undertone. 'But I won't apologise for my need to protect Elias from the damage that you could do.'

Leonidas was pale with fury, his bronzed skin stretched taut over his superb bone structure. 'What do you mean—*deficiencies*?'

'Elias is very precious. What have you got to give him but money? He needs an adult who's willing to put him first, to look after him, but what you cherish most is your freedom. The freedom to do whatever you like when you like would be the first thing you would lose as a father and you wouldn't stick the course for five minutes—'

'Try me!' Leonidas shot back at her in wrathful challenge. 'Who are you to judge me? You have never lived outside your little academic soap-bubble! By what right do you call me irresponsible?'

Although she was drawn and tense, Maribel lifted her head high. 'I've got more right than anyone else I know. You never once called to ask if I was okay after that night we spent together!'

'Why would I have?' Leonidas growled like a bear.

Maribel almost flinched. She refused to allow herself to react in a more personal way and she tucked the hurt of that cruelly casual dismissal away for future reference. 'Because it would have been the responsible thing to do when you knew there was a risk of a pregnancy,' she informed him in a wooden tone.

Leonidas swore in vehement Greek at that retaliation and shot her a censorious glance. 'You walked out on me,' he ground out.

Maribel thought of what had really happened that morning and inwardly squirmed. Walking out would have been the sensible, dignified option, but it was not actually what she had done. He didn't know that, though, and she felt that that fact was none of his business so long after the event. She did not have much pride to conserve over the episode, but what she did have she planned to hang onto.

'It was for you to contact me when you learned that you had conceived,' Leonidas delivered in harsh addition.

'You didn't deserve that amount of consideration,' Maribel told him without hesitation.

Lethal scorn hardened his darkly handsome features. 'I didn't phone—is that what this is all about? So you try to punish me by refusing me contact with my son?'

Maribel looked steadily back at him, her violet blue eyes defiant in the face of that put-down. 'Don't you dare try to twist what I said. Be honest with yourself. Do you really want the hassle of a child in your life?'

Only forty-eight hours earlier, Leonidas would have responded with an unqualified negative to that question. Now a whole new dimension had to be considered. He could not get the image of the smiling little boy in the photograph out of his mind. But his other responses were much more aggressive, because when he looked back at Maribel he could never recall feeling more angry or alienated from her. She had judged him and found him wanting and nobody had ever dared to do that before.

The office door sprang open without warning. 'Why on earth is there a crowd of people hanging around outside?' demanded the older woman with whom Maribel shared the office. 'Oh—sorry. I didn't realise that you had someone with you. Am I interrupting?'

'Not at all,' Leonidas murmured impassively. 'I was about to leave.'

Gripped by a giant wave of frustration, Maribel watched

Leonidas depart. She could not understand why she should feel bereft when he walked away. Her office was no place for emotional discussions. He needed to think about what she had said, as well. Her hand crept up to her lower lip, which was still swollen from the erotic heat of his. It was so typical of Leonidas to try and blur serious issues with sex. He could handle sex. He could handle it beautifully. It was the emotional stuff he couldn't and wouldn't deal with.

Wide-eyed, her colleague hurried back to the doorway. 'Good heavens, was that who I think it is? Was that *actually* Leonidas Pallis?'

A mass of speculative faces peered in at Maribel, as though she were a rare animal on display in a zoo for the first time…

CHAPTER FOUR

MARIBEL could not sleep that night, or indeed during the night that followed.

How long was it since she had fallen in love with Leonidas Pallis? Almost seven years. It sounded like a prison term and had often felt like one, while she'd struggled to feel something—*anything*—for a more suitable man. Her heart might as well have been locked away in a cell, for neither intelligence nor practicality had exercised the smallest influence over what she felt. She had done her utmost to get over him. She knew his every flaw and failing. She did not respect him as a person. Yet helpless sympathy for a male so divorced from his emotions that he did not even recognise grief had led to her lowering her guard after her cousin's funeral. And, to the conception of the son she adored.

Who are you to judge me? She was still pondering that question at dawn on the second day after his latest visit. As she had not expected to see Leonidas again, it had not occurred to her that he would ever find out about Elias. Now that he had, everything had changed and she had been too slow to recognise that truth. Suddenly she was being forced to justify the decisions she had made and she was no longer confident that she had the right to deny Elias all contact with his father. Accustomed as she was to keeping her own counsel, she felt that she was too emotionally involved and that it might be wise to ask for a second opinion from someone she could trust to be discreet.

Later that morning, Maribel went over to see Ginny Bell and finally told the older woman who had fathered her son.

For the space of an entire minute, the older woman simply stared back at her with rounded eyes of shock and disbelief. '*Leonidas Pallis?* The Greek billionaire who's always plastered all over the celebrity magazines? Imogen's ex?'

Red as a beetroot, Maribel nodded affirmation.

'My goodness. You do put new meaning into that saying about being a dark horse!' Ginny exclaimed. 'Leonidas Pallis is really Elias' father?'

'Yes.'

'I never liked to ask who he was, when you didn't seem to want to talk about it.' Ginny shook her head in wonderment over what she had just been told. 'I must be frank. I'm gobsmacked. What prompted you to suddenly tell me about this now?'

'Leonidas has just found out about Elias and he wants to see him.' Maribel compressed her lips. 'I've been saying no.'

Ginny grimaced. 'Surely that's not a good idea, Maribel. Is it wise to get on the wrong side of a man that powerful?'

'He is very annoyed about my attitude,' Maribel conceded unhappily.

'If someone told you that you couldn't see your child,

wouldn't you be angry?' the older woman prompted wryly. 'Try to put yourself in his shoes and be fair.'

'That's not easy,' Maribel confided chokily.

'But why run the risk of turning Leonidas into an enemy? Wouldn't that be more dangerous? I've heard some heart-rending stories about children being snatched away by disaffected foreign fathers.'

Ginny could have said nothing more guaranteed to make Maribel's blood run cold in her veins. 'Don't scare me, Ginny.'

'You're playing with some pretty strong emotional issues here. That's why I would try to be reasonable, if I were you.'

'But I think that Leonidas is just curious. I don't see him getting that involved with Elias,' Maribel said tautly. 'Leonidas has never been that fussed about kids.'

The older woman subjected her to a shrewd appraisal. 'You really know Leonidas Pallis very well, don't you?'

Maribel lowered defensive lashes. 'Reasonably well.'

'Then hang onto that bond before you lose it,' Ginny advised ruefully. 'For your son's sake. Some day, Elias will want to know all about his background and he will want to know his father, as well. Making decisions on Elias' behalf is a big responsibility.'

Shamed into reconsidering her stance, but with all her misgivings still very much in place, Maribel went straight back home and phoned Leonidas on his private number. Leonidas answered the call. The instant he heard her voice, he gave his PA a signal that his meeting with his legal team was on hold until he finished the dialogue.

'Maribel,' he murmured smooth and soft.

'All right, you can see Elias. I was being unreasonable. Just let me know when you would like to see him.'

A wave of satisfaction engulfed Leonidas and a rare smile banished the cold set of his lean, strong features. 'I'll send a car to pick you up in an hour. Okay?'

Maribel swallowed. The immediacy of that request disconcerted her and she would've preferred to stage the meeting on familiar ground. On the other hand, Ginny's warnings had unnerved her and she did not want to be awkward. 'It's short notice, but I don't work on Thursdays, so that will be fine.'

'You've pleased me, *glikia mou*,' Leonidas imparted with approval. 'I'll see you later.'

Maribel came off the phone with gritted teeth. She suspected that had she had four legs like Mouse Leonidas might have rewarded her with a pat on the head and a chocolate treat for her obedience. But surely that was better than being at odds with him? She pelted upstairs with Elias to get changed.

A vast limousine complete with an accompanying carload of what appeared to be security guards arrived to pick her up and filled her with dismay. So much for discretion! Fastened into his car seat in the palatial passenger area, Elias took a nap. Garbed in a turquoise skirt and top, Maribel sat with a mirror and did her make-up while attempting not to be impressed by the cream leather upholstery and the built-in array of entertainment equipment. It was some time before she appreciated that possibly she should have asked Leonidas where their meeting was taking place, because the limo did not head into London as she had expected. Her tension increased when the car swept down a long drive and a vast Georgian mansion appeared ahead. Surrounded by rolling parkland that was furnished with stately trees, it was as picture-book perfect as a film set for a historical costume drama.

Resolving not to be intimidated, Maribel balanced Elias on her hip and strolled into a hall the size of a small football pitch. A manservant spread wide a door for her entrance into an exquisitely furnished reception room. She paused to lower Elias to the ground because he was a little squirming, impatient bundle after being cooped up for so long in the car.

Leonidas saw Maribel first and was immediately distracted, for, as she bent over, the neckline of her top gaped to reveal the creamy swell of her full, rounded breasts. Lust took Leonidas instantaneously and infuriated him. Not for the first time, he wondered why it was that a slight provocative glimpse of Maribel's violin curves should have a more powerful effect on him than a full-on striptease. As she straightened, glossy chestnut tresses fanning back to reveal her vivid eyes and pouting raspberry-tinted mouth, he knew he was going to bed her again. But then as the child who had wandered behind her finally came into view and took his attention by storm Leonidas totally forgot what he had been thinking.

'He's so small,' he breathed gruffly.

Her mouth ran dry when she saw Leonidas. On the brink of pointing out that Elias was actually very tall for his age, Maribel also forgot what she was thinking. Leonidas, garbed in well-cut jeans and a coffee-coloured T-shirt teamed with a designer linen jacket, grabbed the entirety of her attention. Black hair brushed back from his brow, and dark, deep-set eyes intent on Elias below level ebony brows, Leonidas looked jaw-droppingly spectacular. Achingly handsome, fashionable and elegant. Suddenly she felt hot and underdressed—and horribly plain.

'Elias!' Maribel called as the little boy tried to climb

over the big square coffee table. He was at an age where he wanted to scale every obstacle in his path.

'Let him enjoy himself,' Leonidas told her with impatience.

The Pallis approach to parenting, Maribel thought, and then scolded herself for being prejudiced. Leonidas crouched down on the other side of the low table. Clambering upright, Elias gave him a huge grin and fell still halfway in his journey towards the elaborate flower arrangement that had attracted his attention. From several feet away, Maribel watched man and boy exchange eye contact. Elias was fearless and full of beans. Leonidas had only to open his arms for Elias to chuckle and run at him, sensing that fun was on offer.

'Man,' Elias pronounced with approval, for there was none in his world.

'Daddy,' Leonidas contradicted without hesitation, resting his broad shoulders back against the sofa behind him to allow Elias to scramble freely over him.

Maribel parted her lips to object and then sealed them shut again. Leonidas lifted Elias up and held him upside down above him. Elias was thrilled by that manoeuvre. Maribel watched in frank fascination while Leonidas, whom she had never seen make an uncool move in his life, engaged in horseplay on the rug with Elias. They ambushed each other round the sofa. Elias got rolled and tossed about and he clearly adored every minute of such robust handling. Feeling superfluous, Maribel sat down on the arm of a chair. She had expected to act as a connecting point, but neither her son nor his father required her encouragement to get to know each other. The discovery that Leonidas could relax to that extent with a young child astonished her.

'He's amazing,' Leonidas pronounced finally. 'What do I do with him now?'

Exhausted by all the excitement, Elias was draped over Leonidas now like a small crumpled blanket.

'He's ready to go to sleep.'

'No problem.' Leonidas vaulted upright. 'I've got a crib waiting for him upstairs.'

'Do you want me to carry him?'

'No. I need to learn how to manage him.'

'You're doing very well for someone who's not used to children.' Maribel accompanied him up the long, elegant stone-and-iron stairway.

'Elias is different. He's mine.'

The bedroom that contained the crib also contained a uniformed nanny, who could just as easily have competed as an entrant in an international beauty contest. A six-foot-tall Nordic blonde with a pearly smile, she took Elias and cooed over him while attending to him with an efficiency that could only impress. Even so, Maribel was dismayed at the speed with which Leonidas had acquired a member of staff to take care of Elias, and said so.

Leonidas shrugged. 'We have to talk. Elias has to sleep and he needs someone to watch over him. Diane has superb references. Loosen the apron strings, *glikia mou*.'

Maribel was mortified. 'Is that what you think?'

'I want to share the responsibility of raising Elias. Stop worrying. You're not on your own any more.'

'But I've managed fine on my own.'

Ignoring that defensive rejoinder, Leonidas rested a lean hand lightly at her spine and walked her to the end of the landing where a giant window overlooked a fabulous view of the parkland. He knew exactly what he was doing and he was determined to win her agreement. If everything went to plan, she and Elias would be flying out to Greece with him the next morning and he would be introducing his son to the family. 'What do you think of Heyward Park?'

'This place?' Her brow furrowed in bemusement. 'It's—it's magnificent.'

Leonidas turned her round to face him. The sudden intimacy in the air took her by surprise and she went pink, insanely conscious of his masculine proximity. His stunning dark golden eyes glittered in his lean, devastatingly handsome face. 'I would like you and Elias to make this your home.'

Shattered by that proposition coming at her right out of the blue, Maribel froze, her brain going into override while she attempted to work out exactly what he meant. But she could think of only one possible interpretation: he was asking her to move in with him! What else could he possibly mean? It was so typical of Leonidas to behave as though the most important issues were quite inconsequential. He understated, rather than overstated, with a dispassionate cool that few could match. 'Leonidas...' she tried to say, but her voice ran out of steam and croaked into silence again.

'Why not?' Leonidas murmured softly, staring steadily down at her while combing her luxuriant hair back from the sides of her face with surprisingly gentle fingers.

Her breath rattled in her constricted throat. He had never set up home with any woman before and she was very much aware of the fact. So were the newspapers and magazines that recycled incessant stories of how ruthlessly he ended his affairs and maintained his unfettered lifestyle.

But then, nobody had taken account of how the advent of one little boy might affect the Pallis outlook. 'You've really taken me by surprise.'

'You're not fighting me any more.' A charismatic smile curved his wide sensual mouth as she gazed up at him with anxious violet-blue eyes. 'I appreciate your generosity.'

Her heart was beating so fast it felt as if it were in her throat. He was only asking her to move in because of Elias. She couldn't accept on those terms; she couldn't possibly. Didn't she have any pride?

'And I also appreciate you *very* much, *glikia mou,*' Leonidas stressed as though he could read her mind. He lowered his arrogant dark head, his breath fanning her cheek. '*Se thelo*…I want you.'

Shaken by that additional declaration, Maribel blinked in confusion. It felt like too much too soon, but Leonidas was very decisive and he always moved fast. It would be stupid, she told herself, to expect a male as forceful an individual as he to behave like everyone else. The faint familiar tang of his cologne flared her nostrils, releasing an intoxicating tide of intimate memory. She felt weak, wicked. A little inner voice warned her to back off and she ignored it, ensnared by the frisson of anticipation coursing through her. He made her feel astonishingly good. He made her feel sexy. He made her feel totally unlike staid, sensible Maribel, and she would not have exchanged the high she was on at that instant for a fortune in gold and diamonds. It was crazy. He had not seen her in over two years and yet he was inviting her to live with him.

'Are you planning to slap me?' Leonidas husked, pressing his expert mouth to a tender pulse point just below her ear and almost making her knees buckle in the process.

Her clutching fingers curled round his lapel to help her

stay upright and tip him towards her. A low-pitched, sexy laugh was dredged from deep in his throat. He toyed with her mouth. She couldn't breathe for excitement, certainly couldn't think. Time hung in suspension while her heart hammered. His tongue slid moistly between her lips in a sensual plunge that stirred a shocking ache between her thighs. That cautionary voice at the back of her mind was jumping up and down and shouting now. *Stop, don't be stupid...it'll end in tears again!* But she could not resist the temptation he offered. Her disobedient fingers dug into his hair and held her to him as she kissed him back with passionate fervour.

Leonidas hauled her up into his arms with more haste than ceremony, as he was determined to take advantage of the moment. One of her shoes fell off and she giggled. She was all passion and high spirits, and he couldn't get enough of her in that mood. He hadn't been able to get enough of her that night he'd slept with her either. She had put a pillow down the centre of the bed and threatened to scream if he dared to cross it again. As he bore her off to the bedroom he was satisfied that he had played a winning hand. He had not been totally confident that she would agree to his scheme. Ninety-nine out of a hundred women would have bitten his arm off in their eagerness to say yes, but Maribel approached every issue with a shopping list of far from flexible expectations. Add in her old-fashioned streak, and when she dug her heels in it could take dynamite to shift her.

A door thudded shut somewhere. Maribel had yet to open her eyes again. He lowered her to a carpet that was soft and silky below the sole of her foot. She kicked off the remaining shoe and snatched in a jagged breath when he released her reddened mouth from the devouring onslaught of his. He was unbuttoning her cotton cardigan. Long brown fingers anchoring in her hair, he tipped her head back. 'Look at me,' he urged thickly. 'I've waited a long time to get you back into my bed.'

Her lashes lifted on dazed violet-blue eyes. Just like that occasion more than two years previously when she had thrown her principles in the rubbish heap, it was all happening too fast for her and doubts were piling up almost as quickly. He nipped at her tender lower lip with his teeth and made her jerk taut with delicious tension. But that tiny pleasure pain reunited her with rational thought and she muttered feverishly, 'Shouldn't we be talking about what you suggested?'

'Later…'

'But…isn't this a very big step for you?' Maribel prompted worriedly.

'*Ne*…yes,' Leonidas confirmed in husky Greek, uneasy with the topic, determined not to go there unless forced. He'd planned to ease her into the arrangement with every atom of guile he possessed and gloss over the imperfections.

'Are you sure about this? That we're what you want?' Maribel whispered with wide, anxious eyes welded to his darkly handsome face.

'Absolutely.'

'But I'm so ordinary,' Maribel muttered, still unable to credit that he was willing to offer her more than she had ever dreamt he might.

'*Filise me*…kiss me,' Leonidas urged, coaxing her lips apart to let his tongue dart with sinuous skill into the sensitive interior of her mouth and wreak havoc with her self-control. Irresistible sensation made Maribel shudder and a whimper of reaction escaped low in her throat.

By the time Leonidas set her back from him, she was trembling. Not quite knowing what to do, she hovered while he unclipped her bra. Last time she had had two glasses of wine, a lot of turbulent emotion and a sense of recklessness to get her to the brink of intimacy. But guilt and an unplanned pregnancy had given her an instinctive fear of her wanton inner woman and when the swollen bounty of her breasts spilled free of the lace cups his guttural groan of masculine approval only fired self-conscious crimson colour into her cheeks.

'You are magnificent, *mali mou*.'

Maribel still felt incredibly unsure of herself. But then he touched her with strong male hands and helpless physical response enfolded her, stopping her thoughts in their tracks. He moulded the firm creamy mounds and chafed the pouting pink buds that crowned them. His every caress sent tiny little tremors through her while a velvet knot of heat and anticipation uncoiled in her belly. He toyed with her tender nipples and lowered his mouth there to tease the lush, straining tips. Delicious tension gripped her until she was breathing in shallow little gasps, her entire body boneless with simmering, tingling pleasure.

'This is not how I imagined today would turn out,' she confessed unsteadily, a kind of wonder finally daring to blossom inside her and become joy.

Gorgeous golden eyes hot as flames on her oval face, Leonidas tipped her back on the bed. 'Set your imagination free. Today and every day can be what you want it to be now, *mali mou*.'

'Wish-fulfilment,' Maribel muttered, a slim hand curving to a long, powerful male thigh.

'My wish at this precise moment is to be very dominant,

and for you to lie there and allow me to pleasure you,' Leonidas husked in a roughened undertone.

He eased up her skirt in a slow, erotic manoeuvre and nudged her nerveless legs apart. She could feel herself melting like butter beneath a blow torch. Long before he could reach the sweet, damp warmth between her thighs, her excitement was at screaming pitch. Her languorous purplish-blue gaze clung to his bold dark features. 'This once,' she traded unevenly, 'I shall just lie here and think of living with you.'

Leonidas saw disaster hovering on the horizon and almost cursed out loud in his seething frustration. Avoiding the discussion of detail was one thing; lying an impossibility. He rolled over and pinned her in place beneath a muscular thigh. 'We won't be living together,' he murmured. 'This will be your home with Elias and I'll stay only when I'm visiting.'

Visiting? Maribel felt herself freeze in self-protection from the giant rolling wave of pain threatening her composure. Her sense of rejection was acute, but as nothing next to the awful sense of humiliation she experienced. She felt as though she had been slapped in the face with her own stupidity, for he had no desire whatsoever to live with her. He simply wanted to house his son in a luxury dwelling where he could conveniently visit him and occasionally enjoy a little recreational sex with his son's mother. By no stretch of the imagination was he offering her a normal relationship or indeed any form of commitment towards a shared future. Shutting her eyes tight, she tried to pull free of him.

'No…no, you're *not* bolting on me again!' Leonidas growled, catching both her frantic hands in his and pinning them above her head in one of his to hold her in place. 'Calm down.'

'I'm calm,' Maribel declared.

'I'm sorry if I misled you.'

'Let go of me,' she framed tightly between compressed lips.

'Sometimes I could stay the whole weekend with you. Maybe we could even share the occasional vacation,' Leonidas proffered, holding her wildly squirming body captive with the considerable weight of his own. 'It would be good. It would be a very efficient arrangement.'

The last drop of hope inside her died when he voiced that passion-killing word, 'efficient'. 'If you don't let me up, I'll scream.'

Leonidas would much have preferred a scream to the frozen tension of her face and the flatness of her voice. He coiled back from her with extreme reluctance.

Wrapping a screening arm over her bared breasts, tears burning like acid behind her lowered lashes, Maribel slid off the bed, snatched up her discarded clothing and headed straight for the adjoining bathroom. 'I'd appreciate it if you would wait for me downstairs.'

'*Theos mou*…why are you being so bloody unreasonable about this?' Leonidas demanded, vaulting off the bed in one powerful movement. 'Anyone would think I'd insulted you!'

Maribel almost lost her head with him at that point. Had there been anything suitable within reach she would have snatched it up and thrown it at him with vicious intent. Mercifully there wasn't, and she shut the door behind her and simply stared blankly into space. When was she going to learn to keep her distance? Only an idiot would have credited that Leonidas Pallis was offering her a serious live-in relationship. Her eyes burned as she fought back the tears with all her strength. She had almost ended up in bed with him again. Concentrate on the positive, her intelligence told her, not on your mistakes. She could not afford to let go of her emotions. She had to face him again, still had to deal with how two such disparate people—one of whom was a domineering, selfish, spoiled billionaire—could possibly share the upbringing of one little boy.

The instant Maribel entered the drawing room, Leonidas swung round, but before he could say anything she spoke. 'Let's just concentrate on Elias—'

'*Theos mou*, Maribel—'

'That's the only business we have to discuss. We should avoid anything of a more personal nature.'

Leonidas dealt her a fulminating appraisal. 'Elias is not business.'

'Elias is the only reason I am still in this house and speaking to you,' Maribel confided jerkily.

'Very well.' His strong jawline clenched. 'I would like DNA-testing to be done, not because I doubt that Elias is my son, but because there should be no room for any person to doubt that he is a Pallis.'

'All right,' Maribel conceded.

'I would also like your support in having his birth certificate changed to carry my name.'

'If you feel it's necessary.' Although Maribel was feeling totally devastated after what had happened between them, she was doing her utmost to conceal the fact. But it was a challenge to behave normally, when even looking at his lean, strong face actually hurt her. 'Anything else?'

'I'm attending a family wedding tomorrow in Athens,' Leonidas informed her. 'I would like you and Elias to accompany me as my guests. I plan to introduce him to my relatives.'

Maribel stiffened into the defensive mode she had been striving to hold at bay. 'We can't come. Apart from anything else, I'm working tomorrow—'

'I'll take Elias and the nanny, then,' Leonidas traded without hesitation. And she noticed, could really not help noticing, how quickly he was able to dispense with the concept of having her as a companion.

'He's too young to leave me and I won't agree to you taking him out of the country without me. I'm sorry, but that's the way it is for the present,' Maribel told him, her hands lacing restively together when she saw the grim tension tighten his fantastic bone structure. 'I will try to be reasonable in other ways, though. But I would ask you to think again about telling people that you have a son.'

'You have a problem with that, as well?' Leonidas shot back at her, his anger at that request palpable.

'I would prefer it to stay a secret for as long as possible. The press attention and public notice that it would generate could make my life with Elias very difficult.'

'That is precisely why I suggested that you live in one of my properties where your security needs can be met without fuss.'

'But we won't have security needs if you let your connection to Elias remain a private one. I would appreciate it if my life could go on the same way it always has—'

'That's no longer possible.'

'You're not being fair to me,' she protested.

'Less than half an hour ago—for the *right* offer—you were willing to surrender all autonomy over your life, your job and your child.' Leonidas voiced that reminder with derisive emphasis.

Maribel went white at the biting cruelty of that statement. The misunderstanding had mortified her, and only courage stiffened her backbone. 'More fool me,' she muttered with scorn. 'To believe, for even five minutes, that you would make that much of a commitment to either Elias or me! You don't even recognise when I'm trying to be generous—'

'*Generous?*' Leonidas threw up lean brown hands in forceful disagreement. 'When you even object to me taking him to my home in Greece? How is that generous?'

'You're lucky I'm still here after that sleazy proposition you put to me!'

'It was not sleazy. Naturally, I would prefer my son to live in a manner appropriate to his status. I want to take care of both of you.'

'No, you don't. You want the ability to play father any time you like at the cost of *my* freedom—oh, yes, and occasional sex. Was that to keep me happy? Stop me from looking around for long enough to give Elias a stepfather?' she demanded in disgust. 'Or was it just a power-play or a power lay? You *would* sleep with me because you *could*?'

Those twin offensive cracks about stepfathers and power lays sent raw fury roaring through his lean, powerful frame. 'I've offered you more than I have ever offered a woman,' Leonidas intoned with disdain, outraged by her attack.

'But not any kind of a promise that might curtail your freedom. And without that it was a rotten, lousy offer. Elias needs caring and commitment. I'm sorry, but there's no short cut and no quick fix to supplying those. Do you really think that a casual affair with your son's mother would give him a stable, happy home? It wouldn't last five minutes, and when it broke down Elias would suffer. You can't buy access to him through me.'

The coldness of displeasure had hardened the Greek tycoon's bold bronzed features. His dark, deep-set eyes were like black ice. 'I asked you once before not to make this a battle, for whatever it takes I will win.'

As no doubt intended, the threat Maribel perceived in that assurance slid like an ice cube down her rigid spine and settled in her belly, sparking nausea. Fear of losing her son sliced through her, and with it came fierce anger that he should dare to subject her to that level of anxiety. 'And you wonder why I wouldn't even consider letting you take Elias to Greece? Forget the DNA-testing and any change to his birth certificate!' she told him vehemently. 'You have just ensured that I will obstruct any claim you try to make on Elias.'

A white-hot blaze of wrath engulfed Leonidas. He strode forward, the chill in his gaze a formidable warning. 'I won't let you keep me apart from my son. It is madness for you to oppose me in this way. I expected much more from you.'

Stubborn as a mule in the face of intimidation, Maribel stood her ground and surveyed him with furious blue eyes. 'I have to admit that I'm getting more or less what I expected from you. You haven't changed.'

'But you still want me, *glikia mou*,' Leonidas countered silkily. 'I should have appreciated that your sexual compliance would have a major price tag attached. How ambitious are you?'

His sheer insolence made her palms tingle with incipient violence. 'Meaning?'

'Why not put your cards on the table? Were you hoping that I might eventually ask you to marry me?'

A brittle laugh of disagreement was wrenched from Maribel's tight throat. 'No! I don't live in fantasy land. But I must confess that only a wedding ring would now persuade me that I can trust you with my son.'

Leonidas dealt her a sizzling look of derision.

'That was a fact, not a suggestion,' Maribel told him tautly. 'Right now I'm very conscious that you could use your influence and financial power to put pressure on me, but I won't be intimidated. I'll still let you see Elias, but that's all. I don't trust you. I won't give you the chance to take him away from me. I will not let my child out of my sight for five minutes around you, or your employees!'

Leonidas was inflamed by those pledges. He was a responsible adult and Elias was his son. Her attitude incensed him.

A knock on the door interrupted the dialogue. It was Diane, the nanny, with Elias. Sleepy and fretful after waking up in a different room, the little boy held out his arms to his mother. 'Mouse…Mouse,' he muttered tearfully, seeking the security of the familiar pet.

'You'll see Mouse later,' Maribel soothed, folding him close.

'Is Mouse a toy?' Leonidas demanded.

'The dog. '

'You should have brought him.'

Maribel said nothing but almost heaved a sigh. Leonidas was a Pallis and from birth he had been accustomed to instant wish-fulfilment. People went to great lengths to please him and satisfy his every desire. That was not the way she wanted Elias to grow up.

'I'll show him the stables,' Leonidas drawled icily. 'He'll enjoy seeing the horses.'

Maribel nodded without looking near him. 'I'd like to go home at six. It's a long drive back.'

Elias wriggled and squirmed until she lowered him to the rug. He pelted across it to Leonidas and stretched up his arms to be lifted. Hoisted high, he chuckled with pleasure. Even though Maribel knew it was nonsensical, she felt rejected and hurt.

CHAPTER FIVE

LEONIDAS looked down at the old farmhouse as his helicopter flew over the roof to land in the paddock at its side. It was a filthy, wet, windy day and he was in an equally filthy mood. A month had passed since his war of words with Maribel at Heyward Park.

Since then, Leonidas had seen Elias on average twice a week, but it had taken a massive amount of planning to achieve that frequency and he still only managed to see his son for a couple of hours each time at most. Travelling back and forth to Maribel's isolated country home entailed considerable inconvenience and discomfort. Leonidas had not, however, uttered a single complaint. A saint could not have faulted his unfailing courtesy and consideration.

Yet Maribel avoided him during his visits, which made it impossible for him to achieve a better understanding with her. At the same time, his legal team's delicate efforts to negotiate more practical access arrangements had run into a wall of refusal. One month on, nothing had changed: he could see his son only at the farmhouse and could not take him out. He brooded on his conviction that Maribel was hoping he would eventually get fed up and go away.

The racket of the helicopter flying overhead drove

Maribel naked and dripping from the shower. Wrapping a towel round herself, she raced downstairs and found the telephone answer-machine flashing that a message had been received. She didn't waste time trying to listen to it. Evidently Leonidas had made a last-minute decision to visit and, of course, it wouldn't have occurred to him that she might have other plans. Elias, who had already worked out that the sound of a helicopter always signified the arrival of his father, was bouncing up and down as if Santa Claus were about to come down the chimney. She pelted back upstairs and dragged a comb ruthlessly through her wet hair while simultaneously pulling out clothes. She'd only got her panties on before the doorbell went. In feverish haste, she climbed into her jeans. The bell went twice more while she struggled to pull them up to fasten them at her waist. She ran out to the landing and bawled downstairs, 'Give me a minute!'

Elias was whinging with the same appalling impatience on his side of the front door. She yanked on a T-shirt and raced down barefoot.

'Thank you,' Leonidas drawled in a long-suffering tone.

Rattled by his inopportune arrival, Maribel made the very great mistake of allowing herself to look directly at him for the first time in a month of vigilant self-restraint. And that one imprudent glance at him knocked her sideways: he looked amazing. Raindrops glistened on his black hair and classic olive-toned features. His brilliant dark eyes glinted below heavy lashes, his strong masculine jawline and beautifully shaped mouth accentuated by the faint bluish-black shadow where he shaved. Her tummy not only flipped, but performed a series of rapid somersaults.

'I wasn't expecting you—I was in the shower,' she

mumbled, fighting a belated defence action with all her might. Stop it, stop right now, her inner voice of sense was warning her. Don't look at him and don't respond to him, he's pure poison and heartache in a very dangerous package.

'Didn't my staff contact you?'

'I only came home ten minutes ago. I haven't had time to check my messages yet.'

'Your mobile?'

'Forgot to charge it.' As Maribel turned away to close the door his attention was hooked by the distinctly erotic ripple of her voluptuous breasts, which were moulded to perfection by a T-shirt that clung so lovingly to her damp skin that he could see the swell of her pouting nipples. His lean, well-built body reacted with rampant male enthusiasm. He could not shake the deep inner conviction that if he just got her back into bed everything would be perfect.

Maribel watched Elias clawing his way up Leonidas's trouser-legs like a mini-mountaineer. Elias already adored his father. Helped up to chest level, the little boy wrapped two plump arms round Leonidas and covered his face with enthusiastic kisses. He was a very affectionate child, but Leonidas was unused to such physical demonstrations of warmth and liking. The first time Elias had kissed him, Leonidas had frozen in shock. But now Leonidas was trying to reciprocate with occasional awkward hugs. It hurt Maribel to watch, as she knew that Leonidas didn't know how to show or return affection because he had not received it as a child. If anyone was capable of teaching Leonidas how to love another human being, it was her son. That was good, that was healthy. Unfortunately, the more signs of attachment Maribel saw developing between father and son, the more fearful she became of what Leonidas might do in the future.

Maribel would not let herself look again at Leonidas because she was fiercely determined to detach herself from feeling any personal response to him. She had a date, she reminded herself furiously; she was going out on a date in just over an hour. Sloan was an attractive, eligible guy, a research assistant, only a couple of years older than she was. Until Leonidas had arrived, she had been looking forward to the prospect of adult company.

Mouse the wolfhound peered out from below the table and whined in excitement. On his belly, he crawled into view with his long tail banging noisily on the floorboards in a show of ingratiating fervour. Once all of his long grey shaggy body had emerged, Leonidas tossed him a dog treat in reward. Mouse guzzled it down and fixed adoring doggie eyes on his new idol. Maribel didn't think that Leonidas had ever had anything to do with dogs before, either. But once he had registered how important Mouse was to his son, Leonidas had mounted an edible charm offensive to lessen the animal's terror of strangers. And, in common with most challenges that Leonidas set out to meet, he had achieved his goal with brilliance. Bribery, Maribel reflected grimly, worked even in the canine world.

'I have to talk to you,' Leonidas murmured with quiet insistence. 'I can't stay long. I have a flight to catch in a couple of hours.'

'That's good because I'm going out.' Maribel managed a stony smile in his general direction, while remaining wildly and insanely conscious of his every tiny movement. He was so graceful he literally drew the eye to him, and that was even before she noticed the faint husk of his breathing and the dark chocolate tones of his deep sexy voice. 'What do you think we need to talk about?'

Leonidas took up a commanding stance by the fireplace. 'You have to trust me not to try and take Elias away from you.'

'How can I?' Dismay at the directness of that opening salvo made Maribel fall still. 'You've never shared anything in your life; you've never had to. You are number one in all your relationships. It's the Pallis way.'

'Naturally I have to share my son with his mother. I am not an idiot,' Leonidas traded dryly.

'But I'm not doing what you want me to do. Sooner or later, you might persuade yourself that you're entitled to *all*, rather than half, of your son and you could decide to write me out of the picture. You will assure yourself that I have brought that misfortune on myself by my unreasonable behaviour.'

'Where do you get the idea that you know how I think? Or what I might do?' Leonidas demanded with freezing disdain.

Yet, if truth were told, Leonidas was disconcerted by her ability to tap into the deep vein of ruthlessness that powered his aggressive instincts. But he was angered by her flat refusal to accept that Elias stood outside the usual parameters his father observed. Why had she yet to notice that he was making a laudable and heroic effort to put Elias' needs, rather than his own, first?

'Seven years of watching you operate from close up and from a distance?' Maribel shot back at him tightly, torn by conflicting impulses, for when she heard that sincere note in his voice, and watched him unbend with Elias and laugh and smile, she found it hard to say no to him and even harder to police his every move. But two weeks earlier she had taken the precaution of seeking legal advice from a very expensive London solicitor. He had pointed out that Leonidas had almost unlimited power and influence and had advised her to watch over Elias at all times; the law would be of little help if her son were to be taken to a country without a reciprocal agreement to respect UK law.

Leonidas settled level dark, deep-set eyes on her. 'I will give you my word of honour that I will not attempt to remove him from your care.'

Framed by dense black lashes, his eyes had stunning impact, a strong and charismatic key to the level of his sleek, darkly handsome attraction. No matter how hard she tried, her heart was hammering behind her ribcage and her gaze stayed welded to him even as her cheeks burned with colour. 'I can't trust you. I'm sorry. I can't. He means everything in the world to me.'

'He needs you. He's still a baby. I understand that,' Leonidas intoned, strolling lithely closer.

Maribel grew so tense her knees trembled beneath her. 'But he won't always be a baby and I can't keep on changing the rules.'

'If you insist on making rules I'll break them or go round them, *mali mou*,' Leonidas imparted huskily, dark eyes shimmering slices of golden enticement below his lashes. 'I'm made that way.'

'But as I found out that time that you stayed with me in Imogen's house when we were students,' Maribel muttered in a breathless rush, like a deer with a lion stalking around it in an ever-decreasing circle, 'you can follow rules beautifully if it suits you to do so.'

'Maybe I was scared you would slap me again.' The

sexual provocation of his slow-burning smile was an erotic work of art.

Her mouth ran dry. A pulse seemed to be beating low in her tummy. Excitement was building, tensing her every muscle. And then she remembered Sloan and she went into instant retreat, ashamed and angry over her weakness in Leonidas' vicinity. 'I have to get ready. I have a date.'

Lean, hard-boned face taut, Leonidas frowned. 'You have a *date*?'

Still backing, Maribel nodded in vigorous confirmation. 'So if you don't mind I'll go back upstairs and leave you with Elias.'

The atmosphere was heavy, ultra-quiet.

'Okay?' Maribel pressed uneasily.

Pale beneath his bronzed skin, Leonidas fixed his attention on a distant point beyond the window. She had taken him by surprise. But what took him even more by surprise was the tide of anger flooding him. 'Who is this guy?'

'I don't think that's any of your business,' Maribel almost whispered.

Leonidas thought of several very unreasonable responses to that statement. He relived the insulting way in which she had backed away from him. Had that ever happened to him with a woman before? His lean, strong features darkened and set in hard, angular lines. He had been tempted to yank her back to him. He reminded himself that it was not his way to be possessive with a woman. But then Maribel was different, he reasoned just as quickly. Maribel was in a class of her own. Surely it was understandable that he found the very idea of his son's mother becoming intimate with another man deeply objectionable? Elias was tugging at his raincoat now to get his attention. Leonidas had to make an effort to show an interest in the toy train being extended for his admiration. Thinking of how her boyfriend might get to spend time with his son gave Leonidas another cast-iron reason for loathing the whole concept of such a relationship.

His silence in response to a defiant answer shook Maribel rigid, but she didn't quarrel with the reprieve. She hurried away to get dressed. Keen to avoid Leonidas, she even painted her nails to use up more time. Only when she heard Ginny's car pulling up outside did she hasten downstairs to answer the door.

As Maribel reappeared Leonidas glanced up and, in ten seconds flat, minutely catalogued the amount of effort Maribel had made to prepare for her outing. Much more effort than she had ever made for his benefit, he decided, lethal antagonism building on the anger still seething below his unemotional surface. In fact, she had gone to town on her appearance: perfume, chestnut hair straightened into a smooth fall round her pale pink luscious mouth, a pastel girlie top, peach-tinted nails, shapely legs on view in a swirly skirt, sexy high heels.

'This is Ginny Bell, my friend and neighbour who will be looking after Elias while I'm out. Ginny, this is Leonidas Pallis.'

Only when Maribel spoke did Leonidas take note of the woman who had followed her into the room. He rose silently up to his full height. The dark-haired older woman by Maribel's side was staring at him as if she couldn't quite believe her eyes. Agitated as a jumping bean, Maribel watched Leonidas switch on his effortless social charm and wondered anxiously why he had gone so quiet with her earlier. If he was displeased, quietness was in no way typical of Leonidas. Ginny was bowled over by him, couldn't hide the fact and chattered. Leonidas soon established that Maribel was attending a wedding party and was expected home late, so Ginny was staying the night. His mood was not improved by that information, or by the enthusiasm with which Maribel rushed outside before her date could even get his car door open and put in an appearance.

When Leonidas left five minutes after Maribel's speedy departure, rage was sitting like a hard black stone at the heart of him and consuming more of his thoughts with every second that passed. As he headed back to the helicopter Vasos called him on his mobile. His bodyguards, who had watched the farmhouse while he was inside, converged on him.

'I've had a tip-off,' his security chief told him. 'A tabloid newspaper has a lead on Dr Greenaway and the child. You have the connections to kill the story at this stage.'

Shrewd intelligence glittered in Leonidas' hard dark eyes. He pictured the farmhouse under siege by the paparazzi. The press would go crazy: A SECRET HEIR TO THE PALLIS BILLIONS? There would be no place to hide from the storm of publicity and speculation. Maribel would need his help to handle that attention. She would also need somewhere to stay, for there was no way that she could be adequately protected in her current location. Before she knew where she was, she would be putting down roots at Heyward Park, alongside Elias and Mouse and the moth-eaten poultry collection. Satisfaction at that prospect lifted the chilling shadow from his lean, strong face.

'I don't want the story killed.'

'You *don't*?' Vasos was startled, as he was well-acquainted with his employer's loathing for the endless press coverage of his private life.

'We'll use the same source to feed back certain facts. I'll sue if there's any hint of sleaze. Dr Greenaway and my son will also require surveillance and protection from this moment on.' Having referred for the first time to Elias as his son, Leonidas slid his phone back in his pocket. He knew he was being a bastard. But Maribel would never find out. What she didn't know wouldn't hurt her. All that mattered was the bottom line.

In the early hours of the following morning, Maribel slid her shoes off her aching feet, locked up and crept upstairs as quietly as she could.

Tired and disheartened, she acknowledged that she had faked her every smile with Sloan. From the moment Leonidas had arrived and stolen her attention, her chances of having a good time with Sloan had gone downhill fast. She hated herself for the fact. But the relentless pull of Leonidas' attraction had broken through her barriers again.

As she got into bed she reflected that Imogen had never got over Leonidas either and losing the entrée to his exclusive world had devastated her. Only near the end of her cousin's life had Maribel learned that it was Leonidas who had persuaded Imogen to enter rehab; not only had he paid for it, but he'd also settled all her debts at the same time. Only after Imogen had twice abandoned her treatment programme had Leonidas stopped returning her calls.

His grim reserve on the day when Imogen had been buried had warned Maribel that he was finding the occasion a trial. That was the day when she had finally realised that she was surprisingly good at reading Leonidas, who struck other people as utterly unfathomable. At the funeral, she had also noticed his aversion to sycophantic strangers and the women trying to chat him up. He had spoken to her several times while assiduously ignoring everyone else.

Her aunt had asked her to go on and clear out Imogen's house. By then, Maribel had had her own apartment, although she had often stayed with her cousin to look after her. In fact, during that last year, all Maribel's free time had gone into watching over her troubled relative. After the funeral, Maribel had felt bereft, and when she'd reached the house she'd found it in a mess: Imogen's sisters had already sacked her wardrobe and rummaged through every cupboard, taking what they wanted, leaving Maribel to tidy up and dispose of what was left. Maribel had wandered round the silent house and, when she'd come on some old photos, had cried unashamedly while allowing herself to remember the good times.

Leonidas' arrival had been a total bolt from the blue.

'I knew you would be here. You're the only one who genuinely cared about Imo.' Sombre and magnificent in his black suit and overcoat, Leonidas skimmed a knuckle gently across Maribel's tear-streaked cheek and frowned down at her in reproof. 'You feel like ice.'

'I left my coat at my aunt's and the house is cold.'

With a ceremonial flourish, Leonidas removed his coat and draped it round her shoulders. He signalled one of the men stationed by the limo and addressed him in Greek. While she hovered in bewilderment, the gas fire in the front room was lit.

'You should have a brandy.'

'The drinks cabinet was cleaned out a long time ago.'

Leonidas issued another instruction. Within ten minutes

she was sipping a brandy and warming up inside and out. She was further disconcerted when he began talking about the first time Imogen introduced him to her. He was the only person who seemed to understand the depth of her attachment to her cousin.

'Why are you here?' Maribel finally asked.

'I don't know.'

And Maribel saw that he didn't recognise or understand the grief and sense of regret that had prompted him to come to Imogen's house and talk about the past. His incomprehension of his own emotions somehow pierced her to the heart that day.

'It was an impulse,' he finally added. 'You were very upset at the funeral.'

Afterwards, she told herself that the brandy she'd drunk went straight to her head. Of course, there'd also been the exhilaration of Leonidas' full attention and the delight of almost drowning in the sensuality of his kiss. How they'd got upstairs to the guest room that had once been hers, she could not recall. Nothing had seemed to matter but the moment. For a few brief hours she had discovered a happiness more intense than any she had ever known. But the next morning she'd felt terrifyingly scared and oversensitive. His mocking request for breakfast, as though they had shared only the most casual encounter, had hurt like salt in a wound. But had she learnt even then?

No, she had raced out to buy food, as there had been nothing to eat in the entire house. But it had been a foggy morning and, before she'd even reached the supermarket, someone had rammed their car into the back of hers and she'd been injured. It had been hours before she'd recovered consciousness in a hospital bed.

* * *

Two days later, Maribel was wakened by the doorbell.

Assuming it was a special postal delivery, she sighed and got up. The phone started ringing as she opened the door. It was a shock when a bunch of people she had never seen before began running across the lawn towards her shouting and waving cameras. She slammed the door shut again so fast she bashed a microphone being extended towards her.

Her mind blank with shock, she snatched up the phone.

'It's Ginny. My sister phoned me. There's a front-page story on you and Elias in *The Globe*!'

'Oh, no!' Maribel stared in horror at a man peering in through the living-room window at her. She flew over to close the curtains. 'There's a crowd of people in the garden. They must be reporters.'

'I'm coming over. You can't possibly bring Elias to me this morning.'

Someone was knocking on the back door. Every window seemed to have a face at it. She ran around frantically closing curtains and blinds. The phone rang again. It was a well-known female journalist asking if Maribel wanted to sell her story for a substantial cash payment.

'I mean, from what I can see,' the woman commented cheekily, 'Leonidas Pallis isn't exactly keeping you in the luxury you deserve.'

That call was followed by another of a similar ilk, and then she unplugged the phone. Elias had climbed out of his cot and seated himself at the top of the stairs to await a storm of maternal protest over his athletic achievement. Big dark brown eyes alight with curiosity, he watched his mother race about instead in a panic. A hand rapped on the narrow window beside the front door. Maribel ignored it, but nerves were making her feel nauseous. The hubbub outside her quiet and peaceful home horrified her. Mouse would be having a panic attack in his kennel with all those strangers around.

As she pulled on her clothes at speed she peered out through the side of her bedroom curtains and fell still in surprise. Three large thickset men in smart suits were practising crowd control and forcing the photographers to back away from the house itself into the lane. She recognised one of the men as a member of Leonidas' security team. How had they got here so fast? Not that she wasn't grateful for the support, she conceded ruefully.

Her mobile buzzed while she was trying to keep Elias in one place long enough to get a pair of trousers on him. It was Leonidas.

'I understand the press are harassing you, *glikia mou*,' he murmured with audible sympathy.

'It's a nightmare! But your men are out there making them stay back from the doors and windows, which is quite an improvement,' Maribel confided in a rush, feeling in charity with him for the first time in weeks. 'I'm amazed that your bodyguards were able to get here so quickly.'

'The paparazzi are very persistent. You won't find it easy to shake them off. It's a big story.'

'Fortunately, Ginny will be here soon to look after Elias, and now I have the protection of your heavy mob. I'm going to work in half an hour.'

At the other end of the line, Leonidas almost groaned out loud at her innocence. Like a little train on a single track, Maribel would stick stubbornly to her routine, no matter what happened. 'They'll follow you there. Some of my staff will take you. I don't want you trying to drive with those guys tailing you.'

'No, thanks for the offer. But bodyguards would stick out like a sore thumb,' Maribel told him gently.

'I think you may find it very difficult to remain at your home. It might be a good idea to consider a move to Heyward Park.'

Maribel stiffened. 'I don't run at the first sign of trouble, Leonidas.'

'You can't keep Elias locked up out of sight for ever.'

At that salient point, Maribel's face shadowed and she came off the phone in an even more troubled mood.

Ginny arrived while she was giving Elias his breakfast and settled a newspaper on the table. 'There's the article. I decided to buy a copy before I came over. Let me finish feeding Elias. Where did the heavies come from?'

'Heavies? Oh, Leonidas' security men.'

'I should've guessed. They're very professional. They checked me out before they would let me approach the door. It's bedlam out there, though. I don't envy you trying to go to work with a posse behind you.'

BILLIONAIRE BABY BOY! the headline screamed. Maribel was too busy reading the lead story to respond to her friend. An old photo of her taken some years earlier at one of Imogen's parties made her eyes widen. She wondered how on earth it had been obtained and the more she read, the more confused she became. Instead of the shock-horror lies, half-truths and errors she had expected, all her background details were correct, right down to the little-known fact that her late father had been an award-winning scientist who'd chosen academia over financial gain. She was described as a long-standing and trusted confidante of Leonidas Pallis and she rolled her eyes to the ceiling, wondering who had dreamt up that whopper. When had Leonidas ever confided in anyone?

'The article is all right,' Ginny commented. 'It's surprisingly tame and kind. You sound like a cross between Einstein and Leonidas' best friend.'

'It's a disaster,' Maribel muttered wearily. 'I'll never be taken seriously again in the ancient history department.'

Her friend gave her a wry look. 'Don't underestimate the effect of having a very close connection to one of the wealthiest men in the world. Some of your colleagues will be deeply envious and others will suck up to you. Anyway, it's time you went to work. Elias will be safe here with me and Leonidas' men.'

Maribel found it a real challenge to leave her home and drive away with cameras popping and flashing and questions being shouted at her. When she arrived at the department there were more journalists waiting. A crowd began forming around her before she even got upstairs to her office. Even people she knew were stopping and staring and she hated every minute of the attention. Her small tutorial group was uneasy with the number of interruptions that occurred. She couldn't concentrate either. When she emerged from her office in the late afternoon, she had to almost force her passage back out to her car, which was surrounded by photographers urging her to give them a chance to take a decent picture of her. By the time she got away, her hands were trembling on the wheel and her brow was damp with perspiration. Her heart sank when she turned up the lane to her house and saw that there were even more paparazzi encamped than there had been at the start of the day. She was very grateful when the Pallis security team cleared her path to the house.

Ginny was still sitting behind closed curtains in a dim interior. Mouse was now indoors but in a pitiable state, shaking all over and refusing to come out from below the table. Elias had curled up with the dog. Maribel picked him up and cuddled him.

'I'm rather puzzled about something,' Ginny remarked. 'I made coffee for the bodyguards. What do you think I found out?'

'Tell me.'

'One of them let drop that they were detailed to work here the day before yesterday.'

Maribel gave her friend her full attention. 'But that's not possible.'

'Someone must've known in advance that that story was in the pipeline. Leonidas' men were here ready and waiting for the balloon to go up.'

Maribel became very still. It was as if the circuits in her brain were connecting to show her an unexpected pattern. Mental alarm bells began jangling. One too many inconsistencies in recent events forced her to reconsider all of them. Leonidas had been remarkably mild about the paparazzi invasion, and astonishingly tactful and unassuming when he had merely suggested that she should consider moving into his Georgian mansion. Mildness, tact and humility were not typical Pallis traits. In addition, the personal information in the article had been staggeringly accurate and the tone unusually benevolent. That she should suspect Leonidas of prior knowledge and even of having had a hand in destroying her anonymity struck Maribel as appalling. But the suspicion also roused her furious indignation and a strong need to know the truth beyond all doubt.

'Ginny…could you bear to stay here alone with Elias until later this evening?' Maribel asked tautly. 'I need to see Leonidas.'

CHAPTER SIX

MARIBEL was in the private lift being wafted up to Leonidas' office in the Pallis building when her mobile rang. It was Hermione Stratton, and her aunt was in a virulent fury.

'Is it true that Leonidas Pallis is the father of your son?' Hermione demanded in a furious voice of disbelief.

Maribel winced; she had always feared that that revelation might annoy the older woman. 'I'm afraid so.'

'You sly, scheming little witch!' her aunt condemned shrilly. 'He couldn't possibly have wanted you. You couldn't hold a candle to Imogen in looks or personality!'

That verbal onslaught from her closest relative gutted Maribel. 'I know,' she responded gruffly. 'I'm sorry that you've been upset by all this.'

'Don't make me sick! Why would you be sorry? That little boy must be worth a fortune to you! You've been a very, very clever young woman.'

'I think I've been rather stupid,' her niece contradicted in a pained undertone. 'I didn't plan this. This is not how I wanted my life to turn out.'

'Don't you dare get in touch with anyone in this family ever again!' the older woman warned her in a vitriolic rant. 'As far as we're concerned, from this moment on, you're dead.'

After those harsh words, Maribel was pale as snow. She had hoped that time would soften her aunt's attitude to her son and could now see no prospect of that. The lift opened onto a private vestibule. A male PA ushered her into a huge office and informed her that Leonidas would join her when his early-evening meeting had finished. The tall windows displayed the most amazing views of the City of London, lights twinkling against the backdrop of a ruddy sunset. The furniture was contemporary and stylish. First and foremost, however, it was an efficient, custom-designed workspace. Leonidas never mixed business with pleasure. He would probably be less than pleased at her uninvited descent on his business empire.

'Maribel…' Lean, mean and magnificent in a tailored grey pinstripe suit that was enlivened by a red tie, Leonidas wore a rare expression of concern on his darkly handsome features. In a disconcerting move, he crossed the room and reached for both her hands. 'You should have told me that you wanted to see me. I would have sent a helicopter to pick you up. How are you?'

He was a class act, she acknowledged abstractedly, never stuck for the right word for the occasion. In collision with his brilliant dark heavily lashed eyes, she felt positively dizzy. As always, he looked amazing and he made her feel detached from reality, breathless, on the edge of thrills too wicked and wonderful to even think about without blushing. Yet, she had only to think of her son and there was murder in her heart when she gazed back at Leonidas.

'You're being nice because you believe you've won.

You think I've come running all this way in search of your support, don't you?' Maribel bit out shakily, powered by rage and wounded pride.

'Isn't that what I'm here for?' Leonidas surveyed her with resolute cool and satisfaction, for he could think of nothing more appropriate than that she should demand and expect his assistance. Her independence in a crisis infuriated him. 'You've had a very distressing day.'

Maribel snatched her hands free of his in a gesture of rejection. 'Isn't that how you planned it?'

His ebony brows drew together. 'Naturally not.'

'But you were the instigator of that story in *The Globe*,' Maribel fired at him without even pausing to draw breath. 'You were behind it. No, don't you *dare* lie to me!'

Displaying a disturbing amount of confidence in the face of her livid attack, Leonidas lounged back against his designer desk with lithe grace. 'I have never lied to you.'

Maribel spun away from him, literally so angry she couldn't speak. But even turned away from him she could feel the power of him. Nobody could be around Leonidas without becoming aware of the extent of that strength and power. 'The article in the paper was too precise. All the facts were right and there were no scandalous revelations.'

'There is no scandal in your life,' Leonidas pointed out gently. 'Apart from me.'

Angry, incredulous suspicion had brought Maribel to London to confront Leonidas. At the very core of her, though, there had still been room for healthy doubt and an acceptance that sometimes a chain of coincidences could give a misleading impression. But she had accused him and he had not yet voiced a word of denial in his own defence.

Not one single word. The meaning of his silence on that score was finally sinking in on her.

'You did mastermind it—you *were* behind that story about us,' she whispered unevenly. 'It's hard for me to accept that even you could be that selfish and destructive.'

Leonidas was determined not to rise to the bait. He hoped he was not unreasonable: Maribel was entitled to feel aggrieved and he was prepared to let her get that out of her system. While curious as to how she had worked it all out so fast, he was by no means surprised by her swift grasp of the truth. Shimmering dark-as-ebony eyes screened, he scrutinised her, admiring the natural pink of her cheeks and the generous curve of her mouth. Long before he got as far as the ravishing swell of her abundant breasts, his groin was tightening. He was disconcerted by the speed of his response.

'The paparazzi were already onto us,' he pointed out.

'There is no us!' Maribel shot back at him angrily.

'Are you saying that because you're seeing someone else? And don't tell me that's nothing to do with me,' Leonidas urged. 'It is relevant to this situation.'

'I'm not currently involved with anyone else,' Maribel admitted grudgingly.

'Whether you like it or not, we have a connection through our son,' Leonidas asserted in the same outrageously quiet tone. 'How long did you think I could keep on flying down to see Elias without attracting attention? He could not be kept a secret indefinitely, *glikia mou.*'

'I disagree—'

'But—with respect—you don't know what you're talking about. You don't live in my world. It's a goldfish bowl. Even with all my staff and security, my movements are watched and noted in the gossip columns. Sometimes it is wiser to handle the press and shape what is published. The alternative is often a hatchet job, and I felt that when it came to you and my son a sensitive PR spin on the facts was preferable.' Leonidas viewed her with immense calm. 'I stand by that decision.'

Her violet eyes blazed with resentment. She could not credit the extent of his nerve. 'Stop wrapping it up and trying to pretend that you did it to protect us! You weren't planning to tell me the truth and you don't seem to understand or care how much damage you've done!'

At that condemnation, his chiselled jawline clenched. 'I appreciate your annoyance.'

'Like you appreciate me as "a confidante"?' Maribel slammed back at him with scornful force.

The faintest hint of dark blood demarcated the superb slant of his cheekbones. 'You're angry, but my intentions were good. I'm not ashamed of Elias. He's my son. I'm proud of him. I refuse to hide him.'

A shaken and humourless laugh was dredged from Maribel's lush pink lips. The most colossal sense of bitterness was overtaking her. 'And what about our lives? That aspect didn't matter to you, did it? But my privacy has been destroyed and you had no right to do that. I will for ever be associated with a tacky one-night stand and you—'

All relaxation jettisoned, Leonidas strode forward. '*Theos mou*—that night was neither of those things.'

Maribel wasn't listening. 'Wasn't it enough that I let you see Elias? Does everything have to be your way?'

'I want both of you in my life on an open and honest basis,' Leonidas informed her boldly.

'And if you can't get what you want by asking, you'll fight dirty?' Maribel was starting to tremble with rage. 'All you've done is prove is how right I was to distrust you. I'm finished with you, absolutely, totally finished. I gave you a chance and you blew it—'

'You, not I, made this a fight. I won't walk away from either of you.'

'You've been walking away from women all your life and, right at this moment, the son that you pretend to value so much is hiding under the table with the dog!' Her blue eyes were glistening with wrathful tears of condemnation, her anger all-consuming. 'Elias doesn't understand why I'm unhappy, why the curtains can't be opened, why it's dark, why it's so noisy outside, or why he can't go out to play the way he usually does. He's scared and he's upset. You are his father and you did that to him today.'

Leonidas had paled below the healthy bronze of his complexion.

'And why did you do it?' Maribel breathed fiercely. 'Because you are an arrogant bastard, who can't see past winning. Well, today, you lost, Leonidas. You scored a spectacular own goal. I can't trust you. I'm afraid now. You're a threat to me and to my son. You'd have to marry me to see Elias again.'

His ebony brows snapped together. 'What the hell are you talking about?'

'Because that's the only way I could ever feel safe letting you have access to him again! I don't have the resources or the connections to stand up to you. Only a wife could fight you on the same level. As we both know, that's not going to happen, so please leave us alone. With a bit of luck the paparazzi will then get bored and go away. I have no wish to live in the public eye.'

Leonidas was stunned by her attitude. 'You can't bar me from your lives.'

'Why not? I've seen what you can do with your money and your influence. It's my duty to protect my son and I can't compete with you—'

'Elias does not need to be protected from me!' Leonidas closed his hands over her narrow wrists to prevent her backing away from him.

'Doesn't he? What sort of an influence will you be?' Maribel almost sobbed, for rage and sorrow had melded into a combustible mix inside her. 'You own dozens of houses, but you've never lived in a proper home. Even as a child you didn't have rules, you just did as you liked. You had a miniature Ferrari and your own race track at ten years old. You can't give Elias or teach him what you never knew yourself.'

'If you move in Heyward Park and stop being so stubborn and difficult, *mali mou*,' Leonidas breathed in a raw undertone, 'I might learn. That is, if I have anything to learn, and I am not convinced that I do.'

Scorching dark golden eyes blazed down into hers and sentenced her to stillness. There was a sob locked in her throat and a maelstrom of emotion fighting for an exit inside her slim, taut figure. She would never be happy in a casual living arrangement of that nature. He was an addiction she needed to cure, not surrender to. While she adored Elias, she believed that she would have been happier had she never met his father. 'I want my life back. A clean break.'

'No.' Long brown fingers meshed into the fall of her

chestnut hair to angle her head back. He brought his arrogant dark head down and grazed the tender skin of her throat with his lips and the edge of his teeth. Her every skin cell jangled into vibrant, energetic life and an achingly sharp pang of pleasure-pain tightened low in her tummy.

For a split-second Maribel wanted Leonidas so much it hurt. In a devastating burst of intimate images she recalled the passionate weight of his lean, strong body over hers that night in her cousin's house. A passion that had cost her so much she was still paying for it. Just as quickly she remembered her aunt's verbal attack. When was enough enough? Stinging tears at the back of her mortified eyes, she mustered her self-discipline and she pulled free of him. Her oval face was pale and tight with self-control.

'No,' Maribel told him in flat refusal. 'You're bad news for me.'

No woman had ever told Leonidas that he was bad news before.

'I've said all I've got to say.' Maribel walked back to the door, all churned up inside and frozen on the outside. 'Stay away from us. I don't owe you anything. Only a few weeks ago you didn't know Elias existed and you were perfectly happy and content. I wish you had never come to visit me. You lifted the lid on Pandora's box.'

Leonidas stared with brooding intensity at the space Maribel had so recently occupied. She had walked out on him—*again*. Savage frustration roared through his big powerful frame. So, he had got it wrong. Badly wrong. It was exceedingly rare, but he had made a mistake and he was prepared to acknowledge the fact. Why was she always judging him? Even worse, finding serious fault? Walking away, refusing to compromise or even negotiate?

What did it take to please Maribel? If it was a wedding ring, she was destined to disappointment, he reflected harshly, dark eyes hard as iron. What kind of blackmail was that? His chilling anger was tempered, however, by the picture he could not get out of his head—his son taking refuge beneath the table with that pathetic dog. It felt very much like an own goal and that galled him. But what honed his anger to a gleaming razor edge was the knowledge that without Maribel's permission he could not even see Elias.

A week crept past on leaden feet for Maribel.

She was surrounded and ambushed by paparazzi at home and wherever she went. At her request, the police restricted the press presence to gathering at the foot of the lane, but she was still afraid to take Elias into the garden lest a stray photographer pop up from behind the hedge or the fence. She was also tormented by the fear that she had been unfair to Leonidas who, after all, was what he was because he had been horribly neglected as a small child.

In Maribel's opinion, his late mother, Elora Pallis, had had no more notion of how to be a parent than a shop-window dummy. An only child, the volatile heiress to the Pallis fortune of her generation, Elora had racked up four marriages and countless affairs before she'd died of a heart attack in her mid thirties. Non-stop scandal and drug and alcohol addiction had ensured that Elora was a poor mother to the daughter born while she was still a teenager and the son born three years later. Leonidas had only found out who his true father was after the man had died. He had received little in the way of love, attention or stability. When he was fourteen, he had gone to court to demand legal separation from his capricious mother and had moved in with his grandfather. Within three years, however, his mother, his older sister and his grandfather had passed away leaving him alone. And alone was what Leonidas had been ever since, Maribel conceded heavily. At least, until he had met Elias.

Eight days after their London meeting, Leonidas strode into Maribel's office in the ancient history department when she was labouring over a timetable.

'Leonidas?' she queried in stark disconcertion, rising hurriedly upright behind her cluttered desk. Her heart was pounding uncomfortably fast because her once rock-solid nerves had taken a real battering since the paparazzi had begun chasing her around.

Although the lean sculpted face was austere and his dark, deep-set eyes hard as granite, his breathtaking attraction still made the breath catch in her throat. 'If marriage is the only way, I'll make you my wife.'

Shock took Maribel by storm as this was not a development she had foreseen. 'But I wasn't serious…I was only making my point.'

Leonidas looked grimmer than ever and unimpressed by her claim. 'Elias is a powerful incentive. I'm suggesting a business arrangement, of course.'

'Of course,' she echoed, not really sure she knew what she was saying, or indeed what she was feeling, beyond a sense of unreality. 'How could a marriage be a business arrangement?'

'What else could it be? I want access to my son. I want him to have my name. I want to watch him grow up. You won't share him without a wedding ring. I recognise a deal when I get offered one, *glikia mou*.'

'But that's not what I meant. I simply want what is best for Elias.'

Leonidas elevated an imperious brow. 'Yes or no? I will not ask twice.'

Maribel thought very fast. If she married him, she would be giving him legal binding rights over Elias, but she would be around to curb any parenting excesses and watch over her son. If the relationship went wrong she would at least be able to afford the services of a good lawyer. Those were the practical considerations, but what about the personal ones? A business arrangement could only mean that he was talking about a platonic relationship.

Those acquainted with the fabled Pallis cool and control would have been astonished to learn that, at that precise moment, Leonidas was hanging onto his temper by a very slender thread. He had just done what he had always said he would never do: he had proposed marriage. A gold-digger would have accepted before he even finished speaking. A woman who cared about him would have displayed some generous and warm response, he reasoned fiercely. But what was Maribel doing? Mulling the offer over with a serious frown on her face!

Marrying a guy who didn't love her, and who would probably despise her for marrying him on such terms, would not be a ticket to happiness, Maribel ruminated ruefully. It would be a stony road full of disappointments and hurts. So, what was new? On the other hand, if she was destined never to love anyone else, she might as well be with him as be without him. Surely any marriage would be what *she* made of it? Looking to Leonidas to make a constructive matrimonial input would be naïve and foolish.

It would be like unlocking a lion's cage and expecting the predator to come out and behave like a domestic pussycat. Leonidas had had no positive marital role models. Not only did he not have a clue, but she would have to contend with the unhappy truth that he had no intention of changing.

'Yes,' Maribel said gravely. 'I'll marry you.'

'With reservations?' he derided softly.

'Plenty,' she admitted without hesitation. 'I'm a realist and you're unpredictable.'

Leonidas studied her with brooding dark eyes that now glittered like ice crystals. 'I want the wedding to take place in three weeks.'

Maribel blinked. 'Only three weeks from now? For goodness' sake, Leonidas—'

'It'll get it over with. My staff will make the arrangements.'

Maribel worried at the soft underside of her lower lip, her eloquent eyes veiled to hide her discomfiture. *It'll get it over with.* She now knew all she needed to know about Leonidas' view of marriage and it did nothing for her self-esteem.

'I'm off to New York tomorrow,' Leonidas imparted. 'It'll be at least two weeks before I'm back in the UK. I have other stuff to take care of. If you and Elias come to London today, I'll be able to spend some time with him before I leave.'

'Yes…all right.' Her agreement was swift for she had never felt comfortable about keeping father and son apart.

'You'll be spending the night with me.'

Her soft lips parted as though she would have said something, but then finding her mind blank of inspiration, she closed her mouth again. For an instant, she thought he might just mean that she was to stay beneath the same roof, but there was an intimate light in his brilliant eyes that told her otherwise. A dulled flush of awareness illuminated her creamy skin. 'Just like that?'

'I'm not waiting for the wedding night,' Leonidas told her with disdain.

But Maribel was rather confused, for she had reached the conclusion that the marriage he was suggesting was one of convenience alone. 'A business arrangement that includes…er…*sharing a bed*?'

'Think of it as a deal sweetener, *hara mou*.' Leonidas advised, smooth as the most expensive silk. 'Once you've shared my bed, I know you won't back out on me.'

Maribel veiled her expressive gaze, lest he see the growing bewilderment etched there. A marriage that was a business arrangement—of the most intimate sort? And why would she back out? She was not in the habit of last-minute changes of heart. For possibly the first time it dawned on her that Leonidas did not trust her either, and she was surprised by how hurtful she found that discovery.

Long brown fingers tipped up her chin. 'Have we a deal?'

Hot enough to feel as though she were burning up, Maribel gave him a self-conscious nod of confirmation. He lifted her hand and she watched in surprise as he slid a magnificent ruby and diamond ring onto her engagement finger. The jewels shone with dazzling brilliance. 'If I have to do this, I'll respect the conventions,' he breathed curtly. 'This, like the wedding, is part of the surface show.'

Any thrill she might have received from the ring was swiftly squashed by that assurance. It did not even feel like a personal gift; it felt more like a prop she was being allowed to wear for the sake of appearances. 'I'm amazed that you care about the conventions.'

'But you do, and when I say I'll do something, I do it right and I deliver on my side of the bargain.' His keen, curiously forbidding gaze whipped over her taut and troubled face. 'I hope you're equally thorough in the wife stakes.'

Blue eyes sparkling violet at that challenge, Maribel suppressed her misgivings and murmured, 'No doubt you'll soon tell me if I'm not.'

Without warning an appreciative grin slashed his perfectly shaped masculine mouth, instantly putting to flight his icy aura of unapproachability. He bent his handsome dark head and, for a split-second, she actually thought he might be about to kiss her. But he frowned instead and checked his watch. 'A helicopter will pick you up at home at two.'

Maribel nodded slowly. She was so stunned by the idea of marrying him that she was in a daze. 'This doesn't feel real yet.'

Leonidas dealt her a caustic appraisal. 'It'll feel real soon enough. A word of warning—I'll make a lousy husband.'

With that attitude, Maribel believed that this was very probable and she wondered if she was mad to have agreed. After all, he was only willing to make that commitment for his son's sake. The door flipped on his exit, only to be caught before it could close again. Her tutorial group trooped in. She spared a glance down at the enormous ring. It was really exquisite. But essentially meaningless, she reminded herself doggedly, determined not to succumb to any silly flights of fancy.

CHAPTER SEVEN

THE penthouse apartment that Leonidas occupied in central London seemed gigantic to Maribel. A manservant led her across the vast limestone floor of the striking foyer and ushered her into an even bigger reception area.

In the doorway, she set Elias down on his feet. He looked adorable in pale blue cord trousers and a little cotton shirt. Before her eyes could adjust to the bright daylight that flooded in through the long run of windows that comprised the farthest wall, Elias loosed a squeal of excitement and yanked his fingers free of his mother's grasp.

'Daddy!' he yelled, sturdy little legs carrying him across the room in seconds.

A vision of casual elegance in a loose beige linen shirt and chinos, Leonidas scooped the little boy up and closed both arms round him. He was startled by the tide of emotion coursing through him. Elias gave him a big soppy kiss and then struggled to get down again, eager to investigate the mysteries of a strange room.

'He missed you. He asked for you a couple of times,' Maribel admitted guiltily.

Leonidas studied her with keen attention. She had that

refined quality of quintessential Englishness that he had always admired and never quite managed to define to his own satisfaction. Her lustrous chestnut hair was a shining frame for her delicately modelled features and, while her outfit was plain, her simple blue dress threw her violet eyes into amazing prominence. She had a subtle unusual beauty as authentic as her lush sex appeal and he could not understand why it had taken him so long to acknowledge the fact. After all, she had always had the most disturbing knack of immediately attracting his attention even in a crowd.

'Why are you staring at me?' Mirabel muttered uneasily, wondering if she should have used more make-up and put on fancier clothes

'I like the dress, *hara mou*. Of course, I'll like you even better out of it,' Leonidas confided, his dark, rich drawl taking on a husky edge. 'By the way, how has the boyfriend dealt with the relentless pursuit of the paparazzi?'

Her cheeks flaming at that unashamed reminder of the night ahead, Maribel veiled her gaze at that question and jerked a slim shoulder in silent dismissal. Sloan hadn't phoned again and she didn't blame him for the fact. The amount of press interest she was currently drawing, not to mention the exposure of her association with Leonidas, would have scared off the keenest of blokes. The last time she had seen Sloan, he had been gaping in horror at the spectacle of her trying to outrun the photographers to make a fast getaway in her car.

Leonidas got the message that the competition had been decimated and he returned his attention to Elias with a sat-isfied gleam in his dark gaze that would have chilled a block of ice. In the best of humour, he introduced Elias to the toy ride-on car he had bought for him. Elias was ecstatic and got straight into making noisy vroom-vroom sounds and punching the horn and an array of tempting buttons with vigour. While Leonidas was trying not to flinch at the racket, he found himself wondering if Maribel had slept with the boyfriend. He wondered in some bewilderment why he was wondering, but it was far from being the end of that disquieting thought-train, because he was soon wondering how many men there had been since she'd walked out on him two years and two months earlier. Although he continued to devote his attention to his son, all Leonidas' relaxation and satisfaction had drained away.

Lounging back on a gilded sofa with her shoes kicked off for comfort a few hours later, Maribel watched Leonidas roll out a convoy of boats for his son's bath-time entertainment. For a Greek tycoon, whose fortune was based on a vast shipping empire, she supposed an entire fleet was a natural choice, and, certainly, Elias was impressed. Quite deliberately, Maribel was staying in the background. She had tried to leave father and son alone for a while, but Elias, for all his apparent confidence, still needed to check that his mother was present every so often. On the one occasion that Maribel had dared to rove out of sight, her son had shocked Leonidas by screaming the place down. Yet Leonidas was marvellous with Elias and comfortable playing with him. In fact, Leonidas was demonstrating a level of patience and calm with his son that Maribel had never dreamt he possessed.

She was in a guest bathroom large enough to run to several pieces of furniture in addition to the usual fixtures. A stray glimpse of herself in a mirror on the nearest wall made her tense. Her face was pink because she was warm, her hair tumbled, the illusion of straight, smooth locks destroyed by the damp atmosphere that was reviving her natural waves. She stared in dismay, thinking of how ordinary she looked against the grand backdrop, how incongruous a match she was for Leonidas with his jaw-dropping good looks. The idea that she had been fighting day and night since Hermione Stratton's upsetting phone call crept in: Imogen would have looked so much more at home.

For a dangerous moment, Maribel pictured her late cousin, garbed in a designer frock and reclining along the same sofa. With her curtain of silvery blonde hair draped across one shoulder and a mocking smile on her beautiful face, Imogen would have maintained a flow of entertaining chatter. Amusing men had come naturally to her cousin. It was only thanks to Imogen that Maribel had ever met Leonidas Pallis, and if Leonidas had not decided he needed company after Imogen's funeral, Elias would never have been conceived. A sharp pang of discomfiture and unhappiness attacked Maribel as she made herself confront those humiliating truths.

Springing upright, Leonidas hit the call button on the wall and opened the door to Diane, the nanny, whom he had summoned to take over. While Elias was distracted by the new arrival, Leonidas bent down to close a hand over Maribel's and tug her off the sofa and out into the corridor.

Dragged without warning from her troubled thoughts and her comfortable seat, she spluttered, 'I left my shoes in there—'

'You won't need shoes where you're going,' Leonidas told her bluntly.

'But Elias—'

'He's falling asleep sitting upright! But if he kicks up

a fuss, Diane will call us, *hara mou*.' As Maribel hovered indecisively Leonidas scooped her up into his arms to forestall further protest.

As a manservant stepped back against the wall out of his employer's path, Maribel felt totally annihilated by embarrassment. 'Leonidas, it's barely eight o'clock in the evening!' she hissed in a frantic whisper.

'I like to take my time.' Coming to a halt in a spectacular bedroom, Leonidas slid her slowly down the length of his long, lean body.

Just as quickly, brought into lingering physical contact with his strong muscled frame, Maribel was intensely conscious of his potent masculinity. As her breasts rubbed against his broad chest their sensitive peaks tingled. Her stomach grazed the hard, flat slab of his abdomen and his big hands welded to the generous curve of her hips to bring her even closer. Registering the rampant evidence of his desire sent a wanton thrill of anticipation winging through her. Her cheeks flushed with fiery colour, she hid her face against his shirt. It was still damp from Elias' antics in the bath, but Leonidas had the body heat of a furnace and the linen was drying fast. The hard-muscled warmth of his lithe, powerful form and the intrinsically familiar scent of his skin filled her with a sensual awareness that left her legs as weak as matchsticks.

Long fingers speared through her tumbled amber coloured hair to tug her head back. 'I like your hair longer—the way you used to have it. Grow it for me,' Leonidas instructed softly.

'You can't tell me how to wear my hair,' Maribel told him tautly.

'Why not?' His level dark golden eyes didn't leave hers

for a single second. For emphasis he scored her cheekbone with a reproachful forefinger. 'Don't you want to please me?'

'Do you want to please me?' she dared.

'*Ne*—yes, but I don't need any pointers, *mali mou*.'

'But you think that I do?'

'You can't learn if I don't teach you,' Leonidas countered soft and low, his tone eminently reasonable.

'This doesn't sound like much of an equal partnership.'

'I'm a Greek. I have a traditional outlook. So you grow your hair again,' Leonidas repeated, impervious to hints. 'It will be charming.'

His powerful gaze held her as effectively as a chain round her ankle.

'Is this, like, Lesson One in the How-to-be-a-good-little-Pallis-wife course?' Maribel dared unsteadily.

'If you want to think of it that way.' Cupping her *derrière*, Leonidas lifted her against him. 'But there haven't been any good little wives in my immediate family for a long time.'

She was holding her breath even before he bent his handsome dark head and claimed a devouring kiss. Sensation ravished her senses. She found the taste of him utterly seductive. There was a delirious intimacy to the way he made love to her mouth. Tiny shivers darted up and down her spine. Her hands clenched as she held back out of pride from just grabbing him. With the tip of his tongue he explored and delved in the tender interior until she was pushing back against his lean, hard body in helpless, gasping response.

Leonidas pulled free, scanning her with hot golden eyes before he spun her round. He was struggling to rein back his desire, as it had naturally occurred to him that her walkout more than two years earlier might have been her understandable reaction to a less than successful introduction to sex. Although she had acted as though everything was amazing, he was uneasily aware of her predilection for politeness. That sliver of doubt that he had buried since their love-making was beginning to haunt him again because, if that was the problem, he wanted to know. He ran down the zip on her dress and skimmed it very slowly down over her arms while he used his expert mouth to trace a pattern across the tender skin at the nape of her neck.

'Oh-h-h…' Trembling, Maribel closed her eyes and let the tiny little shivers of delicious response ripple through her and gather momentum. At that instant, she could not find an ounce of decent resistance or restraint. Her knees were wobbling. She was melting from inside out.

'I'll make it spectacular, *hara mou*,' Leonidas told her.

A surge of love laced with reluctant amusement overwhelmed Maribel: Leonidas would never knowingly undersell himself.

'Maybe it wasn't quite spectacular the last time,' Leonidas breathed without warning.

Her dreamy eyes shot wide in surprise and she whispered uncertainly, 'I never said that.'

Leonidas was tense. He noticed that she was not contradicting him and he wondered why the hell he had embarked on such a dialogue. It was not his style. 'You were a virgin. It was unlikely to be perfect.'

Maribel flipped round in the circle of his arms and before she could think better of the impulse said, 'I thought it was.'

Dense black lashes lifted on his tawny eyes. 'The first time?'

Even that first times she realised helplessly, but she

didn't think he needed or deserved that ego-boosting information.

Leonidas saw no reason to enquire further. *Perfect?* That rare and very disturbing moment of sexual self-doubt evaporated like a bad dream. His tension banished, he crushed the rosy pouting curve of her lips under his and sent her dress shimmying down to her ankles in a superbly choreographed manoeuvre that came very naturally to a male of his extensive experience. Disposing of the band of lace covering her lush, creamy breasts, he backed her down onto the big bed before she had even registered it was gone.

'You're seriously good at this stuff,' Maribel told him helplessly, feeling shamefully exposed and wonderfully decadent at one and the same time.

Shedding his shirt, Leonidas sent her a wolfish smile that was pure provocation. She watched him stroll back to her and her breath tripped in her throat. He was beautifully built, with wide, bronzed shoulders, a hard, muscular chest and long, powerful legs. He paused to peel off his trousers. The aggressive bulge of his arousal was clearly delineated by his boxers and burning pink blossomed in her cheeks. She felt she should look away and she couldn't. Tantalising heat tingled between her thighs and she pressed them together guiltily. That night, at Imogen's house, she had not even seen him undress, for things had got out of hand incredibly fast after he'd kissed her. They had made love in the dark, on top of the bed, still half dressed, too wild with passion and impatience to take their time. Never in her life had she imagined she could be like that with a man, feel like that, or even behave like that. It was only now that she was even allowing herself to remember how it had been.

Leonidas studied Maribel with raw masculine appreciation. She was all creamy opulence and soft ripe curves. He noticed the abstracted look in her gaze. 'What are you thinking about?'

'That night…er…at Imogen's house.' His unexpected question drew a more honest answer from her than she would have given, had she had forewarning.

'You ripped my shirt off me, *hara mou*…' His smouldering appraisal flamed reflective gold.

'Did I?' Maribel mumbled in a stifled tone, since she had hoped that he had long since forgotten that kind of detail.

'It was mind-blowing…it was the hottest sex I ever had.' After the unchallenged passage of that all-forgiving word, 'perfect', Leonidas was finally willing to concede that fact.

Cheeks fiery, Maribel studied her bare feet.

Leonidas came down beside her and pulled her close with a possessive hand. He lowered his tousled dark head to the inviting swell of her glorious breasts. He teased a straining rosy crest with his lips. He pressed her back and flicked his tongue skilfully over its twin to coax an ever stronger reaction from her. Her fingers sank into the silky black depths of his hair and she gasped, her throat extending. There was a throbbing pulse at the slick centre of her body, beating out the longing that she had suppressed since they were last together. Now her ability to hold back her hunger was being destroyed piece by piece.

'I want my tigress back, *mali mou*,' Leonidas husked, nipping at the base of her ear with his even white teeth, guiding her hand down to the hot velvety length of his erection.

Her slim fingers flexed round his hard male heat. A

sense of vulnerability and the dread that she might be in danger of giving away too much warred with her desire. She truly loved touching him, and adored the intimacy and the thrill of sending him out of control. But, in the aftermath of the one night they had shared, she had also fallen victim to a whole host of humiliating fears. Had she been too bold? Too clumsy in her inexperience? Too keen?

Leonidas groaned out loud. Hot pleasure was shot through with the sudden darkling suspicion that she might have been practising. Anger stirred and sharply disconcerted him, forcing him to shut out the thought. Even so, he slid out of reach of her ministrations.

'What's wrong?' Concerned eyes as purplish a blue as violets questioned him.

'Nothing.' But Leonidas was uneasy with the disturbingly irrational thoughts and responses assailing him. Highly intelligent and pragmatic by nature, he rejoiced in the benefits of cold logic. He had never felt possessive of a woman in his life.

There was hurt and confusion in Maribel's gaze now. With a stifled curse in Greek, Leonidas drove her reddened lips apart in a ravenous kiss that sent her anxiety flying like skittles out of sight and out of memory. Each plunge of his tongue only stoked her yearning higher. A little clenching frisson low in her pelvis made her press closer to him, seeking relief from the ache thrumming at the heart of her desire. She was quivering with that almost agonising awareness long before he removed her last garment to discover the damp, delicate folds beneath.

'*Se thelo*…I want you, *hara mou*,' he breathed in a driven undertone.

'I want you too,' she whispered feverishly.

A whimper of sound halfway between protest and delight was wrenched from her when he stroked the most sensitive place of all. Very soon, she was lost in the dark, pulsing pleasure that he unleashed. Perspiration dampening her creamy skin, she writhed in moaning response to the flood of erotic sensation of which he was so much the master. She was caught up in the irresistible surge of exhilaration. Her blood was hammering through her veins, her heart pounding. Bewitched by his touch, in thrall to his strong sensuality, she was all liquid warmth and seething frustration. Her desire reached a bitter-sweet edge of torment for she could not bear to wait another moment for fulfilment.

In that same instant, Leonidas slid between her thighs. Supplication in her passion-glazed eyes, she was shaking and shivering, pitched to an almost painful pinnacle of need. He entered her at the peak of that longing. Bold and powerful, he forged an entrance into her hot, wet sheath. A surge of ravishing sensation engulfed her for the feel of him within her melting flesh was exquisite. He kissed her and she responded with all the wild passion consuming her. He delved and teased her mouth with his tongue while he took her with long, hard thrusts. She was delirious with a pleasure beyond anything she had ever felt. Excitement flamed through her slim body like a ravenous fire that consumed every ounce of energy and thought.

When she felt the urgent tightening at the very centre of her, she sobbed his name. A split second later she was flung from the whirlpool of passion over the edge into rapture. Dizzy and out of control, she tasted ecstasy and abandoned herself to the rippling tremors of shocking delight that seized her. It seemed like for ever before she felt earthbound again.

'Leonidas,' she mumbled, and in that period of quiet joy and respite all her barriers were down. She did what she wanted to do and gave way to the love she kept locked away inside her. She wrapped her arms round him and hugged him tight. She smoothed his damp hair, landed a kiss on just about every part of him within reach and sighed happily in blissful contentment.

Engulfed in that flood-tide of appreciation, Leonidas froze for an instant, and then he almost laughed, for his son was equally affectionate. In a rather abrupt movement for one so graceful, he pressed his lips in a fleeting tribute to the corner of her mouth and rolled free of her. Almost immediately, however, he reached out across the space between them to close a hand over hers. She turned her head and gave him a huge smile.

Familiarity tugged a cord of memory and his ebony brows pleated. 'Do you know? Until this moment I didn't realise that you resemble Imogen, but now I have seen the family likeness.'

'Have you?' Maribel was sharply disconcerted by that unexpected remark and very surprised, as it had never occurred to her that she was in the least like her cousin. Suddenly she felt as if a giant ice cube had settled in the warm pit of her belly and she lay very still and tense.

'It's not obvious,' Leonidas added lazily. 'I think it's more a trick of expression. Your smile reminded me of her.'

Maribel kept on bravely smiling at that news, even though she felt much more like crying. The coolness inside her was spreading like clammy shock through her limbs and chilling her to the bone. In what way could she possibly resemble the late and very beautiful Imogen? She scarcely needed to be told that it could only have been a trick of expression. After all, Imogen had been six inches taller with classic features, long blonde hair and a slender, perfect figure that looked fabulous in even the most unflattering outfit. When Hermione Stratton had pointed out that Maribel could not compare to her late daughter in looks or personality, she had only spoken the truth. Maribel had always accepted that reality. But she was totally devastated when the man she loved told her that she reminded him of Imogen. Had Leonidas slept with her the night that Elias was conceived, purely because of her elusive similarity to her late cousin? In short, had Leonidas been much more attached to Imogen than Maribel had ever been prepared to acknowledge? Slowly, she eased her limp fingers out of his.

A silence stretched that was heavy and long and when the phone buzzed it sounded incredibly loud. Darkness having chasing the gold from his hard gaze, Leonidas sat up in an impatient movement and reached for it. He switched from English to French. 'Josette?'

Maribel also spoke fluent French and she had no trouble working out who the female caller was. Josette Dawnay, the supermodel, was, according to popular report, one of Leonidas' long-term lovers. A gorgeous brunette with reputedly the longest legs on the catwalk, she had most recently accompanied Leonidas to the Cannes film festival. Her risqué reputation had only been heightened by her well-documented loathing of wearing undergarments with the very short skirts that she favoured.

'At your apartment?' Leonidas murmured sibilantly. 'Why not? I won't make it much before ten, though.'

Maribel breathed in so deep, she felt light-headed. It did not clear the leaden sensation of nausea coiled in her sensitive tummy. She scrambled out of bed. She crawled over the floor, got her dress, forced her way into it and stood up, wriggling violently to do up the zip. All the while, Leonidas talked in idiomatic French and watched her with cool dark eyes as though she were the floor show put on to entertain him.

As she straightened and walked round the side of the bed he murmured, 'What *are* you doing now?'

Maribel said nothing. She lifted the water decanter from the cabinet and upended it on his lap.

With a growl of disbelief, Leonidas sprang out of the bed and finished his call. As magnificent naked as a bronzed Greek god, he shook off water and surveyed her with outrage. 'What the hell is this?'

'You've had your deal sweetener and that's as far as it goes. I think you could term this the cooling-off period. If you decide that you still want me to marry you, we need to get one fact straight beforehand,' Maribel breathed with ringing scorn. 'I will not sleep with you while you are sleeping with other women.'

'*Theos mou*…you presume to dictate terms to me?' Leonidas raked at her with sizzling bite.

'Don't be so prejudiced. This could well be the best offer you've ever had, so think long and hard before you refuse it,' Maribel advised, violet eyes flashing with angry warning. 'Let our marriage be platonic and I will ignore your affairs, because I will not consider you to be my husband. Insist on anything more intimate and I will watch your every move and make your life hell if you betray me!'

'Even as my wife, you will not tell me what to do,' Leonidas intoned with all the chilling assurance of his forceful, arrogant character. He stared at her as she reached for the door handle. 'Walk out of this bedroom before morning and I will be angry with you, *hara mou.*'

'Then you're going to be angry.' After listening to that dialogue with Josette Dawnay and having her every worst fear fulfilled, Maribel was too indignant and upset to linger beneath his shrewd scrutiny. 'I'll check on Elias and sleep in one of the other rooms. Goodnight.'

'As you wish.' His lean, darkly handsome face set in forbidding lines of condemnation, Leonidas made no further attempt to dissuade her from leaving.

Maribel went in to see her son, who was slumbering peacefully in his cot. Exchanging a valiant smile with Diane, who had appeared in the doorway of the connecting room, she departed again. She chose a bedroom just across the corridor and closed the door behind her. She felt dead inside, but her mind was going crazy throwing up wounding thoughts and images.

Reality had burst the bubble of her foolish illusions and she felt that she only had herself to blame. Hadn't Leonidas been honest from the outset?

For business arrangement, read marriage of convenience, she thought heavily. He would continue to have his casual mistresses—the stunning, sycophantic tribe of high-profile women who provided him with sexual variety in his travels round the world. Maribel would wear his ring and raise his son and pretend that it didn't matter that she had nothing else. But just then she knew that what she didn't have, what *he* wouldn't give *her*, would matter very, very much to her...

CHAPTER EIGHT

MARIBEL removed a petal from the flower. 'I love him.' That petal dropped like a little stone to the gravel below the stone seat. 'I hate him,' she breathed and several petals came off in unison and fluttered further afield in the breeze that was blowing across the rose garden. Mouse and Elias scampered past her, chasing along the elaborate maze of box-hedged paths with noisy enjoyment. Maribel ended her idle game with the flower on a note of hatred that made her superstitiously tear that final petal in half before she cast the stem aside.

Nobody needed to tell Maribel that hatred was the dark side of love, but she could not have told a soul at the moment what was in her heart. Yet her wedding day was fast approaching. The event had been so pumped up by press speculation and excitement that she had been forced to take advantage of the privacy on offer at Heyward Park. At his father's country house, Elias could at least play without the threat of a camera lens suddenly zooming out of the shrubbery. The level of curiosity about the most junior member of the Pallis family was alarmingly strong.

Maribel was also virtually homeless since an attempted break-in at the empty farmhouse had left her with no

choice but to agree to the removal of all her personal possessions. The university term had ended and she had
cleared out her desk after handing in her notice. She was
shaken by the speed at which her comfortable, quiet and
secure life had been dismantled. Indeed, the pace of change
engulfing her had left her more than a little shell-shocked
and she was feeling the strain.

In just three days' time it would be too late to back out
of becoming a Pallis, Maribel reflected fearfully. It was
most unlike her, and she had never been a coward, but sometimes she just felt like scooping up Elias and running for
her life. She covered her face with cool hands and breathed
in slow and deep. She couldn't do that to Leonidas; she
couldn't jilt him at the altar just because she was absolutely
terrified that she might be making a very big mistake. He
was so proud, he would never get over the insult. In any
case, everything was organised to the nth degree, right down
to the fabulous designer wedding dress and a string of little
Greek flower-girls and page-boys selected from Leonidas'
extended family circle. Under pressure, Ginny had agreed
to act as her matron of honour, and Maribel had felt forced
to accept the offer of Imogen's sisters, Amanda and Agatha,
as bridesmaids. They were the only family she had left. Had
she snubbed them, it would probably have caused embarrassing comment in the local papers and she knew she owed
her aunt and uncle more than that.

Ginny had accurately forecast how association with a
billionaire might affect the people around Maribel. No
sooner had word of the engagement been made public
than the Strattons had landed *en bloc* on Maribel's doorstep
to mend fences. Her aunt had thought better of cutting off
all contact with a niece on the brink of marrying one of the

richest men in the world. But the Stratton family had decided to acknowledge Elias somewhat too late in the day to impress Maribel and she had felt horribly uncomfortable with such a calculating parade of insincerity.

Her state of mind had not been helped by the fact that she had scarcely seen Leonidas. Since their mutually dissatisfied parting before his trip to New York, Leonidas had been colder than ice. He had spent most of the intervening weeks abroad and had only returned to the UK twice for fleeting visits to see Elias. She did not flatter herself that a desire to see her had figured on his agenda. His scrupulous politeness and reserve had warned her that marriage promised to be an even bigger challenge than she had feared, for he had the resistance of granite towards any attempt to change him. But, on balance, she did know that he very definitely wanted the wedding to go ahead. How did she know that? Well, certainly not by anything he had said, Maribel conceded ruefully.

Every day, Maribel had scoured every magazine and newspaper and had failed to find a single photo of Leonidas with another woman. This was so highly unusual that she could not believe it was a coincidence. For the first time in his notoriously racy existence, Leonidas appeared to be embracing a low social profile. Even the gossip columns were commenting on his new discreet lifestyle and laying bets as to how long it would last. But Maribel could have given them the answer to that question: until *after* the wedding.

It was her belief that Leonidas had decided not to rock the boat until they were safely married and he had finally acquired equal rights over the son he loved. That was surely why he had made the effort to phone her every day. He had also sent her gifts so lavish they took her breath away. On the phone he talked about Elias and did not deviate, even if she tried to throw in a tripwire. Anything more exciting than the weather got him off the phone fast, which she found counter-productive because even when she was furious with him she liked listening to the sound of his voice.

On the gift front, however, she was doing very nicely indeed, and had riches been her sole motivation she would have been ecstatic and ready to sprint down the aisle. To date, she had acquired designer handbags, sunglasses, a watch, a fancy phone, fabulous luggage, a diamond pendant, a superb pearl necklace and matching earrings, two paintings, a sculpture, a jewelled collar for Mouse, a Mercedes car—with the promise of a personalised version to arrive in the near future—the latest books, sundry female outfits that caught his eye. No, Leonidas was not afraid to shop. And so it went on: the gift-giving that she saw as a substitute for what he would not or could not say. To be fair to him, he was very generous, but he was also accustomed to buying loyalty, soothing wounded feelings and pleasing people with the spoils of his wealth. Spending money cost him a lot less effort than other, more lasting and demanding responses.

After all, Leonidas knew why she was angry with him, but he had yet to make the smallest attempt to explain himself or set her fears to rest. The evening she had known he would be with Josette Dawnay, Mirabel had lain awake all night in an absolute torment of anger, jealousy and hatred. She had tortured herself by surfing the net to scrutinise photos of the gorgeous model. A kind of terror of the future had gripped her when she had appreciated that if she married Leonidas and he insisted on his freedom, the torture she was undergoing would just go on and on and on with a series of different faces in the role of rival. Only, how could any normal woman even consider trying to compete with such fantastically beautiful women?

'Dr Greenaway? You have a visitor.' A staff member appeared at the entrance to the rose garden and Maribel stood up in haste, since any distraction from her troubled thoughts was welcome. 'Princess Hussein Al-Zafar is waiting in the drawing room.'

For a moment, Maribel was confused by the impressive title and then a huge smile chased the tension from her soft mouth. Pausing only to gather up Elias and Mouse, she headed back into the mansion at speed. Tilda Crawford! Tilda and her husband, Crown Prince Rashad of Bakhar, had been the only names that appeared on both bride and groom's guest lists. Maribel had been relieved and delighted when she had received an acceptance. Although Rashad remained one of Leonidas' closest friends from his university days, Maribel was aware that Tilda and Leonidas had only ever mixed like oil and water.

Maribel and Tilda had met when Tilda had come to one of Imogen's parties and taken instant refuge in the kitchen when Leonidas had walked in. 'Sorry, I can't stand that Pallis guy,' Tilda confided flatly. 'I once dated a friend of his and, because I worked as a waitress, Leonidas treated me like a gold-digging tart.'

Maribel had found that indifference to Leonidas' status, spectacular good looks and wealth extremely attractive, and she and Tilda had become friends. Since Tilda had married her prince, however, and settled into royal family life abroad, the two women had had little contact. Maribel was guiltily aware that she was partially responsible for that, because the prospect of having to tell Tilda that Leonidas was her son's father had seriously embarrassed her.

'Tilda!' Maribel smiled warmly at the stunningly lovely blonde woman awaiting her arrival. She had paused only to see Mouse into his hidey-hole below the hall table—placed there for that purpose—and hand Elias over to the attentions of his nanny.

Turquoise-blue eyes sparkling, the princess moved forward to greet her. 'Maribel—it's wonderful to see you again.'

'Oh, my goodness, I suppose I should've curtsied, or something. I quite forgot your royal status!' Maribel grasped Tilda's outstretched hands and gave them an affectionate squeeze.

'Don't be silly. That stuff is only for public occasions,' Tilda scolded. 'Is …er…Leonidas here?'

Aware of the other woman's tension, Maribel was quick to reassure her. 'No. You're safe. Leonidas is still abroad.'

Tilda gave her a guilty look of apology. 'Is it so obvious that I want to avoid him? I'm sorry—how horribly rude I'm being!'

'You and he never hit it off. Don't let that come between us,' Maribel told her with complete calm. 'Now how long can you stay for? We have so much to catch up on.'

A tray of tea and delicate little nibbles was brought in and served.

'I was really disappointed that I couldn't come to your wedding in Bakhar,' Maribel confided. 'It wasn't possible for me to leave Imogen at the time. She wasn't well at all.'

'I understood that. You were amazingly patient with her.'

'I was very fond of Imogen.' Even so, ever since Leonidas had confided that Maribel reminded him of

Imogen, Maribel's self-esteem had nosedived. She was crushed by the conviction that she had only ever been a poor substitute for her cousin, and haunted by the suspicion that she had no right whatsoever to expect or ask for anything more than tolerance and acceptance from Leonidas. Surely if she had been the morally decent woman she liked to believe she was, she would have withstood the temptation that Leonidas had offered on the night that Elias was conceived?

'I saw your son walking into the house with you,' the princess remarked softly. 'He looks very like Leonidas.'

'I imagine you were very shocked to find out who his father was.'

Tilda looked troubled. 'How frank can I be?'

'Totally frank.'

'I was very concerned.' Tilda pulled a face and her voice became hesitant. 'I'm probably about to offend you for ever when I tell you why I felt I had to come and see you before your wedding.'

'I doubt that very much. I don't take offence easily, especially not with the people I trust.'

'I was afraid that you might feel you have no choice but to marry Leonidas to retain custody of your son. He's a formidable man and very powerful.' Tilda released her breath in an anxious sigh. 'But you *do* have a choice—I'm willing to offer you financial backing if you need it to go through the courts and fight him.'

'Does Rashad know about this?'

Tilda frowned. 'Rashad and Leonidas have a friendship quite independent of our marriage. I'll be honest— Rashad wouldn't approve of my interference, particularly when there is a child involved, but I have my own money and my own convictions about what's right and what's wrong.'

'You're a dear friend.' Maribel was very much touched by Tilda's offer of monetary assistance. 'But I'm going to marry Leonidas. I could give you a whole host of reasons why. Yes, I do feel under pressure. I do feel I can't compete. But at the same time, Leonidas is wonderful with Elias and my son needs a father more than I wanted to admit.'

'There's more to marriage than raising children,' Tilda said wryly.

A rueful smile touched Maribel's lips and for the first time in weeks she felt curiously at peace with the turmoil of her emotions, because one unchanging truth sat at the centre of it all. 'I've always loved Leonidas, Tilda—even when he was the most unlovable guy around. I can't even explain why. It's been that way almost since the first time I saw him.'

Leonidas returned to Heyward Park late the night before the wedding. He flew in from Greece with a plane-load of relatives. Mirabel chose a classic top and skirt in russet shades to wear with the pearl necklace and earrings, and greeted the arrivals in the front hall. Leonidas entered last, just in time to overhear his bride-to-be chatting quite comfortably with his trio of great-aunts, not one of whom spoke a word of English. Her grasp of Greek was basic but more than adequate for the occasion. A light supper was on offer, but there was also provision for the less lively members of his family who preferred to retire for the night in readiness for the celebrations the next day. Her confidence in dealing with both staff and guests was impressive. But he was quick to notice that her lush curves had slimmed down, and that when she saw him her clear eyes screened and her delicate features tightened.

'My apologies for bringing a large party back at this hour, *glikia mou*,' Leonidas murmured. 'And my compliments for handling them with so much grace and charm.'

'Thanks.' Her acknowledgement of compliments from a most unusual source was brisk. Even a brief encounter with his brilliant dark eyes was sufficient to raise self-conscious colour in her cheeks. She could greet his sixty-odd relatives with equanimity, but one glimpse of him reduced her to a schoolgirlish discomfiture that mortified her. With his stylishly cut ebony hair and lean, sculpted bone structure he looked devastatingly handsome. His black business suit was perfectly tailored to his lithe powerful frame. As usual, he emanated high-voltage masculinity and rampant sex appeal.

Curving a casual arm to her spine to draw her to one side, Leonidas inclined his arrogant dark head. 'When did you start learning Greek?'

'Soon after Elias was born, but I haven't always had the time I would like to concentrate on it.' Although the contact between them was of the slightest, Maribel was as stiff as a stick of rock. 'Excuse me, your great-aunts are waiting for me. I promised to show them some photos of Elias.'

'Don't I have priority?' Astonished at being treated in such an offhand manner, Leonidas closed a staying hand over hers before she could walk away.

Maribel was achingly conscious of the compelling force of his dark golden eyes. He possessed an intense charisma that she could not withstand even when she was angry with him. Her heart was beating very fast. 'Of course,' she said very politely.

The distance Leonidas sensed in her was like a wall. He didn't like it. He had assumed that the passage of time would take care of that problem and he had been wrong. Raw frustration raked through him. He thought of all the women in the past and the present who would have done anything he wanted, who would not have dreamt of angering him or criticising him. Or of making demands he was unwilling to meet. And finally he thought of Maribel who was just…Maribel, and unique. Her ability to wage a war of passive resistance was driving him crazy.

'Tomorrow is our wedding day. In the light of that fact,' Leonidas drawled with sardonic bite, 'I will explain to you that Josette Dawnay has opened an art gallery in the same building as her apartment and I was invited to the opening, along with a lot of other people. If you feel the need to check the date, you should find ample evidence of those facts.'

A tide of guilty pink flushed Maribel's creamy complexion. Relief leapt through her, but it was tinged by a streak of defiance, for she could not see why he could not have laid her concerns to rest at the time. 'I suppose I should say that I'm sorry I drenched you—'

'You should,' Leonidas confirmed without hesitation.

'I'm sorry, but you could have explained.'

'Why should I have? You eavesdropped on a private conversation and jumped to the wrong conclusion,' Leonidas countered with a sibilant cool that was a challenge. 'How was that my fault?'

Maribel was continually amazed at the ease with which Leonidas could infuriate her. He had buckets of unapologetic attitude. Aggressive, dynamic, intensely competitive, he was a living, breathing testament to the power of testosterone. She could feel the eyes of their guests lingering on them. It was one of those times when walking away seemed the wisest option. 'Excuse me,' she murmured again and off she went.

If Leonidas had been astonished by her attitude just minutes earlier, he was even more stunned by this resolute retreat. For the first time in his life, he had made a conciliatory move towards a woman and what was his reward? Where were the abject apologies and the passionate appreciation he had expected to receive? Something touched the toe of his shoe. Eyes smouldering, he glanced down. Mouse had crawled out from below his table. Shaking with nerves at the number of strangers about him, the wolfhound had nonetheless battled his terror to finally sneak out far enough from cover to welcome Leonidas home. Leonidas bent down and patted the shaggy head for that much-appreciated demonstration of loyalty.

Having ensured that all the guests had had their needs attended to, Maribel wasted no time in going straight up to bed. She thought of what Leonidas had told her. All her heartache over Josette Dawnay had been needless, a storm in a teacup that Leonidas could have settled in seconds— had he so desired. That he had not chosen to do so sent her a message, one she would have sooner not received. Leonidas had declared his independence and his freedom. He had spelt out the fact that marriage wasn't going to change his lifestyle.

Her eyes prickled in the darkness. She drew in a deep sustaining breath and scolded herself for being too emotional. She had to learn how to make the best of things, not just for her own sanity but for her son's sake as well. Tomorrow was her wedding day, she reminded herself doggedly. So many people had gone to so much trouble to ensure that every detail would be perfect—the very least she could do was try to enjoy it.

Shortly before six o'clock the next morning, Leonidas was wakened by a phone call from Vasos. Five minutes later, Leonidas was studying tabloid headlines on a computer screen and swearing eloquently in Greek. He raked his sleep-tousled black hair off his brow. PALLIS STAG CRUISE…RIOTOUS REVELRY WITH EXOTIC DANCERS! He flicked on to another page. It only got worse. The photos made him groan out loud in disbelief.

'Who the hell took these pictures?'

Vasos stepped forward. 'Camera phone…one of the dancers Sergio Torrente brought on board for the party. Crude, but effective.'

'Thank you, Sergio,' Leonidas breathed rawly.

Forty-eight hours earlier, his friend, Sergio Torrente, had mustered a crowd of male friends and staged a surprise stag party on his yacht for Leonidas' benefit. Sergio, who loathed weddings, was now safe deep in the jungles of Borneo on one of the Action-Man trips he enjoyed, well away from the furore he had unleashed on the bridegroom.

'I've taken the liberty of removing the daily newspapers from the house,' Vasos admitted.

Dismissing Vasos, Leonidas snapped shut the laptop. He knew Vasos could only be trying to protect Maribel, since nothing shocked the Pallis family. In five hours time, he was getting married. Or was he? Strategic planning and self-preservation came naturally to Leonidas. A business-man to the backbone, he had the Machiavellian genes of a family that had been merchant bankers in the Middle Ages. While over-indulgence in the sins of the flesh had proved the downfall of previous generations of the Pallis family, Leonidas was a great deal more grounded than most people appreciated.

But although plotting and planning were the spice of life to him, he was uneasily aware that Maribel had an intolerant view of such tactics. But would she still go ahead and marry him if she got the chance to read that tabloid trash? How much faith did she have in him? *None*, came the answer. Maribel didn't even pretend to have faith in him. Overhearing a single ambiguous phone call had been sufficient to make her judge and condemn him out of hand.

Leonidas brooded over the problem and, in the interests of fairness, felt duty-bound to ask himself why Maribel *should* trust him. The past three weeks replayed at supersonic speed in his mind. His strong, blue-shadowed jawline squared. Last night he had noticed that she had lost weight. He knew that stress was the most likely cause. She had loved her job and her home and she'd had to surrender both at short notice. Maybe she had been fond of the boyfriend, as well, Leonidas allowed grudgingly. He hadn't wanted to know the details, so he hadn't asked. She had once accused him of only ever doing what he wanted to do and, in this case, he recognised the accuracy of the charge. He had held onto his anger and punished her for daring to stand up to him. He had abandoned her to sink or swim in a world that was very new to her and she was naturally showing signs of strain.

Another woman might have asked him for support, but not Maribel. No, not Maribel, who was as stubborn as he was. Obstinacy was not a good trait for them to share, Leonidas acknowledged, his wide, sensual mouth compressed. A single request for advice or assistance, one little hint that she regretted challenging him, and all would have been well. Generosity in victory was not a problem for him. Unfortunately, Maribel refused to admit defeat. He was beginning to grasp how Maribel could once have said that she didn't like him. That statement had stayed with him in a nagging memory of unpleasantness that he could not forget. But now he had to ask himself: what was to like? He had been callous and cold towards her. He had been absent when he should have been present. And, in refusing to give her a shred of reassurance, he had simply increased her distrust.

Maribel might be as tranquil as a woodland pool on the surface, but she could be amazingly passionate and hasty, he reminded himself grimly. She was a firecracker, who tended to shoot first and ask questions second. That was not a confidence-boosting attribute on the day that he needed her to go to the altar and say yes with a smile. He had already grasped the reality that, in her eyes, he would always be guilty until proven innocent. A refreshing change after a lifetime of women who were too careful to ask loaded questions or make rash demands.

As the hazy morning mist slowly lifted back to reveal the lush green of the immaculately kept grounds and the promise of the glorious summer day yet to come Leonidas reached a decision. He would tell her about the stag-doe fiasco *after* the wedding. A wedding was a once-in-a-lifetime event, and nothing should be allowed to cast a cloud over Maribel's day. Or give her good reason to decide that marrying him might not be in her best interests.

CHAPTER NINE

'REALITY-CHECK here!' Ginny made a comic show of pinching herself while gaping at the dazzling contents of the sumptuous leather case that Maribel had opened. 'A diamond tiara fit for a queen to wear! That will look amazing with your veil.'

'It would look amazing with anything,' Maribel pointed out dry-mouthed, touching the glittering sapphire and diamond jewels with a reverent fingertip. 'But don't you think it might be a touch over-the-top?'

'Maribel…conspicuous consumption goes hand in hand with being a Pallis. The eight hundred guests will expect lots of bling, and most of them will be wearing their jewels.'

Later that morning, finally free of the combined attentions of the hair stylist, the beautician, the manicurist and the make-up artist, Maribel examined her unfamiliar reflection in the bedroom mirror. She was secretly enthralled by her appearance. Every day of her adult life she had played safe with fashion until she'd fallen madly in love with a bold eighteenth-century-style gown in a bridal portfolio. The boned and piped corset top accentuated her tiny waist before flaring out into a glorious full crackling skirt.

Fashioned in rich gold taffeta and silk, it was a wonderfully glamorous dress. The tiara looked superb anchored in the glossy chestnut coils of her upswept hair with a gossamer-fine French lace veil caught at the back of her head.

The church, a substantial building in weathered stone, was on the Heyward Park estate. Its private entrance, allied to the heavy security and a police presence, ensured that the paparazzi could not get closer than the road that lay beyond the solid hedge.

'I admire your calm so much,' her cousin, Amanda Stratton, remarked sweetly, while Ginny and several parents coaxed the enchantingly pretty flower- girls and the lively little page-boys into matching pairs. 'As Mummy says, nine out of ten women would be threatening to leave Leonidas Pallis standing at the altar.'

Maribel frowned. 'Why would I do something like that?'

Ginny Bell leant closer to Amanda Stratton and said something. The pretty blonde went red and stalked off.

'What was she getting at?' Mirabel asked her friend in an urgent undertone.

'Maybe the rumour that Leonidas is marrying you without even the safety net of a prenuptial agreement was more than she could bear. Or, maybe it's the sight of your diamonds. Whatever, its source is the sour grapes of envy and you shouldn't pay the slightest heed to it,' the older woman told her roundly.

Maribel felt as though she had just received a very sensible piece of advice. The sinking spirits she had suffered before midnight had been raised by her natural energy and optimism. Her marriage, she reflected, would be what she made of it. She breathed in deep as the doors were opened and the sweet mellow notes of organ music swelled out into the vestibule. The scent of the massed roses in the church hung heavy on the air.

Leonidas had nerves as strong as steel, but he had not enjoyed the most soothing start to the day and matters had only got worse. He had spent the morning in a disturbing state of indecision unlike anything he had ever experienced. Aware that his supposed stag cruise exploits might well feature on certain television news channels and on various celebrity websites, he had wondered what he would do if Maribel accessed either before she left for the church. On no less than three occasions he had reached the conclusion that he should move fast and give her his version of events first, only to change his mind again.

'The bride has arrived,' his best man, Prince Rashad, delivered in an aside, quietly marvelling at his friend's perceptible tension and unease, and wondering if he was witnessing the reaction of a reluctant bridegroom. It was true that Maribel was a comfortable ten minutes late, but Rashad found it hard to credit that Leonidas could have feared that his wife-to-be might not turn up.

Leonidas swung right round to check that information out firsthand. And there was Maribel, exotic and vibrant in rustling gold-and-white taffeta that provided a superlative frame for her smooth creamy skin and chestnut hair. She lit up the church in a vivid splash of colour and he was so entranced he forgot to turn back again to face the altar in time-honoured tradition.

'Mummy!' It was Elias, who broke the spell by wriggling off his nanny's lap with the speed and energy of an electric eel to hurl himself in Maribel's direction.

Leonidas strode forward to intercept his son and he hoisted the little boy high before he could trip the bride or her attendants up. Laughter and smiles broke out amongst their guests.

Maribel's attention locked to Leonidas and refused to budge. In tails and pinstripe trousers matched with a stylish cravat that toned with her dress, he would have made any woman stare. She met his stunning dark golden eyes and it was as if the rest of the world, and certainly everyone in the church, had vanished in a puff of smoke. All she was aware of was Leonidas. A sweet, wanton tide of warmth slivered silken fingers of anticipation through her slim frame.

Ginny took Elias from Leonidas. Leonidas grasped Maribel's fingers and bent his darkly handsome head to press a kiss to the delicate blue-veined skin of her inner wrist. It was more of a caress than a kiss and, although that contact only lasted for an instant, it sent a tingling sensual message to her every nerve-ending and left her trembling.

She was afraid to look at him again during the service in case she forgot where she was again. Yet she remained aware of him with every fibre of her being. She gave her responses in a clear voice that sounded a lot calmer than she felt. They exchanged rings. Her tension eased the moment they were pronounced man and wife. He retained his hold on her hand.

'You look magnificent, *hara mou*,' Leonidas told her huskily. 'That colour was made for you.'

'I was terrified I would look as if I was starring in a costume drama,' Maribel whispered back, encouraged into a burst of confidence. 'But I just fell totally for the dress.'

'You were rather late arriving at the church.' Leonidas reached down to lift Elias, who was resisting his nanny's attempt to remove him from the midst of things. Tired and fed up with being cooed over and admired, the little boy was starting to get cross.

'It's traditional.' Maribel laughed, touched and pleased by the way Leonidas was beginning to intuitively look out for his son even when Elias was in a less-than appealing mood. 'I could hardly leave you with all that luggage monogrammed with my new married initials.'

Leonidas discovered that his sense of humour wasn't quite as robust as usual. He had a disconcerting vision of those suitcases piled up with all the other gifts he had given her. It would be like Maribel to leave every present behind if she left him. It bothered him that he still felt that edgy. A wedding ring would make any woman stop and think before doing anything foolish or impulsive, wouldn't it? She was a church-goer and she had taken vows and made promises. Even so, all of a sudden, he was wondering at what precise point a marriage became official and binding—before or after the consummation?

In the vehicle that carried them back very slowly to the house, Maribel felt a little uncomfortable with her bridegroom's silence. 'How do you feel now that you've "got it all over with"?' she asked, striving for a light teasing note because she was hoping to receive an answer that would soothe her insecurities.

'*Relieved,*' Leonidas admitted with the emphasis of pure sincerity, although he felt he would be even more relieved when the day was over. He was making a valiant effort to rise above the ignominy of being forced to travel in an open carriage lined with blue velvet and drawn by four white horses prancing along with azure plumes bobbing in their head collars. He was learning a lot about Maribel's bridal preferences and a great deal of it was surprisingly colourful stuff, wholly out of step with her bridegroom's sophisticated tastes.

Maribel felt that, had they just attended a very trying event, she could have understood if he had confessed to a sense of relief. Just as quickly, she scolded herself for being oversensitive. Many men were reputed to dislike the fuss and formality of weddings. Was she getting carried away with the fantasy of her theatrical dress, the church romantically awash with roses, or the thrill of the carriage ride? She gave herself a stern lecture, because a magical wedding day didn't really change anything. It didn't mean that Leonidas would be miraculously transformed into a guy who loved her as much as she loved him. That was the stuff of dreams and she was a practical woman, wasn't she?

When the carriage drew up outside the house, Leonidas sprang out with alacrity and reached up to lift his bride down. But he didn't put her down again. Black lashes curling low over mesmeric golden eyes, he prised her lips apart with a sensual flick of his tongue and set about plundering the delicate interior of her mouth with a carnal expertise that caught her wholly unprepared. Her mind went blank; she was overwhelmed. Sensual firecrackers of response went fizzing and flaring through her bloodstream. The tips of her breasts tingled and her insides turned liquid. Slowly he lowered her again until her fancy golden shoes found purchase on the plush red carpet that ran up to the entrance doors.

Eyes like sapphire stars, Maribel parted her love-bruised lips. She was about to speak when a movement to one side of Leonidas attracted her attention. The sight of a stranger with a camera, signalling her to stay still for another moment, rocked her back to planet earth again with a jarring thump. She had neither noticed nor recalled the team of professionals engaged to film their wedding day for posterity. But Leonidas was a good deal more observant. With perfect timing he had just delivered a perfectly choreographed clinch to mark the bridal couple's arrival at the house.

'*Gone with the Wind* has got nothing on you,' Maribel remarked in a brittle voice, mortified pink highlighting her cheekbones. 'Well, you did promise to ensure a good surface show and that was very much in line with what's expected of a bridegroom.'

Leonidas wondered when she had developed the atrocious habit of remembering everything he had ever said and tossing it back to him like a log on a fire when he didn't feel like a blaze. 'That's not why I kissed you, *hara mou*.'

'Isn't it?'

'No. It is not,' Leonidas framed with succinct bite.

Maribel tossed her head as much as she dared, for she did not want to dislodge her tiara. 'Well, I don't believe you.'

'Why don't we leave our guests to party alone and head straight to the bedroom right now, *mali mou*?' Leonidas intoned that offer in the softest, silkiest voice imaginable. 'I'm ready and willing. Would you believe me then? Would that prove that sexual hunger rather than a wish to pose for the camera-lens powered me?'

Violet-blue eyes wide, her heart thudding at the foot of her throat with shock, Maribel stared up at him aghast. Dangerous dark, deep-set eyes glittered down at her in a ruthless challenge that was all rogue male laced with white-hot sexuality. Her mouth ran dry, for she knew instantly that he wasn't playing games. Indeed she had a horrible suspicion that abandoning their guests and all the hoopla that would go with entertaining them was a prospect that held considerable attraction for Leonidas.

'Yes, it would…er…but I really don't think that we need go that far,' she muttered hurriedly.

'No?' His entire attention was welded to her. Not by so much as a flicker did he betray any awareness of the staff assembled on the far side of the hall to greet them or of the long procession of limousines pulling up outside to disgorge the first guests.

'No,' she whispered unevenly.

Leonidas stroked a blunt brown forefinger across the flush of colour illuminating her creamy complexion. 'No?' he queried thickly. 'Even if it's what I want most in the world at this moment, *hara mou*?'

Her heart was racing. Her breath had snarled up in her throat. His dark, rich drawl, his brilliant, provocative gaze, controlled her. She could feel the wild heat in him igniting a flame low in her pelvis and her legs quivered under her. *Don't I get priority?* he had asked the night before. Suddenly she wanted to give him that priority, no matter what the cost.

'Okay…if that's what you want,' she heard herself say in capitulation, and could then scarcely believe that she had said it.

Surprise and appreciation flashed through Leonidas. At last, *yes*. The strength of his satisfaction astonished him. She was so conventional, so careful. He knew the worth of his triumph and the power of his appeal. Golden eyes smouldering, he grasped her hand and carried her slender fingers to his lips with a gentleness that was rare for him.

'Thank you, *kardoula mou*. But I won't embarrass you like that.'

Disappointment and relief gripped Maribel in equal parts. But people were joining them; introductions had to be made, good wishes and congratulations received. The bustling busyness of being a hostess as well as a bride took over for Maribel, who had gently refused her aunt's suggestion that she take charge for her niece's benefit. When Maribel got her first free moment, she devoted it to Elias, who needed a cuddle and a little time alone with his mother before he would settle down for a long-overdue nap.

She was taking a short cut from the nursery down a rear staircase to the ballroom when she heard a name and a familiar giggle that made her pause.

'Of course, if Imogen had lived,' her cousin Amanda was saying with authority while she fussed with her hair in front of a gilded mirror, 'Maribel would never have got near Leonidas. Imogen was gorgeous and she would never have popped a sprog just to get a guy to the altar.'

'Do you really think Maribel planned her pregnancy?'

'Of course, she did. It must've been right after the funeral—Maribel pounced when Leonidas was drunk, or something…I mean, he *must* have been drunk and upset about my sister!'

Praying that she would not have to suffer the ultimate humiliation of being seen, Maribel began to tiptoe back up the stairs. Unfortunately Amanda's shrill voice carried with clarity after her.

'Imogen thought it was so hilarious that Maribel had the hots for Leonidas that she told him. But I don't suppose my sister would be laughing if she were here today. Did you see that tiara? Did you see the size of those diamonds?

And what does Maribel do to say thank you? She sticks her billionaire in a tacky carriage drawn by horses that looked like they came straight out of a circus!'

Maribel headed for the main staircase at the other side of the great house. Her tummy was knotted with nausea. Had the carriage idea been tacky? How naïve of her not to appreciate that their sudden marriage would create loads of unpleasant rumours! How could anyone think that she had *planned* to fall pregnant? But perhaps this was a shotgun wedding in the sense that she had put Leonidas under pressure with regard to their son. So what right had she to be so thin-skinned?

Some of the comments, however, cut even deeper and hurt much more. Had she taken advantage of the fact that Leonidas was grieving the night after the funeral? They had both been grieving. Even so, that suggestion hit a very sensitive spot. She was still afraid that the only reason Leonidas had gone to bed with her in the first place was that she had reminded him of Imogen. And could it be true that Imogen had guessed how Maribel felt about Leonidas and told him? Made Maribel the butt of a joke? Her cousin, she recalled painfully, had had a rather cruel sense of humour that many people had enjoyed. And none more so, in those far-off student days, than Leonidas. She was cringing at the idea that he might know her biggest secret, might always have known. *Eavesdroppers never heard good of themselves.* She wondered who was responsible for that irrelevant old chestnut. She felt absolutely gutted.

The instant Maribel returned to Leonidas' side, he noticed that something was wrong. Her inner glow had dimmed; her sparkle had dulled. When the meal was served, her healthy appetite had vanished and she picked at her food and evaded his gaze. His tension increased. He knew it had been a big mistake to let her out of his sight. Someone had referred to the stag party and she was upset. He was convinced, however, that she was too well mannered to confront him in public. As he sat there brooding on how best to handle the fallout the appeal of the Italian honeymoon he had organised began to steadily recede. His Tuscan palazzo was exquisite, but there would be airports within reasonable reach as well as towns with easy transport links. Although he always travelled with his own staff, it would be hard to keep the lid on any major marital breakdown. If Maribel decided to be especially lacking in understanding and forgiveness, she would find it all too easy to walk out on him in Italy.

Having reached the conclusion that he might easily live to regret a Tuscan honeymoon, Leonidas decided to take his bride straight back home to the island of Zelos, where he had been born. Surrounded by sea and an army of devoted retainers, Maribel would not be going anywhere in a hurry, or without his consent. He would have all the time in the world to dissuade her from making any hasty or unwise decisions. Inclining his arrogant dark head to signal Vasos over to him, Leonidas communicated his change of heart.

Only when he had done that did he consider the reality that he was making plans to virtually imprison his wife. A very slight frisson of unease assailed Leonidas at that acknowledgement. When he studied Maribel's pale delicate profile, his core of inner steel held him steady. Look what had happened the last time he had given her the freedom to make her own choices! She had only gone through a pregnancy alone and unprotected! A pregnancy with *his* child, which he should have shared in right from the start, Leonidas reasoned fiercely. When she made bad decisions like that, it was hardly surprising that he should feel the need to take control. In any case even Stone Age Man had known it was his duty to protect the family unit.

Tilda insisted on accompanying Maribel when she went upstairs to get changed. 'I owe you an apology for mis-judging Leonidas,' the beautiful blonde murmured with twinkling turquoise eyes. 'Just like the rest of us, he has matured and changed since he was at uni.'

Maribel cast off her private worries to summon up a warm smile that put Tilda at her ease. 'And what brought on that realisation?'

'Apart from the fact that he has been really charming to me today? When I see Leonidas with you and Elias, he is a very different guy from the one I remember,' the princess confessed. 'And while I was astonished when I learned that you and he were a couple, my husband wasn't. He said that you were the only woman Leonidas ever sought out for an intelligent conversation.'

Maribel nodded, but felt just then that intelligent con-versation wasn't a lot to offer to one of the world's most notorious womanisers.

'Is there something worrying you?' Tilda asked gently. 'Is it all that stag cruise nonsense?'

Maribel veiled her startled eyes before she could betray her ignorance on that subject. She concentrated on donning a turquoise and pink dress that was both elegant and com-fortable to travel in. 'Er…no.'

'I knew you would be too sensible to let anything of that

nature bother you. After all, men will be men, and our men in particular will always be paparazzi targets,' Tilda remarked wryly. 'Rashad would have been on that yacht with Sergio and Leonidas, if he hadn't had to take my father-in-law's place at a government meeting.'

Stag-cruise nonsense? Don't go there, Maribel told herself staunchly. None of her business, was it? So soon after that unfortunate misunderstanding over Josette Dawnay, Maribel was in no hurry to suspect the worst. In any case, she was still too much taken up with tormenting herself with the suspicion that Leonidas might always have known that she loved him. She really couldn't bear that idea, she really could *not* live with that possibility, she acknowledged tautly. Without her pride she felt she would have nothing.

Maribel studied the island far below them as the helicopter wheeled round in a turn. There was just enough light left for her to get a good view. Zelos was surprisingly lush and green and there were loads of trees. Long slices of golden sand were edged by the turquoise of the sea that washed the shores. She thought it looked like paradise. A very substantial residence occupied a magnificent site in splendid isolation at one end of the island. At the other, there was a picturesque fishing village with a church and a huge yacht in the harbour. Zelos was where Leonidas had grown up and, for that reason alone, she was fascinated by the prospect of living on the island.

Darkness had fallen when Elias was welcomed into the big sprawling house as though he were royalty. Maribel watched her son being borne off to bed by Diane and her co-nanny, a young Greek woman, closely followed by the housekeeper, the nursery maids and her son's personal protection officer. Slowly she shook her head. 'Elias is never going to be alone again, is he?'

'We Greeks are gregarious by nature. I was alone too much as a child but, just as I was, he will be watched over by everyone on the island. Welcome to your new home, *hara mou*.' Leonidas closed a shapely brown hand over hers. 'Let me show you the house.'

It was as large as Heyward Park, for several generations of his family had built new wings to suit their individual tastes. In a glorious room that opened out onto a beautiful vine-shaded terrace, Leonidas tugged her into his arms with immense care.

'I want you to be happy here,' he told her huskily.

Maribel stared up into his brilliant dark eyes and felt her heart lurch. She had promised herself that she would not stoop to asking Leonidas any foolish questions. But suddenly she could no longer withstand her need to know the truth. 'There's something I want to ask you, Leonidas,' she breathed abruptly.

Leonidas regarded her in level enquiry.

'Did Imogen tell you years ago that I was in love with you?' Maribel completed.

It was the very last question that Leonidas could have foreseen. Having braced himself for a query of an entirely different nature, indeed an accusation, he was bemused.

Maribel stepped out of his loosened hold. 'It's true. She *did* tell you!'

Leonidas frowned. 'You haven't even given me the chance to answer you.'

Maribel drew herself up to her full height. 'You don't need to. Sometimes I can read you like a book.'

Leonidas was anything but reassured by that statement. He had long regarded his famed impassivity as a source of privacy that he could take for granted. Once or twice before, however, she had given him cause to suspect that she did possess a certain rare insight where he was concerned. 'Imogen might once have mentioned something of that nature,' he conceded with the utmost casualness.

'Well, it's not something you need to worry about,' Maribel told him firmly.

'I wasn't worrying.'

'Or think about.'

'I wasn't thinking about it either.'

'Because it's no longer true,' Maribel informed him doggedly, keen to get any such notion knocked right back out of his handsome head again. 'I got over you after that night at Imogen's house.'

His superb bone structure tightened beneath his bronzed skin. 'Why?'

Over two years of pent-up hostility and hurt were suddenly rising up inside Maribel in an unfettered overflow of feelings. 'You remember you asked for breakfast? There was no food in the house, so I—fool that I was—I went out to buy some.'

Leonidas, who had long found his recollections of that same morning offensive enough to ensure he simply buried them, dealt her a cool, unimpressed appraisal. 'Where did you go to shop? Africa?'

'Somewhere rather more convenient. I only drove down the road, but as I turned into the supermarket a car ran into the back of mine. I ended up in hospital with concussion.'

Leonidas studied her in raw disbelief. 'Are you saying that you were involved in a car accident that morning?'

Maribel nodded confirmation.

'Why the hell didn't you phone me?'

'By the time I had recovered my wits enough and had access to a phone you had already left Imogen's house. I took my cue from that fact,' Maribel retorted tightly, her hands clasped together. 'And it cured me of my attachment to you, because I might as well have died for all the interest you had in what had happened to me that day! You didn't even bother to call me.'

Leonidas was still stuck in stunned mode. 'You were hurt…in hospital?'

'Yes, until the following morning.'

The smooth olive planes of his darkly handsome features were taut. Ebony brows pleated with concern, he reached for her hands and drew her towards him. His dark golden eyes were welded to her flushed and defensive face. '*Theos mou,* I am very sorry. If I had known, if I had even suspected that you hadn't returned because something had happened to you, I would have looked for you and I would have been there for you. I thought you had walked out on me.'

Maribel was bewildered. Why would he have thought such a thing? She could not think that he met with rejection of that nature very often. Or was it common for women to behave in such a way after a one-night stand? She didn't want to ask him. She did not want to linger on the subject. She was afraid that her sensitivity might prove all too revealing to a male as shrewd as he was.

Leonidas finally understood why she had said she didn't like him. He was shaken that it had not once occurred to him that she might have had an accident, that there might have been a genuine explanation for her vanishing act. He could not understand why his usual clear-sighted logic should have deserted him that day, or why his reaction had been out of all proportion to the event. But he did recognise the consequences. 'I let you down,' he said gravely. 'I very much regret that, *mali mou*.'

Maribel was taken aback by the sincerity in his lustrous gaze. Her slender fingers smoothed his in a comforting gesture full of all the warmth she would have denied. 'It's all right…you didn't know—'

His wide, sensual mouth twisted. 'It's not all right. I should have enquired. I could have been there with you. But I was arrogant—'

'I know, but you're not about to change,' Maribel told him ruefully. 'Not without an ego transplant.'

Reluctant amusement assailed Leonidas. He lowered his handsome dark head and claimed her soft pink mouth in a passionate onslaught that made the world go into a frantic tailspin around her…

CHAPTER TEN

WHEN the world stopped spinning, Maribel found that Leonidas had propelled her into a bedroom with a soaring ceiling, dimmed lights and a bed the size of a small golf course. 'Is this where you throw orgies?' she asked helplessly.

'You need have no concern on that score. I saw enough of that kind of nonsense growing up with Elora,' Leonidas retorted with derision.

Maribel was transfixed by that frank admission about his late mother. It didn't seem the right moment to tell him that her comment had simply been a bad joke, voiced without thought.

'Aside of the staff, you are the only woman ever to cross the threshold of this room,' Leonidas declared.

Merriment relieved her momentary tension, for she assumed that he was teasing her. 'As if I'd swallow that fairy story!'

'But it is the truth. I have never brought a woman in here before. I have always preferred to keep my bedroom private. It is very rare for me to sleep the whole night through with anyone.'

'You did with me…what was I? An aberration?'

Long brown fingers framed her flushed cheekbones. Her violet-blue eyes subjected him to an unwaveringly direct appraisal. There was no downward and quick upward glance designed to entrap, none of the studied flirtatious moves he was accustomed to receiving from her sex. Instead there was a sincerity he found much more appealing. Slowly a smile began to chase the gravity from his beautifully shaped masculine mouth. 'I would say that addiction would be a more apt description. Here I am back again and that is not like me, *hara mou*. So you must have something unique.'

Something unique? Elias, Maribel filled in ruefully for her own benefit. She could hardly fault him for trying to make his bride feel special on their wedding night. In and out of bed he was too experienced not to know what pleased a woman. He kissed her again with a sweet, intoxicating fervour that soon turned hot and sensual with the dart and plunge of his tongue.

All the tensions of the day found exit in the stormy hunger that took her in a burning tide of desire. Her breath came in short quickened gasps. She stretched up to him, pressing her slim, supple body to his to exchange kiss for kiss with an urgency she could not hold back. He stripped off her dress with impatient hands and lifted her clear of its folds.

Tawny eyes smouldering with purpose, Leonidas stepped back a few inches to get a better look at her. The delicate turquoise lace lingerie revealed rather more than it concealed of her tempting curves and his gaze gleamed with appreciation. 'I like,' he told her sexily against her reddened lips, curving strong hands to her hips to fold her up against his lean, tough, muscular frame.

Even the expensive tailoring of his trousers could not

conceal the hard male heat of his erection. Her breath rasped in her throat. There was an answering tingle of voluptuous response thrumming between her thighs. 'Leonidas…' she gasped under the plundering ravishment of his probing mouth.

'I love your breasts.' He eased the creamy mounds from their lace cups and coaxed the straining rose-tipped crests into almost unbearably tender points. 'The little sounds you make turn me on,' he confided thickly.

Her throat extended as she sucked in oxygen to ease her constricted lungs. But there was no escape from the dark, delirious pleasure that he had taught her to crave with an appetite that could still shock her. Already she was pitched on a high of unquenchable yearning that devoured every sensible thought and destroyed all shame. She was with the man she loved and she liked that very much. He energised her. Insidious heat was whispering through her, every pulse point awakening to the tantalising masculine promise of him, for she knew he would deliver and how.

'Everything about you turns me on, *kardoula mou,*' Leonidas growled. 'You give yourself without pretence.'

He traced the satin wet heat of her beneath the fine material barrier and kneed her legs apart. She shivered violently, every knowing movement of his fingers releasing a cascade of tormenting sensation. She trembled in the high heels she still wore. Every feeling in her body seemed to be concentrated in the tiny sensitive bud at the apex of her thighs. He pushed her unresisting body back against the wall and dropped to his knees to peel off the damp silk. Lean hands cupping the swell of her *derrière*, he brought her to him and indulged in an intimacy that was shockingly new to her.

'No…no,' she mumbled in dismay and dissent.

'Just close your eyes and enjoy,' Leonidas instructed thickly. 'I intend to drive you out of your mind with pleasure.'

The protesting fingers she had dug into his silky black hair lingered to hold him there instead as, all too soon, the sheer seductive delight of what he was doing to her overcame her resistance. She had to lean back against the wall just to stay upright. Her mind was a blank; she was a creature of pure physical response and nothing else mattered. Ripples of wanton pleasure flamed through her in sweet, honeyed waves of rapture. Her blood felt as if it were roaring through her veins. She was gasping, whimpering and out of control when she surged to the point of no return in an explosive climax that shattered her.

Before she had even begun to recover from that erotic onslaught, Leonidas was lifting her to him and bracing her hips back against the wall to tilt her up to receive him. He anchored her knees to his waist. Wildly disconcerted by her position, she looked up at him in confusion. 'Leonidas?'

'All day, every time I looked at you this is where I wanted to be,' he told her with ragged force, plunging his rigid sex deep into the lush, swollen heart of her. 'Inside you, part of you, *hara mou*.'

In that one bold plunge of possession, he deprived her of breath and voice. She was still tender, still descending from the peak of ecstasy, and suddenly he was driving her right back to that same brink for a second time. Extreme sensation returned with blinding force. He slammed into her yielding body with a passion as intense as it was ruthless. The melting, fizzing excitement that seized her was primitive and raw. His fierce passion swept her slowly and steadily to yet another glorious summit where she was overpowered by the exquisite waves of pleasure convulsing her.

'No woman makes me feel as good as you do,' Leonidas whispered in the aftermath.

He carried her over to the bed and settled her down on the cool white linen. He cast off what remained of his clothes and came down beside her. He eased her back into his arms and smoothed her tumbled chestnut hair back from her face. She drank in the aroma of damp musky male that was uniquely him and let her heavy eyes drift closed. She was astonished by the wildness of his love-making, shocked by the level of her response, but content if he was content. She was also overjoyed that he was still holding her.

'You're not going any place, are you?' Maribel felt she had to check after his admission that he preferred not to share a bed.

'Where would I be going?' Leonidas sounded lazily amused.

'Don't want to wake up and find you gone.'

Leonidas remembered emerging from the shower and finding her gone over two years earlier. He had searched the house. He still recalled the sound of the silence, the emptiness that had seemed to echo round him, the hollow sensation inside. The entire episode had seriously spooked him.

'I'll be here,' he confirmed.

'I'm so tired,' she framed drowsily, for now that all her tension had been banished there was nothing left to hold back her bridal exhaustion.

'Happy?' Leonidas prompted.

'Happy,' she mumbled, pressing a sleepy kiss against a smooth brown muscular shoulder.

Leonidas decided that it would be unreasonably cruel to wake her up and tell her about the stag cruise. He would tell her in the morning…some time. He wondered if she would be upset. His arms tightened round her because he really didn't like the idea that any oversight of his might cause her pain.

The third time Maribel woke up the next day, a Greek business channel was playing on the television at the foot of the bed. She flopped back against the pillows with an indolent sigh. It was two in the afternoon. They had break-fasted at seven with Elias and played with him on the shady terrace below the trees. A couple of hours later Leonidas had carried her back to bed. Wakening the second time, she had gone for a shower and he had joined her there. A tender smile curved her reddened mouth. She lifted the television remote and flicked through the channels until she came to a gossipy one about celebrities. She was semi-listening to the entertaining flow of light chatter when Leonidas strolled out of his *en suite* bathroom.

Maribel gave him a rapt appraisal. In a pair of silk boxers and nothing else, he was a magnificent sight.

'Is it worth my while getting dressed again?' Leonidas enquired silkily.

Maribel went pink and gave a little sensual wriggle below the sheet. It would have been true to say that she had not been slow to take advantage of his presence and his amazing stamina.

'I take it that's a no?'

Only the sight of herself in her wedding gown on a tele-vision screen could have distracted Maribel at that instant.

She gaped. 'My goodness…doesn't the dress look marvellous?'

'It wasn't the dress, it was you, *kardoula mou*,' Leonidas asserted. 'But I can't believe you're watching rubbish like that.'

'It's more fun than the business news…' Her teasing voice tailed away to a dying whisper because she was listening to the presenter.

"Predictably Leonidas Pallis enjoyed his final days of freedom with a wild stag party on the Torrente yacht, *Diva Queen*."

A party attended by a bunch of naked women, Maribel registered in horror. Although the presenter didn't specifically mention naked women, Maribel's eyes were glued to the screen and she saw a bare-breasted female dancing on deck and another diving off the yacht in what appeared to be her birthday suit…

'Shut up!' she shouted at Leonidas when his attempted vocal intervention threatened to prevent her from hearing the rest of the item. There was a disturbing reference to the existence of more intimate photos which, it was hinted, were unsuitable for general viewing.

'Give me that…' Leonidas lunged for the remote, but Maribel got there first, throwing herself bodily over the top of it. Unfortunately while she won that potential struggle she also accidentally hit the off button.

'You rat!' she exclaimed sickly as she pushed herself back up onto her knees. 'So you don't do orgies? What were you doing on that yacht?'

'Not what you obviously think,' Leonidas countered with a composure that she felt could only add insult to injury. 'Every move I make is sensationalised.'

'A naked woman is a naked woman, and as sensational as things need to get to offend me!' Maribel launched back at him.

'You have to stop believing implicitly in what you see and what you read. Photos and stories can be fabricated.'

'What about the pictures unsuitable for general viewing?'

'If you really want to push this to the limits, I can show you them as well.' Classic profile forbidding and taut, Leonidas hauled on a pair of faded jeans.

'I want to see them.'

That news spelt out in clear defiance of his wishes, which only made her all the more suspicious, Maribel went into the dressing room to rifle cupboards and drawers for clothing. She was acting on automatic pilot. She was trying to build up the strength to deal with the situation, praying that a momentary respite would rescue her brain and her common sense from the feverish emotional grip of anger, fear and pain.

Leonidas wasn't acting as though he had done something wrong. But then, had she ever seen Leonidas act in a guilty manner? And why should he even feel guilty? Why was it only now that she was remembering that he had still not given her an answer to the choice she had given him a month earlier? A platonic marriage in which he would retain his freedom or marital monogamy. Was this his answer? Or just another attention-grabbing paparazzi spread that a sensible woman would rise above and disbelieve as Tilda had suggested? Although Maribel couldn't help feeling that it was rather easier for Tilda to have taken that stance when her own husband was not involved.

Clad in white linen trousers and a fitted white waistcoat

top, Maribel emerged again. Her eyes were a very bright blue against her pallor. Across the depth of the room Leonidas slung her a charged look. The atmosphere was electric with aggressive undertones. He tossed a newspaper down like a statement on the tumbled bed. 'Looking at those pictures is only going to annoy you and give you the wrong impression.'

The tip of her tongue snaked out to moisten her full pink lower lip. 'But I'll always wonder if I don't look at them now.'

'It's a question of trust,' he breathed tautly. 'Who do you believe?'

At that, Maribel lifted her chin. 'I would have believed you if you'd told me about this before I heard about it on television.'

'Was that how you would have preferred our wedding day to begin? With a load of tabloid sleaze aimed at selling a few more papers?'

Discomfiture made Maribel redden and shake her head. 'But when *were* you going to tell me?'

'I foresaw this scenario, *glikia mou*. I have to admit that I wasn't in a hurry.' Golden eyes semi-screened by lush black lashes to gleaming blades challenged her.

'So…er…what are you asking me to believe? That you were kidnapped and forced aboard your friend's yacht where you were subjected to the unwelcome attentions of loose women?'

'Sergio happens to be very into partying right now…he's a friend, a good one. It was a stag do. So, it wasn't to my taste!' Leonidas proclaimed in a raw undertone, lean, strong face set into hard, angular lines of hostility. '*Theos mou*… that ring on my finger doesn't mean that you own me or that you can tell me what I can and can't do!'

'So if I decide to go partying on a yacht with a bunch of half-naked men, that'll be fine with you. You won't ask any awkward questions afterwards. You will fully respect my right to do as I wish. I'm glad we've got that established,' Maribel retorted crisply.

Leonidas froze. Scorching golden eyes locked with hers on a powerful wave of anger. It was like sailing too close to the sun, but she stood her ground. The silence somehow managed to howl around her, laced as it was with intimidating vibrations. Finally, Leonidas spoke. 'That would not be acceptable to me.'

Maribel was not at all surprised by that news. 'And why would that be?'

'You're my wife!' Leonidas grated.

'So you do as you like and I do as you like, too?'

Leonidas refused to take that bait. He surveyed her with dark glittering intensity as if daring her to disagree.

Maribel wondered how they had contrived to roam so far from the main issue and blamed herself for backing away in fear of asking what was undoubtedly the only important question. 'Did you sleep with anyone on that yacht?'

His black brows pleated, the forceful angle of his hard jawline diminishing. 'Of course not.'

Maribel didn't say anything. She was studying the beautiful rug beneath his feet. She felt sick with tension and terror, and dizzy with relief. With a rather jerky nod of acknowledgement she swooped on the paper and went out through the open doors onto the terrace. She was ashamed of how shaken up she was and the reality that her eyes were wet with tears.

Leonidas, who had not been prepared for her to walk out, raked his black hair back off his brow, dissatisfaction seething through him. If he went after her there would be another scene. He had a lifetime of experience at avoiding messy confrontations. All his early memories were of the constant hysterical scenes his late mother had staged with everyone in her life. It was sensible to give Maribel time to calm down. So why, he asked himself in bewilderment, did he want to go after her? Why did the very knowledge that she was alone and unhappy bother him so much? A few minutes later he strode outdoors, only to discover that she was no longer within view.

Maribel made her way through the extensive gardens, plotting a path below the mature trees that shaded her from the sun. The newspaper still felt like a burning brand under her arm. When she reached the beach, she kicked off her shoes and sat down on a rock. The photos weren't quite the shock she had expected. It might have been a party in his honour, but Leonidas looked downright bored. There was one shot of him, lean, bronzed features cold and set, a beautiful skimpily dressed blonde giggling beside him. Maribel knew those facial expressions of his; she knew them so well. She knew he didn't like strangers getting too close and, in much the same way, he disliked women who flung themselves at him. Drunken familiarity really repulsed him. He was a Pallis, an aristocrat born and bred, and he was both fastidious and intolerant of lower standards.

Her throat was thick with the tears she was choking back. She flung the newspaper down. In one sense she was the one with the problem, not him. She was insecure, but she was only getting what she had asked for. He had married her, hadn't he? But he had only put that ring on her finger for Elias' sake. How safe and secure had she expected to feel in those circumstances? He had had a

perfect right to enjoy a stag do within reasonable boundaries and to expect his new wife not to make a big deal out
of it. He was also entitled to expect her to trust him to some
extent at least. How long would their marriage last if she
continually made unjust accusations? She was jealous and
insecure, but he should not have to pay the price for that.
Those feelings, Maribel reckoned painfully, were the price
of marrying a guy who didn't love her.

Footsteps crunched across the sand. A long shadow fell
over her as Leonidas drew level with her.

Maribel stood up. 'I'm sorry,' she whispered jaggedly.
'I wasn't giving you a fair hearing.'

Leonidas expelled his breath on a hiss and pulled her
into his arms. He rested his brow on the top of her head.
'On my honour, I swear that nothing happened. Do you
believe me?'

'Yes.' Maribel gulped. 'You look awfully fed up in
those photos.'

'That was the lifestyle I grew up with and it wrecked
the family I might have had. Drugs destroyed my mother,
Elora's health and infidelity ruined her relationships. My
older sister followed in her footsteps,' he acknowledged
grimly. 'Elora conceived me by one man on the same day
that she married another. By the time the truth came out,
my real father was dead and the man I thought was my
father turned his back on me. How's that for screwing up?
But I have always wanted and needed more from my life.'

'I know.' She found his hands and squeezed them. When
she thought of how hard she tried to protect Elias from hurt
she was filled with angry regret on Leonidas' behalf. He
had been forced to learn hard lessons at too young an age.
'You're strong. But I need to trust you. I know that.'

'It's my fault that you couldn't.' Leonidas regarded her with level dark golden eyes. 'I should have told you before the wedding but I was too proud—I don't want anyone else but you, *hara mou*.'

Maribel was unprepared for that admission. She swallowed hard and closed her eyes tight. Suddenly her heart felt light and the shadows were lifting from her. He was telling her so much more than he was saying. He really did want their marriage to work. He was prepared to make the effort. She thought back to her blind foolishness the day before, when she had informed him that she no longer loved him, and she almost groaned out loud. How short-sighted she had been! It was time that she ditched some of her pride and defensiveness.

'With a wife who wakes me up during the night to have her wicked way with me, where would I get the energy?' Leonidas murmured teasingly.

Maribel flushed to the roots of her hair. 'I didn't mean to waken you. It was dark—I wasn't sure where I was—'

'Excuses…excuses.' Leonidas treated her to a smouldering visual appraisal that made her tummy turn a somersault. 'But tonight it'll be my turn, *mali mou*.'

Elias was fast asleep on his stomach with his bottom in the air. Maribel gently rearranged him into a cooler position. Exhausted, he did not even stir. Her son's days were packed with adventure, for the Pallis estate was a wonderful playground for a child as active as he was. From dawn to dusk Elias was on the go, playing in the pool with his parents or just running round with Mouse, who was now travelling on a swanky pet passport.

Maribel dressed up for dinner. It was a special evening

because it was to be their last night on Zelos for a while. For the past week, Leonidas had been flying in and out on business at all hours in an effort to extend their stay on the island for as long as possible. He seemed as reluctant as she was to leave, as they'd had a magical honeymoon.

Certainly, Maribel conceded, she had never dreamt that she might find such happiness so quickly with Leonidas. She had first seen him discard his famous reserve with his son, but with every week that had passed since she'd become his wife he seemed to relax his guard more with her. She noticed the little things the most. If he had to work in his office for a while, he would come looking for her afterwards. He wakened her to have breakfast with him at an ungodly hour because he clearly wanted her company. He liked her to see him right out to the helipad and he really loved it if she waited up for him when he was late home.

And she had begun to appreciate that all his life he had been horribly starved of genuine affection and any form of conventional home-based routine. Things she took for granted, like sitting down to eat a meal with Elias, he set a high value on. He enjoyed the simple pleasures—a walk with Elias through the citrus orchards to the shore, where their son would toddle in the waves and shout in delight when he got wet. Leonidas liked the little rituals of family life that she had naïvely feared he would consider boring, restrictive or outdated. What he had never had he wanted Elias to have, and he adored his son. Nobody watching Leonidas smile as Elias raced to greet him could have doubted that.

Seeing Greece through his eyes, she had fallen more in love with it than ever, after he had taken her off the tourist track on his yacht. In his company she had explored some fascinating ancient archaeological sites. He had shown her his favourite places, some hauntingly beautiful and almost all deserted. He had also taught her that, if the food was good, he was happier eating at a rickety table in a tiny taverna in a hillside village than he was in an exclusive restaurant. They had picnicked and swum in unspoilt coves that could only be reached from the sea. Above all, he prized his privacy and even though he was almost always recognised his countrymen awarded him that space.

Maribel had worked hard at losing the habit of making unfavourable comparisons between herself and Imogen. She had accepted that it was stupid to continually torment herself with such ego-zapping thoughts and she had concentrated instead on recognising what she did have with Leonidas. And what she had, she reflected dreamily, was a lot more than she had ever dared to hope for. He was her every fantasy come true in the bedroom. He was highly intelligent, great, cool company and very witty. She was learning how dependable he was, how straightforward he could be once the barriers came down. He could also be wonderfully gentle and considerate.

A slim, stylish figure clad in a strappy emerald-green sundress, Maribel strolled out onto the terrace that overlooked the bay. It was gloriously cool below the spreading canopy of the walnut trees. Only a few minutes later, Leonidas came out to join her. His mobile phone was ringing, but he paused only to switch it off and set it aside. The staff knew better than to interrupt him with anything less than an emergency. Her dark blue eyes locked to his lean, darkly handsome face. His presence always created a buzz and, true to form, he looked amazing in a cream open-necked shirt and jeans.

'We've been together one calendar month, *hara mou*,' Leonidas filled two flutes with champagne and handed a jewel box to her. 'That calls for a celebration.'

Taken aback, Maribel lifted the lid. Her breath caught in her throat at the beauty of the diamond bracelet with the initials MP picked out in sapphires. She now knew how much he enjoyed giving her presents and she no longer scolded him for it.

'It's really gorgeous, Leonidas. Put it on for me,' she urged. 'Now I feel bad because I've got nothing to give you!'

Leonidas looked down at his wife with sensual dark eyes. 'Don't worry. I'll come up with something that doesn't cost you anything but lost sleep.'

Maribel blushed and grinned and extended her wrist until the light filtering through the trees glittered over the jewels. 'Thank you,' she told him.

He passed her a champagne flute. 'Before I forget to mention it, your cousin Amanda phoned to ask us to a dinner party in London. I was surprised she didn't ring you.'

Maribel wasn't surprised. Amanda was as ruthless at making use of influential contacts as her mother was and would have deliberately contacted Leonidas in preference to her cousin. 'I think I'll make a polite excuse,' she said uncomfortably. 'My relatives are going through a bit of an adjustment period just now. It's probably best if I let them have some time to get used to the fact that you're my husband.'

Leonidas quirked an eloquent black brow. 'What on earth are you talking about? Why should they need time?'

Maribel winced. 'The Strattons were rather like the spectres at our wedding feast,' she admitted ruefully. 'I'm afraid my aunt was initially very upset when she realised that you were Elias' father—'

His brilliant dark eyes flashed gold.' How was that her business?'

'I know it's a long time ago, but you and Imogen were once an item.' It was a reluctant reminder, for Maribel was already wishing she had chosen to be less frank on the subject. The habit she had recently developed of telling Leonidas everything had gone deeper than she appreciated.

'No, we weren't.'

'Possibly not on your terms.' Maribel was performing a mental dance to choose the right words to explain how her relatives felt. 'Had you had a child with anyone but me and married that person, it wouldn't have bothered them. But when it's me, they can't seem to stop thinking that I somehow poached on Imogen's preserves.'

Leonidas frowned. 'But I didn't date Imogen.'

Maribel stared fixedly at him. 'Maybe you didn't call it dating, but you were involved with her for a while—'

'Sexually?' Leonidas cut in. 'No, I wasn't.'

Gobsmacked by a statement that turned years of conviction upside down, Maribel shook her head as though to clear it. 'But that's not possible. I mean, Imogen herself *said*—I mean, she talked as if—'

'I don't care what she said, *hara mou*. It didn't happen. *Ever*,' Leonidas said dryly.

'Oh, my goodness.' Maribel gazed wide-eyed back at him. 'She let everyone think that you had been lovers.'

'No doubt she liked the attention it brought her, but she didn't appeal to me on that level.'

Maribel nodded like a marionette, because she could scarcely get her mind round the obvious fact that

Leonidas had been more attracted to her than he had ever been to her beautiful cousin. 'But…but *why* weren't you attracted to her?'

'She was good fun, but she was also neurotic and superficial.' A frown line pleated his fine brows as if he was engaging in deeper thought as well. 'To be blunt, I knew she wanted me. I assumed that that was why you said you weren't interested when I kissed you—'

Maribel was bemused and momentarily lost. 'Kissed… me…*when*?'

Leonidas shrugged. 'When I was a student staying in Imogen's house.'

'You mean that was a genuine pass…not just some sort of a bad-boy joke?' Maribel stammered, her mind leaping back almost seven years.

'Is that what you thought?' Leonidas gave her a wry look. 'You pushed me away and it was the right thing to do. Back then, I would definitely have screwed up with you. I didn't know what was going on inside my own head. Imogen would have got in the way as well. I realised even then that if she couldn't have me, she didn't want you to have me either.'

Maribel was hanging on his every word. Discovering that Leonidas had been attracted to her that far back, at the same time as she learnt that he had never wanted Imogen, transformed Maribel's view of her entire relationship with him. Only now could she see that there had been a definite history between them before they had first shared a bed.

'Remember the night I told you about my sister? That was when I realised that I wanted you because, afterwards, I didn't know what I had been doing there in your room talking about all that personal stuff—'

'Drunk and in Greek,' Maribel slotted in helplessly.

'But I'd never done anything like that before with a woman.' Leonidas mimicked an uneasy masculine shiver. 'It…it disturbed me that you had this mental pull on me that I couldn't explain. It was too deep and I wasn't ready for anything deep at the time.'

'I know,' Maribel said feelingly, but the joy was rising steadily inside her, as she would never again have to feel as though she was second-best to her cousin. Imogen had lied about the level of her involvement with Leonidas—which didn't really surprise Maribel when she thought about it.

'Imogen told me you cared about me and it was supposed to be a joke,' Leonidas confided, dark golden eyes resting tautly on her. 'But I liked the idea and it drew me to you even more, *kardoula mou*.'

Her cheeks were a warm peach. Unsure what to say, she breathed, 'But you were upset after Imogen's funeral.'

'At the waste of her life, yes. It took me back to when my mother and my sister died. I tried to help Imogen and I failed,' Leonidas murmured gravely. 'When she abandoned rehab, I turned my back on her because I refused to watch her die.'

'You did your best and you weren't the only one. Nothing worked,' Maribel breathed with tears glistening in her blue eyes.

'But you did watch over her and support her long after other people gave up on her. That level of loyalty and love is very rare. I recognised that, even if her family didn't. When I saw you again at the funeral, nothing would have stopped me seeking you out.'

'What are you saying?' Maribel whispered.

'That if it hadn't been for your cousin, we would never

have met. But once I met you, no other woman really had a chance with me because there was so much in you that I admired.'

'Even if you weren't quite ready for all that stuff you admired in me?' Mirabel prompted unevenly.

'Even then. You were clever and gutsy and not at all impressed by me or my money. Our first night together was very special—'

'Special? All you did was ask for breakfast afterwards.'

Leonidas spread lean brown hands in an expressive gesture of reproach at that judgement. '*Theos mou*, I didn't know what to say. I didn't even appreciate that anything needed to be said in that moment. I suppose I was out of my comfort zone. All I knew was that I was in a wonderful mood. I felt so natural with you. I was devastated when I came out of the shower and found an empty house!' Leonidas admitted in a raw undertone. 'No note, no phone call—nothing!'

Maribel stared at him in horror. 'D-devastated?'

'And then very angry with you because you'd walked out on me. I took it as a rejection and I wouldn't let myself think about it because it *hurt*…' That last word cost him such an effort to get out that it was almost whispered.

Tears were trickling down Maribel's cheeks. 'Oh, Leonidas…'

He removed the champagne glass from her fingers and set it aside so that he could pull her close and comfort her with a tenderness that made her cling to him for a few minutes. 'Of course, I went to the memorial service looking for you without even admitting that to myself. And then when I did, telling myself that it was only because we'd had great sex.'

Maribel sniffed and stole a hanky off him. 'If only I hadn't had that accident,' she sighed.

'But we're together now and I will never let you go.' He admitted how nervous he had been on their wedding day over the bad publicity concerning the stag cruise. Maribel, who had thought he didn't have nerves, was entranced by the idea that she had that much influence over him. When he confided that they had ended up on Zelos, rather than in Italy, because he had been afraid that she might try to leave him she broke down into helpless giggles.

Leonidas slid lean fingers into her chestnut hair and tipped her head back to scan her with steady dark golden eyes of appreciation. 'I know, it's hilarious. Loving you does fill my head with freaky thoughts and fears.'

Maribel stopped laughing. 'Loving me?' she parroted.

'I really, really do love you,' Leonidas declared huskily.

Maribel gazed up at him in wonderment.

'I fought it hard. But there was no escaping it,' Leonidas said ruefully. 'You put me through an emotional wringer— telling me what a lousy father I would be and how irresponsible I was. That was a massive shock to my system and a challenge. I went haywire for a few weeks. Why do you think I engineered that story in the newspaper to expose our relationship? I was seriously jealous of your boyfriend.'

'Sloan? You were jealous? We only had one date.' But Maribel was thrilled that he had been roused to jealousy, for it made her feel wonderfully like a *femme fatale*. 'You truly love me?'

'Didn't I marry you without demanding DNA tests for Elias? Or the safety net of a pre-nup? Didn't you appre-

ciate how much I had to trust and value you to do that?'
Leonidas gave her an appreciative appraisal, his dark eyes
rich and mellow as honey. 'And why do you think I let you
blackmail me into marrying you?'

'To get me back in bed?'

'There is that angle,' Leonidas was honest enough to acknowledge, a wolfish grin curving his handsome mouth.
'But it is what I wanted too, so I let myself be blackmailed.
I would have got around to asking you eventually, but you
got in first. That allowed me to save face.'

Maribel couldn't stop smiling and only just remembered that she had something to say too. 'I was lying when
I said I got over you. I've been in love with you for so long,
you're like a fixture in my heart.'

Leonidas had tensed. 'You lied? You *mean*—'

'Now don't take it so personally. A girl's got to do what
a girl's got to do sometimes and, after all that stuff you
talked about our marriage being a business arrangement and
demanding sex up front, you didn't really deserve a confession of true love.' Maribel eased caressing hands of distraction beneath his shirt. 'But I do love you very very much.'

'Is that the truth?'

Maribel was touched by his uncertainty. 'Yes. I love you.'

'Your penance for withholding that information is that
you don't get to eat. We're going to bed, *agape mou*.'
Leonidas took her ripe lips in a single hungry kiss of heated
intent that left her breathless and with weak knees. Then
he peeled her off him again and closed a hand over hers to
urge her back indoors. She had absolutely no quarrel with
his plan of action.

A long time later, Maribel lying comfortably wrapped
in his arms and hand-fed with appetising nibbles and sips

of wine to conserve her strength, Leonidas confessed that he was sad that he had missed out on the whole experience of her being pregnant, not to mention the first months of their son's life.

'We could have another baby,' Maribel conceded.

'I'd like that, *agape mou*.'

'But not just yet.' Maribel ran a possessive hand over his lean muscular torso and buried her cheek there. 'When I'm pregnant, I spend most of the time wanting to sleep.'

'Not just yet,' Leonidas agreed with a ragged edge to his dark drawl.

Two years later, Sofia Pallis was born.

Mirabel's second pregnancy suffered from none of the anxieties that had burdened the first. With staff to help at every turn, she retained her usual energy right up until the last few weeks. Leonidas took a great interest in every development. It brought them even closer and she really enjoyed carrying her daughter. When her due date came close, Leonidas wouldn't go abroad in case she went into labour early and he stayed with her when Sofia was born. His delight in their daughter was the equal of her own.

Sofia took after both her parents. She inherited her father's lustrous dark brown eyes and her mother's delicate features. Now three-and-a-half years old, Elias was fascinated with his baby sister, but rather disappointed that she couldn't even sit up to play with him.

'She's so little,' Elias lamented with all the drama of a Pallis.

'Sofia will grow,' his mother consoled him.

'She yells a lot.'

'You did too when you were a baby.' Having settled her

infant daughter for the night in the nursery next door, Maribel tugged back the duvet to encourage Elias into bed. He climbed in with a truck tucked under one arm.

Leonidas appeared in the doorway while Maribel was reading a bedtime story. She smiled across the room at him, her heart in her eyes, for he had made her extraordinarily happy and she was not a woman to take that good fortune for granted. When the story was finished, Leonidas walked across the room and opened the door of the built in closet. Mouse unfolded his shaggy limbs and got up to greet him with innocent enthusiasm.

'Dad!' Elias wailed in protest.

'Mouse sleeps downstairs.'

'You're getting so tough,' Maribel told her husband outside their son's bedroom door.

Leonidas laughed softly. 'But Elias was clever hiding the dog like that.'

'No, he was sneaky and so I shall tell him tomorrow when I have the time to explain the difference,' Maribel told him staunchly.

'Who says cunning is always wrong?' Leonidas studied her with smouldering dark golden eyes of appreciation. 'Didn't I take advantage of you on the night that Elias was conceived? There you were all weepy and emotional and lonely and I made the most of the occasion.'

Maribel was shaken by that take on the past. 'I never thought of it that way before.'

'And as long as I live I won't regret it, *agape mou*.' Leonidas breathed with raw sincerity. 'I have you and Elias and Sofia and you are the most precious elements in my world. I cannot imagine my life without you.'

It was the same for Maribel. Her heart was full to overflowing at that instant. He told her how much he loved her and she responded with the same fervour, for they both knew that the strong bonds they shared were very precious. Once Leonidas and Maribel had moved out of sight and hearing, Mouse slunk back upstairs and back into Elias' room again.

The Italian Billionaire's
Pregnant Bride

LYNNE GRAHAM

CHAPTER ONE

SERGIO TORRENTE walked into the Palazzo Azzarini for the first time in ten years.

A magnificent mansion in the Tuscan hills, the palazzo was as famous for its grand Palladian architecture as for its legendary Azzarini wine label, which had spawned a massive empire with vineyards all over the world. Sadly, recent financial reverses had taken their toll: the breathtaking collection of treasures that had once filled the house was gone and the grandeur had become shabby. But it belonged to Sergio now. All of it. Every stone, every inch of rich productive earth, and he was rich enough to turn the clock back and remedy the neglect.

He had regained his birthright; it should have been a moment of supreme triumph. Yet Sergio felt nothing. He had stopped feeling a long time ago. At first it had been a defence mechanism but it had soon become an engrained habit he nourished. He liked the clean, efficient structure of his existence. He did not suffer from emotional highs and lows. When he wanted something more, when he felt the need for a certain buzz to bring him alive, he got it out of sex or physical challenge. He had climbed sheer rock faces in blizzards, trekked through jungles in appalling conditions and engaged in extreme sports. He had not found fear. But he had not found anything he really cared about, either, he acknowledged grimly.

Sergio strolled through the echoing empty entrance hall at an unhurried pace. Once the palazzo had been a happy place and he had been a loving son, who took family affection, wealth and security for granted. But the fond memories had long since been wiped out by the nightmare that had followed. He now knew more than he had ever wanted to know about the depths of human greed. His strong, handsome features set in forbidding lines, he strolled out onto the rear terrace, which overlooked the gardens. The sound of footsteps turned his head. A woman was walking towards him.

Platinum-blonde hair rippled back from Grazia's perfect face. The white slip dress clinging to her pouting nipples and outlining the mound at the junction of her thighs left little to the imagination: she was naked beneath the silk. Grazia had always known what appealed most to a man and it wasn't conversation. He got the message: it was basic and it was instant.

'Don't throw me out.' Her languorous turquoise eyes proffered an invitation that both teased and begged. 'There's nothing I won't do for a second chance with you.'

Sergio raised a derisive ebony brow. 'I don't do second chances.'

'Even if this time I offer you a free trial? No strings attached? I can say sorry with style.' With a provocative look, Grazia folded fluidly down on her knees in front of him and reached for the clasp on his belt.

For a split second, Sergio was taut and then he vented an appreciative laugh. A consummate survivor, Grazia had the morals of a whore but at least she was honest about it. To the winner went the spoils. And without a doubt she was a prize many men would kill to possess, for she was beautiful, sexually adventurous and an aristocrat born and bred. He knew exactly what Grazia was, as once she had been his. A heartbeat later, however, when his bright prospects were destroyed, she had been his brother's. Love on a budget had had zero appeal for Grazia; she went where the money was. And time had wrought dramatic changes, since Sergio was now a billionaire and the Azzarini vineyards were just one small part of his enterprises.

'You're my brother's wife,' he reminded her softly, angling his lean hips back to lounge indolently against the wall a tantalising few inches out of her reach, 'and I don't do adultery, *cara mia*.'

His mobile phone rang. 'Excuse me,' he murmured with perfect cool and he walked back indoors, just leaving her kneeling in sensual subservience on the tiles of the terrace.

The call was from his security chief, Renzo Catallone, in London. Sergio suppressed a sigh. Once a senior police officer, the older man took his job very seriously. Sergio had a valuable chess set on display in his London office and, a few weeks ago, he'd been startled to see that someone, in blatant disregard of the 'Do Not Touch' notice, had solved the most recent chess puzzle he had laid out on the board. Since then, every subsequent move Sergio had made had been matched.

'Look, if it's bothering you that much, hide a surveillance camera nearby,' Sergio suggested.

'This nonsense with the chessboard is bugging my whole team,' Renzo confessed. 'We're determined to catch this joker out.'

'What are we going to do with him when we catch

him?' Sergio enquired drily. 'Charge him with challenging me to a game of chess?'

'It's more serious than you think,' the older man countered. 'That vestibule is in a private area right beside your office, yet someone is walking in and out of there whenever they like. It's a dangerous breach of security. I checked the board this afternoon but I couldn't tell if any of the pieces had been moved again.'

'Don't worry about it,' Sergio told him gently. 'I will know immediately.'

Not least because he was playing a highly innovative opponent, ready to use a game to attract his attention. The culprit could only be an ambitious member of his executive staff, keen to impress him with his strategic skills.

The young man was so busy staring at Kathy that he almost tripped over a chair on his way out of the café.

'You're seriously good for business.' Bridget Kirk's round, good-natured face shone with amusement. A bustling brunette of forty-one, she was the manager. 'All the men want you to serve them. When are you going to pick one of them to go out with?'

Her green eyes veiled to conceal her awkwardness at the question, Kathy forced a laugh. 'I haven't got time for a boyfriend.'

Watching the youthful redhead pull on her jacket to go home, Bridget suppressed a sigh. Kathy Galvin was drop-dead gorgeous and only twenty-three years old, but she lived like a hermit. 'You could always squeeze one in somewhere. You're only young once. All you seem to do is work and study. I hope you're not worrying about old history and how to explain it. That's all behind you now.'

Kathy resisted the urge to respond that the past was still with her all the time, physically in the shape of a livid scar on her back, haunting her in nightmares and shadowing and threatening her even during daylight hours with a sense of insecurity. She knew now that if you were unlucky you didn't even need to do anything bad to have everything taken away from you. Her life had gone badly wrong when she was nineteen years old. As far as she knew nothing she had done had contributed to that situation. Indeed, when she had been least expecting it, calamity had come out of nowhere and almost destroyed her. Although she had survived the experience it had changed her. Once she had been confident, outgoing and trusting. She had also had complete faith in the integrity of the justice system and an even deeper belief in the essential kindness of other human beings. Four years on, those convictions had taken a savage beating and now she preferred to keep herself to herself, rather than invite rejection and hurt.

Bridget squeezed the younger woman's slight shoulder. It was a stretch for her because Kathy was a good bit taller than she was. 'It *is* behind you now,' the brunette murmured gently. 'Stop brooding about it.'

Walking home, Kathy reflected how lucky she was to work for someone like Bridget, who accepted her in spite of her past. Unhappily, Kathy had discovered that if she wanted to work that kind of honesty was a rare luxury, and she had learnt to be inventive with her CV to explain the gap in her employment record. To survive she had two jobs: evenings as an office cleaner, day shifts as a waitress. She needed every penny to pay the bills and there was nothing left over at the end. Even so, long, frustrating months of soul-destroying unemployment had taught

Kathy to be grateful for what she had. Few people were as generous and open-minded as Bridget. Although Kathy had qualifications, she'd still had to settle for unskilled and poorly paid work.

As always, it was a relief to get the door of her bedsit safely shut behind her. She loved her privacy and relished the fact that she had no noisy neighbours. She had painted the bedsit's walls pale colours to reflect the light that flooded through the window. Tigger was curled up on the sill outside awaiting her return. She let the elderly tortoiseshell cat in and fed him. He was a stray and half-wild and it had taken months for her to win his trust. Even now he would panic if she closed the window, so no matter how cold it was it stayed open for the duration of his visits. She understood exactly how he felt and his health had improved greatly since she had begun caring for him. His coat had acquired a gloss and his thin lanky frame a decent covering of flesh.

Tigger reminded her of the pet cat that her family had once cherished. An only child, Kathy had had a chequered early history. Abandoned by her birth mother in a park when she was a year old, Kathy had been adopted as a toddler. But by the time she was ten tragedy had struck again when her adoptive mother had died in a train crash, and soon afterwards a debilitating illness had begun to claim her father's health. Kathy had become a carer in her teens, struggling to cope with looking after the older man while at the same time running a home on a tight budget and keeping up with her schoolwork. Her love for her surviving parent had strengthened her and if she had any consolation now it was that her father had died before the bright academic future he had foreseen for his daughter had been destroyed.

A couple of hours later, Kathy entered the office block where she worked five nights a week. She had got to quite like cleaning. It was peaceful. As long as she got through her work on time, nobody bossed her about and there were very few men around to harass her. She had soon discovered that hardly anyone paid much heed to the maintenance staff: it was if their very lowliness made them invisible and unworthy of notice, which suited Kathy right down to the ground. She had never been comfortable with the way her looks tended to attract male attention.

As there were still some employees at work, she dealt with the public areas first. Even the stalwarts were packing up to go home when she began on the offices. She was emptying a bin when an impatient masculine voice hailed her from the far end of the corridor.

'Are you the cleaner? Come into my office—I've had a spillage!'

Kathy spun round. The man in the smart business suit didn't bother to look at her before he swung on his heel. As she hurried in his wake with her trolley he vanished through the doorway that led into the swanky private office suite where the pretentious chess set was on display. The 'Do Not Touch' notice was still in a prominent position. Her mouth quirked and her gaze skimmed the board as she moved past. Another move had been made by her unknown opponent. She would make hers during her break when she was the only person left on the floor.

The big office was huge and imposing and it had a fabulous view of the London City skyline. The man had his back turned to her while he talked on the phone in a foreign language. He was very tall with broad shoulders and black hair. Those observations concluded her interest, for she finally spotted the spillage he had mentioned: a porcelain coffee jug with a broken handle that had spread its contents over a wide area. She soaked up the dark liquid as best she could and then went to fill her bucket with fresh water.

Sergio ended his phone call and sat down at his glass desk. Only then did he notice the cleaner, who was down on her knees busily scrubbing the carpet on the other side of the office. The long hair clasped at her nape was an eye-catching metallic mix of copper, amber and auburn shades.

'Thank you. I'm sure that'll do,' he told her dismissively.

Kathy glanced up. 'It'll stain if I leave it,' she warned.

She settled huge green eyes on him. They were fringed with lashes like a cartoon fawn's, Sergio found himself thinking abstractedly. Her face was heart-shaped and unusual and so spectacular in its beauty that he who never stared at a woman stared. Even a shapeless overall could not conceal the grace of her slender long-legged figure. Just as quickly he was convinced that she could not possibly be an authentic cleaner. She had to be an out-of-work actress or a model. Women that beautiful didn't scrub floors for a living. How had she got past Security?

Had one of his friends set him up for a joke? Neither of his best friends was a likely candidate, Sergio acknowledged wryly. It would be too juvenile a trick for Leonidas, and Rashad had become alarmingly unadventurous since he had acquired a wife and children. Of course he had other friends. But it was equally likely that the lady was trying to set him up for her own reasons.

For a split second when she focused on the male behind the desk, Kathy had gawped like a startled schoolgirl because he was a dazzlingly handsome guy. He had gleaming cropped black hair, brilliant eyes like polished jet set below level brows, high sculpted cheekbones and a strong patrician nose. The whole was connected by smooth planes of olive skin that roughened and darkened around his hard jaw line. Her heart slowed to a dulled heavy thud that seemed to get in the way of her breathing normally.

'The carpet?' she framed unevenly, the effort of even remembering the task she had been doing a challenge as she scrambled to her feet, ready to leave.

Sergio was committing her flawless features to memory. Stunning women were not a novelty to him. So, he was still trying to work out what it was about her face that gave it such amazingly powerful appeal that it was a challenge to look away from her. He lounged back in his seat with deceptive indolence. 'Go ahead and clean it,' he urged huskily. 'But before you do, answer one question. Which one of my friends sent you here?'

Her delicate brows pleated and she hovered with perceptible uneasiness. Pink tinting her pale ivory skin, she dragged her attention from him only to be shaken by the compulsion to look afresh. It was as though a piece of indiscernible elastic were tightening and trying to jerk her eyes back to him again by force. 'I'm sorry—I don't understand. Look, I'll come back and finish this later.'

'No, do it now.' Sergio arrested her retreat in its tracks with the command. Her apparent bewilderment at his query was making him question his initial suspicions.

Arrogant, demanding, oversexed…Kathy gave him a rude label inside her head, a flush of angry embarrassment colouring her cheeks. She wanted out of his office: she wasn't stupid. She knew why he had asked if one of his friends had sent her. On another occasion a male member of staff had asked her hopefully if she was a strippergram girl. It infuriated her that such insulting assumptions should be made purely on the basis of her appearance. She was doing her job and she had the same right as anyone else to be left in peace to get on with it! As she knelt back down again she accidentally collided with black eyes that flared as golden as flames and momentarily held her transfixed. For a timeless moment she was still, breathing held in suspension, mouth running dry. Then she blinked, tore her attention free again with difficulty and discovered that her mind was a total blank, for his sensationally attractive image was now stamped there in place of rational thought.

Sergio was watching her every move and she made no effort that he could see to put on a show designed to draw his notice to her. Her clothing was unremarkable, the overall all-concealing. She was not provocative and her movements were very quiet, so why was he still watching her? There was something different about her, an unknown element that stood out and grabbed his attention. The pale pink blush of awareness that had swept her ivory complexion had sent his healthy male hormones on a rampant surge. Her amazing eyes were as green as the bitter-sweet apples his English grandfather had once grown and there was a surprisingly direct look in them. A lingering appraisal of the lush pout of her crushed strawberry mouth was sufficient to arouse him to a serious level of discomfort.

Kathy kept on working at the patch of carpet that she knew needed more specialist attention than she could give it. She was really fighting to think straight but she was amazed by her response to him. No man had had that effect on her since Gareth—and Gareth had never left her so bemused that she scarcely knew what she was doing. But then she had been in love, a dreaming teenager drifting along on a raft of foolish romantic expectations. Her reaction to the guy in the business suit, she reasoned feverishly, was just a reminder that Mother Nature had blessed her with the same physical chemistry as every other human being and sexual attraction was just a part of that. Maybe she should be welcoming the discovery that a broken heart and disillusionment hadn't entirely killed off her ability to feel like a normal woman.

'Excuse me…' she muttered with careful politeness, moving across the room to leave.

Instinct made Sergio spring upright. Near the doorway she lifted her bright head, her apple green eyes telegraphing her tension. The words of amused protest he had been about to voice to retain her presence went unspoken. *Madonna diavolo*, she was a cleaner and he a Torrente! His strong bone structure tautened, rigorous self-discipline reinstated. What was he thinking of? But he still could not accept that it was a coincidence that such a strikingly beautiful woman should be working so close to his office and conveniently available at his first call. It was even more unusual for him to work late without his customary support staff in attendance. It *had* to be some kind of a set-up!

Sergio was well aware that his fabulous wealth made him a constant target. Women frequently went to extreme lengths to catch his eye. Vital pieces of clothing slipped so that he could see what was on offer and how easily available it was. Any shade of gallantry in his character had turned to hardened cynicism while he was still a teenager. Too many maidens in distress had vied for his attention with fake incidents that ranged from cars that had broken down, doors that wouldn't unlock and flights that had been mysteriously missed to last-minute accommodation problems and sudden attacks of illness. Innumerable women had used the tactics of guile and trickery just to get the chance to meet Sergio and spark his interest. A seemingly respectable and very bright PA had once stripped down to her saucy lingerie to bring him coffee, while several others had used late meetings and business trips to get naked and raunchy for his benefit. At the age of thirty-one, he had received countless sexual invitations, some subtle, most of them bold and a few downright strange.

The door safely shut behind her again, Kathy drank in a quivering breath of oxygen to replenish her starved lungs. She wondered who he was and then discarded the thought again. What did it matter to her who he was? On the way past the chessboard, with its pieces fashioned of polished metal and glittering stones, she hesitated, studied the state of play and swiftly sacrificed a pawn, hoping to tempt the other player into relaxing their guard. Was it *him*? She thought it highly improbable: there were two other large offices linked to that inner hallway and one of them contained half a dozen desks. A posh guy with gold cuff links and a cold upper-class accent that just shrieked an English public school education struck her as a very unlikely candidate for exchanging long-distance chess moves with a total stranger. She sped back down the corridor to continue the work he had interrupted.

Sergio was closing his laptop when the phone rang.

'We've got the mysterious chess joker on camera, sir,' Renzo revealed with satisfaction.

'When did you manage that? This evening?'

'The incident took place last night. I've had a man checking the surveillance footage for hours. I think you'll be surprised by what I've found out.'

'So, surprise me,' Sergio urged, stifling his impatience.

'It's a young woman, one of the maintenance staff, who works nights—a cleaner called Kathy Galvin. She started here a month ago.'

Incredulity awakened in Sergio's cool dark features and was swiftly followed by strong curiosity. 'Send the relevant images to my computer.'

Sergio ran the footage on screen while keeping Renzo on the telephone, and there she was: the ravishing redhead. He watched her get up from the sofa in the vestibule where she had evidently been taking a nap and stretch. With a cursory glance down at the board she moved the white knight. Was it sexist to suspect that someone much cleverer was advising her by mobile phone on her skilful game? She then began to tidy her tousled hair, unclasping it and pulling out a comb. He was put in mind of a mermaid showing off her crowning glory to tempt sailors onto the rocks. He wondered if she knew the camera was there while he feasted his attention on her exquisite face and froze her image on screen.

'It's misconduct, sir,' Renzo told him eagerly.

'You think so?' Sergio got up from his desk, taking the portable phone with him as he strolled out to take a look at the chessboard. Evidently she had abandoned caution and made another move directly after leaving his office. Why? No doubt she was keen to help him to speedily unveil her identity and take the bait. Illicit napping on the job aside, the humble toil of cleaning duties had to be a serious challenge for a woman only doing it in an effort to cross his path.

'She'll be disciplined, probably sacked by the contract company when we lodge a complaint—'

'No. Leave this matter with me and be discreet about it,' Sergio interposed softly. 'I'll handle it.'

'You'll handle it, sir?' his security chief repeated in audible astonishment. 'Are you sure?'

'Of course. I also want that surveillance camera put out of commission right now.' Sergio tossed the phone down. His astute dark eyes were shot through with derisive gold. So she wasn't a genuine hard-working salt-of-the-earth cleaner worthy of his respect. Why had he been willing to believe she was for even five minutes? Put that glorious face and body in tandem with the creative chess game aimed at attracting his attention and he had yet another gold-digger in hot and original pursuit.

Open season for the hunt, Sergio mused with sardonic amusement. He was a hell of a good shot and he intended to have some fun. And sooner rather than later, because he was leaving London the next day to compete in a cross-country skiing marathon in Norway. After that he had business to attend to in New York. It would be ten days before he was back in the UK.

Rising to his full imposing height of six feet three inches, Sergio strode out of the office and down the corridor in search of his quarry. He found her dusting a desk. Her fabulous hair glittered in multi-shaded splendour below the ceiling lights. When she straightened and saw him in the doorway, an expression of surprise grew on her delicate features. Grudging amusement assailed Sergio: she knew how to stay in role all right. Looking at that frowning air of enquiry, nobody would have dreamt that she had been teasing and tantalising him with a game that he considered very much his own for almost three weeks.

'Let's play chess in the real world, *bella mia*,' Sergio

suggested with silken cool. 'I challenge you to finish the game tonight. If you win, you get me. If you lose, you still get me. How can you lose?'

CHAPTER TWO

KATHY stared at Sergio Torrente for a good ten seconds. Her every expectation was shattered by that challenge coming at her out of the blue, and from such a source as the powerfully built male confronting her. For a long time now, she had protected herself by never taking a risk and never stepping out of line to be noticed. Sudden unexpected attention from a stranger and the belated realisation that she had foolishly invited it unnerved her.

Yet she was mortifyingly aware that it was his bold, dark masculine beauty that claimed her attention first. Win or lose, he was on offer? Was he serious? If he was, would she dare to take him up on it? While she'd worked she had told herself that he could not have been half as attractive as she had thought he was. Now here he was again in the flesh to blow that staid and sensible belief right out of the water. Just looking at the proud, chiselled planes of his darkly handsome features gave her the strangest sense of pleasure. A frisson of dangerous exhilaration gripped her while butterflies fluttered in her stomach. She parted her lips without even knowing what she intended to say. 'I—er—'

Glittering black eyes centred on her with laser beam intensity. 'Backing down from a face-to-face contest?' he murmured with unconcealed scorn.

Anger shot through Kathy with a power and sharpness that she had forgotten she could feel and she lifted her chin in answer. 'Are you kidding?'

Sergio stepped back to allow her to precede him from the room. 'Then let's go and play.'

'But I'm working,' Kathy pointed out with a slow bemused shake of her head. 'For goodness' sake, who are you?'

A mocking ebony brow quirked. 'Is that a serious question?'

'Why wouldn't it be?'

'I am Sergio Torrente and I own the Torrenco Group,' Sergio delivered drily, wondering whether she thought it was clever to make what he considered to be an outrageous claim of ignorance. 'Every company in this block belongs to me. I find it hard to believe that you're not aware of those facts.'

Kathy was paralysed to the spot by that revelation. It had not even occurred to her that he might be that important. But, even so, she had never heard of him before. She had never been on any floor other than the one she was on now and she had had no interest whatsoever in the business world or the personalities that powered the huge building during the hours of daylight.

'So will you play?' Sergio prompted with impatience.

An adrenalin rush was firing self-preservation skills in Kathy. It was clear to her that she had picked the wrong chessboard to get familiar with and the wrong guy. Why had she not even suspected that he might be her opponent? His smooth urbane façade had deceived her, she conceded tautly. He radiated an aura of sophisticated ease and cool.

But the breathtaking elegance of his designer suit concealed a purebred predator, for he was a highly aggressive and clever player who took advantage of every tactical opportunity to attack. In short, he was very much an Alpha male incapable of ignoring any perceived challenge to prove his strength. Not a guy to tangle with, not a guy to offend.

'I could take my break now,' Kathy told him, ready to get her punishment over with, as instead of beating him in two moves as she had previously planned she decided that it would be wiser to let him win.

Sergio nodded, hooded dark golden eyes nailed to her because he had yet to work out what script she was trying to follow. Was he really supposed to credit that she didn't know who he was?

'I've had the board moved into my office so that we can play undisturbed.'

Her heart was now beating very fast with nervous tension. He thrust open the door of his office, then stood back. Momentarily she was close enough to catch the faint evocative scent of some expensive male cologne. She snatched in a charged breath. 'How did you know it was me? How did you find out?'

'That's not important.'

'It's important to me,' she dared.

'Surveillance camera,' he supplied.

Kathy lost colour. There was a security camera in that hallway? She was appalled by that news. She took her breaks there and, once or twice, when she had been very tired, she had set the alarm on her watch and taken a nap on that sofa. Proof of those facts would be sufficient to put her out of a job.

'Would you like a drink?'

Her slender figure now tense as a bowstring, Kathy hovered in the centre of the carpet. A pool of light shone across the board and the sofas in one corner. It was a very intimate backdrop. If the supervisor came looking for her and found her in such a situation she would get totally the wrong idea and alcohol was a sackable offence. 'Are you trying to get me fired?'

'If you don't talk, I won't,' Sergio countered with lazy indifference.

An automatic negative was on Kathy's lips, but suddenly a spirit of rebellion sparked inside her. With the proof he already had of her stealing a nap during her break, there was little point splitting hairs. 'You're only young once,' Bridget had scolded that same day. But Kathy had never really known what it was to be young and carefree. Since she had regained her freedom she had followed every rule she met everywhere to the letter, no matter how small the rule, no matter how petty. The habit had become engrained in her, the new secure framework by which she lived. The chess game had been the only deviation and only because she couldn't resist the temptation of reliving the challenges her late father had once set her. In truth she could not even recall when she had last tasted alcohol and that made her feel pathetic, sad and defiant. She named a fashionable drink that she had seen advertised on a billboard.

'You seem very tense.' Sergio passed her a glass. Translucent green eyes rested on him, providing an alluring contrast to her alabaster skin and copper and red streaked hair. Predictably, he went straight for it. 'Don't stress, *bella mia*. I find you incredibly attractive.'

The annoyance and embarrassment that Kathy usually felt at such moments was entirely absent. So, he had been serious. She felt as if her heart were pounding right at the foot of her throat. She was shaken by the discovery that she was thrilled by his approach. Her fingers tightened round the glass, her hand shook a little. She sipped and swallowed, sipped and swallowed again, to conceal the reality of her physical weakness. It was so uncool to be so excited. Locked into his stunning dark golden gaze when she finally raised the courage to look up, she could not have breathed to save her life.

Unhurriedly, Sergio angled his lustrous dark head down. He was testing the boundaries, amusing himself. The delicate fresh scent of her skin made his strong, hard body tauten. Arousal slivered through him with a force that surprised him and speedily tipped him out of teasing mode. He claimed her luscious pink lips with hungry urgency and that first taste only whet his appetite for more.

Kathy couldn't credit what she was doing, but she wouldn't have shifted an inch to prevent it happening, either. A storm tide of feeling engulfed her and she couldn't get enough of it. It was as energising as hitching a ride on a rocket and it left her equally dizzy and disorientated. He kissed her and fireworks of sensation shot through her and she pulsed and tingled with response. Honeyed warmth pooled in her tummy, a tightness forming at her pelvis. She shivered violently when the sensual glide of his tongue probed the tender cave of her mouth. The throb of desire that flashed and stabbed through her slim length was almost too much to bear and she moaned in protest.

'You are so hot, you burn,' Sergio framed and, as his deep, dark drawl roughened, a faint Italian accent broke through to mellow the syllables with a lyrical edge. 'But we have a game to finish.'

Kathy wasn't quite sure her legs would keep her upright long enough to reach the sofa at her side of the board. She would have found it easier to fall back into his arms than walk away, an acknowledgement that shook her up even more. Her body felt tight, overheated and unfamiliar. She was aware of it in ways that were new to her. All the time her brain was set on enumerating her mistakes. She shouldn't be in a room alone with him, shouldn't have allowed him to kiss her, and certainly shouldn't have encouraged him by responding. But while her intelligence knew each and every one of those things, the hunger he had awakened and the dissatisfaction he had left behind had an even stronger hold on her.

Two moves later, the chess game was over.

When Sergio won, his black brows drew together and then anger illuminated his narrowed gaze to gilded bronze. 'Either someone else has been telling you how to play for the past three weeks, or you just deliberately threw the game to let me win!'

Kathy was dismayed by his discernment but determined to tough it out. 'You won…okay?'

'No, it is not okay. Which was it?' Sergio countered icily.

The silence felt suffocating. Tension made it hard for her to swallow. She scrambled up. 'I should get back to work.'

Hauteur stamped on his lean hard features, Sergio vaulted upright, well over six feet of lean, muscular male. 'You will go nowhere until you give me an answer.'

Kathy dealt him a troubled glance and screened her green eyes. His cold anger took her aback. 'My goodness, it's only a game,' she mumbled.

'Answer me,' Sergio commanded.

Kathy heaved a sigh and shifted her hands in a dismissive gesture. 'I let you win…all right?'

Sergio could not recall when he had last been so outraged by a woman. 'Is that what you believe I wanted or expected from you? Do you think I am so vain that I need a fake victory to bolster my ego?' he shot at her with stinging contempt. 'I don't need that kind of sacrifice and I don't like flattery. This is not the way to please me.'

Temper like a red-hot flame was darting through Kathy's willowy form. 'Well, then, you should stop throwing your weight around and behaving like a bully!' she launched back at him half an octave higher. 'How do you expect me to behave? How am I supposed to cope with you? Let's not pretend that this is a level playing field or that you gave me a choice—'

'Don't shout at me,' Sergio breathed glacially while inside he reeled in stunned disbelief from that condemnation.

'You wouldn't be listening otherwise. I'm sorry I touched your stupid chess set, but it was only meant to be a harmless piece of fun. I'm sorry I let you win and offended you. But I wasn't trying to please you—I couldn't care less about pleasing you!' Kathy flung back at him in disgust. 'I was trying to *placate* you…I'm supposed to be working. I don't want to lose my job. Can I get back to work now?'

Her attitude shone a bright revisionist light on the confrontation for Sergio. He had a brilliant penetrating mind and an unequalled talent for strategy. In business he was invincible, for he united the survival skills and killing instincts of a shark with a similar lack of emotion. He had learned early not to accept people at face value. But would a woman out to impress him shout at him? He had no evidence of anything calculated in Kathy Galvin's behaviour. Why should she have known who he was?

Sergio reached a decision on the basis of the facts. 'You really are just the cleaner.'

An affronted flush coloured Kathy's face as she wondered what on earth that comment was supposed to mean. Had he perhaps thought she was an undercover spy? Or a hooker moonlighting with a mop? 'Yes,' she said tightly. 'Just the cleaner—excuse me.'

As the door flipped shut on her quick exit Sergio swore softly in Italian, because he had not intended to humiliate her. The phone rang.

It was Renzo again. 'I've been running a check on the cleaning lady with the chess fetish—'

'Unnecessary,' Sergio interposed.

The older man cleared his throat. 'Galvin has a dodgy CV, sir. I don't think she's what she says she is. Although she's a very bright girl with a fistful of top grades from school, her employment record only contains some very recent restaurant work. It doesn't add up. There's a gap of three years and no adequate explanation for it. According to the résumé she was travelling all that time, but I don't buy it.'

'Neither do I.' His lean, strong face hard, Sergio considered the fact that for the first time in a decade he had almost been conned by a woman.

'I think she's probably another bimbo on the make, or even a paparazzo. I'll ask the cleaning company to remove her from the rota. Thankfully, she's their problem, not ours.'

But Sergio was unwilling to let Kathy Galvin off so easily. When had he ever walked away from a challenge?

Kathy worked at speed in an attempt to lose her troubled thoughts in energetic activity. The treatment she had received had left her angry and bewildered. Sergio Torrente was a gorgeous guy with an attitude problem. A rampant snob and very proud. Cool at best, he was colder than ice when he was crossed. But when he had kissed her, pure naked excitement had made mincemeat of all his faults. Had he momentarily contrived to forget that she was *just* the cleaner? He must have done. He was probably at least thirty years old and way too mature for her. She rammed the mop into the bucket with noisy unnecessary force. She had nothing in common with some super-rich older guy who owned a building and made a big fuss when some lesser mortal dared to muck around with his chessboard!

She began to wonder if she was fated to die a virgin. Year after year, life was steadily passing her by. Sergio Torrente was the first bloke she had fancied since Gareth had dumped her. How clever was that? Sexual chemistry was very strange, she mused ruefully. Why hadn't she warmed to one of the many men who had tried to chat her up at the café? Obviously she was being rather too fussy. Even so, she was convinced that nine out of ten women would find Sergio Torrente pretty much irresistible. She had never gone for boyish men or the type who might almost be described as pretty. His lean dark features contrived to unite classic good looks with a raw and compelling masculinity that was seriously sexy, Kathy ruminated dreamily, wielding her mop with less and less vigour.

'Kathy…?'

Her head flew up, light green eyes preoccupied. When she saw the subject of her most intimate thoughts standing just ten feet from her she did a double take. As she felt her wretched skin colouring up in a wave of guilty heat she wanted the ground to open up and swallow her alive. 'Yes?'

'I owe you an apology.'

Kathy nodded in firm agreement.

Sergio, who had been awaiting a flattering protest at that statement, laughed with reluctant appreciation. She was turning in a prize-winning performance in the sincerity stakes. Was her candour supposed to strike him as a refreshing quality? Appeal to his jaded billionaire palate and need for novelty? He didn't know and he didn't care. The fawn-like lashes swept down on her amazing eyes and desire dug talon claws of need into his groin. What did it matter if she sold her story afterwards to some tacky tabloid? One glimpse of her exquisite face and the most basic of male instincts took over. His reaction to her was atavistic and stronger than anything he had felt in a long time. To look at her without touching her almost hurt. He knew that the only thing that would satisfy him now was bedding her. He had never been into self-denial.

'Will you play another game with me when your shift ends?' Sergio asked silkily.

Kathy was astonished by the apology and the renewed invitation. In a wary and fleeting collision with brilliant dark eyes as crystal-clear and cold as an underground lake, she sensed the danger of him: the powerful personality reined in below the surface. Clever, ruthless, definitely not the sort of male anyone would want as an enemy. It dismayed her that even sensing those hard-nosed qualities she should still find him incredibly attractive. She swallowed hard, struggling to pay heed to her misgivings. 'I'm afraid I don't finish until eleven o'clock.'

'It's not a problem.'

'No?' Temptation was tugging at her with relentless force.

'No. I haven't eaten yet. I'll send a car to pick you up when you're finished.'

'Can't we just play here?' Kathy gave way but only on terms that she felt would be comfortable for her. She didn't want to risk being seen with him. Nor did she want to climb into some strange car to be taken heaven knew where and possibly left to find her own way home again in the early hours of the morning.

His surprise was patent. 'If that's what you want.'

'It is.'

Kathy watched his long fluid stride carry him out of her sight. She was in a daze, not quite able to accept that he had talked her round with very little effort. It was only a game of chess, she told herself in sudden exasperation. He was still set on winning. If he kissed her again, she would…well, she would just make sure that they didn't get that close. It would be pointless, him with his business empire and her with her history. And she didn't want to be kicked in the teeth again, did she? There was no point literally queuing up to get hurt. But nor was there any harm in pitting her wits against his.

Five minutes before eleven, Kathy freshened up in the cloakroom. She folded up her overall and dug it into her bag. Her turquoise cotton T-shirt clung to her minimal curves. She turned sideways, breathed in deep and arched her spine. Her bosom remained disappointingly slight from every angle. Meeting her own eyes in the mirror, she flushed in embarrassment and concentrated on brushing her hair instead.

Kathy was twenty-three years old but, just then, she felt more like a nervous teenager. That lowering feeling of ignorance and insecurity annoyed her. The years between nineteen and twenty-two, when she might have acquired a little more experience, had been stolen from her. As soon as that bitter thought occurred to her, she buried it again, for she tried never to look back in that spirit; it did her no good to dwell on what could not be changed. She had spent three years in prison for a crime she had not committed and still bore the scars, mentally and physically. But few had been willing to believe in her innocence and indeed had often judged her more harshly for daring to make such a claim. Get over it, she told herself firmly; leave it in the past, move on.

When she walked into his office, her lissom figure and endless long coltish legs merely enhanced by a T-shirt and jeans, Sergio was startled by her impact. The exotic slant of her cheekbones was more obvious with her glorious hair tumbling in loose waves round her narrow shoulders—hair the colour of tangerine marmalade in sunlight, glinting with amber and ochre shades that acted as a superb showcase for her white skin and apple-green eyes.

'Have you ever been a model?' he asked while he poured her another drink.

'No. I don't fancy walking half naked down a catwalk. I like food too much, as well. Could you spare a packet of crisps?' Her tummy grumbling with hunger, Kathy had noticed the snacks in the snazzy drinks cabinet that stood open.

'Help yourself. You seem more relaxed than you were earlier,' Sergio remarked.

'I'm on my own free time.' Kathy curled up on the sofa and munched crisps while she played. The salty snack made her thirsty and she had to keep on sipping her drink. She only allowed herself to study him closely several moves into the game when he seemed unaware of her attention.

But no matter how much she looked at him, Sergio

Torrente still took her breath away. He was drop-dead beautiful. Hair and lashes with the sheen of black silk, mesmeric dark eyes, a strong sensual mouth. He had shaved since she had last seen him—the faint bluish shadow of stubble had vanished. She wondered if that meant he planned to kiss her again. Heat pooled in her tummy and warmed more intimate places with a physical awareness that took her aback. She reminded herself that she had come to play chess, not to flirt.

Sergio glanced up. 'Your move.'

Her lashes dropping in a protective screen over her eyes, she studied the board.

Sergio watched her demonstrate a skill, speed and assurance that made it clear that she was well able to hold her own. 'Who taught you to play?'

'My father.'

'So did mine.' His lean strong face shadowed. Silence lay before he matched her on the board and then, noticing her empty glass, he rose to refill it.

Her light green eyes rested on him throughout the exercise. Everything about him fascinated her: the classy cut of his hair, the designer *élan* of his suit, the discreet gleam of gold at his wrist and cuff, the fluid way he moved his lean brown hands when he spoke. He was very elegant and very controlled.

'If you keep on looking at me like that, we'll never finish the game, *bella mia*.'

Kathy reddened and took the glass he extended with a hand that wasn't quite steady. He had read her so easily it embarrassed her. It also reminded her of how little she knew about him. As she thought of what she should have asked at the outset she tensed. 'Are you married?'

Surprise made Sergio quirk an ebony brow. 'Why are you asking?'

'Is that a yes or a no?'

'I'm single.'

Although her head was swimming a little, Kathy sidestepped the trap he had set for her on the board and shot him a victorious smile.

'You're good,' Sergio conceded, amused by the suspicion that she too might have set out to play a very fast game. 'We have a tie. Tact or fact?'

'Fact.'

Her cheeky grin of challenge brought out the caveman in him.

He leant down, closed a hand into her tumbling copperstreaked tresses to raise her face to his and drove her delectable pink lips hungrily apart, making love to her mouth with devastating expertise.

That sudden taste of him took Kathy by storm. Desire exploded through her slender length like a depth charge that ignited on impact. Shards of sensation rippled through her. He kissed with an eroticism that was spellbinding. As he pulled her up against him her arms went round him to steady herself because she was dizzy. The alcohol? She shut down that suspicion, suddenly determined not to succumb to her need to play safe again. She was breathless with excitement, her heart pounding like mad. For the first time that she could remember she felt young and fearless and alive.

'I can't keep my hands off you,' Sergio told her softly.

'We were playing chess,' Kathy reminded him in a breathless whisper.

'I want to play with you instead, *delizia mia*.'

That was a touch too blunt for her. Her cheeks flamed, her confusion patent. With a sardonic laugh, he raked smouldering golden eyes over her exquisite face. He lowered his handsome dark head again. The invasive stab of his tongue inside her mouth was deliciously sensual and she pressed helplessly closer to his hard masculine frame for more. Against her lower stomach she could feel the hard, intimate proof of his arousal and she shivered. Her hands fixed to the wide, steely strength of his shoulders. Her response overwhelmed and ensnared her. A tight little knot of desire was unfurling low in her pelvis, filling her with yearning and impatience. Even her senses seemed to have gone into hyperactive mode: her fingers filtered through his springy black hair and rejoiced in the silken texture while the already familiar scent of his skin acted on her like an aphrodisiac.

Sergio had planned to finish the game first and it had finished on schedule. Sergio always planned everything. But desire was a raging fire in his blood and that driving intensity was novel to him. Her slim body slotted into his lean powerful frame as though she had been born to make that connection. What he was feeling was addictive and he wanted more of it and *all* of her. He lowered her down on the sofa and discarded his jacket and tie.

That temporary separation made Kathy tense and question what she was doing. Even though her mind was fuzzy, she told herself to get up. Hair spread in a burnished mass of Titian splendour round her head, she looked up at him, eyes glazed with passion and uncertainty, her generous mouth rosy red from the attention of his. He chose that particular moment to smile down at her. 'You are gorgeous,' he told her and it was a smile of such charismatic power that she felt as though her heart were bouncing like a rubber ball inside her chest.

A tiny pulse was going crazy at her collar-bone. Sergio put his mouth to the delicate blue-veined skin and she gasped and arrowed up to him. Her body was thrumming like an engine that was raring to go and she didn't know how to handle the stress of it. He found the bare skin below her T-shirt and closed his hand to a tiny, sweet pouting mound. For an instant she went stiff because she had forgotten that she had no bra on and there was no warning before he found the part of her body that she was least confident about. He pushed the turquoise fabric out of his path and exposed her small breasts to his appreciative scrutiny.

'Ravishing,' Sergio pronounced with satisfaction, catching a pouting nipple the colour of a tea rose between thumb and finger and chafing the delicate bud until a smothered sound of response was wrenched from her. He used his tongue to moisten the distended crest and it was only the beginning of a slow process of sensual torment. Her hips jerked and shifted with increasing frequency, her thighs pressing together on the ache of emptiness that was stirring between them. Her breath rasped in her throat as he toyed with the sensitised nubs until they were stiff and taut and wildly responsive to his every caress.

Reaction was piling onto reaction too fast for her to bear. She was on the heights of a frantic anticipation that utterly controlled her. He coiled back from her to peel off her jeans. For an instant awareness returned to her when she rocked back up into sitting position to blink in vague surprise at the sight of her bare legs. Tiny tremors of frantic desire were quivering through her. She met hot golden eyes and burned inside and out, sensible thought sizzling into nothingness.

'Sergio,' she whispered wonderingly.

That fast he recaptured her attention. He meshed long brown fingers into the vibrant fall of her hair and kissed her with devouring passion. She resented the distraction when something caught in her hair and pulled it hard enough to make her mutter in complaint.

'Be still. Your hair's caught,' he groaned, unclasping his designer watch to disentangle her from the bracelet and removing the timepiece to toss it aside.

Kathy struggled with the buttons on his shirt until he leant back and wrenched it off for her. 'You need practice,' he told her thickly. 'I'll give you all you can handle, *delizia mia.*'

The hair-roughened contours of his warm muscular torso felt amazing beneath her palms. She wanted to explore further, but he pushed her back against the arm of the sofa to take her mouth with ravenous need. At the same instant that he discovered the moist, swollen heart of her, conscious choices evaporated for her. She had never been touched there before and never dreamt that she could be quite so sensitive. But he had the erotic skill to show her. Exquisite sensation engulfed her in mindless pleasure and she shivered and writhed and whimpered.

Sergio had never been so aroused by a woman. There was no thought now of who she was or what she might be. Her passionate out-of-control response exploded his customary cool like dynamite. Once his powerful sensuality was unleashed, he was all decisive action. He came over her in one slick movement. She trembled, suddenly aware of the feel of his hot, probing intrusion in that most tender place. Her eyes widened and she tensed in disquiet at virtually the same moment as he entered her with an earthy groan of satisfaction. She was unprepared for the sharp stab of pure piercing pain that provoked a cry of dismay from her lips before she could bite it back.

Ebony brows pleating, Sergio stared down at her with frowning golden eyes of enquiry. '*Per meraviglia*…I am the first?'

'Don't stop.' Kathy shut her eyes tight. It was like being in the grip of a whirlwind, for even as the pangs of pain receded her body still signalled a powerful craving for the urgency of his.

He sank his hands below her hips to ease his passage with a slow sexual skill that was breathtakingly erotic. Her heart hammered as he taught her his sensual masculine rhythm with a boldness that delighted her senses. The excitement flooded back even stronger than before. Ripples of pleasure began to build, gripping her tighter and tighter in a torment of need she could not withstand. She reached for the ultimate and shattered in a climax that consumed her at hurricane force and plunged her into a free fall of delight.

The delight was short-lived.

Sergio held her close. 'It's a long time since any woman made me feel so good, *bellezza mia*,' he murmured raggedly.

Kathy was still shell-shocked by the entire experience and revelling in a sense of physical connection that was seductively new to her. 'I've never felt like this…ever,' she added helplessly.

'I have one vital question.' Sergio stared down at her with disturbingly cool and assessing dark eyes. 'Why did you give me your virginity?'

Kathy was dismayed by that direct question, particularly as he was suggesting that she had made some kind of a decision while she was all too uneasily aware that she had been considerably less mature in the nature of her giving.

Taut with suspicion of her motives, Sergio shook his handsome dark head. 'It was a very gratifying experience and not one I ever expected to have,' he confided flatly. 'But I know and I accept that any special pleasure always comes at a cost and I would really prefer to know right now up front what you want in return.'

Her smooth brow furrowed. 'Why should it cost you anything?'

'I'm a very rich man. I can't recall when I last enjoyed a freebie,' Sergio countered with sibilant derision.

When Kathy finally grasped his meaning she was appalled. She snaked her slim body free of his weight in an irate gesture of repudiation. How could she have shared her body with a guy who seemed to think that she would want to reap a financial reward from the activity? She could not have felt more ashamed had she been forced to walk down a street naked with the word *whore* written on a placard and hung round her neck.

Forced back from her by her sudden unanticipated retreat, Sergio had discovered another even more immediate source for concern. He cursed under his breath in Italian. 'Are you using birth control? In any form?'

Kathy was feeling dizzy and sick and distraught. She could not credit what she had done. She could not credit how stupid she had been. But while she was still in his presence she would not allow herself to think about those realities. All her energy was now concentrated on beating a very fast retreat from the scene of her worst ever mistake. She reached for her clothing. 'No—but you used contraception.'

Lean dark features uniformly grim, Sergio was getting dressed. 'The condom tore.'

Kathy flinched and turned paler than ever but she said

nothing in response. Indeed she refused even to look at him. This is what it's like when you get intimate with someone you don't know—awkward, humiliating, shaming, she reflected painfully. She fought her way into her panties with trembling hands, hauled on her T-shirt and wrenched on her jeans with so much force that she scratched the skin on her thighs.

'Obviously that doesn't bother you too much,' Sergio growled, outraged that she was simply ignoring him.

'What bothers me most at this moment is that I had sex with a truly horrible guy. I know I'm going to live with this mistake for a long, long time,' Kathy shared in a low-pitched tone of fierce regret. 'Getting pregnant by you would add a whole new dimension to this nightmare and I can't believe that even I could be that unlucky.'

'I doubt if that will be your reaction if it happens. Having my child could be a very lucrative lifestyle choice,' Sergio drawled with icy bite.

'Why do you think everyone's out to rip you off?' Kathy demanded in the rage that was steadily banishing any desire she might have had to take refuge in a small dark corner. 'Or is it just me you reserve the offensive accusations for? You really shouldn't mess around with the cleaning staff, Mr Torrente. Your nerves aren't cut out for it!'

'You need to calm down so that we can discuss this like adults.' Sergio breathed, glittering dark eyes locking to her with determined force, his expectations once again turned upside down by her behaviour. 'Sit down, please.'

'No.' Kathy shook her head vehemently, her wildly tousled copper-streaked hair flying back from her flushed cheekbones in vibrant splendour. 'I don't want to discuss anything with you. I had too much to drink. I did something I wish I hadn't done. You have been very, very rude to me.'

'That was not my intention.' Sergio aimed at striking a peaceful note, while he continued to watch her with shrewd concentration. Her heated distress was convincingly real and she was definitely slurring her words a little. She looked very young and quite magnificent.

Kathy loosed an unimpressed laugh, for she was not taken in by that smooth inflection. 'No, you couldn't care less if you were rude or not! You think you can get away with it.'

'You could well be right,' Sergio drawled in the same even tone. 'It's an unfortunate fact that gold-diggers target me—'

'You *deserve* a gold-digger!' Kathy snapped with furious conviction. 'If you think for one minute that that explanation excuses you for talking to me as if I was a prostitute, you're seriously out of line!'

'I wasn't aware that I made an excuse.'

Scornful dismissal flamed in Kathy's shimmering gaze. 'You haven't even got the manners for that, have you?'

'If you could rise above my failings in that department, I believe we have more important things to consider—'

'I doubt if I'll be pregnant, but if the worst was to happen, you don't need to worry,' Kathy tossed at him glibly as she walked to the door. 'I wouldn't even consider going for the "lucrative lifestyle choice" option!'

'That's not funny,' Sergio intoned grimly.

'Neither are your assumptions about me.' Kathy marched down the corridor, and when she registered that he was following her she hastened into the lift at speed. There she stabbed repeatedly at the button that closed the doors but he still made it past them to join her. The enclosed space felt unbearably claustrophobic. Hostility radiating from her in waves, her willowy figure rigid, she ignored him. She could not understand why he refused to get the message and leave her alone.

Sergio glanced down at his watch only to discover that he was no longer wearing it: he had left his sleek timepiece behind in his office. 'It's late. I'll take you home.'

'No, thanks.'

As the lift came to a halt Sergio imposed his lean powerful frame between her and the doors opening. 'I'll take you home,' he told her steadily.

'What is it about the word *no* that you don't understand?'

Sergio shifted closer. His intent dark gaze flared gold over her mutinous face. Her continuing defiance and refusal to be reasonable was so far outside his usual experience with women that he was astonished.

'You're in my way. I'm getting annoyed with you,' Kathy warned him, an unevenly drawn breath rasping in her throat as she fired an unwilling glance at him. His dark gaze flashed down into hers like a livewire connection. Excitement came at her out of nowhere. Her heartbeat broke into a sprint, her mouth ran dry.

'But you feel the burn between us the same way I do, *bella mia*,' Sergio husked, reaching out to frame her cheekbones between shapely brown hands, his thumbs delicately smoothing over her fine creamy skin.

For the merest instant she was frozen there, tantalised by his approach and teased by his touch. She was extraordinarily aware of the intimate ache between her thighs and his intense sexual magnetism. Her brain had no control over her body. It terrified her that he could still win that response from her and angry defensiveness overcame her paralysis and forced her into urgent denial. 'I don't feel anything!'

Sidestepping him in an impulsive move that took him by surprise, Kathy stalked across the brightly lit empty space of the vast foyer and headed straight for the exit doors. She was in total turmoil, deeply disturbed by what she had allowed to happen between them.

'Kathy,' Sergio grated, his patience on the ebb since he had not believed that she would actually walk away from him.

'Get lost!' Kathy told him roundly, impervious to the fact that they had an audience. One of the two night security guards on duty, both of whom had been studiously staring into space, abruptly unfroze to hurry forward and thrust a door wide for her. She walked out onto the street.

Renzo Catallone moved forward from his discreet position in the shadow of a pillar to intercept his employer. A stocky man in his forties, he looked unusually ill at ease. 'I—'

'While I appreciate that it is your job to take care of my security, your zeal is occasionally more than I require,' Sergio informed his security chief drily. 'No more enquiries or checks on Kathy Galvin. She's off limits.'

'But—sir—' Renzo began with a frown of dismay.

'I don't want to hear another word about her,' Sergio instructed in a flat tone of finality. 'With the exception of one piece of information: the lady's address.'

CHAPTER THREE

KATHY LAY IN BED sleepless far into the night.

She tossed and turned, her emotions reeling between anger, hurt, shame and resentment. Above all she was disappointed in herself. Why hadn't she paid heed to her misgivings? Bored of the dullness of her life, she had rebelled like a headstrong teenager. She had lived too quietly, played too safe and Sergio Torrente had been more temptation than she could withstand. But she blamed the alcohol for making her reckless. Why had she pretended that the only attraction on offer was a game of chess?

She splayed apprehensive fingers across her concave tummy. The very idea of falling pregnant terrified her: taking care of her own needs was enough of a challenge. She told herself off for panicking. What was that going to achieve? Why did she always expect the worst? It was true that she had suffered some serious bad luck in recent years, but then, she reasoned doggedly, everybody had to live through bad times at some stage.

The next morning she fed Tigger and tried to think only resolutely upbeat thoughts. It was her day off and she could not afford to waste it. She needed to do research at the library for an essay. For the past year she had been studying for a degree with the Open University. On the way to the library, however, she called into a pharmacy and read the small print on the back of a pregnancy test to work out how soon she could use one.

She was queuing for the bus when her mobile phone rang. The cleaning company had received a complaint about her performance at the Torrenco building and, as a result, her services were no longer required.

Being sacked hit Kathy like a bolt from the blue. Sergio Torrente had had her fired! How could any guy sink that low? But, then, was such callous behaviour really that unusual? She suffered an unwelcome recollection of being dumped—not by Gareth but by his mother—and her tummy lurched in humiliated remembrance. Her childhood sweetheart had not even had the courage to tell her himself. He had abandoned her at a time when his support had felt like her only hope. His lack of faith in her had made her imprisonment for a crime she had not committed all the harder to bear.

Her memory dragged her back to the summer she had finished school. Her plans to study law at university had been on hold because her father was dying. After he had passed away, she'd had six months to fill before she could take up her deferred university place. She had accepted a live-in job as a career for Agnes Taplow, an elderly woman whom Kathy had been told was suffering from dementia.

When the old lady complained to Kathy that pieces of her antique silver collection were going missing, Agnes Taplow's niece had assured Kathy that her aunt was imagining things. But items had continued to disappear without trace. The police had been called in to investigate and a small but rare early Georgian jug had been found in

Kathy's handbag. That same day Kathy had been charged with theft. Initially she had been confident that the true culprit, who could only have hidden the jug in her bag to implicate her, would soon be exposed. Caught up in a web of deceit and lies, and with no family of her own to fight her corner, Kathy had been unable to prove her innocence. The court had found her guilty of theft and she'd had to serve her prison sentence.

But those events had taken place at a time when she was too immature and powerless to act in her own defence, Kathy reminded herself urgently. Since then she had learned how to look after herself. Why should she allow Sergio Torrente to get away with putting her out of work? It was hard to see how she could prevent him. He had wealth, status and power and she had none of those things. But even if she couldn't change anything she had the right to tell him what she thought of him. Indeed standing up for the sake of her self-esteem felt like the only strength she had left.

'I'm afraid there's no sign of your watch, Mr Torrente. I've searched every inch of your office,' the security man reported ruefully.

With a faint frown marking his sleek ebony brows, Sergio rose from behind his desk because he had a flight to Norway to catch. Of course there would be a simple explanation. When he had discarded his watch the night before, it must have fallen somewhere beneath the furniture. Searches were rarely as thorough as people liked to think they were. The watch was mislaid, rather than missing, and theft was an unlikely possibility. He did not suffer from Renzo's paranoia about strangers. It would, however,

Sergio felt, be naïve to overlook the fact that his platinum watch was extremely valuable.

His entire personal staff was engaged in an urgent whispered consultation by the door. He was exasperated by the cloud of stress and indecision that hung over them. His efficient senior executive assistant was on vacation and her subordinates seemed lost without her. Finally, one broke away from the group and approached him in an apologetic manner. 'A woman called Kathy Galvin is out in Reception, sir. She's not on the approved list but she seems convinced that you will want to see her.'

Cool, hard satisfaction stamped Sergio's darkly handsome face. As he had suspected, Kathy's big walk-out had been an empty gesture. He was relieved that he had not sent her flowers, for conciliatory gestures were not his style. 'I do. She can travel to the airport with me.'

The PA could not conceal his surprise, since Sergio never saw anyone without an appointment and the women in his life invariably knew better than to interrupt his working day. A pleasurable sense of sexual anticipation building, Sergio began to plan his return to London in a fortnight's time. He strolled out to the private lift that would whisk him down to the car park.

Her vibrant head held high, soft colour defining her slanting cheekbones and bright green eyes, Kathy stepped through the door that had been opened for her. Her heart was beating very fast. Having assumed she was being granted a private meeting with Sergio, she was dismayed when she saw him standing with other men in the corridor. Tall, broad shouldered and dark, he dominated the group in more than the physical sense as he had the potent presence of a powerful man.

As Kathy had no intention of telling Sergio Torrente what she thought of him in front of an audience she was forced to contain her temper. The effort required made her feel like a pressure-cooker on the boil. Nor was her anger soothed by the discovery that that lean, hard-boned face of his could still send a jolt of response through her that was the equivalent of an electric shock. Imperious dark eyes unreadable, he directed her into the lift ahead of him. A positive aristocrat of good breeding and manners, she labelled inwardly, her teeth gritting. She was not impressed by the surface show.

'I suppose your aim is to get me out of here with the minimum of fuss,' Kathy condemned hotly.

Sergio was still engaged in tracking his glittering gaze over her gorgeous face and the amazing lithe, long-legged perfection of her body. His companions had studied her like a row of gobsmacked schoolboys. A striking effect, he acknowledged, for a woman who wasn't wearing either make-up or designer clothes. 'No, I'm heading to the airport. You can keep me company on the journey.'

'Don't waste your time with the charm offensive. I can hardly stick being this close to you in a lift!' Kathy hissed back at him at the speed of a bullet. 'You complained about me and I've been sacked. I'm only here to tell you what I think of your despicable behaviour—'

The lift doors glided open again on an underground car park. 'I lodged no complaint.'

'Someone did. But I didn't damage your chess set and I always completed my work targets—'

'It is possible that the enquiries made about you by my security advisors may have been construed as a complaint,' Sergio conceded, striding out of the lift. 'Given the tempo-

rary nature of your contract, your employer may have decided
that dispensing with your services was the wisest option.'

Hurrying along by his side, Kathy didn't know whether
to believe that interpretation or not. 'If that's the case, then
you should play fair and sort it out for me.'

But Sergio had a different take on the situation. He was
not disappointed by the news that she would no longer be
cleaning the Torrenco building. He thought that was definitely
a development to be welcomed. If she was about to figure in
his life in any guise she could not be engaged in such lowly
work. 'I'll fix you up with something more appropriate—'

'I don't want you fixing me up with anything!' Kathy
was incredulous at that cool response. 'I'm not asking for
favours either, only fair treatment.'

'We'll discuss it in the limo,' Sergio intoned smoothly.

Disconcerted by that proposal, Kathy finally dragged
her attention from Sergio for long enough to notice her immediate surroundings. A uniformed chauffeur was holding
wide the passenger door of a huge gleaming limousine,
while several men with the build of professional bodyguards hovered in a protective circle. Extreme discomfiture assailed her; she felt out of her depth. Even so, she also
recognised that getting into the car with him was the price
of continuing the dialogue. She climbed in and tried hard
not to gawp at the opulent leather interior and the sleek
built-in bank of business and entertainment equipment.

'Naturally you're annoyed. It is most regrettable that
you should have suffered unjust treatment,' Sergio intoned.

The dark, deep timbre of his voice sent a sinuous little
frisson snaking down Kathy's spine. But it also crossed her
mind that he was clever enough to know exactly what to
say and how to say it on any given occasion. Distrust

slivered through her and she stiffened like a cat stroked the wrong way. 'I'm glad that you recognise that it was unfair.'

'You don't need to worry,' Sergio countered with supreme assurance. 'I'll ensure that you get another job. '

'Easier said than done. I've only got a good reference as a waitress.' Kathy was already planning to take on extra shifts at the café to make ends meet. But the cracking pace of waiting tables for longer hours would exhaust her and her studies would suffer, so that option would only be useful in the short term.

'Would you prefer to work in the catering trade?'

'No.' Kathy closed her hands together in a taut movement. Even though it was his fault that she was in a tight corner she had a lot of pride and found it very hard to ask anyone for help. But if he had the influence he seemed to think he had, there was a chance that just for once a piece of bad luck could be turned into something more positive. 'I would love an office job,' she confided in a rush. 'It doesn't matter how junior it is. Even a temporary position would do, because it would give me some experience. I've got good IT skills…and a rather empty CV.'

'It's not a problem. I own a chain of employment agencies. I'll organise it today.'

'I'm not asking for any special favours,' she said defensively.

'I'm not offering any.' Sergio closed a confident hand over hers, unfurling her taut white fingers to tug her closer.

Her green eyes were wary. 'Look, I'm not here for the seduction routine.'

'Your pulse says otherwise, *bella mia*,' Sergio traded huskily, his thumb and forefinger encircling her fragile wrist while he challenged her with smouldering dark golden eyes.

That single look was so hot that Kathy felt as though she were burning inside her skin. A lightning strike of desire slivered through her, stinging her nipples into straining needle points, creating a knot of tension in her pelvis. In a sudden compulsive movement that had nothing to do with thought she leant forward and found his shapely sensual mouth for herself. A split second later she could not believe that she had made the first move, but she could no more have resisted that primitive prompting than she could have stopped breathing.

His powerful libido ignited by that boldness, Sergio drove her soft pink lips apart with answering passion. He delved into the moist interior of her mouth with a rhythmic eroticism that drove her wild with longing. Her fingers raked through his gleaming black hair, holding him to her. One kiss only led to the next and the exchange was frantic, increasingly forceful and infuriatingly unsatisfying for both of them. With a groan of frustration he hauled her slim body closer, closing his hand over hers to guide it down to the furious power of his erection.

Her fingers spread over the swell of his male arousal, outrageously obvious even through the fabric of his trousers. Wanton damp heat flowered at the tender heart of her body and she quivered, shot through and weak with sheer longing and excitement. She knew what he wanted and she knew what she wanted to do, though it was something that had never before had the slightest appeal to her. The shock of that sexual intensity made her eyes fly open.

It was disconcerting to recognise that it was still broad daylight and that they were in a moving car in traffic. She had forgotten everything, where she was, who she was. She felt out of control and it scared her. Tearing her reddened mouth from his, she sucked in a steadying breath and shifted her hand onto his long powerful thigh.

A lean brown hand closed into her copper hair to stop her moving back out of reach. Scorching golden eyes held her fast. 'You shouldn't start anything you're not prepared to finish.'

'I've got work to do.' Kathy lifted her chin, her cheeks burning.

Accustomed to instant compliance with his wishes, Sergio studied her with shimmering dark eyes of hauteur. Then he flung his arrogant head back and vented an appreciative laugh. He liked her nerve. 'What work?'

'I have another part-time job. I'm also studying.'

'And I have a flight to catch.'

Her heart thudded heavily inside her ribcage. He ran a slow caressing forefinger across the swollen curve of her lower lip. Her nerve-endings prickled with awareness. It took all her self-discipline not to lean forward and invite a greater intimacy.

'I'll see you when I get back to London—in a couple of weeks, *delizia mia*,' Sergio murmured softly.

'A couple of weeks?' Kathy queried in bemusement.

He explained his schedule. Intense disappointment filled her that he would be abroad for so long. She veiled her eyes, irritated by her juvenile response, her previous doubts setting in again. What was the point of seeing him again? Did she have novelty value? Even if he was interested in her, it would only be for all of five minutes. She needed no great experience of men to know that all she had to offer on his terms was her face and body. Was that enough for her?

Sergio checked his watch, only to rediscover for the tenth

time that morning that it wasn't on his wrist. Fortunately a replacement awaited him at the airport. 'I took off my watch last night. Did you notice where I put it?'

Her smooth brow furrowed. 'It was lying on the carpet. I stepped over it. Look, us seeing each other again isn't a good idea—'

His dark stare was unnervingly direct. 'Try keeping me away.'

'I'm serious—'

Sergio lifted the phone and punched in a number. A moment later he was talking in rapid Italian.

'Would you be interested in becoming a receptionist?' he enquired in casual aside.

Kathy nodded in immediate eager acknowledgement. After a brief further dialogue he replaced the phone and gave her an address to go to the following morning. 'For an interview?' she asked.

'No, the job's yours for three months. Longer, if you make a good impression.'

'Thanks,' she muttered awkwardly as the limo came to a halt.

'I owed you.' Sergio stepped out.

Uncertainly Kathy climbed out, as well, but he didn't notice; he was already walking away with two of his bodyguards following close behind him. His departure was the epitome of casualness. Before she sank back into the limo, she noticed a stocky older man on the pavement treating her to a flinty appraisal. His gloomy face was vaguely familiar and she knew she had seen him before, even if she could not recall where. When he got into the car behind, which previously had disgorged the bodyguards, she realised that he must work for Sergio.

The chauffeur captured her attention by asking her where she wanted to go. As the luxury vehicle moved off again to drop her at the library, she was in a happy daze at the prospect of starting a new job.

Almost two weeks later, Sergio arrived back in London. He was in an excellent mood.

Grave-faced, Renzo Catallone met his employer off his private jet and passed him a slim file.

'I realise I'm putting my job on the line here. But I can't be in charge of your personal security and keep quiet,' the security chief declared tautly. 'It's vital that you take a look at this dossier. I'm convinced that your watch has been stolen.'

CHAPTER FOUR

EYES AS BRIGHT AS STARS, Kathy studied her reflection in the mirror.

'Put on a pair of sunglasses and a bored expression and you'll be taken for a celebrity!' Bridget Kirk teased, her cheerful face wreathed in smiles.

Kathy was dressed in a vintage sixties dress the zingy yellow of a citrus fruit. It was a sleeveless sheath that hugged her slight curves as though it had been custom-made, and Kathy thought it gave her an amazingly classy look. She felt that that was an important consideration for a date with a guy who had been born into a family with a history that stretched back several centuries. While she was by no means intimidated by Sergio Torrente's background, which she had checked out on the internet, she had cringed at the reality that he might well wince if she turned out to see him in another pair of jeans. In actuality her wardrobe contained nothing fancier than black trousers.

And trying to remedy that problem on her income in the first weeks of a new job was out of the question. The struggle to survive until she received her first pay as a receptionist was proving a major challenge, even though she had worked almost every night at the café. She was very lucky that Bridget had come to her rescue with the suggestion that she might borrow an outfit from the café manager's vintage fashion collection accumulated from various charity shops.

'I don't know how to thank you.' Kathy enveloped the older woman in an impulsive hug. 'I know how proud you are of your clothes and I promise I'll look after the dress.'

Delighted to see Kathy so animated and talkative, Bridget returned the hug with enthusiasm. 'I'm pleased that you're finally going out on a date!'

'But it won't last five minutes with Sergio.' Kathy delivered that forecast with a shrug of a narrow shoulder to show how low her expectations were and reached for her jeans, intending to get changed. 'I think he's just curious about how the other half lives.'

'Will you tell him?'

Kathy paled and tensed. She knew immediately that Bridget was referring to the prison sentence that the younger woman had served. 'I don't think Sergio will be around long enough for a heartfelt confession to become necessary. But if he asks too many awkward questions, I won't lie—'

'Give things a chance to develop first,' Bridget advised hurriedly.

'He's too sophisticated and well travelled to fool. If I tried to pretend I spent all that time abroad I'd soon trip myself up,' Kathy countered gently.

'He's not going to ask for map references, Kathy,' the little brunette scolded. 'Don't go spilling it all out when there's no need. You're entitled to a few secrets until you know him better.'

Bridget was very much a romantic and Kathy

wouldn't have had her any other way, but Kathy had not been able to bring herself to the point of confessing to her friend that she had already been intimate with Sergio. In fact, the more Kathy thought about that, the more disturbed and ashamed she became over her behaviour. She was annoyed that she had not had more sense. The fear that there might be consequences from their contraceptive accident was one she kept pushed to the back of her mind; she was planning to do a pregnancy test in a couple of days.

Surprisingly, Sergio had actually phoned her four times since he had left London. He had called her from Norway and talked with astonishing enthusiasm about white-outs and skiable peaks. Whether he was telling her about living rough in a wilderness of snow fields, frozen lakes and forest or revealing an abiding passion for what she had discovered was the world's most expensive coffee, Sergio could be very entertaining.

Kathy had, however, satisfied her curiosity about him on the internet and had been both intrigued and troubled by what she learned. Born to an almost royal existence of extreme privilege in a vast Italian palazzo, Sergio had evidently led a charmed life until he became mysteriously estranged from his father while he was still at university. Although virtually disinherited in favour of his younger half-brother, Sergio had still contrived to make his first million by the age of twenty-two and he had hogged the fast lane of energetic high-powered achievement ever since. Super-rich and super-successful, he maintained the same hectic pace in his private life. He had a rather chilling reputation with women. When he wasn't doing his utmost to kill himself in dangerous sporting activities, he was staving off boredom with a relentless parade of beautiful women, all of whom belonged to the celebrity and socialite sets.

As Kathy caught the bus home from work the following evening, she was striving not to dwell too much on those unpalatable truths because, by finding her employment, Sergio had single-handedly contrived to transform her life. Her new job was in a busy advertising agency, which buzzed with activity at all hours of the day and she absolutely loved it. A quick learner, she had already been complimented on her work. It was the opportunity she had so badly needed to prove her ability and gain experience. But without Sergio's intervention she knew that she would not have been given that chance. That did not mean she planned to sleep with him when she saw him that night, but it did mean that she would probably continue to hold back and not beat him if they ever played chess again.

Amused by that idea, Kathy donned the citrus-yellow dress. A car collected her on the dot of eight and took her across the city to a very exclusive residential block. Shown into the lift by the driver, she was tense and uncomfortable. Where was she being taken? Not unnaturally she had assumed they were going out. Maybe he didn't want to take her anywhere. Maybe he was afraid that her table manners or appearance would let him down.

Bright coppery head held high, Kathy walked across the marble hall and through the open door facing her into a stunning reception room so large that it seemed to stretch into infinity. Her heartbeat was moving up tempo, colour warming her cheeks.

'Kathy…' Sergio strolled forward to greet her.

And the definitive word to describe him, she thought dizzily, was *gorgeous*. His fashionable suit was the colour of dark chocolate and, worn with a fawn T-shirt, it struck a wonderfully classic and casual note. Just one glimpse of the hard, masculine planes of his lean bronzed face unleashed the butterflies in her stomach. It took tremendous self-control for her to rise above those promptings and say out loud what was on her mind.

'Is this your apartment?' Kathy asked stiffly.

Sergio ran veiled dark eyes as cold as ice over her and, even though he was disgusted by what he now knew about her character, he still could not deny her stunning physical appeal. The bright yellow dress set off her glorious hair and her green eyes shone like polished jade against her pale porcelain complexion. He knew at a glance that the outfit was designer faux-vintage and had no doubt at all in deciding where she had got the money to buy it: from the sale of his watch.

'Yes. Why?' he tossed back smooth as glass.

'Are we going out?' Kathy asked tautly.

Sergio gazed steadily back at her. 'I thought we'd be more comfortable staying here.'

'Either we go out somewhere, or I go home.' Kathy tilted her chin and sent him a look of disdain, angry hurt and strong pride powering her. 'I'm not an easy option you call up when you feel like sex. If that's all you're interested in, I'm leaving. No offence intended.'

His dark scrutiny kindled to gold as though she had tossed a burning torch on a bale of hay and provoked a blaze. 'You can't leave until you've answered certain questions to my satisfaction.'

Kathy froze. 'What are you talking about?'

'Let's keep it simple. You stole my watch. I want to know what you did with it.'

'I...*stole* your watch? Are you crazy?' Kathy exclaimed, barely able to credit that accusation coming at her out of the blue. 'I remember you asking about it before you left London but—'

'You were the last person to see it in my office. It can scarcely be a coincidence that you should also have a criminal record for theft.'

Her delicate natural colour ebbed to leave her an ashen shade. Without warning he was plunging her back into the nightmare that she had believed she had left behind. He *knew* about her past. She felt sick and cornered, and under attack. He believed she was a thief and that only she could be responsible for the disappearance of his watch. For a few taut seconds her mind was in turmoil and her throat was so tight she could barely get oxygen into her lungs.

For an instant Sergio wondered if she might faint. She'd turned as white as snow, her pallor in stark contrast to her vivid hair and dress. She was terrified, of course she was. He did not regret choosing the short, sharp shock approach. He liked results and he liked them fast.

'I didn't steal your watch,' Kathy framed shakily.

'Are lies a wise move at this point?' Sergio traded, unimpressed. 'I could call the police right now and let them handle it. But I would prefer to deal with this in a private capacity. Keep two facts in mind: I have no pity for those who try to take advantage of me and I have never regarded women as the weaker sex.'

'I didn't touch your watch!' Her protest was vehement. A pulse was beating so fast at the base of her throat that still she found it difficult to catch her breath. That reference to the police terrified her, bringing back memories she would have done anything to forget and which she had no wish to relive. With her history as a former offender, how could she possibly hope to combat an accusation from a very rich and powerful man?

Sergio regarded her with cold, steady determination. 'I won't let you leave this apartment until you have told me the truth.'

'You can't do that!' Kathy told him in disbelief. 'You don't have the right.'

'Oh, I think you'll give me the right to do whatever I like, *cara mia*,' Sergio countered silkily. 'I believe that you will do virtually anything to keep the police out of this. Am I correct?'

As she received that very shrewd assumption Kathy's teeth almost chattered together. Yet, while fear was making her skin clammy, rage was sitting like a lump of red hot coal inside her. 'How did you find out that I had served a prison sentence?'

'My security chief started checking you out when he saw you making chess moves on the surveillance camera. He's very thorough.'

'Is he?' Kathy raised a fine brow in disagreement. 'I would say that I make a very convenient fall guy—'

'Renzo Catallone doesn't operate like that,' Sergio asserted. 'He used to be in the police force.'

'Even better!' A bitter laugh was wrenched from Kathy's dry throat before she could bite it back. 'He saw that I had a criminal record and that was that, wasn't it? Investigation over!'

'Are you denying that you stole the watch?'

'Yes, but clearly you don't believe me and I don't have any way of proving that I didn't take it. Obviously, you have a thief in your office. It might just be someone in a smart business suit, someone who was tempted, even someone who wanted a thrill. Thieves come in all shapes and sizes and in all walks of life.'

Sergio rested brooding dark eyes of derision on her. The crime for which she had once been convicted filled him with distaste. Far from being the refreshingly natural and unspoilt girl he had come to believe her to be, her beauty hid a rotten core of serious greed. In the position of carer and companion, she had abused the trust of an elderly invalid and had systematically robbed her charge over a period of many months. She had been prosecuted for the theft of the single item found in her possession, but she had almost certainly been responsible for stealing and disposing of other valuable antiques that had disappeared without trace during her employment.

'I don't need you to tell me the obvious,' Sergio responded drily. 'In this case I'm confident that I'm looking at the culprit.'

'But then you're confident in every sphere.' Kathy slowly shook her head. Her copper and amber hair glittered with bright streaks, forming a metallic halo that accentuated the pallor of her ivory complexion.

Dully she recognised that she was in shock. In the space of minutes he had torn her newly learnt self-belief to shreds. He had tempted her out of the safety of her quiet life only to threaten to destroy her. She hated him for it. She hated him for the arrogant assurance that convinced him that he was right and she was in the wrong. She hated herself for believing, however briefly, that she could aspire to dating a guy like him. What sort of an idiot had she become? Did she believe in fairy stories, as well? She had surrendered her defence mechanisms when she'd put on the pretty yellow dress. Within the anger and the fear lurked a very strong sense of humiliation.

'Let's keep this clean and straightforward. I want to know what you did with the watch,' Sergio repeated grimly. 'And don't waste my time with tears or tantrums. They don't work with me.'

An insidious chill ran down her taut spinal cord as she recorded the cruel lack of emotion stamped on his lean, dark, handsome features. He would never listen to her story of the injustice she had suffered—he would have neither the faith nor the patience. He had no time for her or her explanations, since he dealt in black and white facts. As far as he was concerned, she was a convicted thief and she might have served her sentence, but he was not prepared to give her the benefit of the doubt.

'I didn't take it, so I don't know where you expect to go with this. I haven't got the information you're asking for,' Kathy framed tightly.

Implacable dark as ebony eyes rested on her. 'Then I hand you over to the police.'

All Kathy could think about was the threat of being sent back to prison. For a split second she was back there in a cell with endless empty hours to fill without occupation or privacy. She was back in the grip of the powerlessness, the despair and the fear. The scar on her back seemed to pulse with remembered pain. Perspiration broke out on her short upper lip, gooseflesh on her exposed skin. Unlike Bridget's daughter, who had never come home again, Kathy had coped and she had survived. But the prospect of being forced to cope a second time with the loss of all freedom and dignity was too much for her to bear.

'I don't want that,' she admitted half under her breath.

'Neither do I,' Sergio confided lazily. 'Having to admit that I shagged the office cleaner would be tacky.'

Her facial muscles tightened at the insult, while her brain discarded the degrading words as an irrelevance. Her mind was on a frantic feverish search for any solution that might persuade him not to involve the police. Only something unusual was likely to appeal to Sergio Torrente. He liked danger and he liked risk and he loved to compete.

'If I can beat you at chess tonight, you let me walk away,' Kathy shot that proposition at him before she could lose her nerve.

That sudden turnaround in attitude took Sergio by surprise. In that one reckless sentence she'd acknowledged her guilt as a thief and bargained with him for her freedom. But she'd done both without apology or explanation. He found her audacity a turn-on. 'You're challenging me?'

Her green eyes were alight with defiance, but deep down inside she was a mass of panic and insecurity because she knew that she was literally fighting for the chance to keep her life from falling apart again. 'Why not?'

'What's in it for me? A good game?' Sergio derided. 'That watch was worth at least forty grand. You set a high rating on your entertainment value.'

Consternation gripped Kathy at that news. *Forty thousand* pounds? It had not occurred to her that the missing item might be so valuable. Her apprehension increased. 'The choice is yours.'

'If you lose, I want my watch back,' Sergio delivered with sardonic bite. 'Or, at the very least, the details of where it was disposed of.'

As he asked for the impossible again Kathy was careful not to meet his astute eyes in a direct collision. But his tacit agreement to her challenge sent the adrenalin zinging through her veins again, loosening the fierce tension in her spine and lower limbs. He would play her and whatever it took she had to win. If she lost she would be right back where she had started out, with the added disadvantage that he would be outraged when she was unable to provide either the watch or the information that might lead to its return.

'Okay,' Kathy agreed, toughing out the pretence that she could deliver that deal because he had given her no other choice.

'And I think that, whatever the result, I should enjoy a reprise of the best entertainment you can offer, *delizia mia*,' Sergio murmured, lifting the phone to request that a chess set be brought in.

Her fine brows pleated. 'Sorry?'

Sergio dealt her an appreciative glance. Her outfit gave her the tantalising femininity of a delicate tea rose but her suggestion that they play for what was, after all, *his* watch was as ingenious as it was in-your-face impudent. 'We finish the contest in bed.'

Kathy went rigid, colour splashing her wide, high cheekbones, anger rising and soaring high within her. She was shattered by that demand, for she thought it was utterly unfair. 'Regardless of who wins?'

'There has to be something extra in it for me.'

Kathy focused on the superb view through the nearest window and thought of the lack of view she would have in a cell. Her tummy flipped, her skin chilled at that realistic acknowledgement of who held the true power. He had the whip hand while she had only her wits as ammunition. 'All right.'

A manservant appeared with a polished antique wooden

box and laid out a board table with stylish carved chess pieces. A maid arrived to serve refreshments. Kathy took her seat. Even though she had not eaten since lunch time, she refused the offer of a drink and the tiny tempting canapés that accompanied it. It was all so civilised that she almost laughed out loud. On the face of it she was an honoured guest, but she knew she would be playing for her very survival.

Sergio lifted a white and then a black pawn and closed his hands round them. Kathy picked a fist and won white to play. She told herself it was a good omen and her concentration went into super mode. She had no sense of time, only of the patterns and combinations on the board in front of her. He was an aggressive player, who made a steady advance. But her strategy was more intricate, her moves lightning-fast to push up the pace. She let him capture her bishop and then slid her knight behind his.

'Check,' she breathed softly and a short while later she trapped his king.

'Checkmate,' Sergio conceded, stunned by the level of her brilliance and incensed that she had concealed the extent of her skill during their two previous games.

Kathy snatched in a slow quivering breath. It was over; she was safe. Her skin was damp with stress. Adrenalin was still pumping through her on a high octane charge. Pushing back her chair, she got up.

Dark golden eyes shimmering, Sergio followed suit. 'You fixed the tie last time we played,' he condemned.

'Maybe it was my way of flirting with you.' Kathy threw her head high, reacting to the electric tension in the air. 'Guys don't like being beaten, do they?'

'Some prefer a challenge,' Sergio traded.

'But you're not one of them,' Kathy dared with scorn. 'Your past features a remarkable number of airheads.'

'Horses for courses,' Sergio rhymed unabashed. 'Is this the real Kathy Galvin? Or is there yet another Kathy waiting in the wings? You're full of astonishing contradictions.'

Annoyed he had not reacted angrily to her taunt when she was keen to keep him at a distance, Kathy was non-committal. 'Am I?'

'A cleaner, when you could be a model. A virgin. A chess player, who could make an Olympic team, and a thief.' Sergio lifted a hand and laced lean brown fingers into the luxuriant thickness of her amber and copper streaked hair. 'I don't like what you are but you fascinate me, *cara mia*.'

His thumb stroked the delicate skin below her ear and she trembled. He was so close she could smell his cologne, a fragrance that had already acquired an aching familiarity that awakened her senses. The proximity of his lean, powerful body was impossible to ignore. Her mouth knew the taste of him. Her body was already remembering him and wantonly keen to relive the experience. Her breasts felt warm and heavy inside her bra. Her breath fluttered in her throat as she fought the treacherous demon of her own sensuality.

He tipped her head back. Merciless golden eyes assailed hers and forced a connection. 'You keep the watch…and tonight I keep you,' he reminded her with ruthless precision. 'But I don't want a martyr in my bed.'

Kathy had no intention of playing the victim and she was too proud to try and reason with him again. She knew how he operated. If she ruled the chessboard, he would rule the bedroom. She had made the deal and she refused to let herself think and react with her emotions: she was tougher than that. Life had gone wrong again, but she would handle it just as she had before, she told herself fiercely. He closed a hand over hers and led her into the hall and down a corridor.

The master bedroom suite overlooked a big roof garden. She could hardly credit that something as beautiful as that garden could exist so many floors above street level. She focused on it while he unzipped her dress and spread back its edges. Her heart starting to hammer like a road drill, she watched his reflection in the sunlit wall of glass. He bent his proud dark head and pressed his expert mouth to a narrow white shoulder blade. He found a place she didn't know existed and triggered a frisson of response that slivered through her, shocking her back into awareness of him.

Sergio laughed softly. 'I don't want a woman behaving like an exquisite automaton. I want you wide awake, *delizia mia*.'

'What do those words mean?' she whispered.

'My delight—and you are. Wildly inventive dreams about you have disturbed my sleep ever since I left London,' he confided thickly.

'So my being a thief really didn't make much difference to you?'

His big powerful frame tensed behind hers. He spun her round to look him. Forbidding dark eyes flared down into hers.

But Kathy was untouched by that silent censure. Indeed she was almost provoked by the anger she could feel contained within him, firmly controlled by self-discipline. 'You're more sensitive than you might seem.'

'Where is your shame?' he demanded.

'Are you ashamed that you are using your power over me to get me into bed again?'

Sergio dealt her a fulminating appraisal and then he

startled her with a shout of laughter. 'No,' he conceded, his strong, hard-boned face spectacularly handsome as grim amusement splintered his usual sombre mien. 'But then why would I be? You want me just as much.'

'Don't men always tell themselves ego-boosting stuff like th-that?' Her voice succumbed to a slight nervous jerk as he eased her dress down over her wrists and lifted her free of the rich brocade fabric as easily as if she were a doll.

In answer, Sergio bent his arrogant dark head and kissed her. The moist curl and flick of his tongue against the roof of her mouth made her shiver. The emotion she had walled up inside her burst out in a hungry surge. She wanted, wanted, *hated* wanting him, refused to surrender to it. As her defensive stiffness grew he gathered her close and tasted her soft pink lips with an intoxicating sweetness that was so unexpected it transfixed her. He followed that tantalising assault with a passionate urgency that sent sparks of fire dancing through her veins. With a roughened sound in his throat, he wrenched her bra out of his path and closed a hand over the silken soft curve of her breast. Her knees went weak, her body burning.

'You want me too,' Sergio husked against her reddened, love-bruised mouth. 'Admit it.'

'No!' Her green eyes flashing like polished emeralds, she pulled free. Picking up the yellow dress, she shook it out and laid it carefully across a chair.

'Even though it might pay to please me?' Sergio traded, smooth as silk.

'You get one night and that's it—you don't ever come near me again!' Kathy hissed back at him like a bristling cat. 'You got that?'

'I got it, *delizia mia*,' Sergio intoned, sweeping her up

into his arms to carry her over to the bed. 'Whether or not I'll accept it is another question. I dislike doing what other people tell me.'

'Tell me something I don't know.' Finding herself sprawled on the bed clad only in her briefs, Kathy became suddenly less strident. Uncomfortable with her semi-unclothed state, she flung a look of dismay at the sunlit windows. 'For goodness' sake, close the curtains!'

Amused by that sudden lurch from feisty cool to panic, Sergio hit a button and flicked another to put on the lights. He shed his jacket and his tie while he watched her with the single-minded golden gaze of a predator. Her beautiful eyes were wary, her colourful hair tousled. He recognised her extraordinary magnetism. On his bed she was as unusual and exotic as a tiger strolling through a drawing room.

Beneath that forceful scrutiny, Kathy was uneasy and she twisted away to conceal her bare breasts. Her shyness infuriated her, for she saw it as yet another weakness and her conscience was already shouting at her. She had kissed him back with more than toleration. How could she have responded with that much enthusiasm to a guy she loathed? On the other hand, wasn't it as well that she could? But *why* could she still respond to him?

'*Madonna mia,*' Sergio was staring in shock at the jagged scar that marred the white skin of her back. 'What the hell happened to you?'

When Kathy realised what had grabbed his attention she thrust herself back against the pillows so that that part of her body was hidden again. She was mortified that he should have seen the ugly evidence of the attack she had suffered three years earlier. 'Nothing—'

'That was not nothing—'

Her vivid green eyes were screened, her lithe, slender length taut. 'But I don't have to talk about it if I don't want to.'

Clad in designer boxers, Sergio came down on the bed. He was tall, bronzed and boldly masculine, his powerful muscles laid over the lean, strong frame of an athlete. 'Are you always this ready for a fight?'

Kathy was feeling incredibly tense. 'If you don't like it, send me home.'

Dark golden eyes intent, Sergio stared down at her with the aggressive potency of a hunter. She couldn't take her attention from him. In response, he curved lean fingers to the nape of her neck. 'Maybe I could get to like fighting, *delizia mia*,' he husked, tipping up her mouth to the wide, sensual promise of his.

Her nerves were as lively as jumping beans; she was rigid. But the kiss was a teasing provocation that enticed and promised. Her breath feathered in her throat. The taste of him intoxicated her but she fought that truth, determined to endure his attentions rather than respond to him. He found the delicate swell of her breasts and massaged the velvet peaks to sensitive rosebud crests. Arrows of exquisite sensation were slivering through her. But still she struggled to withstand his sexual mastery.

Sergio tugged her down into his arms to combat her resistance. There was more urgency than patience in the possessive stroke of his hands over her slender curves. There was greater demand in the heated force of his mouth. She twisted and turned beneath the onslaught of his increasing ardour. No matter how hard she tried to stay separate he was sweeping her up into the same storm of passion where pride had no place and only fervent need ruled.

'You want me too,' he told her thickly. 'It's reciprocal. I saw it in you the first time you looked at me.'

Her lashes swept down to conceal her apple-green eyes. She wouldn't answer but she was powerless to control the desire he had aroused. Her fingers were digging into his wide brown shoulders. The aromatic scent of his skin entranced her. At first meeting he had imprinted on her senses and she had recognised him on every level since then. The bewildering strength of that initial bonding scared her and infuriated her but it also exhilarated her.

'You are so stubborn,' Sergio growled in the simmering silence.

'I'm not here to stroke your ego!' Kathy declared.

He ground her lips apart with devouring heat and punished her with pleasure. Every nerve-ending in her body leapt in response. He worked his erotic path down over her squirming length, lingering on the rosy crowns of her breasts with his tongue and his teeth and exploring the hidden places to discover the exquisite sensitivity of her most tender flesh. The excitement became overwhelming. Her heart pounded in her eardrums, for in no time at all the yearning became a ravenous need. His caresses pushed her to an edge of frustrated torment that she found unbearable.

'Sergio…'

'Say please,' he urged breathlessly.

She gritted her teeth. 'No!'

'Some day I'll make you say please,' he swore.

But Kathy wasn't listening. Trembling with desire, she was already pulling him closer. Hot and impatient, Sergio required little encouragement. Golden eyes ablaze, he slid between her thighs and entered her with energising heat and strength. She cried out in startled acknowledgement of his invasion. He had made her burn with an irresistible hunger and now the dark, delirious pleasure began. It was glorious and her capacity for enjoyment knew no limits. His passionate intensity drove her wild with excitement. Sensation gradually became a raw, sweet agony until he sent her careening to a tumultuous peak of explosive release.

There was a timeless moment of pure ecstasy and joy. In the sensual ripples of delight that followed, she felt wonderfully close to him, transformed and at peace. And then her brain kicked back into action and blew all those fine feelings away again. She remembered how things really were between them and felt angry, mortified and earth-shatteringly bitter. As a deep sense of hurt threatened to surface she squashed it flat and wrenched herself free of his arms in a fierce gesture of rejection.

'Can I leave now?' Kathy asked, snaking over to the far side of the bed and sliding her legs off the edge with an eagerness to depart that spoke more clearly than any words. 'Or are you really going to insist I stay the whole night?'

Sergio was accustomed to women who voiced compliments and witty remarks in the aftermath of intimacy. He thought her attitude offensive.

Kathy didn't wait for an answer from him. She rose upright in a hurry and was quite unprepared for the wave of dizziness that engulfed her. The room tilted in front of her bemused eyes and the floor threatened to rise and greet her. Her face damp with perspiration, she swayed and staggered before she sank hurriedly back down on the bed again.

'What's wrong?' he asked.

Kathy was fighting an attack of nausea while taking slow, deep breaths in a desperate effort to clear her swimming head. 'Maybe I stood up too fast.'

'Lie down.' Sergio pressed her back against the pillows. 'I thought you were going to faint.'

'I haven't eaten in hours. That's all that's wrong,' she muttered, feeling foolish at having her big exit halted in its tracks. 'I'll be fine in a minute.'

'I'll order food.' Sergio used the phone by the bed and began getting dressed.

Kathy refused to look at him. 'I just want to go home.'

'As soon as you've eaten something and you're feeling better.' Lean, dark face sombre, Sergio spoke with scrupulous politeness.

Gripped by an overwhelming weariness that was as unfamiliar to her as the dizziness, Kathy swallowed hard and said nothing. She knew that there was no way she was going to feel better in the near future. He had destroyed her peace of mind and devastated her pride. What if her worst fear came true and she was pregnant? Pregnant by a guy whom she hated like poison?

CHAPTER FIVE

THE next morning, Kathy woke up feeling sick again.

Although she was afraid of using the pregnancy test she had bought too soon and wasting it, her nerves would no longer stand the prospect of a longer wait. It shook her that it took so little time to perform a test that was of earth-shattering importance to her life. A few minutes later and she had the result that she had dreaded: she was going to have a baby. Her tummy flipped with panic and nausea and she had to make a dash for the bathroom. In the aftermath, even a morsel of toast was more than her tender digestive system could contemplate.

Had she but known it, Sergio was not having a very satisfactory start to his day, either. He had only just arrived at the Torrente building when his senior executive PA, Paola, and his security chief, Renzo Catallone, requested an urgent meeting with him.

Paola laid the watch that Sergio had never expected to see again down on his desk. 'I'm really sorry, sir. I'm very upset about this. I came into the office very early on the morning I went on holiday because I wanted to check that I'd taken care of everything before I left. I saw your watch lying on the floor of your office and I locked it in a drawer in my desk for safe keeping—'

'*You* found my watch?' Sergio interrupted with incredulity. 'And said nothing?'

'I was in a hurry to leave. There was nobody else around. I did email another staff member to say where your watch was, but evidently the message was overlooked,' the troubled brunette explained unhappily. 'When I came back to work this morning, someone mentioned that your watch had gone missing and that everyone thought it had been stolen. It was only then that I realised that nobody knew what I'd done.'

That morning, Kathy could not help noticing every pregnant woman in her vicinity and she was amazed by how many of them there seemed to be. Even though the reality of her predicament had yet to sink in she could feel panic waiting to pounce on her. Other women managed to cope with unplanned pregnancies and so would she, she told herself doggedly. She had to consider all the options open to her and stay calm. But if she chose to be a single parent she would not be able to manage without financial help—*his* financial help. That lowering prospect made Kathy stiffen with distaste. She could not forget Sergio Torrente's crack about how having his child would be a 'lucrative lifestyle choice.'

'Call for you,' Kathy was told by her colleague on Reception.

'Why are you not answering your mobile?' Sergio enquired, his rich dark drawl thrumming down the line and paralysing her to the spot.

'I'm not allowed to take personal calls. I'm sorry I can't talk to you,' Kathy told him flatly and cut the connection, furious that he had dared to phone her. Was there no limit to his arrogance? Was he incapable of appreciating that she wanted nothing to do with him? The night before he had left her in peace to get dressed and eat the meal that was brought to her. She had travelled home in a limo and cried herself to sleep. Of course, she would have to speak to him sooner or later, she acknowledged reluctantly. But just then later had much more appeal to her than sooner.

Mid-morning a spectacular designer flower arrangement was delivered to her. Kathy opened a card signed only with Sergio's initials. Why was he phoning her and sending her flowers? Uncomfortably aware of the amount of attention the extravagant vase of exotic tiger lilies and grasses was generating, she tried to hand it back to the delivery man. 'I'm sorry but I don't want this—'

'That's not my problem,' he told her and off he went.

An hour later, another phone call came from Sergio, but she refused to take it. At noon, her supervisor approached her and took her aside to speak to her in a low voice. 'You can take extra time for your lunch break today. In fact, I've been told to tell you that it'll be fine if you want to take the rest of the afternoon off.'

Kathy studied her in bewilderment. 'But why?'

'The boss received a special request from the CEO. I believe Mr Torrente's driver is waiting outside for you.'

Kathy flushed to the roots of her hairline. She wanted to sink through the floor. But as she parted her lips to protest that she did not wish to see Sergio and had no wish whatsoever to be singled out for special treatment the other woman went into retreat, her uneasiness palpable. Sergio had the subtlety of a ram-raider, Kathy thought in outraged embarrassment as she squirmed beneath the covert glances and low-pitched buzz of comment that accompanied her departure from the agency. What Sergio wanted he had to have and he refused to wait.

Fizzing with fierce resentment, Kathy climbed into the waiting Mercedes. Should she tell him that she was pregnant? Or did she need to deal with her own feelings before she made an announcement? Fifteen minutes later, she was set down in front of an exclusive hotel. A doorman ushered her into the opulent interior. One of Sergio's bodyguards greeted her in the foyer and escorted her into the lift. She was shown into a palatial reception room.

Sergio strolled through the balcony doors that stood ajar and came to a fluid halt. As an entrance it was unrivalled in the performance stakes, for he was a dazzlingly good-looking guy. Her heart jumped and her breath shortened in her throat. No matter how she felt about Sergio, or how often she saw him, his physical impact did not lessen. Her response was involuntary. She looked at him and she knew she would look again and again and again. It was as if some wanton, rebellious sixth sense of hers had already forged a permanent connection with him.

'What do I say?' His dark drawl as rich and smooth as vintage wine, Sergio spread graceful lean brown hands. 'I am rarely at a loss, but I don't know what to say to you—'

'Well, believe me, I'm not stuck for words!' Kathy broke in to tell him roundly. 'How dare you put me in a position where I had no choice but to come here and see you? I liked my job. But what you did today—going to the boss to demand that I get out of work—was the equivalent of career suicide!'

'I needed to see you and I made a polite request. Don't exaggerate.'

'I'm not exaggerating.' Her apple-green eyes were

bright with indignation. 'I didn't know that you owned the advertising agency, as well as the recruitment company. A request from the CEO is the same as a demand. Now you've made it obvious that we have some kind of personal connection, I'll be the equivalent of a plague-carrier at work! After this, nobody's going to take me seriously and my colleagues will be counting the days until my temporary contract ends.'

Sergio expelled his breath on a measured hiss. 'If there is a problem, I'll secure employment for you elsewhere.'

Her slim white hands knotted into fists of frustration. 'Nothing is that simple. Is that really all you have to say?'

'No. I had to see you today to apologise.' His astute dark eyes were level and unflinching. 'My watch was not stolen, it was misplaced. Please accept my sincere regrets for accusing you of something which you did not do.'

That change of subject and the information that his watch had been found momentarily distracted Kathy and her brows pleated.

'But there is one thing that I cannot understand,' Sergio continued with a slow shake of his handsome dark head. 'Why on earth did you admit to stealing my watch in the first place?'

'What else could I do? You didn't believe me when I told you I hadn't taken it!'

'You didn't persist in pleading your innocence for very long. When you offered to play me for my watch, I naturally took it as a confession of guilt and I acted accordingly.'

'You acted *appallingly*.' Anger drove colour up over Kathy's slanted cheekbones as she voiced that contradiction.

'I'm not a soft touch. If you offend me I fight back. Circumstances weren't in your favour. You are a convicted thief and it did colour my judgement.' Sergio traded that defence without hesitation. 'But if you had not challenged me to that game on the terms that you did, I would not have slept with you last night.'

Kathy trembled with rage. 'So, even though you have apologised, it's really all my own fault?'

'That was not what I said. I fired my security chief over this affair today—'

'The ex-policeman? You gave him the sack for jumping to the same conclusion about me that you did?' Kathy exclaimed in disgust. 'How can you be so unjust?'

Disconcerted by that reaction, Sergio breathed, 'Unjust? How?'

'Unlike you, that man never met me and had no personal knowledge of me. He was only doing his job. You should blame yourself for misjudging me, not him.'

'Your compassion for Renzo surprises me. Why don't we discuss our differences over lunch?'

'I'd have to be starving to eat with you!' Kathy flung back, unimpressed.

'I love your passion, but I am less fond of drama, *cara mia*.'

Powerful dissatisfaction gripped Kathy, for she felt like a wave trying to batter a granite rock into subjection. He was stonewalling her. Her accusations had washed clean off him again. Her pain and anger were rising in direct proportion to her inability to break through his ice cool façade. 'Last night I was afraid you would call the police. I was terrified of ending up back in jail. That's the only reason I slept with you and I truly *hate* you for it—'

'You're angry with me. I accept that and I'm prepared to make amends by whatever means are within my power. But I do not accept that you only shared my bed out of fear.'

Fury roared through Kathy in an energising flood. 'Of course, you're going to say that!'

'But we both know that that claim is untrue.' Sergio rested glittering golden eyes on her in a challenging look as scorching as his touch.

The atmosphere was electric.

Kathy was so tense her muscles ached. Her heart thumped inside her tight chest. She sucked in a ragged breath. 'Don't tell me what I know.'

'Then admit the obvious. The sexual chemistry between us is extraordinarily strong. Don't you know how rare it is to feel this much excitement just being in the same room with someone?' Sergio murmured huskily.

Her legs felt weak and wobbly. The butterflies were back in her tummy and her mouth was running dry. 'That doesn't matter—'

'It always matters.'

A fleeting encounter with his brilliant predatory gaze pierced her with a flood of erotic awareness. The sensitive peaks of her breasts tingled. She remembered the taste and the urgency of his mouth on hers. Her slender hands tightened into defensive fists. Excitement was like a dangerous drug in her veins, powering a sensual awakening. She shivered in the grip of that madness and fought her weakness with all her might, her anger surfacing again. 'I don't want anything more to do with you—'

'But if I touched you now you'd burn up in my arms, *delizia mia*,' Sergio savoured that forecast with blazing assurance.

'Don't even think of getting that close!' Her reaction was raw in tone. 'I'm not stupid. I know how you think of me. You were too quick to remind me today that I'm a convicted thief. You said that in virtually the same breath as you apologised for accusing me of stealing your watch.'

Sergio rested unrepentant dark eyes on her. 'I won't lie or prevaricate. How do you expect me to feel about your history as a former offender? It's not acceptable. How could it be?'

Kathy was stunned to feel a prickly surge of tears threatening the backs of her eyes. She wasn't the tearful sort, but around him she was not her rational self and her emotions were in a chaotic tangle. How would he react when she told him that regardless of her shameful history she had conceived his child? Just then she couldn't handle the thought or the prospect of that humiliation. She focused studiously on the balcony where she could see the corner of a table and a crystal wineglass. 'I hope I'm getting a lift back to work,' she said tightly. 'I only get an hour for lunch and I'm already late.'

'I want you to stay,' Sergio spelt out.

'You can't always have what you want.' Kathy was struggling to control the see sawing thoughts and feelings attacking her in waves. 'Things have become more complicated than you appreciate.'

'What things?' Impatience stamped his lean dark features and his intonation.

His only use for her was sexual, Kathy thought in bitter mortification. But no doubt his ease of conquest had encouraged that attitude and she knew she could not blame him entirely for that. Even so, the base line was that he had the blue-blooded arrogance of wealth and privilege and her criminal conviction made her the lowest of the low in his eyes. That would never, ever change. She wondered why she was holding back on telling him that she was pregnant, for the passage of time would alter nothing. Indeed, she reasoned heavily, breaking the bad news and giving him the chance to come to terms with the idea was probably the more dignified plan of action to follow.

'I'm pregnant,' Kathy told him flatly. 'I did the test at home this morning.'

The silence that fell was bottomless, absolute and endless to her fast fraying nerves.

The instant she spoke, Sergio had veiled his keen dark gaze. His olive skin took on a faint ashen tone that she put down to shock. But that was his sole visible reaction, for his reserve and self-discipline triumphed. 'A doctor should check out that result,' he drawled without inflection. 'I'll organise it right now.'

Disconcerted by his cold-blooded calm, Kathy gave an uncertain nod of agreement. He was already using the phone and a few minutes later he told her that he had arranged a private medical appointment.

'If it's confirmed, have you any idea what you want to do?' Sergio enquired.

Her tension increased at that warning glimpse of a guy who preferred to solve every problem at speed. 'I don't want a termination,' she said in a taut undertone, feeling that it was only fair to tell him that up front.

'I wasn't going to suggest that option.' Sergio escorted her from the suite.

Lunch, she noted, was no longer on his agenda. In the lift, she said awkwardly, 'You don't need to come with me to see the doctor.'

'We're in this together.'

'The doctor can confirm the result. That's all you need to know at this stage.'

'I was trying to be supportive.'

Kathy shrugged a narrow shoulder, reluctant to be drawn. She didn't trust him. She didn't want to be put under pressure. The very fact that he was being careful not to betray his true feelings about her condition put her on her guard.

'I'll see you tonight, then,' Sergio conceded.

'I'd like a few days to think over all this.'

'How many days?'

As the uneasy silence thundered Sergio closed a hand over hers. 'Kathy…' he prompted.

'I'll phone you.' She tugged her fingers free from his, setting a boundary as much for her own benefit as for his. Although he did not voice his dissatisfaction the atmosphere had acquired a distinct chill.

Little more than an hour later, the smoothly spoken middle-aged gynaecologist confirmed that she was pregnant and warned her that she was underweight. A nurse gave her a sheaf of advisory leaflets. There and then, the new life Kathy carried within her began to seem rather more real to her. Back at the advertising agency she tried not to seem conscious of the curious looks she was receiving and the sudden silences when she passed by. Quite deliberately, she stayed late to make up the time she had missed over lunch.

The following morning when she arrived at work a colourful weekly gossip magazine was lying on her chair. Carefully folded open at the relevant page, it showed Sergio emerging from a New York nightclub with a famous young film actress clinging to him for support. A voluptuous blonde, Christabel Janson was reportedly very taken with her latest lover. Her throat so tight that it ached and her mood plummeting, Kathy forced a smile onto her lips that felt like concrete and dropped the magazine into the bin. Well, that was that. Someone had done her a favour in drawing that picture to her attention. It had certainly nipped any foolish expectations or romantic fancies in the bud. She might be expecting Sergio Torrente's child, but that really was the sum total of any continuing relationship that they now had.

That evening when Kathy took her break at the café, she told Bridget everything.

During that confessional, Bridget made several brusque comments about Sergio and gave the younger woman a reassuring hug. 'Falling pregnant is not the end of the world, so stop talking as though it is—'

Kathy gulped. 'I'm terrified—'

'It's the shock. Not to mention the fright Sergio Torrente gave you when he assumed that you had stolen his watch,' Bridget muttered tight-mouthed. 'When I think of what you've already gone through, his attitude makes my blood boil.'

'At least he was honest,' Kathy muttered heavily. 'But I hate him for it. How fair is that?'

'Forget about him. I'm more concerned about you.'

'Why am I crying all the time?' Kathy lamented, hauling out a tissue to mop at her overflowing eyes.

'Hormones,' Bridget answered succinctly.

Over the next forty-eight hours Kathy discovered two missed calls from Sergio on her mobile and she kept it switched off because she didn't want to speak to him. That evening she had an unexpected visitor when Renzo Catallone knocked on the door of her bedsit.

'I'd like to speak to you. Will you give me five minutes?' the former police officer asked bluntly.

Pale and stiff with unease, Kathy gave him a grudging nod.

'Mr Torrente has given me my job back as his chief of security,' Renzo volunteered. 'I understand that I have you to thank for that change of heart.'

Kathy was astonished by that assurance. 'But I only pointed out that it wasn't fair to blame you for misjudging me when you didn't actually know me.'

'In the circumstances, it was very generous of you to make that point on my behalf,' the older man told her warmly. 'I wanted to thank you and tell you that if there is ever anything I can do for you, please don't hesitate to ask for my help.'

Kathy went to bed that night feeling a little more cheerful and a little less ashamed of the past she could not change. The next day was Saturday, and she was serving breakfast at the café when Sergio strode in. His hard dark gaze raked across the room and closed in on her with punitive force. For a split second she stared and the edge-of-the-seat excitement was there, instant and powerful, sizzling through her slender taut frame like an electric charge. Her face flamed and she hastened into the kitchen with her order and lingered there.

Bridget put her head round the door. 'Kathy? We'll have to do without you today. Let Sergio take you home.'

'Bridget, I—'

'You have to talk to him some time.'

Kathy supposed that that was true. But it did mean stifling a seething desire to storm out and tell Sergio exactly what she thought of his two-timing cheating habits. With a baby on the way, she needed to take a long-term view, she told herself doggedly. Sergio was single and he could do as he liked. Her pregnancy was an accidental development. Now that the intimate side of things was over between them, establishing a civil connection with the future father of her child made better sense. Having given herself that quick mental pep talk, she emerged from the rear of the café clutching her bag and jacket.

The epitome of cool elegance in a black business suit teamed with a gold silk tie, Sergio was poised by the cash desk and incongruously out of step with his pedestrian surroundings. A bodyguard stood by the door, while two more hovered on the pavement outside.

Dark deep-set eyes alert, Sergio studied Kathy. As thin and pale as a wraith with her vibrant copper and red hair anchored in a casual pony-tail and her apple-green eyes hostile, she looked barely out of her teens. Yet not one of those facts detracted in the slightest from the power of her haunting beauty.

'You were supposed to wait for me to phone,' Kathy complained as she got into the limousine.

'That's not my style,' Sergio murmured lazily, the smoky timbre of his dark drawl ensuring that she remained outrageously aware of his sensual charisma. 'You need to collect your passport—we're flying to Paris this morning.'

Already shaken, her studied air of detachment evaporated entirely at that statement. 'Paris? Is this a joke?'

'No.'

'But to go all that way just for one day and when I'm supposed to be working…' Her voice ran out of steam because the minute she thought about it, the more she wanted to do it.

Sergio elevated a fine ebony brow. 'Why not? We have to talk and you're stressed. I would like you to relax today.'

CHAPTER SIX

THE opulent interior of Sergio's very large private jet took Kathy's breath away.

The main cabin was furnished with inviting seating areas and adorned with modern art. The interior also offered a purpose-built office, a movie theatre and several *en suite* bedrooms. In her casual beige corduroy jacket and denim jeans, she felt seriously at odds with the cutting-edge style of her surroundings.

'Wherever I am I have to be able to work. I spend a lot of time travelling and I usually have several staff with me,' Sergio explained over the delicious lunch that was prepared for them by his personal chef.

By the time the meal was over the jet was getting ready to land, for it was a very short flight.

'Why Paris?' Kathy asked in the limo that ferried them away from the hustle and bustle of CDG airport.

'France has strict press privacy laws. Many public figures find the media less intrusive here and a private life is more easily maintained,' Sergio advanced smoothly.

'So where are you taking me?'

'It's a surprise—a pleasant one, I hope, *cara mia*.'

Their destination was the island of Ile St-Louis, one of the most exclusive residential areas in Paris. The car came to a halt on a picturesque tree-lined quay in front of an elegant seventeenth-century building. Her curiosity rising by the second, Kathy accompanied Sergio inside. Sunlight fell from the tall windows and illuminated an elegant hall and stair-case complemented by strikingly contemporary décor.

'Feel free to explore,' Sergio murmured softly.

Kathy made no attempt to hide her bewilderment. 'What's going on? Why have you brought me to this house?'

'I have bought this house for you. I want you to raise my child here.'

Kathy was stunned by the concept and the wording. *My* child, not our child. She noted the distinction but tried to regard it as an encouraging sign of his wish to be involved in his baby's future. Slowly she shook her head, her glorious hair sparkling like polished metal in the intense light, her green eyes alive with incredulity. 'You want me to move to another country and live as your dependant? Am I supposed to clap my hands with joy, or something?'

'Let me explain how I see this,' Sergio urged.

Kathy swallowed back another outburst on the score of his single-minded arrogance and audacity. She understood that she was supposed to be impressed to death by the sheer grandeur and expense of a surprise that must have cost him millions. Maybe he thought he was being clever, generous and creative in a difficult situation. Maybe he believed that she was a problem that could best be cured with a liberal shower of money. Regardless, she felt humili-ated and offended as once again he contrived to underscore the differences of wealth, class and status between them while insisting on making all her choices for her.

'Some wine?' Sergio suggested, indicating the bottle

with the elegant label on the table. 'It's a classic Brunello from the Azzarini vineyards, which have belonged to the Torrentes for centuries.'

Her generous mouth compressed. 'I'm pregnant... alcohol is not supposed to be a good idea,' she extended when he continued to view her without comprehension. 'Don't you know anything about pregnant women?'

Sergio frowned. 'Why would I?'

Kathy folded her arms. 'Tell me why you think it would be a good idea for me to move to France.'

'If you remain in London, you will always be handi-capped by your past.'

'My prison record, you mean.' Her tummy gave a nauseous lurch as if reacting to her sudden increased tension and discomfiture.

Lean, strong face grim, Sergio surveyed her with level dark golden eyes. 'With my help you can rewrite that history and bury your past. You can change your name and move here to embark on a new life. It would be a second chance for you and it would also provide a less contentious background for my child.'

His candour really hurt. Sucking in a steadying gulp of air, Kathy walked over to the window. Her nails were biting purple crescents into her palms as she fought to retain her composure. 'And you think that that's what I should do?'

'If you remain in London our association will inevitably be exposed by the press. Once that particular genie gets out of its bottle, it can't be put back.'

In an abrupt movement, Kathy spun back. 'I've listened to you, and now you have to listen to me. I went to prison for a crime I didn't commit. I did not steal that jug, or any of the other stuff that vanished from Mrs Taplow's collection.'

Dark as midnight eyes cool and uncompromising, Sergio released his breath on a long slow hiss. 'You made a mistake. You were very young and you had no family support system. Let's move on from there and deal with the current challenge.'

Losing colour, Kathy stared back at him. She was cut to the quick by his flat refusal to even consider that she might be innocent. 'Can't you even give me a fair hearing?'

'You had that hearing in a court of law before a judge and jury four years ago.'

Pale as death at that hard-hitting response, Kathy looked away from him, feeling as though he had slapped her in the face. She tried to open a door but he slammed it shut and then locked it for good measure. He refused to listen to her claim of innocence. He wasn't interested in hearing her story because he was convinced of her guilt.

'My concern relates to the future,' Sergio continued. 'Let's stay on track.'

Her vivid green eyes clashed head on with his, her anger unhidden. 'You're not concerned about me, except in so far as you want to control my every move without making a commitment in return.'

'This house is quite a commitment for me. Think of the life you could have here.' Sergio closed the distance between them to reach for her knotted hands and enclose them in his. 'A fresh start, no financial worries, the best of everything for you and your child. Why are you arguing about this? These practicalities have to be dealt with before we can consider any more personal angle.'

'I told you that I would *never* go for the "lucrative life-style choice" option.' Her voice was jerky because she was trying without success to work up the will-power to step back from him. On every level her senses craved physical contact, even if it was only the masculine warmth of his hands on hers. She was in total turmoil, wanting to do the right thing while being terrified of making the wrong decision.

'I should never have made that comment, *delizia mia*. I was on edge that evening and aggressive without cause. You are now carrying my child. Who else should take care of you?'

Sergio was so close she could see the ring of bronze that accentuated his dark pupils, the spiky ebony lashes that lent his gaze such mesmerising depth and impact. Antagonism and hurt slivered through her like warring wounding blades. She could hardly breathe for wanting him. There was a quivering knot of intense longing locked inside her. She could feel the euphoric effect of his proximity threatening to shut down her brain cells, as she had no desire to think or to deny herself or to drive a further wedge between them. It was an abysmal moment to appreciate that her feelings for Sergio Torrente ran much deeper than she had been prepared to admit.

'Kathy,' Sergio husked in an intonation that was pure predatory enticement.

'Look, I haven't even decided if I'm going to keep this baby yet.' Kathy had to force out that statement, because it took that much effort to think straight and suppress an acknowledgement that threatened to tear her apart with self-loathing.

As Sergio froze in surprise his lean brown fingers tightened round her narrow wrists. 'What are you trying to suggest?'

Her oval face defensive and deeply troubled, she pulled free of his hold. 'I may yet choose adoption—'

'Adoption?' Sergio was shattered by the word and the concept.

'I was adopted and I had a very happy childhood. If I'm not certain that I can give as much to my baby, I will consider adoption as a possibility. Because one thing I *do* know!' Kathy reasoned in a surge of heartfelt emotion. 'This is not about houses and appearances and money! Nor is it about what you want. It's about my ability to love and care for my baby!'

His lean, darkly handsome face clenched taut. 'Of course it is. But you will not be alone in that undertaking. You will have my support.'

'You won't be here for the tough stuff. You'll stay in the background and you'll visit only when it suits you to do so. Can't you understand that I don't want to be a hanger-on in your world? I don't want you paying my bills and telling me what to do at every turn—'

'That is not how it would be.'

Kathy was quick to challenge him again. 'No? So I'd be free to move another guy in here if I met one?'

His dark eyes flamed sizzling gold. He was taken by surprise and his hostile distaste to that idea spoke for him.

'Obviously not. You would expect me to live like a nun—'

'Or content yourself with me.'

'Oh…' Kathy trembled, tension forming like an iron bar in her spine as her rage climbed. 'So you're not just talking about being an occasional supportive parent. There would be sexual strings attached to this arrangement, as well.'

'That's a tacky observation. I can't see into the future. I don't know where we're going.' Sergio lifted a shoulder in a sophisticated shrug. Intensely charismatic, he was Italian to his manicured fingertips, but he was also cool as ice under pressure and he refused to be drawn into dangerous waters.

'You know exactly where we'd be going and that would be nowhere,' Kathy condemned shakily. 'From what I can work out, you haven't been in a relationship that went anywhere in living memory. And you're certainly not going to break that habit for a convicted thief!'

Sergio cornered her between the window and the wall and studied her with smouldering golden sensuality. 'Even if I can't keep my hands off you when you're annoying the hell out of me, *delizia mia*?'

But Kathy was too afraid of his magnetism to relax her guard for a moment. 'Did you tell Christabel Janson that too? Or did she qualify for a less critical approach?'

The classic lines of his hard-boned features were impassive while the teasing light had evaporated from his astute gaze. 'Don't go there,' he advised. 'I don't answer to any woman.'

'Then where do you get the nerve to demand anything from me?' Kathy was so incensed she was shaking. 'I absolutely refuse to be some dirty secret in your life!'

His stunning eyes flamed gold. 'I did not ask you to be.'

'Yes, you did. You're ashamed of me but you still want to sleep with me. I won't accept that *ever*. You wasted my time and yours bringing me here,' Kathy flung at him furiously and she stalked back to the door. 'I want to go back to London.'

'This is childish, *bellezza mia*.'

Kathy sent him a shimmering emerald glance, afraid to let go of her anger in case it weakened her. 'No, I'm being sensible.'

'We have to agree a way forward.'

Kathy dealt him a fiery appraisal. 'I can't talk to you

feeling like this—maybe we could talk on the phone and be polite in a few months' time.'

'In a few months?' Sergio splintered in raw disbelief at that liberal time frame. 'You need me *now*!'

'No, I don't.'

'*Maremma maiale*…you're not even looking after yourself properly!' Sergio condemned without warning. 'How many hours a day are you working? You can't keep up two jobs while you're pregnant and stay healthy.'

Kathy gave him a frozen look. 'I'll cope and I'll manage. I learned a long time ago not to rely on a man.'

'Who taught you that?'

'The love of my life—Gareth.' Her lush pink mouth curled as she deliberately stoked that bitterness to make it into a further barrier between them. 'We grew up next door to each other. There's nothing I wouldn't have done for him. But he was no use at all in a tight corner and you're not going to be any different—'

Outrage flashed in Sergio's hard-boned features. 'I'm doing everything possible to support you.'

'No, you're throwing money at me and trying to ship me out to a foreign country where I am less likely to cause you embarrassment. If that's what you call support, you can keep it!' Kathy reached out to open the front door in an effort to end the confrontation.

'*Madonna diavolo!* What about this? Will you do without this, as well?' Sergio caught her into his arms and crushed her soft full mouth beneath his with a passion that devastated her resistance.

He knotted one hand into her copper hair to hold her fast and clamped her slender body to his like a second skin. His heart pounded against hers. Urgently aware of his mascu-

line arousal, she quivered in that hard embrace and exchanged kiss for kiss with a hunger as fierce, hot and lethal
as a fever. But nothing could assuage the sadness within
her and the ache at the heart of her. When he let her go she
staggered back against the wall.

'I was supposed to drink the classic wine and go upstairs
with you to celebrate, wasn't I?' Kathy was still fighting
even though her knees didn't feel up to the challenge of
holding her upright. 'But I'm not so desperate that I need
to share a man and I never will be!'

Sergio was already using his phone. He did not deign
to reply to that sally. His detachment was as effective as an
invisible wall. The silence was suffocating. She felt shut
out, pushed away and she found it unbearable. Even when
she was so mad with him that she could have screamed she
wanted to be back in his arms. He flipped the key to the
door. She gave him a tiny split second to speak. He said
nothing. He did nothing to prevent her from leaving, either.

'I hate you—I really, *really* hate you,' she whispered fierily
as she left and, in that instant, she meant every word of it.

The door snapped shut behind her. There was not even
the suspicion of a slam.

Conscious that Sergio's protection team were watching
her every move and had to be wondering why she was
leaving alone ten minutes after their arrival, Kathy endeavoured to look composed. Then suddenly, from the house
behind her, she heard the unmistakable noise of glass
smashing and splintering. The vintage wine bottle hitting
the fireplace? Her narrow shoulders straightened, her chin
came up. Eyes sparkling with satisfaction and with a new
purpose in her step, she headed for the waiting car.

Over the next two weeks, however, Kathy grew steadily

more exhausted. Tigger died in his sleep without fuss or fanfare and she was inconsolable at the loss of her elderly pet. While she fretted about the future and grieved for her cat, her morning sickness spread to other times of day and she began lying awake at night worrying. Being pregnant and ill was more of a struggle than she had expected and she had to cut back on her hours at the café. Aware that Kathy was already struggling to pay her bills, Bridget offered Kathy her spare room, but Kathy was determined not to take advantage of their friendship.

Kathy would have vehemently protested any suggestion that she was waiting for Sergio to make another move. But when she discovered that Sergio was fully engaged in making moves that had nothing to do with her whatsoever, she had a rather rude awakening to reality. Travelling into work on the bus, she caught an infuriating flash of Sergio's face on a newspaper page. She wasn't close enough to see what the article was about and, while she told herself that she shouldn't care, she was only human. As soon as she got off the bus she bought the tabloid and paid the price for her curiosity.

Sergio, she learned, was the owner of a giant yacht called *Diva Queen* and he had thrown a stag party on board for his friend, Leonidas Pallis, the Greek billionaire. An exotic dancer talked of a 'non-stop orgy on the high seas.' Kathy studied the grainy photo of Sergio, shirt hanging open, engaging in dirty dancing with a pneumatic semi-naked blonde. Even drunk and carousing he still looked gorgeous and she swallowed hard. He really did like blondes, she thought dully. He also looked as if he was having fun. No doubt it beat the hell out of chess.

This was not a guy any woman would choose to have

an unplanned baby with, Kathy acknowledged heavily. Yet, how could she fault him when he had already accepted responsibility and was ready to help her financially? At no stage had he told her how he actually felt about the prospect of becoming a father and now she realised that he didn't need to tell her when his behaviour spoke so clearly for him. He was trying to ship her off to France to live under an assumed name where their paths would only cross at his instigation. And Sergio's riotous partying was making headlines round the world, while prompting an anonymous source to admit surprise at the sheer scale of his recent bad-boy activities.

Kathy believed that Sergio was reacting to the situation he had found himself in. He didn't want to be a father and he was even less happy that the mother of his child was a convicted thief. Those were the unlovely facts and it was time she learned to live with them and matched his independence. A good first move would be sorting out her immediate future on her own, for at this stage of her pregnancy there was no need for Sergio to be involved. In any case, a cooling-off period would probably do them both the world of good, she reflected painfully. She needed time and space to make her mind up about what she wanted to do after the baby was born. Hanging around in the hope that Sergio Torrente would somehow provide an answer for all her doubts and fears was a sure path to disappointment.

That evening she ate with Bridget at her apartment and outlined her intentions. 'I'll have to leave London. If I stop working at the café I won't be able to make my rent,' she confided ruefully. 'And I don't want to depend on Sergio for help.'

'Why not?'

Kathy dug into her tote bag and passed the newspaper across the table.

Bridget perused the article, raised her brows and set it aside without comment. 'If you don't mind kids and cooking, you can go to my god-daughter in Devon,' she said abruptly.

'Your god-daughter?' Kathy repeated with a frown. 'The estate agent?'

'Nola's energetic and practical just like you. You'll like each other. Her husband's a journalist and hardly ever at home. She's heavily pregnant with her fourth child and desperate for help,' the other woman said. 'Her nanny got married, and in the past two months two au pairs have come and gone. The first was so homesick she couldn't stop crying and the second quit because the house was too far out of town. What do you think?'

'I'll consider any option,' Kathy answered. 'There's nothing to keep me here.'

CHAPTER SEVEN

KATHY had just walked into the estate agency where Nola worked when the first pain hit.

With a muffled gasp, she clutched the edge of a desk to steady herself. The fear that engulfed her was much worse than the slight cramping sensation that gripped her lower abdomen.

'What's wrong?' Nola demanded, breaking off her conversation with another employee.

'I think the baby's coming!' Kathy whispered shakily, white as the wall behind her. 'But it's too soon.'

Nola Ross, a sensible brown-eyed blonde in her thirties, pressed Kathy down into a chair. 'Breathe in and out slowly. It may just be a Braxton-Hicks contraction.'

But the pains kept on coming and the two women decided that Kathy should go to the local hospital. There, Kathy insisted that Nola went back to the agency because she knew that the other woman had clients to meet. The doctor gave Kathy medication in an effort to stop the contractions and made arrangements to have her transferred to a facility with a neonatal unit. By that stage several hours had passed. As there was no bed free, she was kept on a trolley while she waited for the transportation to arrive.

Lying there, Kathy prayed and struggled to keep panic at bay. She was only thirty-five weeks pregnant and knew that her little girl would be at risk if she was born too early. The past seven months seemed to run on fast forward through Kathy's mind. She had not worked as Nola's domestic support for very long. No sooner had Nola had her own baby than her husband had taken off with another woman, plunging the Ross family into chaos. During that testing time, Nola and Kathy had become firm friends. By now Kathy had recovered from her early pregnancy sickness and helped out at the estate agency while Nola was briefly on maternity leave. She'd discovered that she was a whizz at selling houses! It was now three months since Nola had engaged a full-time nanny and hired Kathy as a saleswoman instead. In every way that mattered, Kathy's move from London to a small market town in Devon had proved an unqualified success.

But now Kathy was fast sinking into a pit of dread and self-blame. Determined to establish a secure base for herself and her child, she had worked hard because a career with prospects was the best possible safety net for a single parent. But had she worked too hard? Stressed too much? Rested too little? Once those preliminary bouts of nausea had melted away, she had felt amazingly healthy. Slowly but surely, her unborn baby had become the most important element of her world. The discovery that she was having a little girl had simply intensified her feelings. It had never once occurred to Kathy that her own body might let her down.

'Kathy...?'

As she recognised that unforgettable dark-timbred drawl shock flooded Kathy's taut length. She turned her head on the thin pillow, her apple-green gaze alight with astonishment. Sergio Torrente was poised several feet away just staring at her with sombre dark-as-night eyes.

'Are you okay?' he breathed tautly.

'No…' She squeezed out the word and it got tangled up in her vocal cords, and the next thing she knew she was sobbing as though her heart would break. In recent months, rigid self-discipline had prevented her from giving way too often to unproductive thoughts. His actual presence, however, was much more challenging at a moment when her defences were down and her emotions were out of her control. 'Go a-away!' she told him chokily.

In answer, Sergio made an unexpected move that had all the hallmarks of spontaneity. He smoothed her tangled hair off her damp brow and gripped her trembling hand in his. 'I can't leave you alone. Don't ask me to do that again.'

Kathy made use of the hanky he had produced for her use. 'How did you find out I was here?'

'Right now that's not important. I've already talked to the doctor. No doubt the staff has done their best, but you are lying unattended on a trolley in a corridor,' Sergio murmured in a wrathful undertone. 'That is not an acceptable level of care.'

'It's a small hospital and there's nothing more they can do for me at present,' Kathy mumbled unsteadily.

His hold on her fingers tightened. 'I have an air ambulance on its way and an obstetrician waiting to take charge. Please let me help.'

Kathy did not even have to think about how to respond to that offer, because in terms of treatment it was superior to anything else immediately available to her. Her spirits also received an immediate boost from the obvious fact that he placed as much importance on the safe birth of their child as she did. 'All right.'

His lean, darkly handsome features were tense and he made no attempt to hide his surprise. 'I thought you'd make me sweat through every possible argument.'

'All I care about is what's best for my baby,' Kathy admitted tightly. 'At this moment our differences don't matter.'

Everything moved very quickly after that. Attended by paramedics, she was stretchered onto the air ambulance. For the first time in months, she found herself actually worrying about what she looked like and she couldn't get over how silly and superficial she was being. How could she waste energy worrying that her eyelids and her nose might be pink and swollen? Or wondering if her large tummy equalled Mount Everest while she was lying flat? At best, she knew she had to look tired and tousled like most heavily pregnant women after a more than usually trying day. Even Sergio was a touch less perfect than usual, she reasoned in desperation. He had loosened his silk tie, dishevelled his black hair with impatient fingers and a blue-black shadow of stubble was beginning to define his stubborn jaw line and strong, sensual mouth. But he still looked totally amazing to her.

Just then he frowned with concern, visually questioning her lingering appraisal.

Cheeks reddening, Kathy shook her head to indicate that there was nothing wrong and shut her eyes tight. But the image of the guy she loved stayed with her. She loved him to bits, hated his guts for all sorts of reasons, as well, but she was still as possessed by a bone-deep longing for him as a starving woman sighting life-giving food. She knew he was bad for her, knew too big a dose of him was dangerous, but he was in her blood and in her mind and, no matter how hard she tried, she couldn't shake free of his influence over her.

In what seemed to her a remarkably short space of time, and with impressive efficiency, she was transported to the opulent comfort of a private London hospital. There she was given an ultrasound scan.

'I'd like to stay,' Sergio said flatly.

An objection was brimming on her lips and a glimpse of his taut profile warned her that that was exactly the response he expected from her. She swallowed back her protest because he was doing everything within his power to help and excluding him yet again seemed unfair. As she steeled herself to have her tummy exposed another thought occurred to her and she tugged at the sleeve of his jacket to get his attention.

Sergio angled his arrogant dark head down to her.

'We're having a girl,' she whispered.

Fine ebony brows drawing together, Sergio lifted his head and stared at her before comprehension sank in. Suddenly and entirely unexpectedly, a smile curved his wide sculpted mouth.

When the procedure commenced, she realised that she need not have worried about baring her swollen belly because Sergio's fascination was wholly reserved for the images on screen. A shot of the baby's face made him marvel out loud in Italian and reach for her hand. 'Awesome,' he finally murmured in roughened English. 'She is awesome.'

Tears dampened her eyes and she blinked them back fiercely. Some tests were carried out and a foetal monitor was attached to her, before she was finally slotted into bed in a luxurious private room. The obstetrician soothed her worst fears by telling her that babies born after the thirty-fourth week of gestation had a high rate of survival and less chance of suffering long-term complications. Even so, there were no guarantees and the longer her baby stayed in the womb the healthier she was likely to be. With Kathy still at risk of going into labour, the treatment plan was bed-rest and hydration.

Minutes after leaving with the obstetrician, Sergio reappeared.

'I thought you'd gone,' Kathy commented.

'*Per meraviglia*…I hope that's a joke.' Astute dark-as-night eyes rested on her. 'But it's not a joke, is it?'

Kathy sidestepped that issue, for she had not intended to annoy him. 'Well, now that we're on our own, at last you can tell me how long you've known where I was living.'

'I found out today at the same time as I heard you had been hospitalised.' Lean bronzed features bleak, Sergio studied her from the foot of the bed. 'I was last in the chain. Nola—whoever she is—contacted Bridget Kirk, who decided to pass the news on to Renzo Catallone.'

'Bridget told Renzo?' Her brows pleated in surprise. 'I didn't even know they'd met.'

'They've met all right. Evidently your friend is good at keeping secrets. When I spoke to her months ago, she swore that she had no idea where you were.'

Kathy was very much disconcerted. 'She didn't tell me you'd contacted her, either.'

'Renzo kept in touch with her and finally it paid off. But he also believed that she didn't know where you had gone.'

'I'm surprised that Bridget chose to tell Renzo.'

'Are you? With you on the brink of giving birth or possibly even losing my child, it was time to stop playing games.'

Kathy registered the cold core of his anger. The very fact that he was struggling to hide it, that his diamond-hard façade was no longer impregnable, warned her how deep his hostility had gone. 'Bridget was only respecting my wishes and trying to protect me—'

'From me?' Sergio sent her an almost raw glance and strode over to the window, his broad shoulders radiating his ferocious tension, before he swung back to look at her. 'Do I deserve that? Did I frighten you in any way?'

'No,' Kathy conceded.

'Perhaps something I did upset you…'

The verdant green eyes resting on him veiled. 'You're fishing.'

'I need to know. I don't want you pulling another vanishing act,' Sergio traded in a direct challenge.

Kathy contemplated the swollen mound of her tummy and opted for honesty. 'You asked for it.'

The silence fairly leapt and jumped and throbbed.

'Are you saying what I think you might be saying?' Sergio was studying her in disbelief. 'Was that a reference to the stag cruise I organised for Leonidas Pallis? That event was blown up out of all proportion by the press. But was that what upset you?'

'Lose the word, *upset*,' Kathy advised, a shade tart in tone.

His brilliant dark eyes shimmering scorching gold, Sergio spread lean brown hands in a gesture that expressed his incredulity. 'You were so angry about the cruise that you took off and put me through more than seven months of hell?'

'*Angry* isn't the right word, either—'

'How about…*revenge*?'

'I suppose there was a degree of that, although I didn't see it at the time,' Kathy conceded ruefully.

Sergio bit out a humourless laugh.

'I think I'd just had enough of you. I didn't want to be shipped off to France,' Kathy confided. 'There I was, throwing up every day and so tired I could hardly keep my eyes open at work and you were partying—'

'I can explain—'

'Don't waste your time. In any case you don't owe me any explanations,' Kathy fielded with resolute brightness. 'It's simple—I needed to get on with my life just the same as you were.'

Sergio dealt her a measuring appraisal. 'You don't just get mad, you get even, *delizia mia*.'

Kathy experienced a very strong desire to get out of bed and slap him for his arrogance. 'It's not all about you— why do you think everything is about you? Stop trying to twist what I said into a backhanded compliment! I had no good reason to stay in London.'

Lean, darkly handsome face taut, Sergio stared down at her with brooding force. 'You can't afford to get mad with me at present. You're supposed to stay calm and avoid all stress.'

In a frustrated movement, Kathy pushed her copper hair off her brow. 'Then rewind my life and wipe the bit where we met!'

'Even if I could I would not,' Sergio admitted without hesitation. 'I want that little girl. I also want you.'

Kathy was hugely unimpressed by that claim. Her green eyes glinted, her full rose-pink mouth curled with disdain. She was very tempted to tell him that the boat had not only sailed, but also sunk with all hands on board. He hadn't wanted her enough when it had mattered. He hadn't wanted her enough when she had been as available as a free sample. She said nothing, though, for telling him that would only make her sound sad.

'And whatever it takes, I intend to have you,' Sergio delivered in the same even tone.

Kathy blinked, for she was not quite sure she had heard that. Her curling lashes lifted high. She collided with the hot gold challenge of his gaze and it was like being hauled down into a whirlpool of heat and hunger. He made no attempt to hide the desire etched on his lean strong face and sheer shock paralysed her to the bed.

'Okay. Glad we understand each other at last, *delizia mia*,' Sergio murmured smooth as silk as he pressed the bell on the wall. 'I asked for a meal to be brought and I'd like you to try to eat something.'

But when the meal arrived, Kathy was unable to oblige for she had no appetite at all. Sergio took a seat at the far end of the room and unfurled a notebook PC with a disturbing air of permanency, while she lay on the side she had been told to lie on and fretted. Why was it that every time she got her life back on track something happened to derail it again? She reminded herself that she had played a very active part in this particular derailment.

Frustration filled her at the awareness that the dependency she had been so determined to avoid was now being forced on her. Lying in bed in London wasn't going to pay her bills. If her baby was born early and in need of specialist care, she would be even more dependent on Sergio's goodwill and support to survive. She had planned to work right up to the last minute. How long would she be tied to London? For how long could she expect Nola to hold her job open? What about her rent? Her possessions?

'Why are you frowning?' Sergio enquired lazily.

'Promise me that if I'm stuck in here for weeks, you'll collect my belongings and keep them safe for me,' Kathy urged abruptly.

With a wondering shake of his handsome dark head, Sergio sprang upright and strolled with lithe grace towards the bed. 'What could possibly make you worry about something like that?'

'I'm not fit enough to take care of it myself and everything I own is at Nola's.'

'But why on earth would you imagine that it could become a problem?'

'When I was arrested four years ago, I lost everything I owned while I was in custody,' Kathy admitted tightly. 'Family photos, keepsakes, clothes, *everything*. I don't want it to happen again and it could so easily.'

Sergio frowned. 'How did that happen?'

'There was nobody to take responsibility for my things while I was in prison, so what I owned was either dumped or sold. Gareth promised that he would store my stuff for me, but then he let his mother ditch me and I never heard from him again—'

'His mother?' Sergio studied her in astonishment.

'She visited me in prison to tell me that her son was finished with me. I wrote to him and my landlady, but neither of them bothered to reply.'

'I'll have your possessions collected for you the moment you say the word. Believe me, you won't lose a single item.' Lean brown fingers curling to the footboard on the bed, Sergio surveyed her with disturbingly intent dark eyes. 'We share a mutual distrust of our fellow man. How can I prove to you that although I have my faults you can trust my word?'

'You can't.' Kathy was tense because she was experiencing a tightening sensation that she was afraid might be the forerunner of the contractions that had faded away some hours earlier.

'Even if I ask you to marry me?'

Her heart gave a slow, heavy thud and she stared at him fixedly. 'Are you asking?'

'Yes, *bellezza mia*.' Sergio met her startled appraisal with rock-solid calm. 'You're having my baby. It's the most rational solution.'

'But people don't get married just because—'

'In my family they do,' Sergio cut in.

Kathy contemplated the armchair he had vacated. She didn't want to snatch at his offer and give his ego an unnecessary boost. If she considered his proposal purely in terms of security and common sense, however, it answered her every practical need, for she would no longer need to worry about how she would manage as a mother. Indeed if she married Sergio the luxury of choice would enter her world again and her little girl would never have to make the sacrifices her mother had. Her adoptive parents had instilled enough of their principles to ensure that marriage had much more appeal for Kathy than the worry of having to go it alone with her child. If he was willing to commit to that extent to their daughter's future, she reckoned that he was much more responsible and reliable than she had given him credit for.

Kathy tried not to grimace as the sensation in her abdomen became definite enough to warn her that she was going into labour again. It was a very vulnerable moment and she fully recognised the fact. He didn't love her, but he was willing to be there for her as the father of her child. Just then that mattered to her as much as the knowledge that if she said yes, he would stay with her.

'Okay…I'll marry you,' she muttered jerkily.

'I'll organise it.' His lean dark features serious, Sergio's smooth response bore the infuriating hallmarks of a male who had not expected any other reply. 'We'll organise the ceremony before the baby's born—'

'I don't th-think so,' Kathy gasped as another pain rippled in a wave across her lower body, returning stronger and faster than she had expected. 'My contractions have started again. Our baby's going to get here first.'

Momentarily, Sergio dealt her a look of consternation, but then he unfroze and wasted no time in summoning assistance. Events moved fast from that point. Both of them were filled with dismay when the surgeon decided that a Caesarean section would be the safest, speediest option for the delivery. Kathy was frightened for her child and Sergio made an enormous effort to keep her calm. His strength and assurance helped her a great deal. Clad in green theatre scrubs, he held her hand throughout the procedure and talked her through every step. He looked very pale but the delivery went without a hitch. Only in the instant after Sergio first saw their daughter did Kathy fully appreciate how much of a front he could put up, and that his anxiety had been equal to her own, for his stunning dark deep-set eyes were lustrous with tears.

Their newborn infant was checked over with great care. She had slight breathing problems, so was immediately placed in an incubator and whisked away.

Kathy was returned to her room. 'I'd like to call our

daughter Ella after my mother,' she said tautly, keen to personalise their child with a name, so that even if she couldn't hold the tiny girl at that moment she could feel closer to her.

'Ella Battista…after mine,' Sergio suggested.

The effects of stress, exhaustion and medication were steadily piling up on Kathy and making her eyes very heavy. Sergio went to check on Ella and came back to report on her progress before Kathy finally let herself fall asleep.

Nola Ross phoned the next morning and sent flowers. Bridget arrived and joined Kathy in the special care baby unit, where quite some time was spent admiring Ella with her silky fluff of coppery curls and fine features. 'Are you annoyed with me for getting Sergio involved?' Bridget asked worriedly, once Kathy had been conveyed back to her room and the two women had the privacy to talk.

Kathy was grateful to be distracted from her ever-present worry about her baby's health. 'Of course I'm not. But why didn't you mention Sergio's visit or Renzo's?'

Bridget winced. 'I knew it would stress you out if you realised that Sergio was making a big push to find you, and then things got really complicated…'

'How?'

'Don't mention it to Sergio yet, but I'm dating Renzo.'

Kathy gave her a bemused look, and then she began to laugh. The brunette made Kathy smile with her story of how the middle-aged Italian's regular visits to the café had led to a friendship that had warmed into something more serious.

'I'd pretended I didn't know where you were at first. Then I had to keep up the pretence because Renzo was too loyal to Sergio to be trusted with the truth—'

'You should have told me.'

'You had enough on your plate. To be fair to Sergio, the guy hasn't stopped looking for you since you left London.'

'Guilty conscience. I should've left him a note telling him not to worry and that I'd be fine,' Kathy conceded wryly.

'But the dramatic silence and the walk-out was much more your style, *bellezza mia*,' Sergio interposed from the doorway. 'Mrs Kirk…I hope Kathy has invited you to our wedding.'

The older woman's eyes expanded like saucers. 'What wedding?' she exclaimed. 'You two are planning to get married? That is wonderful news!'

'I hadn't got around to mentioning it yet.' Beneath Sergio's sardonic appraisal, Kathy squirmed and flushed. She had found it impossible to find the right words with which to make that announcement when deep down inside she felt as though agreeing to marry him was a betrayal of her principles and her pride. 'It won't be for ages yet anyway,' she added. 'I mean, we'll have to wait until Ella's strong enough to leave the baby unit and I've recovered from the Caesarean.'

In actuality, Ella finally gained her release from medical care only three days before her parents were due to marry and, by then, she was seven weeks old. The little girl had overcome the breathing problems caused by her under-developed lungs only to be diagnosed with anaemia. At one stage, a worrying infection had kept Kathy at the hospital with her daughter day and night. With a vast business empire demanding his attention, Sergio had been unable to be on the spot as often, but he had shared every crisis with Kathy and his daughter. It was Sergio's strength that Kathy had learnt to rely on at the lowest moments. His courage in the face of adversity and his refusal to contemplate a negative outcome had grounded Kathy and given her hope when she had been most afraid for their child. Once the danger passed, however, Sergio had gone back abroad.

He had suggested that Kathy move into his apartment, but a suite in the quiet hotel across the road from the hospital had proved to be more convenient and she had seen no reason to move out before the wedding. That physical separation, allied to the need to concentrate solely on Ella's problems, had created a polite distance between Sergio and Kathy. In addition, Sergio had been determined to keep the press from finding out about Ella and his marital plans before he chose to make an official announcement. As a result their meetings had acquired a level of discretion that had ensured that they invariably only saw each other at the hospital. And there they had been virtually never alone.

Although Sergio had belatedly attempted to break the stalemate, Kathy had made endless excuses about needing to stay with Ella or being too tired while she recovered from her op. Kathy was miserably convinced that all the secrecy was aimed at keeping her shameful past hidden for as long as possible. So, how could Sergio really want to risk being seen out with her in public? Wouldn't it only hasten her exposure as a convicted thief? The paparazzi followed Sergio's every move with intense interest. Kathy reckoned that about five minutes after she was revealed as the new Mrs Torrente her criminal record would be dug up and paraded in newsprint for all to see. The very thought of it made her feel sick with dread. But worst of all was the knowledge that Sergio would also feel that humiliation—and that some day her daughter would, as well.

In the background, the wedding arrangements had been handled by experts who worked in tandem with Sergio's staff. Italy had been chosen as the ideal location and every detail had been kept under wraps. Kathy only had Bridget and Nola on her guest list, and her friends were over the moon at the prospect of a luxury weekend in the sunshine. The one item that Kathy had chosen for herself was her wedding gown.

Forty-eight hours before the wedding, the hotel reception called Kathy's suite to inform her that Mr Torrente was on his way up to see her. Surprised because she had not expected to see Sergio before she flew out to Italy with her friends the next day, Kathy stopped packing Ella's clothes and rushed to check her hair instead. She was astonished when she opened the door to a stranger, because the stringent security precautions Sergio insisted on meant that nobody she didn't know should even get as far as the lift.

A portly man with receding hair and rather sad brown eyes smiled at her. 'I'm Abramo Torrente, Sergio's brother.'

'My goodness…' Kathy had the tact not to say that she had quite forgotten that her bridegroom even had a brother. 'Please come in.'

'You should check my credentials first.' Abramo extended his passport as evidence of his identity. 'You can't be too careful nowadays.'

Certainly the brothers bore little resemblance to each other. Abramo looked more cuddly than sexy and, where Sergio was in the physical peak of condition the younger man had a grey indoor pallor. She had to strain her memory to recall that Sergio was the child of his father's first marriage and Abramo the child of the second.

'My brother hasn't told you anything about me, has he?'

Abramo, Kathy registered, was shrewder than he seemed at first glance. 'I'm afraid not.'

'It's eight years since Sergio spoke to me. He refuses to see me. He's an old-world Torrente in the style of our late father—stubborn and hard as iron,' Abramo commented heavily. 'But we are still brothers.'

'Eight years is a long time. It must have been some family feud.'

'Sergio was the innocent victim of my mother's lies,' Abramo admitted ruefully. 'My father favoured him and she resented that. I loved my brother but I envied him too. Once I saw how Sergio's fall might give me a chance with Grazia, I was no better than my mother. I stood by and did nothing to help him regain what was rightfully his.'

'Grazia?' Kathy prompted in fascination. 'Who's Grazia?'

'Surely Sergio has mentioned her to you?'

'No.'

Abramo contrived to look stunned by that oversight. 'When Sergio was twenty-one he got engaged to Grazia. I too loved her,' he confided with a grimace. 'When Sergio was deposed as heir to the Azzarini wine empire and I took his place, Grazia panicked and changed her mind about marrying him. I didn't waste the opportunity. I married her before she could change her mind.'

Kathy marvelled at his honesty and at his evident hope that Sergio would absolve him from what must have been a devastating double betrayal. 'I'm not sure I understand why you're telling me all this.'

'Sergio is about to marry you. You have a child. All our lives are in a different place now. I want to offer my good wishes for your future. I have a great need to make peace with my brother.' Abramo gave her a look of unashamed appeal. 'Will you speak to him?'

Ella wakened in the room next door and her cries created

a welcome diversion. Kathy lifted her tiny precious daughter from her cradle and hugged her gently close. Family ties were important, she reflected helplessly. Although Abramo's sincerity had impressed her, she was reluctant to interfere in a situation about which she knew so little. She took Ella out to meet her uncle. He was one of those men who absolutely adored babies and was enchanted with his niece. Kathy was surprised to learn that he had no children of his own.

'I'll have a word with Sergio after the wedding,' Kathy said finally. 'But that's all I can promise.'

Abramo gripped her hands in a warmly enthusiastic expression of gratitude and swore she would not regret it. As soon as he had left, Kathy made use of the internet and did a search for Grazia Torrente. A startling number of websites came up: Grazia was a celebrity in mainland Europe, the fashionista daughter of an Italian marquis with an alarmingly long name. Up came a picture of an ethereal blonde with the face of a Madonna and a figure that would make even a sack look trendy. As couples went, Abramo and Grazia matched like oil and water, whereas Sergio and...Her face tight with discomfiture, Kathy closed the page and scolded herself for snooping. After all, it was *eight* years since he had been engaged to the woman who was now married to his brother.

That night the cheerful nanny whom Kathy had picked from a short list arrived to help with Ella. The next day, they departed for the airport, where they met up with Bridget and Nola. Ten minutes later, Kathy's mobile phone rang.

'I hear you're having a good time,' Sergio murmured teasingly.

Kathy stiffened. 'Have you got your security team spying on me now?'

'No need, *delizia mia*. I can hear the giggles from where I'm standing and it sounds very much like a hen-party.'

'From where you're standing?' Kathy froze and looked up. Her searching gaze fanned round before it homed straight in on Sergio's unmistakable tall, well-built frame. Sun shades in place, he was talking on his phone about fifty yards away. 'I didn't know you were here—'

'No, don't come over. Ignore me,' Sergio urged as she began to rise from her seat. 'We're travelling separately. You're flying to Italy in a Pallis jet to keep the paparazzi off our trail.'

'Is your friend Leonidas throwing in male strippers to enliven our flight?' Her apple-green eyes were bright as danger flares. 'Maybe I want to do more than have a giggle over a cup of coffee during my last hours as a single woman.'

Across the concourse, Sergio raised lean brown fingers to his lips and blew on them as though he had been burnt. 'You are never going to let me forget that stag cruise, are you?'

Chin at an angle, Kathy lifted and dropped a slim shoulder in an exaggerated shrug. 'What do you think?'

'I think that christening my yacht *Diva Queen* was an act of prophecy, *delizia mia*,' Sergio drawled. 'By the way, be nice about Leonidas. He and his wife are hosting our wedding…'

CHAPTER EIGHT

A COURTEOUS steward escorted Kathy and her party onto the Pallis jet.

Kathy was surprised to find two women waiting on board to greet them. A shapely chestnut-haired girl with violet eyes and a ready smile introduced herself as Maribel Pallis and her stunning blonde companion as Tilda, Princess Hussein Al-Zafar. They were the wives of Sergio's friends from his university days, Leonidas and Rashad.

'The guys are like this…' Tilda meshed her fingers together in a speaking gesture to explain the strength of the men's friendship. 'We couldn't wait until you got to Italy to meet you.'

'I always thought it would take a big game hunter to land Sergio,' Maribel teased.

Kathy resisted the urge to comment that a six-pound baby had accomplished that feat all on her own and without the use of a weapon. It might be the truth, she thought heavily, but it would also be a conversational killer when Tilda and Maribel were making a wonderful effort to extend a friendly welcome. Then Ella opened her baby version of her mother's unusual light green eyes to inspect their new acquaintances and any remaining barriers fell, for every woman present was a mother and there was plenty of common ground to share. That led into Maribel asking soon after takeoff if there was any chance that Kathy fancied a night out rather than a sedate pre-bridal early night.

Kathy gave Maribel a look of surprise. 'Any sort of a night out would be a thrill,' she confided ruefully. 'I stayed in while I was pregnant and after the birth I was tied to the hospital until last week.'

Tilda and Maribel exchanged smiles. 'Let's go for the thrill.'

'Sergio always does.' Kathy spoke her thoughts out loud and then blushed at that revealing comment, which her companions were too tactful to pick up on.

When the jet landed in Tuscany, Ella and her nanny were borne off to the Pallis country estate while Kathy and her companions headed into the medieval splendour of Florence for a whirlwind shopping trip. There Kathy finally got to make use of the credit cards Sergio had given her and that breathless, chattering tour of exclusive boutiques was a lot of fun. It soon transpired that the night out was a pre-planned event that had merely required her approval. The five women enjoyed the comfort of a luxury hotel suite as a changing room and sashayed out to dinner in style.

Maribel took a picture of Kathy with her phone. Kathy's new turquoise dress was a fabulous foil for her colouring and very long legs. 'One for the album, I think.'

Within five minutes of that picture being taken, Kathy's mobile phone rang. It was Sergio. 'I couldn't believe it when Ella arrived without you. Where are you?'

'Enjoying dinner. I'm having a hen-night,' Kathy told him chirpily.

'It feels like you've been kidnapped. I don't know what

Maribel and Tilda are playing at, but it's inappropriate to stage that kind of event this close to our wedding,' Sergio informed her with censorious cool.

Chagrined colour surged into Kathy's cheeks and she excused herself from her companions to move to a more private area where she could speak without being overheard. 'I wasn't aware that I asked for your opinion!'

'My opinion comes free of charge. You have to be exhausted; you've only just recovered from your delivery. Just tell me where you are. I'll come and collect you,' Sergio responded, his hard shell of self-assurance impervious to her furious response.

'Forget it! Wouldn't that be a great way to thank Maribel for her kindness in organising entertainment for me?'

'Is that why Maribel sent me a photo of you in a very short dress? And told me not to wait up for you because you were going clubbing?' Sergio queried, unimpressed. 'My take on this would be that this is payback time for the stag cruise I organised for Leonidas—'

'Well, even if it is, you can be sure that we'll be doing something more fun and more intelligent than getting off our faces on booze and carousing with half-naked dancers!' Kathy blazed down the phone in an incandescent rage before she cut the connection. 'You know why? We've got more class and imagination!'

As Kathy stalked back across the restaurant her phone pulsed and lit up. She switched it off quickly and thrust it into her bag. He was so incredibly bossy. Did he think she was a feckless teenager in need of a curfew?

'Was that Sergio on the phone?' Bridget enquired.

'He wants us to have a brilliant time!' Kathy fibbed with a set smile.

The women entered the nightclub by a rear entrance where they were welcomed by the management team. Flanked by a platoon of security guards, they were swept into an interior extravagantly modelled on a Moroccan Kasbah with exotic lights and very private seating areas embellished by colourful silks and fat cushioned divans.

Kathy was coming off the dance floor with Nola when a tiny curvaceous blonde in an eye catching white short suit intercepted her. 'I'm Grazia Torrente,' she announced. 'Abramo's wife.'

A bemused smile crossed Kathy's expressive mouth, because she had not appreciated that Grazia would be so much smaller than she was. Nola excused herself and returned to their party.

'I've been dying to meet you ever since I heard about you. Come and sit down with me.' Grazia linked arms with Kathy in an intimate fashion and made it quite impossible for her to walk away again without administering a pointed snub.

Kathy disliked the lack of choice extended to her, but natural curiosity about Sergio's former fiancée won. 'How did you know who I was?'

Languorous turquoise-blue eyes rested on her and the chill there sent a frisson of unease darting through Kathy. 'You're out on the town with an army of bodyguards in the company of Maribel Pallis and the Crown Princess of Bakhar? Who else could you be but Sergio's bride? As to how I found you, I have connections.'

'I'm sure you do and it would be lovely to sit and chat, but I can't leave my party for long. We're leaving soon,' Kathy responded.

'Sergio is only using you to punish me, Kathy.' The tiny blonde's turquoise eyes were bold and sharp as knives, her voice full of soft scorn. 'He's not a forgiving man. I let him down when I married his loser brother and now I have to pay the price and watch him marry you. It really is that simple— an almost biblical act of revenge. Only when Sergio decides that I've suffered enough will he snap his fingers and allow me back into his life on a permanent basis.'

Flushed and taut, Kathy studied Grazia, whose perfect features were framed by silken wings of silvery blonde hair. The other woman was even more beautiful than she had looked in pictures. 'I think you're the one with the problem. Maybe you never got over Sergio—'

Grazia vented a sarcastic laugh. 'I'm warning you. You're way out of your comfort zone—a clueless little English girl with no idea how a complex man like Sergio operates. You're caught up in something that has nothing to do with you and you can't win because I will *always* be the girl he idolised at eighteen.'

'For goodness' sake, you're married to his brother!' Kathy breathed in reproof, losing patience with the blonde's drama and standing up to leave.

'I'm in the process of divorcing Abramo—as Sergio told me to do,' Grazia declared with a pitying smile. 'Don't be fooled. Sergio may act like he despises me, but he is still determined to have me. So, he's marrying you to give his daughter his name, just like his father did a generation ago for Abramo. But what's a ring on those terms worth? A comfortable divorce settlement? Sergio can afford it.'

Kathy walked away feeling hollow with uncertainty and angry that she had even listened. But the news that Grazia and Abramo were divorcing had come as a shock. Even so, she reasoned, that did not necessarily mean that there was an ongoing connection of any kind between Grazia and

Sergio. Her temples were tight with tension. She lifted her hand to massage the taut skin. Maribel suggested that perhaps it was time to call it a night. Bridget asked Kathy if she was tired and she admitted that she was.

Grazia told a good story, Kathy acknowledged unhappily. Sergio had enough powerful pride, ferocious strength of will and a dark, deep secretive nature to nourish the concept of revenge. He kept his emotions in a private place. And nobody knew better than Kathy how closely love, hate and sexual hunger could interconnect until it was impossible to define the boundaries. Grazia did indeed have terrific connections, since not only had she known where to find Kathy that evening, but she was also one of the select few who knew about Ella's existence.

Leonidas and Maribel Pallis owned a huge country house outside Siena. Kathy scrambled out of the car, eager to see Sergio even if it meant a confrontation. But there was no sign of the men. Maribel took Kathy to the nursery to see Ella, who was sleeping soundly in her cradle. Kathy was then shown into the superb private suite set aside for the bride's use and left alone. Feeling incredibly weary and free to finally show it, Kathy simply sagged like a worn rag doll. Even the thought of getting undressed was a challenge.

The door opened and she jumped. A tall dark male appeared on the threshold and her heart pounded like a road drill in an instant leap of pleasure and relief.

'I won't say I told you so,' Sergio murmured lazily.

Her attention closed in and clung to him. He was the image of natural elegance in a well-cut jacket and designer jeans. She stamped down hard on an anxious thought about Grazia, determined not to panic into asking stupid questions that would only create friction. 'About what?

'Maribel and Tilda have no idea how exhausted you are, *delizia mia*. You had a difficult birth and weeks of round-the-clock worry about Ella, and it will take time for you to get over that.'

Guilt assailed Kathy, for when he had phoned her earlier she had assumed that he was objecting to her going out on the town when it was obvious that concern had motivated him. 'I could've said no to the night out.'

'How often do you go for the sensible option around me?'

A dulled flush of chagrin lit Kathy's drawn features, for it was true. She was so vigilant in fighting her own corner that her choices often related more to a statement of independence than practicality. He moved forward and lifted her up into his arms with easy strength to carry her through to the bedroom where he set her down on the bed. She fought an urgent desire to touch the arrogant dark head momentarily level with her knees as he bent to tug off her shoes. She wanted him to stay; she wanted him to stay so badly she dug her hands like talons into the bedspread. But she said nothing because she was determined not to be a clingy, needy woman.

'You need all the rest you can get for the wedding.' In the act of straightening, Sergio paused to swoop down on her ripe pink mouth and claim it in a kiss that startled her and rocked her with a pleasure that made her pulses race. 'And for me, *dolcezza mia*.'

She lay in bed in the darkness drowsily reliving that erotic thrill. At the same time she was ashamed of herself for not telling him about Abramo's visit or Grazia's poisonous forecast. Keeping secrets from the guy she was about to marry didn't feel right. On the other hand, if she wasn't careful he might think she was the jealous type, liable to turn into a bunny boiler. She was painfully aware that he didn't love her and was only prepared to marry her for Ella's benefit. What if a reference to Grazia sparked off a change of heart on his part? Kathy despised herself for being so fearful. When had Sergio become so precious to her that the prospect of life without him loomed like a death sentence?

Kathy was truly enjoying her wedding day.

Maribel's efficient planning had ensured that everything ran like clockwork, from the moment Kathy wakened to a delicious breakfast in bed to the arrival of a parade of beauticians eager to groom the bride to perfection. The pure white off-the-shoulder dress clung to her delicate curves and small waist before flaring out into a full skirt and a swirling embroidered train worthy of a royal wedding. The gown was rather more adaptable, however, than its traditional style suggested.

Mid-morning, Kathy employed reverent fingers to examine the magnificent jewellery that had been brought to her. It had arrived complete with a note from Sergio asking her to wear the emerald and pearl suite worn by generations of Torrente brides. Kathy slowly shook her head in wonderment. 'I'll glitter like a Christmas tree.'

'Who wouldn't like the problem?' Bridget quipped.

'It will look amazing. That's a spectacular set and your dress is plain enough to carry it,' Nola opined.

The church was an ancient medieval building shaded by massive trees on the slopes of a sleepy hill village. When Bridget and Nola assisted Kathy from the limo, Sergio was waiting outside to give Kathy a glorious bouquet. As Sergio descended the steps the bridal couple were so busily engaged in looking at each other that in the exchange the flowers almost fell to the ground.

'I like the dress,' Sergio breathed tautly.

Kathy collided with his dark deep-set eyes. Lean, strong features serious, he was so dazzlingly handsome and so achingly familiar that she felt almost dizzy with delight. She didn't even notice Bridget putting out a hand to steady her hold on the flowers. Moving into the dim cool of the church with the heady scent of roses heavy on the still air and the magic musical notes of a harp swelling to greet them, Kathy was conscious only of Sergio.

An interpreter translated every word of the lengthy service for her benefit. Every word had meaning for her and she could feel a kind of peace stealing over her: her life and her future seemed more promising to her than it had in a very long time. She wanted to believe that the dark times were over. She had her precious little daughter and now she was marrying the man that she loved. Just at that moment she refused to qualify those beliefs with a single negative connotation.

Walking down the aisle on Sergio's arm and out into the sunshine, Kathy was radiant. 'How do you feel?' she asked him.

'Grateful it's over,' Sergio murmured with all the off-the-cuff immediacy of serious sincerity. 'I don't like weddings, *dolcezza mia.*'

That sobering little speech engulfed Kathy like an unexpected deluge of cold water. It made her feel foolish and naïve. It knocked her right off her fluffy bridal cloud of contentment and back down to earth again. 'It's going to be a long day for you, then. Leonidas and Maribel are really pushing out the boat for us.'

Sergio laughed softly as he lifted Kathy into the wonderful fairy-tale flower-bedecked carriage awaiting them. 'Maribel knows how I feel about weddings. She has a terrific sense of humour and she's making the most of the opportunity.'

His irreverent attitude did nothing to raise her spirits. Drinks were served back at the imposing house where many more guests were arriving. Innumerable introductions followed and when the swamp of people seeking them became too pressing, Sergio swept her off to take a seat at the top table in the magnificent ballroom. Kathy paused only to remove the detachable train from her gown. She laughed in appreciation when she saw that the wedding décor was based on a chess motif with witty touches—that idea could only have originated with Sergio. She was pleased that he had had the interest to make that choice.

After the two best men, Leonidas and Prince Rashad had made brief and amusing speeches, Bridget said just a few words in which she described Kathy as the daughter of her heart. As she spoke the two women exchanged a look of warm affection and Sergio later asked his bride when she had first met the older woman.

Kathy tensed. 'I don't think you want to know.'

'You're my wife,' Sergio said levelly. 'There's nothing you can't tell me.'

Kathy resisted the urge to remind him that he had refused to listen when she had told him that she wasn't a thief. She was all too well aware that plenty of other people would share his scepticism.

'Bridget's daughter died in custody ten years ago. She took her own life,' Kathy told him in a hesitant undertone. 'Ever since then, Bridget has volunteered as a prison visitor. We met when I was in hospital in the second year of my sentence. She's a wonderful woman and she became my lifeline.'

Sergio closed a lean masculine hand over her slim fingers, which she was involuntarily clenching and unclenching on her lap in an unconscious betrayal of tension. 'I'm grateful she was there for you, *dolcezza mia.*'

After the meal, Kathy went off to freshen up. It was time to allow her highly adaptable wedding gown to enter its final reinvention. She removed the full constricting skirt of her dress to reveal a shorter, more fitted skirt and returned with Maribel to the ballroom in fashionable style. When he saw her, Sergio stilled in surprise and admiration before moving forward to greet her, brilliant dark eyes intent on her stunning face. He swept her out onto the floor to dance. 'You look spectacular in the family jewels.'

'So would most women.'

'But they wouldn't have your hair, your face or your astonishing legs, *bella mia,*' Sergio husked. 'You look gorgeous.'

Two hours later, Kathy came downstairs with Maribel after checking on Ella, who was sleeping soundly. Maribel and Tilda had put their children to bed, but not without some protest. Sharaf, Bethany and Elias had made a concerted and comical effort to push bedtime back another few minutes. With her green eyes sparkling and laughter still on her lips, Kathy was in the best of spirits when she returned to the ballroom. That mood took a sharp downturn at the same moment that she spotted the exquisite blonde seated at a table by the edge of the dance floor.

It was Grazia. At first Kathy couldn't believe the evidence of her own eyes. It didn't help that a whole host of people were also exhibiting surprise at the appearance of the bridegroom's one-time fiancée. Indeed, as Kathy watched with growing disbelief, Grazia responded to the attention with little nods and smiles and even lifted a hand in acknowledgement very much like visiting royalty. Evidently she was a late arrival.

'What's wrong?' Maribel Pallis asked, because Kathy had stopped dead and fallen silent.

'Was Grazia Torrente on Sergio's guest list?'

'I'll check.' Maribel signalled a staff member. 'Who is she? A relative?'

'She's still married to Sergio's brother, but Sergio used to be engaged to her,' Kathy framed shakily, high spots of colour beginning to bloom over her taut cheekbones. 'I can't believe she had the cheek to come to our wedding—'

'Are you sure you're not mistaking her for someone else?' Tilda prompted.

'No chance! Once met, never forgotten.'

Both women followed the path of Kathy's gaze and Maribel exclaimed, 'My goodness, isn't that the same woman who approached you at the club last night?'

Kathy shifted her hands in a hasty dismissive gesture. 'Don't worry about it, Maribel. I'm being silly.'

But that was only a polite plea for Maribel's benefit, because Kathy did not want to make her hostess feel that she was in any way responsible for Grazia's unwelcome appearance. No, Kathy knew exactly who she should be tackling on that score and she wasted no time in tracking down Sergio. She found him talking business in a secluded corner with Leonidas and Rashad.

Kathy headed for Sergio like a high-velocity bullet aimed at a target. 'Could we have a word?'

Leonidas Pallis gave her an amused appraisal. 'That sounds ominous.'

'I don't think so,' Sergio drawled, smooth as glass.

'Trust me,' the Greek tycoon urged his friend with lazy mockery. 'I've been married longer.'

'Leonidas,' Prince Rashad interposed on a wry note.

Sergio strolled back into the crowded ballroom by Kathy's side. 'Is there a problem?'

'Did you invite your ex-fiancée to our wedding?' Kathy questioned tautly.

Sergio stilled. 'Who are you referring to?'

Suspecting that he was deliberately sidestepping a direct answer to her query, Kathy lifted her coppery head high. 'Grazia! Who else?'

'I wasn't aware that you even knew she existed,' Sergio remarked in the most deflating tone.

Kathy folded her arms in a defensive movement and recalled how keen Grazia had been to ensure that Kathy knew exactly who she was. 'Oh, yes, I know all right. She's creating quite a stir.'

His lean, dark, handsome face cool and unrevealing, Sergio looked across the ballroom. Grazia was leaning back against a table flirting like mad with a bunch of young men, her aura of sensual allure a magnetic draw. Even in the middle of a crowd she was a high-profile presence who attracted attention. 'I'm afraid I don't know what the problem is.'

Kathy snatched in a deep jerky breath. She was so worked up that it was an effort. At that instant she could not even explain why she was getting so angry so quickly. All she knew was that Grazia's presence felt like a very public slap in the face. She felt humiliated and insecure and unnerved. She was now thinking that there might be a great deal more to Grazia's utterances than mere sour grapes. 'Don't you? She shouldn't be here. Why did you invite her?'

'I didn't,' Sergio murmured levelly. 'But she's with her cousin, who *was*. Perhaps he brought her as his guest.'

It was not a good moment for Kathy to be forced to appreciate that Grazia and her relations had an ongoing social entrée to his exclusive world. Inevitably that meant that a network of other connections could still link Sergio back to the beautiful blonde.

'I want her out of here,' Kathy confided and her voice shook because it was a struggle to keep her voice low in pitch.

'You're a Torrente now. That is not how we treat guests, welcome or otherwise.' Sardonic dark deep-set eyes held hers.

Her heart-shaped face flushed with embarrassment. 'I'm not joking, Sergio. Get rid of her. I don't care how you do it, just *do* it. '

There was hard resolve in his steady appraisal. 'No,' Sergio countered. 'Now calm down.'

Kathy walked away from him. She was trembling with hurt and anger and resentment. She lifted a glass of wine to occupy her restive hands. Her mind and her imagination were on fire with suspicions and fears that there was more going on between Sergio and Grazia than she knew. What was she supposed to think? That everything Grazia had said was true? That Sergio was content for the other woman to attend his wedding because it was part of his revenge? After all, his brother was surely no less guilty of betrayal, but Sergio refused even to speak to Abramo, never mind see him. Grazia, however, was now getting a divorce and, if she was to be believed, that was at Sergio's request. Was that divorce her first step back into Sergio's affections?

Suddenly Kathy was totting up facts and fearing the worst. What was the explanation for Grazia's amazing insider knowledge? How had she known where Kathy would be the night before? Or about Ella's existence? Was Grazia in regular communication with Sergio? Her skin turned clammy. How could Grazia just appear at Kathy's wedding? Why was Sergio protecting the other woman? On this particular very special once-only day, which should have been Kathy's day alone?

All smirking smiles and pearly teeth, Grazia sauntered up to Kathy. 'Trouble in paradise already?' she mocked, making it clear that she had been watching the bride and groom closely.

The next few seconds were for-ever after etched in Kathy's memory. Someone nudged her from behind and tipped her forward. Her arm jerked and, although she contrived to retain her hold on the glass, red wine flew out of it and splashed in a wide arc across Grazia's white dress, leaving stains like drops of blood.

'Oh, my goodness, I'm so sorry!' Kathy gasped, reaching out in haste to snatch up a napkin from the nearest table.

Grazia shrieked as if she had been attacked and refused to let Kathy near her. While the blonde examined the stains with enraged turquoise eyes she hissed at Kathy in vitriolic Italian. Kathy just didn't know what else to do or say but then, mercifully, Maribel surged up out of nowhere like a one-woman rescue squad. Undeterred by Grazia's noisy histrionics, Maribel swept the blonde woman off through the crush and out of sight. A transitory silence as sharp as a thunderclap lay across the ballroom like the quiet before the storm. Then the whispers broke out and grew into a buzz of comment.

A hand closed over Kathy's and drew her round, detaching her fingers from her death grip on the napkin. She looked up at Sergio in bewilderment. Lean, powerful face impassive, he swept her out onto the dance floor in silence.

'It was an accident,' Kathy told him unevenly.

Sergio said nothing. He didn't need to. His dark golden eyes radiated disbelief.

'Say something,' Kathy urged tightly.

'I'm not into arguments as a spectator sport,' Sergio delivered silkily.

Her spine became more rigid. Pain and fury melded inside her until she was literally shaking with the force of her feelings. She pulled back from him with a fixed smile designed to fool any interested onlookers. Engaged in a fierce effort to keep her emotional turmoil hidden, she walked away.

Eyes stinging with tears, Kathy hurried upstairs to the suite she had occupied. Sergio strode through the door only seconds in her wake. 'What the hell did you think you were doing?'

'I didn't throw it at her. Honestly, I've had it with you,' she breathed rawly. 'You won't speak to your brother even though he's a nice guy, but you roll out the red carpet for that spiteful witch at my wedding!'

'When did you meet my brother and reach that conclusion?' Sergio shot at her.

'You're never there when you're needed and you always assume I'm in the wrong,' Kathy told him thickly, ignoring his question. 'Grazia cornered me when I was out last night and bitched at me. She knows too much, she even knows about Ella. This was supposed to be my day and you've wrecked it!'

His ebony brows pleated in surprise. 'Last night? You ran into Grazia in Florence?'

'You wreck everything…every single thing,' Kathy added, mentally piling up his every sin, laying them out for judgement and finding him guilty at that moment without any possibility of forgiveness. 'Now I'm going to pack and I'm returning to London—'

'Kathy—we have just got married,' Sergio pointed out.

'So?' Kathy hurled back wrathfully. 'I can already see that I've made a dreadful mistake and I'm not too proud to admit it!'

Sergio rested incredulous golden eyes on her. He lowered lush black lashes, his gaze intent. 'You're not thinking this through—'

'You picked a weak moment to ask me to marry you. I was in labour, for goodness' sake! If I'd been my normal self I'd never have agreed to be your wife. I'm leaving you—'

Sergio moved at speed to plant his lean powerful frame squarely between her and the door. 'No, you're not, *delizia mia.*' He took out his mobile and made a call.

'What are you doing?' Kathy demanded.

'We'll leave together. I may have ruined your day, but that's no reason why we have to share our misery with our hosts and our guests.'

Kathy studied her case, which was already sitting packed in readiness for their departure. She sank down at the foot of the bed. 'You're making me unhappy—'

Sergio moved forward at a measured pace. 'It's early days yet. Obviously, I'm far from perfect. But in my own defence I have to ask why you didn't tell me that you'd met Abramo. Or Grazia?'

'I didn't want to spoil the wedding,' Kathy mumbled in a wobbly voice. 'If you'd wanted me to know about them, you'd have told me about them, right?'

'Please don't cry,' Sergio breathed gruffly, taking a step closer to her. 'Obviously I owe you a little family history…'

His mother had died when he was eight years old. Five years later, his father had married his mistress, Cecilia, who already had a ten-year-old son: Sergio's half-brother, Abramo. Unfortunately, marriage to a man several decades older, who was inclined to frown on her extravagance, failed to meet Cecilia's expectations and she took a series of lovers.

'I minded my own business—' Sergio's lean strong features darkened '—but when my father was receiving cancer treatment, Cecilia began an affair with the family lawyer, Umberto Tessano. He was my father's closest friend and in charge of our business interests.'

Kathy winced. 'What age were you then?'

'Twenty-two, and in my final year at Oxford University. I found my stepmother in bed with Tessano at our London apartment. I felt that I had no choice but to tell my father, but Cecilia and her lover got their story in first.' Sergio vented a bitter laugh of remembrance, his classic profile settling into grim lines.

As the silence dragged Kathy breathed, 'And what was that?'

'That for some time I had been harassing my stepmother with sexual attentions—'

'Oh, no!' Kathy exclaimed with a feeling grimace

'—and that that particular day I made a drunken assault on her virtue from which Tessano gallantly rescued her.'

'Surely your father didn't believe such nonsense?'

'When his lifelong best friend confirmed that sordid account, I had no hope of being believed,' Sergio breathed heavily. 'I had a playboy reputation and Cecilia was beautiful. I can't blame my father because he was a sick man and he loved her. At the time he was dying. I didn't know that but they did. In so far as my father was able within the law, and with Tessano's encouragement, I was disinherited in favour of Cecilia and Abramo. My stepmother married Tessano three months after the funeral.'

His story rocked Kathy out of her self-absorption; she was appalled. There was, she was discovering, a great deal more unpleasantness to the events that had torn Abramo and Sergio apart than she had innocently imagined. The greed and envy of his stepmother and his half-brother had combined to tear Sergio's life asunder. 'Having your father turn against you when he was so ill must've been a nightmare for you.'

'It shattered me.' A muscle pulled taut at the edge of Sergio's wide sensual mouth. 'He died two months later still believing their lies. Up until that point, my life had been easy and privileged. At birth, I was the little prince, the heir to the Azzarini estates and I took it all for granted. Then it was all taken away from me.'

In a quick movement, Kathy got up and reached for his hands in a spontaneous gesture of sympathy, because she had been deeply attached to her own father and she knew how much that misjudgement and rejection from one so close must have tormented Sergio. Her softened green eyes clung to the bold angularity of his bronzed masculine features. 'You should have told me about your family ages ago. But then you don't tell me anything.' Her voice grew more hesitant as she registered that he had finished talking and had still not made a reference to Grazia's role. Feeling self-conscious, she made an abrupt movement to withdraw her hands from his.

'That can change, *dolcezza mia*.' Sergio snapped long brown fingers round her narrow wrists before she could back away again.

Uncertainly, Kathy looked up at him. She was being torn in two by the pull of his white-hot sexual attraction and the need to protect herself from further hurt and disappointment. 'You know you think you're great just the way you are—'

'Until you came along and somehow I consistently manage to live down to your lowest expectations,' Sergio traded.

'Your aversion to weddings…how do you think that made me feel today?' Kathy fenced, jerking her hands free, walking away and turning back with an agitation that betrayed her tension.

'I was a selfish bastard. But, believe me, it wasn't intentional. Grazia jilted me at the altar. It made an indelible impression.'

Shell-shocked by the sheer unexpectedness of that flat admission, Kathy stared up at him.

'Only my closest friends know about that. My father had recently passed away and the wedding was to be a small quiet affair in London. She didn't turn up.' His stunning eyes were dark and reflective. A saturnine smile slashed his hard, handsome mouth. 'Don't look so surprised. Grazia was a luxury I couldn't afford.'

Her lashes veiled her gaze. Her nails carved little crescents into her palms as she recalled Grazia's smiling air of complacency, for the other woman was very much aware of her pulling power. Sergio had wanted her once, loved her enough to want to marry her and lost her again. It could only have added salt to the wound when she decided to marry his brother instead. But it troubled Kathy that both brothers seemed to accept without comment that Grazia put money first.

'Surely she didn't believe that claptrap about you and your stepmother?'

'Naturally not.' Sergio reached out and pulled her up against him with the bold self-assurance that was so much a part of his nature. 'Are you still bent on leaving me?'

Disconcerted by that sudden change of subject, Kathy tipped her coppery head back and he meshed his fingers into the luxuriant fall of her hair to hold her there. Hot golden eyes struck hers and desire pierced her as sharply as a knife. Her tummy flipped and her knees went weak. That fast her physical awareness rose to a level of almost painful sensitivity. His high-voltage male potency got to her every time. She wondered if there had ever been any real chance that she would walk out on him. She wondered if that was a little fantasy she used to console her pride, for at that instant it would have taken brute force to tear her away from him.

'Is it too late to strike a deal?' Sergio husked, tracing the full pout of her lower lip with a caressing fingertip. 'Grant me a trial run until the end of the honeymoon?'

'How flexible are you when it comes to change?' Kathy asked half under her breath. 'Will I need to set objectives? Award points for performance? Come up with rewards for inspirational outcomes?'

'All of the above, *dolcezza mia*.' Brilliant eyes alight with appreciation, Sergio curved her slim body to his. 'Rewards work with me.'

The brisk staccato knock that sounded on the door provoked a groan of frustration from him. 'I said we were leaving immediately.'

CHAPTER NINE

'SO WHAT do you think?' Sergio demanded before Kathy had got more than fifty feet from the helicopter that had delivered them to the Palazzo Azzarini.

Even from the air, the architectural magnificence and size of the building that crowned the hill had disconcerted Kathy. Sergio closed a hand over hers to walk her up the steps to the terrace. 'This house has been in my family for centuries. For the best part of a decade it belonged to Cecilia and Abramo but I bought it back last year. Right now, it's a work of art in progress because the restoration is ongoing. This will be where we base our lives—our home with Ella.'

Kathy cleared her throat gently. 'Objective one, Sergio. Major decisions should be discussed.'

An unholy grin slashed his handsome mouth. 'Of course I'm not going to make you stay here if you hate it. But you're a country girl; you know you are—'

'And when did you reach that conclusion?'

'Maybe I know more about you than you think. You'll love the estate and the people here, *bella mia*.'

Kathy wondered whether to mention that his second objective should be not making assumptions about *her* feelings. But that reference to Ella had tugged at her heart-strings and acted as a distraction. 'I miss Ella already.'

'I'm sure she will be fine without us for a week,' Sergio interposed. 'Maribel is terrific with children.'

Kathy knew that was true. But even though intelligence told her that they needed time alone together as a couple, the habit of constantly fretting about her baby was hard to unlearn and resist. Clearing her mind of those anxious thoughts, she reminded herself of the very sensible pair of nannies also placed in charge of their daughter's care, not to mention the doctor engaged to make daily visits as a safeguard. She rested her hands on the worn stone balustrade, which was still warm from the heat of the day. The silence was bliss after all the hoopla of a big wedding. It was early evening and a soft mist of light lay across the lush valley over which the palazzo presided. Nothing she could see reminded her of the twenty-first century: the rolling hills were covered with dense woodland, vineyards and dotted here and there was the indistinct silvery foliage of olive groves. The view was utterly breathtaking.

She walked below the massive arched portico and wandered wide-eyed into a huge circular reception hall ornamented with faded frescos and towering columns. Like the view, it was an amazing sight and the prospect of living amid such grandeur made her laugh. From somewhere she could hear faint strains of music and she recognised a popular song. Slim hips swaying to the beat, hair glittering like burnished copper and falling back from her high cheekbones, she executed a couple of dance steps.

Sergio fell still and watched her. Kathy met his intent dark eyes and stopped dancing. Although she was pink with embarrassment she gave him an irrepressible grin.

'You have so much life that it bubbles out of you, *bellezza mia*,' he murmured thickly. 'You also look astonishingly beautiful.'

'Who's playing that radio?' she stage whispered.

'Apart from the security outside the house, we should be totally alone here.' Sergio pushed open a door on a big bare room that had scaffolding erected along one wall. A workman's radio was playing in one corner. He switched it off and strolled back to her.

'Thank you. Your first objective at all times,' Kathy instructed cheekily, 'is to make me happy.'

Sergio was much amused. 'And the reward is?'

'Keep me happy and you get an easier life, because you should know by now—I don't suffer in silence.'

Sergio slid out of his jacket and let it fall.

'Oops,' Kathy gasped. 'I think this is a very male take on what makes a woman happy.'

Sergio tugged loose his tie and backed her in the direction of the splendid stone staircase.

'Although you could be on the right track,' Kathy conceded half under her breath, her attention locked to him as he unbuttoned his shirt. 'Of course we could play chess first…'

Sergio was thrown enough by that possibility to frown.

Kathy smiled like the cat that had got the cream. 'Just checking how keen you were. If you'd agreed, I wouldn't have been impressed.'

'*Maremma maiale*…I couldn't concentrate,' he confided.

Her attention rested on the muscular slice of bronzed, hair-roughened torso visible between the parted edges of his shirt. She did not believe that she could have concentrated, either. A delicious frisson of anticipation was already running through her slender body and self-consciousness claimed her, for she wasn't yet used to feeling like that.

Sergio was infinitely more at ease with the ambience. With infinite cool and casualness, he laced his fingers with hers and walked her up the stairs. 'I am not really familiar with shy women—'

'I've never been shy in my life!' Kathy objected, kicking off her shoes there and then on the landing as if she was making a statement.

'Except with me.' Unimpressed by her claim, Sergio lowered his arrogant dark head and let his expert mouth travel a sensual path from her ear lobe to the extended length of her neck and the tiny pulse beating like mad at the centre of her delicate collar-bone. 'And it's okay. I find it unbelievably sexy, *delizia mia.*'

The master bedroom suite was set behind huge double doors and on the same massive scale as everything in the palazzo. Kathy took one look at the gilded four-poster bed and scrambled onto it, bouncing back against the heaped pillows with an ecstatic whoop of appreciation. 'Oh, that's amazing—I've always wanted a bed like this!'

'And although I almost didn't recognise it until it was too late, I always wanted a girl like you in it,' Sergio informed her huskily.

Her ready smile lurched a little and she was quick to lower her lashes to conceal her expression, as she knew that someone like her could not aspire to dream-girl status. She was so different from Grazia in looks, style and experience. As Grazia had cruelly pointed out, she would always be the girl he had idolised as a teenager. There was a history there, a pull of familiarity, background and youthful attachment that Kathy knew she could never hope to equal.

Sergio sank down beside her and undid the clasp of her emerald and pearl necklace, setting it aside before embarking on the tiny hooks on her fitted bodice. Her narrow spine tensed because she was thinking about the moment when he would see the scar on her back. 'That's okay…I can manage!' she said hurriedly, wriggling out of reach with the dexterity of an eel.

Sergio tugged her back to him. 'How did it happen?'

The level of his insight unnerved her and her delicate profile tightened. 'In prison. Someone thought I'd grassed them up and jumped me in the showers.'

He closed his arms round her. 'Nobody will ever harm you again.'

'You can't make promises like that.' Her eyes were hot and scratchy with tears but she wouldn't give way to her emotions. Being absolutely crazy about him was one thing, even dropping a hint of it something else entirely.

Sergio turned her round to look at him. 'You are so terrified of trusting me—'

Her apple-green eyes flashed. 'I'm not terrified of anything!'

Dark golden eyes smouldering, he leant forward and drove her soft lips apart with the passionate demand of his sensual mouth. After so long the taste of him chased through her like a chain reaction. Heat uncoiled in her pelvis while the rest of her turned to jelly. Angling his proud dark head back, he sprang up to peel off his shirt. Her heart thudded while she watched him undress. Light caught the wedding ring on his finger. The reminder that he was her husband was welcome and it strengthened her again.

She slid off the bed in a fluid movement and turned round. 'I need your help to get out of this…' she said gruffly.

He ran down the zip on the fitted skirt and it dropped to her feet. She stepped out of it. He shifted her hair round her slim white shoulders and touched his lips to a sensual pulse point at the vulnerable nape of her neck. 'You're trembling…'

'It's been a long time,' she said breathlessly.

'How long?' His question was abrupt and a sharp little silence fell. 'I did wonder *if*—'

'Don't go there. It's none of your business,' Kathy interposed waspishly. 'Did I ask you for chapter and verse on what you did on your stupid flashy boat?'

'I offered and you refused to listen. Tell me, if I sank *Diva Queen*, would you stop going on about the stag do?' Sergio enquired dulcetly.

Kathy giggled. 'No, I'd tell you how extravagant and wasteful you were, and I still wouldn't forget.'

He let the boned bodice fall and an almost inaudible gasp escaped her when she realised that the jagged seam of her scar was visible. 'You have skin like satin, all soft and silky and white as snow,' he murmured with silken intimacy. 'Your hair looks like flame against it and I can't believe you're so anxious about one small imperfection…' He smoothed over the roughened skin and she shivered, narrow shoulder blades protruding defensively.

'It's ugly,' she pointed out. 'And my skin is so pale it really shows.'

'The only ugliness is in the person who did this to you,' Sergio asserted. 'If it bothers you so much that you feel you have to hide it, a good plastic surgeon could probably make it vanish. But as far as I'm concerned, it's nothing, *bella mia*.'

'You're quite good at saying the right thing when you have to,' Kathy teased, all her tension evaporating, her spine curving as she leant back against him. 'So, no doubt if you put your mind to it, you can be equally good at being married.'

'Is that an order or a request?'

Kathy winced. 'A hint?'

Sergio laughed with rich appreciation and curved possessive hands to her tiny waist. 'It was way too bossy to be a hint.'

His hands closed over the pert swell of her small breasts. She leant back against him with a helpless little moan, shaken by how sensitive she was to that first light touch. The hunger she had fought while Ella needed all her attention was breaking free of her control. A score of times she had watched Sergio walking towards her and she had blocked out the sexual response that had once betrayed her so badly. Those artificial barriers crumpled once she reminded herself that they were married, that, in spite of all the mishaps that had gone before, they were now together. Her soaring sense of relief at that truth made her dizzy.

Filled with sudden impatience, Kathy turned herself round clumsily in the circle of his arms and stretched up on tiptoe to find his mouth for herself. That stolen taste of him was impossibly seductive. He hauled her to him and kissed her with bruising passion, answering the fierce need in her with an accuracy that shook her. He lifted her onto the bed and reached for the silk panties that hugged her hips to peel them off.

Panting for breath, her rosy lips swollen from his attention, Kathy gazed up at him with anxious eyes. Even though she had never felt more naked or exposed, she made no attempt to cover herself up because she accepted that he wanted to look at her. She held her breath in fear that a shadow would cross his face as he suddenly appreciated that she was too skinny and lacking in curves to compete with tiny, curvaceous Grazia, and that her body was marred by the scars of her past and of childbirth.

'You have the most wonderful figure.' Wholly intent on her, Sergio skated an undeniably admiring hand down over her narrow ribcage to a slender thigh still clad in lace-topped white hold-up stockings. 'Elegant, graceful...'

Kathy stretched so that he could better admire her from all angles and ready amusement curved his handsome mouth even as his gaze marked her every move with very masculine appreciation. He shed his boxer shorts without ceremony. She looked at him in turn, for he was beautifully built. The lean, hard, muscular lines of his powerful bronzed body bore out his reputation for being as super fit as an athlete. Her attention rested on his rampant state of arousal and colour warmed her cheeks.

'This is the first place we make a deal, *delizia mia*,' Sergio murmured, pulling her up against his long, sleek, masculine frame

'A deal?' Her green eyes flew wide.

'While I concentrate on what pleases you outside the bedroom you can concentrate on what pleases me *inside* it.'

Kathy studied him in honest wonderment. 'Are you really that basic?'

Sergio nodded affirmation without hesitation. 'I want to spend the entire week in bed,' he growled. 'I am so hungry for you I almost dragged you off from the church.'

Kathy was blushing like mad. But she really liked the idea of being lusted after; a man making her the focus of his erotic intent was most unlikely to be thinking of another woman at the same time.

'Under the table at the reception…into another room… up against the wall…on the floor,' Sergio enumerated thickly. 'In my fantasies you're insatiable, *delizia mia*.'

'Am I?' Kathy whispered a split second before the hungry onslaught of his mouth silenced her.

Fizzing little signals of response darted through her bloodstream and fired inside her with every wicked probe of his tongue. Her body was hypersensitive and geared up for him. For the first time she was eager to touch him and conduct her own explorations. For the first time she was confident enough to be his lover. She traced the solid wall of his chest with admiring fingertips, traversed the taut flatness of his muscular stomach, and when she hesitated he took over to guide and teach her and she learned that it was astonishingly easy to make him groan.

'Enough,' he growled. 'This is our wedding night. I want to give you pleasure.'

'You're so traditional.' Eyes bright as stars, empowered by newly learned skills that had done wonders for her assurance, Kathy flopped back against the pillows. Breathless, she watched him, her gaze clinging to his lean, strong face. There was a wicked tight knot of longing clenched at the heart of her. All he had to do was mention pleasure and she was boneless with expectation.

'No, I've waited too long to lie here and keep my hands off your beautiful body,' Sergio breathed roughly.

Hot, hungry golden eyes assailed her and her mouth ran dry. He spread her beneath him and smoothed a possessive hand over the swollen pink peaks of her breasts. She shivered. A wicked smile of knowledge slashed his strong, sensual mouth.

'You are so ready for me, *amata mia*,' he told her, dipping his tousled dark head to lock his mouth to the tiny taut, straining buds that betrayed her arousal.

Kathy gasped out loud, her hips squirming into the mattress. With controlled passion and endless skill, he traced his sensual path down over her slender twisting length, deliberately not touching her in the one place where she most yearned to be touched. As if in compensation other areas seemed to become much more sensitive in response while the blood thrummed in her veins and her heart pounded faster and faster. A river of elemental fire was flowing through her, burning and scorching everything within its path.

'Sergio…' She almost wept with impatience.

'No orders, instructions or even hints allowed, *cara mia*,' Sergio warned huskily. 'This is one of those occasions when I really do know what I'm doing.'

And she learned things she didn't know about herself. She learned she liked things she had never dreamt she might like. She also learnt a level of response that was terrifyingly powerful. When she believed she could stand no more she found she had no voice to tell him so. He wrested all control, all reasoned thought from her. The ache of need was overwhelming. She was shaking with desire when he chose the optimum moment to take her enjoyment to its zenith. Easing her under him, he plunged into her tender depths with potent power.

Irresistible sensation seized her in a tempestuous flood. He said her name and she moaned a response, locked to him in wild arousal. In thrall to his sexual energy, her excitement soared to a dizzy high. His desire for her was unquenchable, energising. She was all liquid heat and craving. Caught up in a delirium of spellbinding pleasure, she arched her spine and cried out at the height of release. Melting waves of delight followed and left her rocked to the core of her being over the strength of what she had experienced.

'I think I'm going to like being married,' she whispered blissfully, both arms wrapped round him as she hugged him tight with instinctive affection.

An ocean of love and forgiveness was washing round Kathy's heart. She breathed in the musky perfume of his skin and sighed with contentment. He pushed her hair off her brow and kissed her and studied her with slumberous dark-as-night eyes fringed by spiky black lashes. Just looking at him she felt weak. 'You were right,' she added, feeling that just this once a small compliment might be due. 'You don't need instructions.'

The silence lingered and she wondered what he was thinking about. Grazia? The idea and the name came at her out of nowhere and dropped like a giant rock on her floaty feelings to crush them flat. Wasn't it odd that he hadn't even asked what Grazia had said to her the night before? He was certain to have thought about Grazia after seeing her today, Kathy reasoned uneasily. He was only human, but she didn't want him to be only human, and she definitely didn't want him thinking about his former fiancée and soon-to-be-ex-sister-in-law.

'Were you madly in love with Grazia?' Kathy asked abruptly, and she was so horrified by the nosy question that had simply leapt from her brain to her tongue that she almost cringed in front of him.

Sergio released his hold on her and sat up. 'What do you think?'

On the might-as-well-be-hung-for-a-sheep-as-a-lamb principle, Kathy added with equal abruptness, 'Did you speak to her today?'

His jaw line squaring, Sergio groaned out loud. 'No, I think she was only in the building for about ten minutes.'

Her face burning at what might or might not have been an unkind allusion to the incident with the red wine, Kathy muttered, 'She mentioned that she's divorcing your brother.'

Sergio shot her a sudden shuttered glance. Lean, extravagantly handsome features sombre, he vaulted out of bed. 'I need a shower.'

'And you're the guy who's going to change and share things with me?' Kathy flung, cut to the bone and wishing she could shut up—but quite unable in her sense of humiliation and abandonment to make herself shut up.

'*Madonna diavolo*—not stuff like that!' Sergio countered without hesitation.

The bathroom thudded shut. Lesson one, don't mention Grazia, Kathy reflected unhappily. Even after eight years there was unfinished business there. But grilling him like a silly jealous schoolgirl had scarcely been the subtle route to take. She wished she had kept quiet. She wished she hadn't spoiled that lovely precious moment of closeness with prying questions. And over and over again she kept on seeing that hard, closed look on his face.

Ten minutes later, Sergio emerged, black hair slicked back, a towel wrapped round his lean hips. 'Come here, *amata mia*.'

Kathy dealt him an aggrieved look while simultaneously admiring his incredible physique. 'No, I'm sulking,' she confessed from the depths of the four poster.

'Wouldn't you like to cool off in the pool?'

'I can't swim,' she admitted stonily.

Sergio could not hide his surprise. 'Okay. But you'll be safe with me.'

Kathy wondered if there would be shallow steps at one end on which she could sit, because she was very warm and the prospect of cool water on her overheated body was extremely tempting. She hovered between a desire to make him suffer, hurt pride and acceptance.

'I have champagne on ice waiting downstairs.'

'I'm really not into all that vintage stuff,' she told him huffily. 'You're never going to educate my palate.'

'I also have your favourite Swiss chocolate.'

Sergio had saved the best and most seductive offer for last. Her taste buds salivated. As he had discovered one night at the hospital when she had been too afraid to leave Ella to eat, she simply adored chocolate. Her head flipped over, light green eyes arrowing across the room. 'All right— but there is a ground rule. You are not allowed to touch me.'

'Let's see who surrenders first,' Sergio murmured lazily.

Six weeks later, Sergio guided Kathy into a room at the palazzo. As instructed her eyes were tightly shut. He spun her round to heighten the tension.

'Can I look yet?' Kathy demanded.

'Go ahead.'

Kathy blinked: he had taken her out of bright sunlight and it took a while for her eyes to adjust to the dimness. What she saw sitting on a table in front of her was a dolls' house that appeared to be the identical twin of the one she had owned in her childhood, but that she had believed she would never see again. Disconcerted, she simply stared, unable to fathom the coincidence, for she could not believe that it could actually be hers.

'Say something,' Sergio urged.

'It can't be mine…' But she discovered that she was

wrong. When she put out a hesitant hand and opened the front of the miniature house, she found all the little bits and pieces of furniture lined up in tidy ranks for inspection. She lifted the familiar little plastic doll with one leg and dressed in an overlarge knitted frock that her late adoptive mother had made for it.

'It is yours,' Sergio confirmed.

Her attention expanded to encompass the other things on the table-top. She set down the doll to study the collection of cat ornaments, one or two of which had had tails glued back on after getting broken in house moves. There was a bag of girlish keepsakes from her teen years and a little box of jewellery. Beside that sat a collection of photo albums and she leafed through them, suddenly frantic to reach the most important one and there they were—her adoptive parents' photos intact and even spruced up from the faded pictures she recalled. Tears were running down her face without her even realising it.

'Where did you get all this stuff from?' she prompted chokily.

'Your ex-boyfriend still had them—'

'Gareth?' she exclaimed.

'Although his mother sent him to the dump with your possessions, he managed to hide this stuff in the attic. Hey…' Sergio ran a knuckle lightly down her tear stained cheek. 'I wanted to make you smile, not cry!'

'I'm just overwhelmed!' she sobbed, breaking down altogether. 'You don't know what this stuff m-means to me.'

Sergio eased her up against him and stroked a hand through her hair until she had calmed down again. 'But I do. When my father changed his will and deprived me of most of what was to be my inheritance I lost everything below this roof but my clothes. Cecilia and Umberto liquidated the paintings, sculpture and furniture collected by my ancestors, as well as quite a few personal items that I wasn't able to prove belonged to me.'

'You can hardly compare my cat ornaments to a world-renowned art collection—'

'But it was only when I listened to your story that I appreciated how fortunate I was to be in a position to trace and buy back so much of what I lost.'

'If Gareth still had my things, why didn't he answer the letter I sent him after I got out of prison?'

There was a slight hesitation before he responded to her question. 'His mother probably got to it first.'

Kathy paled and looked away from him, conscious that he was uncomfortable with anything that reminded him of her criminal record. 'Did you actually meet Gareth? When?'

Her question acted as a useful distraction because an unholy grin curved Sergio's mobile mouth. 'Last week when I went to London on business. Gareth's mother slammed doors and ranted at him throughout my visit. He leads a dog's life, but at least he had the courage to admit that he still had your possessions and hand them over.'

Kathy was incredibly touched that he had gone to so much trouble on her behalf. 'I can't tell you what this means to me. It's like getting my roots back. When your family's gone, sentimental things mean a lot.' She drew in a deep breath, her green eyes suddenly filling with determination. 'I honestly believe that you should at least talk to your brother and hear what he has to say—'

'I'm not the sentimental type.' His tone was impatient, for it was not the first time she had tried to open the controversial subject.

'You haven't even asked me what Abramo said when he came to see me in London—'

'I'm not interested.'

'He feels really bad about the past and he wants to make peace with you—'

'He almost bankrupted this estate and he's down on his luck. Of course he wants my forgiveness in terms of financial support.'

His cynicism provoked a reproachful look from Kathy. 'He seemed sincere and unhappy and he didn't look at all well,' she sighed. 'All right, I won't say anything more, especially when you gave me such a great surprise.'

'It was nothing.' Sergio curved lean hands to the feminine swell of her slim hips to tug her closer to him. 'Besides, I like it when you think about other people. You have a tender heart, *bella mia*.'

His keen dark eyes held hers and emotion welled up inside her. Sometimes she loved him so much it hurt. Although he had grown up with many privileges he had gone through tough and testing times, just as she had. He set a high value on loyalty, for, while many of his friends had dropped away after his father changed his will, Rashad and Leonidas had demonstrated their support by standing by Sergio and backing his first business ventures.

She understood the experiences that had given him his granite hard core, single-minded sense of purpose and cynicism. The acquisition of a wealth much greater than his own father had ever known had encouraged Sergio's arrogant, ruthless outlook on life. Yet, when he went out of his way to do something that pleased her, Kathy recognised and appreciated how much he had changed where she was concerned. She could hardly credit that six weeks had passed since their wedding because the time had flown in. But then, life didn't stand still around Sergio for longer than five minutes and it was now time for him to get back to his London office. The following day they were due to return to the UK.

Kathy was reluctant to leave Italy because she had been so happy there. The honeymoon had begun with Sergio giving her swimming lessons while banning her from even sitting on the pool steps when he wasn't in the water. He had taken her rock climbing in the Dolomites, as well, teaching her how to sail a catamaran. When she'd got seasick he had made her work through it and she had ended up having a lot of fun. She suspected that her keen sailor husband was determined to get her on board the *Diva Queen*, to which Kathy had taken a fierce dislike sight unseen. She was willing, however, to acknowledge that in physical terms they were both very active and well matched. He was equally convinced that she would love skiing and had already pencilled a winter break into his schedule for that purpose.

Sergio was also encouraging her to take an interest in the charitable trust he had set up and plans had been made for her to accompany him on a trip to Africa to publicise the work being done there. In all the ways that mattered, Sergio was making space for her in his busy, energetic life and sharing his interests to a degree that she had never dared to hope he would. But he had yet to beat her at chess.

Ella remained the centre of their world, the meeting point that continually drew them together and united them. She was beginning to realise that during the first precarious weeks of their daughter's life she had bonded with Sergio at a level she hadn't grasped at the time. They had so shared much and it had added depth to their relation-ship. Although they had had a fabulous first few days alone as lovers, Sergio had missed Ella as much as Kathy and they had brought her home to join them early.

That afternoon Kathy cuddled Ella and tucked her into her cot for a nap. With her black hair, ever more green eyes and little button nose, Ella was super cute and sometimes Kathy had to force herself to put her daughter down to sleep. She had yet to forget the occasions when it had not been possible for her to hold her baby close.

An hour later, Kathy was just out of the shower when Bridget phoned her to announce that Renzo had asked her to marry him. 'Oh, my goodness, I'm so happy for you!' Kathy exclaimed, anchoring her towel beneath her arms. 'You did say yes, didn't you?'

'Of course I did. He's a good man,' Bridget said fondly. 'He didn't want me to tell you but I think you should know. He's been checking out all the facts of your conviction and the court case and he's been following up every lead for months now.'

Kathy was astonished. 'But why?'

'He accepts that you're innocent and he wants to help. There's some good news, as well. A couple of silver items stolen from old Mrs Taplow's collection were recently acquired by an antique trader in Dover. He listed them on his website and Renzo spotted them. If he can trace them back to whoever sold them, he might be able to identify the real thief.'

Kathy frowned. 'It's really kind of him to take such an interest, so please tell him how much I appreciate it. But I think too much time has passed. People won't remember anything—'

'Don't be so pessimistic,' Bridget scolded. 'The trader called in the police and it's already being investigated. The guy bought the silver in good faith and he stands to lose a lot of money. Aren't you dying to know who the thief is? Of course you are!'

Kathy grimaced, for she had long since worked out the likely identity of the thief. Only one person had had the opportunity to lay the fake trail that had led to Kathy being convicted of a crime she hadn't committed. But Kathy did not know how she could possibly prove the fact. Rather than burn up in self-destructive bitterness, she had chosen to get on with her life. Four years on, she had little time for false hopes and accepted that she would have to live with a criminal record to the end of her days.

'Let's hope for the best,' Kathy responded with tact. 'So when do you think you'll be getting married?'

'Well, we don't want to wait long.'

'I think it's past time we let Sergio in on the secret—'

'Renzo didn't think it would be *professional* to admit that we were a couple before your wedding,' Bridget shared ruefully. 'Men!'

'What secret?'

Thrown off balance by the interruption, Kathy spun round and saw Sergio poised in the doorway. His lean dark features were grim. 'Kathy…I asked you a question.'

His commanding tone made Kathy redden with annoyance. Wondering what on earth was the matter with him, she made a hurried excuse and promised to call Bridget back later. She set the receiver down and moved forward. 'Bridget and Renzo have been dating for months and he's just asked her to marry him. That was the secret but it wasn't mine to share.'

Sergio regarded her closely, not a muscle moving on his lean strong face, his shrewd dark eyes unrevealing. 'I had no idea that they were seeing each other, but Renzo's private life is not my concern.'

Her tension increased, for she could tell that something was wrong. 'Why are you angry with me?'

'I'm not angry. But I'm afraid there's been a change of plan. We're leaving now, not tomorrow morning.'

Her smooth brow indented. 'Now? Like, *right* now? I'm just out of the shower!'

'I would really appreciate it if you were ready to leave in ten minutes,' Sergio drawled.

'But I haven't even packed!'

'The staff will deal with that. Just get dressed.'

Obviously something had happened. Anxious now, she put on a green dress that he had admired on her a few days earlier and paused only to pin up her damp copper hair with a clip. Sergio was on the terrace talking urgently into his phone. One glance and her husband still took her breath away. Black hair gleaming in the sunlight, his classic profile in evidence, he was the living image of sleek Italian sophistication in a caramel linen jacket worn with the sleeves pushed up and teamed with pale fitted jeans.

Kathy approached him as he switched off the phone. 'Please tell me what's up.'

'Nothing unexpected, *amata mia*.' Stunning dark golden eyes rested on her worried face. He strolled over to her and bent his arrogant dark head to crush her full pink lips beneath his.

The erotic probe of his tongue set off an alert through every nerve-ending in her slender body. At her most vulnerable, she quivered in bewildered response. Her senses singing, she leant into the muscular heat of his tall, powerful frame. Freeing her again, he closed a hand over hers and urged her down the steps to the helipad.

'You never said where we were going,' Kathy said breathlessly.

Sergio helped her into the helicopter. Ella was already snuggled in a safety seat demonstrating her amazing ability to sleep like a log through every interruption and noise. 'No, I didn't, did I?'

The mystery was cleared up within the hour. The pilot flew out over the Mediterranean and just as the light was fading in rosy golden splendour across the sky landed on a vast ocean-going yacht.

Fifteen minutes later, Ella was stashed in another cot in a cabin with her excited nannies in tow. Kathy joined Sergio in the dazzlingly plush décor of the main reception area. 'So what's going on?' she pressed, fed up with being kept in the dark…

'Leonidas has a lot of media connections. He warned me that tomorrow a tabloid newspaper is running a story on your criminal record,' Sergio explained, his strong jaw line clenching. 'I decided it would be a good idea to keep you and Ella somewhere the cameras can't get near you. While *Diva Queen* stays out at sea, you're safe.'

Shock hit Kathy in a wave of physical reactions. The colour drained from her complexion and nausea upset her tummy. Feeling sick and dizzy, she sank down on the nearest seat in silence. A split second after that, other responses kicked in and they hurt her a great deal more, for she discovered that she no longer had the courage to meet her husband's gaze for fear of what she might see there. Revulsion, anger, derision? How could she blame him for loathing the public exposure of her shameful, embarrassing past? What decent man wanted it known that his wife had once been prosecuted for stealing from a sick old lady?

Yet there was nothing, absolutely nothing, Kathy acknowledged wretchedly, that she could do to change the situation.

CHAPTER TEN

'I'M SORRY about this,' Kathy admitted tightly.

'I believe we were both aware that this situation was on the cards,' Sergio countered levelly. 'But I'm surprised it's happened so quickly.'

Kathy had still to look at him. Coffee was served. Her heart was thumping in what felt like the foot of her throat and the sick hollowness in her tummy was refusing to abate. Oh, yes, she was sorry all right. Even though she had served her time in prison her conviction was still the equivalent of a giant rock anchored to her ankle. And it seemed that it always would be.

But what was really tearing her apart was the change in Sergio. He was not a male who could ever have envisaged having a wife who was a social embarrassment. She could not forget that he had once tried to persuade her to change her name and move to France to escape her past. Now his forecast of public humiliation was coming true and it was a miracle that her Alpha male had yet to voice a single I-told-you-so. A total miracle, Kathy conceded miserably. His cool façade of formality could only be concealing the furious frustration that he felt he had to contain.

'Fortunately, I did prepare for this eventuality,' Sergio informed her.

'Am I going to disappear at sea?' Kathy mumbled, for in her opinion only a bigger scandal would wipe out the one about to break.

The silence was electrifying.

Sergio released his breath in a slow hiss. 'That's not funny, Kathy.'

Kathy had rarely felt less like laughing. There was an intolerable ache of tears in her throat. Only hours earlier, she had been naively rejoicing in her contentment. In so far as he was able, Sergio had contrived to forget her prison record. But it would be foolish to ignore the fact that Sergio had conservative views on crime and punishment. He abhorred dishonesty. He was ashamed of her now. How could he not be? He was striving to be sympathetic, but she could sense his reserve like a wall inside him.

How had he felt when Leonidas Pallis had warned him of the story about to break? The cringe factor during that conversation must have been high, she thought guiltily. Leonidas might be one of his oldest friends, but men didn't like showing a more vulnerable side to each other and a wife who was a former jailbird could only be a source of severe embarrassment. How much shame could any marriage stand? How could he continue to respect her? For how long would Sergio overlook her past without thinking of her as a liability he could do without? He was very proud of the Torrente name and here she was dragging it through the mire. He had wanted her past to stay hidden to protect their child. All of a sudden she was seeing how events could conspire to destroy their relationship.

Kathy made a courageous effort to pull herself together. 'You were saying,' she muttered in a wobbly undertone, 'that you had prepared for this?'

'*Maremma maiale,*' Sergio groaned, crossing the room to propel her up out of her seat and into the protective circle of his arms. 'We'll get through this, *bella mia*. It's a matter of damage limitation.'

Held close and comforted, Kathy gulped back the tears threatening and nodded vigorously into a broad masculine shoulder. He felt strong and familiar and she wanted to stay in his arms for ever.

'My PR team have come up with a press statement that strikes the right note,' Sergio declared, settling her down onto a sofa. 'It will end the speculation. Next week someone else will be the target.'

Kathy wasn't quite sure she understood what he was saying, but his concern for her had banished her fear of losing him and strengthened her. 'All right.'

His spectacular dark gaze was intent. 'It's not what you have done, but how you handle it once it's in the public arena that matters.'

Kathy gave him an uncertain nod. 'This statement…'

'I have a copy of it here.' Sergio extracted a sheet of paper from a file and extended it for her perusal. 'It's standard stuff and with your agreement, it will be released to the press.'

Kathy had only read the first sentence when her heart started to sink. It was basically an acknowledgement of her conviction for theft, a reference to the fact that she had served the sentence for her wrongdoing and the assurance that she had learned her lesson. An everyday tale of retribution and redemption.

'I can't allow you to release this to the media,' she whispered tautly.

'Public apology—that's what it takes now. It may seem

glib and pointless, but people will respect you for being honest about your past.'

'Sergio…' There was a desperate plea for understanding in Kathy's troubled gaze. 'I am not a thief. I didn't take that silver. I went to prison for something I didn't do. I can't agree to this statement being made on my behalf because it would be a lie.'

'That press release will draw a line under the whole affair and take the steam out of the story.'

'Did you even listen to what I just said?'

'You already know where I stand on that issue,' Sergio breathed in a driven undertone. 'Maybe you need to forgive yourself for what you did before you can come to terms with it. But right at this moment we have something more immediate to deal with—'

Her cheekbones flushed with annoyance, Kathy flew to her feet. 'I can't believe you just said that to me!'

An expression of hard resolve was stamped on Sergio's lean, darkly handsome features. 'You made a mistake when you were young and you had no family to support you. Many teenagers have made similar mistakes, put them behind them and gone on to live law-abiding lives just as you have done. You should be proud of that achievement.'

'Stuff the pep talk! There's only one little problem—I didn't make that mistake in the first place!' Kathy fired back at him. 'You've never even let me tell you what happened.'

'You avoid the subject like the plague.'

Kathy froze in surprise. She was dismayed that her desire to stay away from a controversial issue during their honeymoon had given him that misleading impression. And a heartbeat later she was furious with herself for being so craven.

'Don't treat me like your enemy. I'm trying to help you,' Sergio spelt out grimly.

Kathy compressed bloodless lips. 'I know.'

'Will you agree to the statement?' Sergio demanded.

Kathy turned as pale as a martyr at the stake. 'No, never.'

Sergio dealt her a forbidding appraisal. 'This problem will run and run. It won't go away. It has to be dealt with.'

The expectant silence that stretched was like an icy hand trailing down her taut spine, but she defied that intimidation. Her apple-green eyes alight with resolve, she tilted her chin. 'But not like this. Not with me making a fake confession and a fake apology for something I didn't do. I served my full sentence because I wouldn't lie and express remorse for someone else's crime.'

Sergio surveyed her with cold, hard censure in his challenging gaze. The trauma of that moment made her stop breathing. Without another word, he turned on his heel and strode out of the room. Pulling in a jagged breath, she collapsed down on a seat and stared into space. *What if this costs me my marriage? What if I lose him?* Her mind was awash and adrift on terrified thoughts and fears.

It didn't help that she could see his point. He had decided she was guilty at a very early stage of their relationship when he hardly knew her, and he was as stubborn as a mule. He had even got as far as explaining her criminal behaviour to his own satisfaction—youthful mistake, no family backup. In trying circumstances, he had not voiced a single word of blame or complaint. And now he was engaging in what he had called damage limitation in an effort to protect what little remained of her reputation. Determined to keep her safe from the paparazzi, he had marooned her on his yacht. He was doing what came most naturally to him: taking charge, making decisive moves to handle the crisis and trying to protect her, as well. But instead of being grateful for his advice, she was being unreasonable and refusing it. She dashed the tears from her eyes with a trembling hand.

An evening meal was served in the dining room. Although the table was set for two and she waited and the steward hovered in readiness, Sergio didn't appear. She ate hardly anything and at her request was shown to a huge stateroom. Desperate to fill the time, she ran a bath in the amazing splendour of the marble bathroom. She had only lowered herself into the warm scented water when the door she had forgotten to shut opened wider to disclose Sergio.

A dark shadow of stubble roughening his hard jaw line, black hair tousled, his shirt hanging loose from his jeans, he had so much raw bad-boy appeal he made her heart bounce like a ball inside her chest. As she sat up in haste, hugging her knees to her breasts, he regarded her in nerve-racking silence.

'I'm sorry…' he said grittily.

Those two words were like the blade of a knife slicing between her ribs, as she didn't know what was coming next. Even worse where he was concerned, she was in negative mode and expecting bad news. What was he sorry for? An inability to live with a woman publicly branded a thief?

Sergio shrugged a broad shoulder. His gorgeous tawny eyes were strained. 'I don't know what to say to you.'

Kathy was frozen there in the bath like an ice statue, the gooseflesh of fear breaking out on her skin and a clammy sensation in her tummy.

'You see it was your fatal flaw,' he added incomprehensibly.

'What was?'

'I've always had this theory that everyone has a fatal flaw. Yours was a criminal record,' he shared. 'It all connected, it made sense—'

'What made sense?' Kathy was hanging on his every word and wishing they would connect in an understandable way.

'You were beautiful, clever and sexy, but you were working in a menial position for low pay. Why? You had a criminal record.' Sergio flattened his strong, sensual mouth. 'I'm a cynic. I always look on the dark side. It never occurred to me to doubt that you were a thief.'

'I know,' she agreed heavily.

'And for months I didn't think about it because when I thought about it I got annoyed,' he breathed almost roughly. 'When I found you again and Ella was born, I let that knowledge go—I buried it.'

Her green eyes only accentuated her pallor. Her supposed guilt had been buried like a body because that was the only way he could live with it and her.

Sergio shifted an eloquent brown hand to signify his regret and then said something that disconcerted her entirely. 'But although a jury found you guilty and you went to prison you are not a thief.'

Her smooth brow indented. 'What did you just say?'

'I believe you. You've convinced me, *dolcezza mia*.'

Kathy continued to stare at him in wordless disorientation, for that change of heart and opinion knocked her sideways.

'You're innocent. You've got to be. It doesn't make sense any other way. I'm sorry I wouldn't listen.'

'I don't understand why you're willing to listen now,' she admitted unevenly.

'I weighed up the crime with everything I know about

you and all of a sudden it was clear to me that you had to be telling me the truth.'

'Have you been talking to Renzo, by any chance?'

'No. Why?'

Sergio had no idea that his security chief had been looking into her case, acquainting himself with the facts and chasing up every possible lead. When Kathy explained, his lean powerful face shadowed. 'So, even Renzo believed you when I didn't.'

'I imagine Bridget wouldn't have given him any choice in the matter.' The relief of knowing that Sergio finally had faith in her brought a tidal wave of tears to the back of her eyes. She studied the water fixedly and blinked like mad. 'Let me finish my bath. I'll be out in five minutes.'

Sergio frowned. 'Are you going to cry?'

Kathy raised a delicate brow, her eyes bright as jewels. 'What do you think?'

'I need to know what happened to you four years ago. Your arrest, the whole story.'

'It's not likely to make you feel any better.'

'Do you think I deserve to feel better?'

'No,' she said honestly.

Kathy didn't cry. He had given her good news. At last he believed that she wasn't a thief. It had only taken him the guts of a year to reach that happy conclusion but, hey, later was better than never. She put on a crisp blue cotton robe and went into the bedroom to join him.

'I was hired to act as Mrs Taplow's companion and provide her with basic meals by her nieces, Janet and Sylvia. I hardly ever saw Sylvia because she worked. They lived in the village about a mile away,' Kathy told him, curling up on the giant bed. 'Mrs Taplow lived in a big old house. On my first day Janet explained that her aunt was suffering from the early stages of dementia and that I should pay no heed to her stories about her things disappearing.'

Sergio elevated an ebony brow and sat down on the bed beside her. 'Didn't that make you suspicious?'

'No. I was too glad of the job and somewhere to live. The old lady did seem a little confused sometimes but she was very nice,' Kathy confided ruefully. 'Janet asked me to clean the silver, which was kept in a cupboard, and she told me that it was very old and valuable. There was a lot of it and, to be honest, I barely looked at the stuff as I cleaned it.'

'But no doubt you put your fingerprints all over it.'

'A few weeks later Mrs Taplow got very upset and claimed that two pieces of silver had gone missing. I couldn't have said either way, but I mentioned it to Janet and she said her aunt was either imagining things or that she had removed them herself and hidden them somewhere. She insisted that Mrs Taplow had done that before. Mrs Taplow wanted to call the police, but I dissuaded her,' Kathy recalled unhappily.

Sergio closed a reassuring hand over hers. 'What happened next?'

'The same thing again—but I noticed the pieces that had gone missing and I searched all over the house for them without any luck. I started feeling uncomfortable, but Janet told me not to be silly and that the items would turn up eventually. I had no reason to doubt her. I had a day off. I was supposed to be meeting Gareth and I was getting dressed when the police arrived,' Kathy whispered, sick at the memory of the moment when her world had begun to come crashing down around her. 'They searched my room and the

Georgian jug was found in my handbag. I was charged with theft. I thought maybe the old lady had put it in there, but then I was told that she didn't suffer from dementia.'

'*Madonna diavolo*…you were hired and set up, so that her niece could steal from her and ensure that you got the blame.' His dark eyes were grim.

'But there was no way of proving it when Janet denied it. It was my word against hers and she was a church warden. There was a large amount of money involved in the silver that had gone missing.'

'But the evidence was circumstantial.'

'Three different solicitors dealt with my case, but I was still convinced that I'd be proved innocent. I didn't really understand how much trouble I was in,' Kathy admitted shakily. 'I was in shock for days after the guilty verdict and it was too late then. There was nobody on the outside to fight my corner.'

Sergio tried to retain a hold on her hand but she trailed her fingers free and turned her head away. He sprang upright and moved back into her field of vision. 'It must have been a terrifying ordeal.'

Kathy lifted a narrow shoulder in a jerky shrug.

Tall, dark and impossibly handsome, Sergio hovered at the foot of the bed. 'I had no idea, *amata mia*. I feel like a total bastard.'

'Don't. Let it go. I don't blame you for thinking the worst. Plenty of other people have reacted the same way,' she told him ruefully. 'But it consumed too many years of my life and I don't want to waste any more time on regret.'

'However long it takes I will clear your name. I swear it,' Sergio intoned in a raw undertone.

'Is it that important to you?'

Sergio dealt her a questioning look. 'Of course it is. You're my wife.'

It was the early hours before Sergio came to bed that night and she noticed that he didn't reach for her the way he usually did. In fact, it was the very first night they had ever spent together when they slept so far apart that they might as well have been in separate beds. The next morning he was gone when she awakened and she thought unhappily that that might be for the best.

While Kathy had no desire to read what the newspapers made of her criminal conviction, she had the sinking suspicion that Sergio would read every word and feel the humiliating sting of it to the primal depths of his macho soul. As a result she had no appetite for breakfast and she passed most of the day with Ella, worrying about the future of their marriage. After all, while he might accept that she had been wrongfully convicted, he still had to live in a world where everybody else would most assuredly believe his wife was guilty as charged. He wasn't in love with her, so there was no safety net to strengthen them when things went wrong; there was no reservoir of forgiving love and tolerance to draw on.

Late afternoon, Sergio strode in, dressed in a black business suit teamed with a gold tie. He looked extraordinarily handsome and unusually tense and pale. Black lashed dark eyes inspected her. 'I've been flat out all day but you usually walk in and out of my office when I'm working, *bella mia*. Where were you?'

In the strained atmosphere, Kathy veiled her troubled gaze. She had lost the confidence to assume that she would be welcome. In addition, his personal staff had flown in early that morning and would presumably have read all about their employer's jailbird wife. On a day when she really just wanted to hide herself away a brave smile of indifference had proved too much of a challenge. She had also feared that her presence would embarrass him. 'With Ella…I forgot you were going to London tonight.'

'Twenty-four hours max and I'll be back. I don't like leaving you.'

'I'm fine,' Kathy hastened to protest, for a woman who needed looking after like a child could hardly be an attractive prospect to a male as independent as he was.

'By the way, that newspaper article? It was nothing.' Sergio shrugged but failed to meet her gaze. 'Don't worry about it.'

But she did; she couldn't help it. Guilty or otherwise, she had become a source of embarrassment. His reserved manner warned her that events had hit him hard. Both Tilda and Maribel rang her that evening and proved their worth as loyal friends. Tilda invited her and Sergio to spend a weekend in Bakhar and Maribel offered to stay on the yacht with Kathy for a few days. Kathy thanked her and gently refused. The next day, Sergio phoned and told her that he would be away longer than he had expected.

Forty-eight hours after that, Kathy flicked on the television in the bedroom and up came the Italian news channel that Sergio always watched. Before she could change station, her husband's picture appeared on screen and her hand stilled on the remote control. That was swiftly followed by film of Grazia emerging from a hotel and Sergio emerging from what looked like the same building. Her grasp of Italian wasn't good enough to translate the accompanying commentary. She had to use the internet to check the report out and, although there was very little information available, what she found out shattered her.

The night before, Sergio had spent a couple of hours in the same London hotel as Grazia, both of them leaving by separate entrances in an evident effort to avoid detection. There was talk of a reanimated affair with reference made to Grazia's divorce and Sergio's marriage described as being 'in turmoil' after unsavoury revelations about his wife's past.

The phone rang.

The instant Kathy heard Sergio's deep pitched drawl she interrupted, 'What were you doing in a hotel with Grazia?'

'Malicious gossip travels faster than an avalanche,' he murmured smooth as glass. 'I'll be with you in an hour.'

'You didn't answer my question.'

'I have company, *cara mia.*'

At her end of the phone, she reddened fierily in receipt of that clarification. Time had never seemed to move more slowly than in the minutes that followed. She left the bedroom and waited in the entertainment-sized lounge, where she paced the floor. Eventually she walked out onto the deck where the blue sky was beginning to shade with warm hints of peach as the sun began to go down.

She could not imagine life without Sergio, but she was wondering if, at the end of the day, that might also be how Sergio felt about Grazia. A fatal attraction that he despised, but ultimately couldn't resist. Would that explain why was he was so reluctant to talk about his former fiancée? He had still to ask what Grazia had said to his bride the night before their wedding. Kathy could only feel threatened by that reality.

Her heart started beating very fast when the helicopter came in low to land. Lean, powerful face serious, Sergio emerged.

'For once, I have good news,' he informed her levelly. 'Janet Taplow was arrested this afternoon.'

That being the last topic she had expected him to open the conversation with, Kathy simply stared back at him. 'Are you serious?'

'The police got a search warrant and found the old lady's missing silver in her house. Mrs Taplow died last year. Janet only began selling off the silver a few months ago when she thought it would be safe to do so. But as you're already aware, Renzo was able to identify a piece of it and the trail led straight back to her.'

'My word…' Her legs hollow with shock, Kathy weakly sat down on the arm of a designer sofa. 'After all this time, the truth is coming out—'

'An antique dealer has made a positive identification of Janet, and her cousin is also willing to give evidence against her because she's furious at being robbed of a large part of what should have been a shared inheritance. I've got my best lawyers working on this. It'll take time but they are certain that you will eventually be able to prove your innocence.'

Kathy pressed cooling hands to her shaken face. 'I can't believe it. I don't know how to thank you—'

'This is all thanks to Renzo's efforts. He's the hero here. But for your intervention, he would no longer be on my staff. I've done nothing,' Sergio declared. 'The tabloids are already onto this development. A wrongful conviction is more newsworthy than the original story. You'll probably be inundated with requests for interviews about your experiences in prison.'

Kathy pulled a face at the idea. 'No, thanks.'

'How do you feel?'

'Shocked.' Kathy hesitated. 'What about Grazia?'

Sergio raked long fingers through his cropped black hair. 'I had no choice but to do a deal with her face to face. But I should've guessed she would have the paparazzi standing by to capture those photos at the hotel. Grazia never misses out on free publicity.'

Kathy frowned. 'What sort of a deal?'

'Abramo was in London because he's been receiving treatment for leukaemia. He's not well at all,' Sergio told her heavily.

'Oh, my goodness, you finally got in touch with your brother!' Her lovely face sobered as she registered what he had said. 'Leukaemia?'

Sergio grimaced. 'His chances are roughly fifty-fifty. He doesn't need the stress of a contested divorce right now, so I bought her off.'

'That's what you mean by a deal? You gave Grazia money?'

'In return for certain undertakings all legally signed, sealed and delivered.' Sergio withdrew a document from his jacket and unfolded it. 'Our hotel rendezvous was supported by a team of lawyers. They did well. I would have paid twice as much.'

Kathy was nodding like a puppet in rapid succession. 'What undertakings?'

'Grazia has agreed to return the family jewels in her possession and give Abramo a quiet divorce. She has also promised not to approach you again.'

Her green eyes widened in surprise. 'You mean you were annoyed when she cornered me at that club?'

'Of course!'

'Well, why didn't you say so then?'

Sergio regarded her with bleak dark-as-night eyes. A faint veil of colour accentuated his hard cheekbones. 'I felt very guilty about what happened and guilt made me lash out. She upset you before our wedding and almost ruined the day—'

'How did she even find me that night?'

'The nightclub manager tipped her off.'

'She knew about Ella.'

'But not from me,' Sergio countered, letting her know that he understood her concerns.

'Grazia said you told her to divorce Abramo.'

'No, that was a lie. But it was my fault that she made you the target of her venom,' Sergio said gravely.

'How could it be your fault?'

'Grazia's a vulture. When she tried to get back into my life, I didn't discourage her as much as I could have done and her vanity was her undoing,' Sergio revealed with visible reluctance. 'Her pursuit amused me. It was before I met you and I didn't see why I shouldn't play her along as she had once done to me—'

'You wanted revenge?' Kathy was startled by a possibility that she had not considered before, and uplifted by the belated awareness that he was no longer interested in the beautiful blonde.

Sergio shifted a dismissive brown hand. 'I would never have sought her out on my own behalf; I didn't care enough. But I was angry when she dared to approach me last year. I didn't have to do anything to settle old scores— just stand back and watch while Grazia plotted and planned to get me back.'

Kathy released a shaken sound of consternation. 'But she was Abramo's wife.'

'Grazia goes where the money is and the minute Abramo lost his, he was yesterday's news. He knows that as well as I do and I do believe he is over her now. What kind of a woman deserts her husband when he's ill?'

'A ruthless one—the sort of woman I thought you admired.'

'But she'd never beat me at chess in a million years, *delizia mia*. She'd never dream of telling me I can't climb Everest because it's too dangerous and I might get killed— by the way, I did it a few years ago. I think it's fortunate that I took in certain experiences before I met you because there's a long list of manly sporting pursuits which bring you out in a rash of anxiety, isn't there?'

Kathy had turned pink with mortification, not having appreciated that her terror at the prospect of anything happening to him was quite so obvious.

Sergio rested dark golden eyes on her and reached for her hands. 'Grazia would have encouraged me to follow dangerous sports because she'd have enjoyed being a merry widow more than wife. How could you think I'd want her back for even five minutes when you were around?'

'You and I sort of fell into a relationship. Nothing was planned—especially not Ella.' Kathy's voice was uneven. 'But you chose Grazia. You wanted to marry her.'

'Per meraviglia,' Sergio sighed in a tone of regret. 'I was twenty-one and she was a trophy my friends envied. I loved her to the best of my ability then. I was a boy, but now I'm a man and I have a very different take on what I want in a wife. But until I met you I didn't know what I wanted—'

'All you wanted was sex,' Kathy told him bluntly.

'That may be how I first saw us, but you taught me to want other things that I didn't even know that I needed.'

'Like what?' she prompted.

'Ordinary things like laughter, honest opinions, arguments...'

'You think you needed someone to argue with?'

'Opposition is good for me now and again. And the occasional intelligent dialogue that did not relate to jewellery, clothes or diet was very welcome, *amata mia*,' Sergio confided. 'Of course, I didn't properly appreciate what a catch you were until you vanished for seven and a half months and I found out what it was like to miss you.'

Kathy was enthralled, for at first she had thought he was teasing her but now she was recognising the sincerity that lay behind the self-mocking delivery. 'You missed me?'

'And it was too late. You were gone. Now if Grazia had played that card she would've shown up again within a couple of weeks, but, you being you, you were gone for good.'

'I thought it was for the best at the time.'

'The knowledge that I came that close to losing you for ever still haunts me. The stag cruise was a disaster. No...' Sergio groaned when she suddenly snatched her hands from his. 'You have to let me talk about this—'

Her face tight, Kathy stepped back from him. 'No, that kind of stuff is better left buried. It was before we were married and none of my business.'

Sergio strode forward and swept her up off her feet. 'Oh, I like that when it's still being held against me and thrown up at every opportunity!'

'When did I last throw it up?' Kathy yelled.

'You didn't see the judgemental look on your face when you got on this boat for the first time...'

'Maybe your conscience made you imagine that. For goodness' sake, put me down!'

'No. I didn't get horrendously drunk on that stag cruise. I didn't even kiss anyone. Okay?' he demanded. 'You were inside my head to such an extent you might as well have been with me. You were the only woman I wanted.'

Shocked by that burst of confession, Kathy let him carry her downstairs to their stateroom. 'I didn't like you very much then.'

Sergio laid her down very gently on the bed. His brilliant dark eyes were bleak. 'I know and it's what I deserved, totally what I asked for. But I'll never be like that with you again because I love you. Even if you were a thief I would still be married to you and I would still feel the same way.'

Kathy was stunned by the raw emotion stamped in his face. 'You fell for me?'

'Probably the first time we met and my brain started malfunctioning. I was all over the place, assuming this, assuming that about you. The sex was amazing, but so were you. When I was in Norway, the rest of the guys were in stitches at the number of times I phoned you.'

'Yes, you did phone quite a bit,' she acknowledged.

'And the move to France may not have appealed to you, but it was my first fumbling attempt at a committed relationship in a decade,' Sergio argued in his own defence.

'I'm glad you used the word *fumbling*.'

'And I blew any remaining goodwill with that stupid stag do. I accept that. But when I couldn't find you, I was devastated. That's when I knew how I felt about you. That's why there was nobody else all that time…'

'Nobody?' Wide-eyed, Kathy turned her coppery head to study him. 'Not one single woman in all those months?'

'Call it retribution for the night I made you sleep with me. I haven't been with anyone else since I met you and

I'm amazingly proud of that fact.' His rueful smile tilted her heart on its axis. 'I did get you to agree to marry me in a weak moment. It was deliberate. I knew I wouldn't feel secure until you were my wife. I would have done virtually anything to get that ring on your finger.'

Kathy was smiling back, flattered by such eagerness to marry on his part. 'So it was really just the wedding hoopla you disliked? Not the act of getting married to me?'

'Is that what you thought?' Sergio grimaced. 'It wasn't meant that way, *bella mia*. I thought I could make you happy——'

'You did.'

'But all the time I was making the worst mistake I could in not believing in you. I feel very guilty about that.'

'It's true you've got flaws, but I love you anyway——or maybe even because of them. I don't think I could stand you if you never did anything wrong but don't take that as an invitation to stray.' A luminous smile curved her rosy mouth while he studied her in wonderment. 'Because as you know——the stag thingy——I'm not forgiving about stuff like that——'

On his knees on the bed, he hauled her to him and kissed her with a passionate intensity that made her blink back tears of happiness.

'And what is more, a good husband keeps his energy for his wife,' Kathy told him dizzily, yanking off his tie.

Sergio pitched off his jacket and wrenched at his shirt with considerable enthusiasm. 'How the hell did you manage to fall in love with me?'

'You're annoying, but very good-looking, sexy, entertaining…' Kathy spread admiring fingertips on his bronzed and muscular chest, but her eyes were soft and bright and loving. 'I have to confess that when I beat you at chess it gives me a thrill—'

In answer Sergio tipped her back against the soft pillows and kissed her breathless. His rampant enthusiasm met with a most encouraging reception.

Almost three years later, Kathy put the finishing touches to her make-up, smoothed her vibrant copper hair into place and stood back to get the full effect of her shimmering golden ball gown.

Within the hour, everybody who was anybody would be arriving at the Palazzo Azzarini, because Sergio Torrente was throwing what was being described as the party of the year. Why? A miscarriage of justice had been declared in Kathy's case and her wrongful conviction as a thief quashed. The judge during the original court case was also deemed to have misdirected the jury, thus preventing her from receiving a fair hearing. She had had the support of a wonderful legal team, who had had to work long and hard to achieve that successful result even though Janet Taplow had finally owned up to planting the jug in Kathy's bag.

Indeed Janet Taplow had ironically already served her sentence and won her release by the time Kathy contrived to clear her own name. But Kathy had not been bothered by that reality. It was enough for her that the truth be known. When she received compensation for her imprisonment she planned to donate it to a charity that helped former offenders to settle back into the community and find work.

No longer haunted by painful bitter memories, she was at last managing to leave the past behind her. Little by little, she was regaining the easy confidence and friendliness that had once been so much a part of her personality. Her happiness had contributed most to that process.

Bridget and Renzo had recently celebrated their second wedding anniversary. Bridget was now the mother of a little boy of six months, a development that had surprised and delighted the older woman, who had assumed she was at an age when a pregnancy was an unlikely event. Abramo had recovered from his illness and started dating again. Sergio was slowly forging stronger bonds with his half-brother and had put him in charge of one of his smaller companies. Grazia had collected a small fortune off Sergio and had gone on to become the fourth wife of a fabulously wealthy Egyptian. Like Cleopatra, she was said to bathe in milk and honey.

Kathy had spent most of the first two years of her marriage based in London so that she could take classes and complete the business degree she had been working on when she had first met Sergio. Maribel Pallis had become one of her closest friends. Sergio and Kathy also regularly visited Bakhar to enjoy Rashad and Tilda's lavish hospitality with Maribel and Leonidas. Their children all knew each other very well.

Kathy put on her jewellery, a recent birthday present from Sergio. The contemporary diamond pendant glittered with white-fire brilliance at her throat and the earrings caught the light with every movement. She went to say goodnight to Ella, with her pet Siamese cat, Horace, padding fluidly in her wake. Already Horace was like her shadow and he had almost—but not quite—filled the space left by his much-missed predecessor, Tigger.

Ella was still awake and complaining about Elias Pallis, who was almost three years older. In truth, Elias and Ella frequently fought like cat and dog. Elias liked to lay down the law and Ella couldn't stand being told what to do. Tilda's son, Sharaf, was always the peacemaker, very much a future diplomatist and ruler in the making while Bethany, his little sister, was as feisty as Ella. Soon, Kathy reflected dreamily, resting her hand against the very slight curve of her tummy, there would be another child in the group. Boy or girl, she didn't mind. She was looking forward to telling Sergio her good news.

Lethally tall, dark and handsome in a dinner jacket, Sergio joined Kathy on the gallery at the top of the stairs. 'I love the dress. Gold is your colour. Is Ella asleep?'

'Yes, don't disturb her,' Kathy advised. 'She'll only start muttering about Elias again. They're a double act from hell. Ella's cheeky to him, he winds her up, she loses the plot and he laughs.'

Sergio tugged her into the shadows. 'Isn't that the way you are with me, *delizia mia*?'

Assailed by teasing dark golden eyes, Kathy laughed. 'Only when I first knew you. I've grown up quite a bit since then—'

'So you're not the woman who slammed down the phone on me last week when I couldn't get home in time for dinner?'

Kathy went pink with embarrassment and squirmed. 'Well, obviously that was an exception and I was in the wrong—'

'Oh, you can slam the phone down on me any time you like. I'm tough as granite,' Sergio husked, one hand splaying to her hip to curve her into connection with his long powerful thighs. 'And you said sorry very nicely in bed that night.'

Her guilty blush hit her hairline.

Sergio stared down at her with appreciative eyes. 'I love you, Kathy Torrente. You and Ella are the sunshine in my life—'

'And you're going to have to share that sunshine in the near future,' Kathy told him playfully, wanting to make her announcement before they joined their guests for the evening.

'You mean Horace, the most spoilt cat in Italy, is finally getting a mate?'

Kathy giggled like a drain. 'No, I'm pregnant!'

Warm satisfaction burnished his brilliant smile. 'You are an amazing woman.'

'I'm glad you think so.' Kathy locked her arms round his neck. Eventually they emerged from the shadows and she was lamenting that she would have to renew her lipstick. But she was laughing and he was watching her every lively change of expression with the intensity of a man very much in love. It was a while before they joined their guests...

Intense passion and glamour from our bestselling stars of international romance

Lynne Graham
Passion

Available 20th May 2011

Sandra Marton
Pleasure

Available 17th June 2011

Miranda Lee
Seduction

Available 15th July 2011

Sharon Kendrick
Satisfaction

Available 19th August 2011

Polo, players & passion

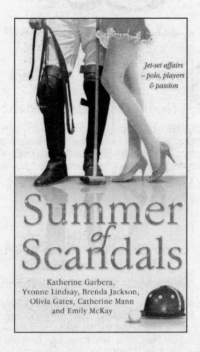

Jet-set affairs – polo, players & passion

Summer of Scandals

Katherine Garbera,
Yvonne Lindsay, Brenda Jackson,
Olivia Gates, Catherine Mann
and Emily McKay

*The polo season—the rich mingle,
passions run hot and
scandals surface…*